THE SIEGE OF SORCERY

"Archers! Now! Set the towers afire!"

They strove to obey Branra's order. At first the fire-arrows and gobbets of balled fire bounced away uselessly as they had before. But as the barrage kept on, Danaer felt an odd pressure building, a tautness in the air and a crackling.

Lira? Hurling her magic against the mighty Markuand wizard?

Danaer's talisman was quiet, but he sensed Lira's presence though he could not see or hear her. The tension in the air grew, and an eerie blue glow limned the enemy siege towers—the unseen barrier becoming solid!

And then it burst. All at once the fire-arrows struck home, and so did the catapults' missiles. Their white clothing in flame, the Markuand warriors fell like living torches.

Indeed, it *was* a battle now, true and untainted by wizardry at last!

Afire with scenes of battle, intrigue, romance and occult duels—Juanita Coulson's new novel is a pulse-pounding triumph of heroic fantasy. . .

The Web
of Wizardry

Juanita Coulson

A Del Rey Book

BALLANTINE BOOKS • NEW YORK

A Del Rey Book
Published by Ballantine Books

Library of Congress Catalog Card Number: 78-67659

ISBN 0-345-27337-0

Manufactured in the United States of America

First Edition: October 1978

Cover art by Boris Vallejo

FOR
MARION ZIMMER BRADLEY

CONTENTS

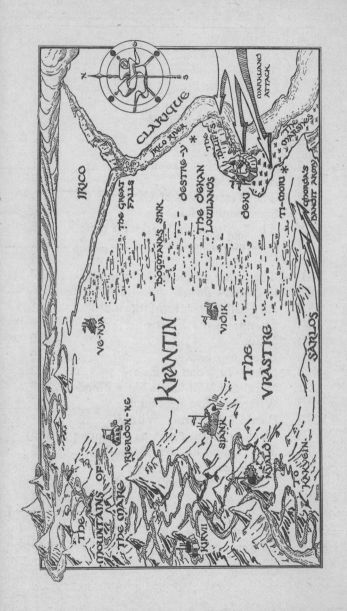

I

WIZARDRY OF MARKUAND

THE SEASON OF BITTER DARKNESS HAD COME TO Markuand. Snow fell from lowering, slate-gray clouds, drifting across barren fields and the chalky ridges. Even at midday, the country was a twilit white. Stark shadows fell upon peasants' huts and villages and towns and the castles of the warlords. Though it was not a time of travel, the warlords had left their citadels, journeying from all quarters, obeying the imperious summons that could not be refused.

Now the warlords' sledges were drawn up in the courtyard of the Emperor's palace. Cruel winds lashed at the waiting teams while drivers and lackeys burrowed for warmth into the straw heaped against the gateposts. Dumb brutes and menials shivered helplessly, and the snow continued to fall.

White dominated Markuand, a cruelty of nature, a thing which had always been. Snow would ever come to blanket the land, and in the warmer season soil and rocks would be revealed in their pale dustiness. This was Markuand's fate in the schemings of the gods, and men and beasts accepted their lot.

But now a new and quite different pallor had stolen through Markuand. This was not the familiar, coldly beauteous sweep of windblown flake. By the Emperor's decree, standards and garb and all accoutrements of his warlords and soldiery were white henceforth—an absence of any color, a bleeding dry of the many hues which once had marked the Emperor's own. With that whiteness came fear more profound than any Markuand had suffered. The wave radiated from the palace, engulfing the land in whiteness, numbing hope, as the dark seasons had numbed flesh for countless generations.

1

In the pillared throne room of the palace, great fires crackled on the hearths and the Emperor sat swathed in costly fur cloaks; his concubines and favorite pages were permitted to draw near his presence, but others who attended him must wait below his dais. Along the outer walls stood rows of white-clad sentinels, seemingly immune to cold and fatigue. At the Emperor's back, half hidden in shadows and curtains, certain men and women lurked, their eyes glittering, their whispering ominous. An immense water clock splashed away the time, each drop into the carven bowl beneath the urn magnifying sound. The repetition added to the restlessness of the men of battle waiting below the throne. Yet none dared voice his impatience. The warlords were petty kings in their own right, jealous of prowess and territory. Now their pride was bent to a thing more powerful than any strength of arms. They closed ranks, staring with mutual loathing at the Emperor.

Childlike, he smiled in return, and his concubines laughed at the warlords' discomfiture. In face and form, the Emperor was a paragon, the very image of his illustrious sire. Tall and well formed, he was as well blessed with a fair and open countenance of godly mien. The blood of Markuand's most esteemed dynasty flowed in his veins, and this was to be the flower of that seed. His sire had been a leader warlord most bloody, and all had hoped the son would rule Markuand unto still greater glory.

The paragon gazed over the gathering and giggled inanely. His pale eyes were empty of any mature wit. One of his women fussed with his cloaks and he pouted and waved her away, not wanting to be distracted in his game.

The warlords must suffer the humiliation, though each longed to draw blade and strike down this half-wit in tyrant's guise. Not merely loyalty to the late Emperor and fear of the guards' pikes made them stay an attack on the imperial presence. Rather they watched the shadowy stirrings along the drapes behind the throne, that place where the bright-eyed apprentices were waiting.

At long last, the heavy curtain was thrown back and servants rushed forth, carrying a chair and brazier and placing these at the foot of the throne. They kindled fire and then spread a golden cloth upon the chair, making it a rival for the Emperor's own. The simpleton perched on the edge of his throne and clapped his hands in excited expectation, peering intently toward the curtains.

He was not disappointed. With a flourish, the master wizard made his entrance, bowing very low to the Emperor. As he straightened he made a negligent flutter with his hand and produced a singing bird from the tips of his fingers. The Emperor squealed with delight and reached out for the creature, only to have the thing transform into a glittering, golden chain ere he could touch it. His squeals became gasps of awe, and he allowed the master wizard to twine the ornament about his royal shoulders. It nestled amid many a similar gaud, all gifts bestowed by the same hand.

While the Emperor and his favorites cooed over this new trinket, the wizard seated himself, not asking permission. He was a man of middle years, and luxury had put only a bit of fleshiness upon his sturdy frame. If he had chosen, he might have been a puissant warlord, for his limbs were well formed, his shoulders broad. His features could have been quite ordinary, save that an essence of some terrible, arcane knowledge shone through his dark eyes; it was a fearsome quality that held the waiting warlords in utter thrall.

He studied them and did not honor them with their titles when he addressed them. "Perhaps you are curious to know why his Most Perfect Highness and I bade you come to us. I will explain our whim to you." Behind him, those wizardly apprentices, men and women, formed a curtain of flesh, silent, listening to every word, now and then nodding or smiling in a fashion that made the warlords shudder.

The sorcerer steepled his forefingers and said, "It has come into our thoughts to look with covetousness upon the Lands Across the Great Western Sea."

He let a moment lengthen, probing their reactions. The warlords began to forget their dread, greed quickening their pulses, though some doubt clung to them.

"We . . . we know of them, Master Wizard," one ventured to say. "Their boats are blown to our shores now and again, but it is far across that sea, and how may we know the strength of this enemy, Master?"

A condescending smile answered them. "There are ways. I do not rashly slay such boatmen who are brought to *my* attention, my lords. I find methods to learn of their lands and peoples. They revealed many, many things before they were granted death's release."

Once more the wizard let silence serve as his weapon, and an evil leer curved his full lips. A few of the warlords made surreptitious signs in an attempt to ward off his magic. Uneasily, they mulled what he had said.

"They told me many things," the wizard repeated, "and much they would not have offered under mere torture." He enjoyed the collective shiver that went through their ranks, then continued. "The Lands Across the Sea are rich and fertile, ripe for the conquest. There are precious metals and timber such as Markuand's rocky hills have not known for half of twelve generations. There are gems and beasts and goods which will glorify His Most Perfect Highness's realm immeasurably. And of course, there will be slaves, alien women of exotic coloring and habits to brighten your dull households, my generals . . ."

"Oh, show these things to me!" the Emperor exclaimed.

The master did not take his attention from the warlords but left such display to his apprentices. Each was most skilled in the magical arts, though they had given over their lives to his commands. Now his silent bidding moved them. One by one, they conjured transformations upon themselves and took on the form of peoples far away. A dark and hulking male apprentice wizard became a tall, golden-haired fisherman, whose nets held a weighty harvest. A scrawny young woman changed herself to a well-fleshed beauty, small, with curling dark hair and tanned flesh; her lands, she said, were prosperous and green and warm throughout the year. Another of the wizard's talented minions spread a veil of illusion over his being. This representation of an alien people was very tall and, though young, his hair was white; he held an ax, and the magician conjured the prey of that ax, showing the warlords magnificent trees which seemed to burst through the ceiling, towering out of sight. A fourth had his turn and assumed the shape of a strong, dark man of middle height. He cast several images about himself. The warlords saw first a seemingly endless grassland where countless fat herds grazed. Heavily laden wagons traveled across the vista, their cargoes rich in gems and shining cloth and pure white and yellow metals from deep mines within towering mountains.

Their master gave no signal that the warlords could see, but he had tired of the game, and in an instant his minions were once more Markuand. They eased back into the shadows as he spoke. "Rich lands, Most Perfect Highness, and rich in population. They will make good slaves, those we choose to spare, and their labor will fill Markuand's coffers."

The warlords grimaced, and one of them said, "And are there not warriors in these alien lands? That fisherman did not look weak, nor did the hewer of trees or the miner, nor even that small woman."

"And did not the Gnarly Folk of the Broken Fields resist you, my generals? Where are they now? Their domain is ours and the people are dust," the wizard reminded them. "What of the Cave Fastnesses and the redbeards who ate from skulls? They were slain by our soldiers, our white-clad army that feels no pain. So shall the Lands Across the Sea fall to us."

"These . . . these alien lands . . . we do not know their languages and their ways. There may be dangers there foreign to Markuand, their customs a mystery to us . . ."

"Not to me."

A bit desperately, one of the bravest of the warlords found his voice and said, "But it is madness to attack them, in their own lands, upon several fronts. Surely we cannot hope to overwhelm them easily."

The wizard held out his hand and the words caught in the challenger's throat. But the curse or enchantment he had dreaded did not come. Instead an incantation began, a droning chant among the wizard's apprentices, and a new set of images flowed from the fire of the brazier, took form, and leaped outward, crouching on the marble floor.

As one, the warlords shrank back. Even the Emperor forgot his amusements and gibbered in terror, and his women and pages shrieked and hid behind his throne.

A foursome of scaly abominations confronted the generals. They stood on the hindmost of six pairs of limbs, and forked tongues thrust out between slavering fangs. These were things of nightmares and a man's worst deliriums, brought up from the bowels of darkness and given life.

Few could bear to look directly upon them. Fear boiled out into prayers as the generals called upon their gods to protect them. Men snatched their cloaks out of the groping claws and fell back, scrambling across the cold floor, courage fleeing.

The master wizard employed his arts, a frown creasing his broad forehead, and a fifth creature appeared from the brazier and took flight. Larger than an ox, the winged snake soared in the smoky air, and light and shadow rippled across its leathery white wings—white like the imperial uniforms of the guards.

Now the wizard sent his bird-snake flying toward the nearest of those soldiers. The guard threw up his spear to fend off the assault, fighting well. A long, vicious beak lined with teeth snapped at him, sundering the spear to splinters. The great wings rustled and wafted a stench through the room as the bird-snake closed with its prey. In stark horror, the warlords saw the soldier draw knife and try to strike, only to have the iron blade break against the magical beast's hide. Talon and beak ripped at the soldier, rending him like carrion. Potioned with the wizard's brew, he did not cry out in pain or fear but continued to strike futilely at the creature even as his vitals were destroyed. Within a few heartbeats, he lay dead, flesh and bone scattered as in a slaughterhouse.

Though the warlords were well hardened to battle

and had seen many a lopped limb and split head, this was something beyond mortal understanding. They clasped hands to their mouths to contain their vomit and turned away from the scene. The snake-bird croaked and hopped amid the carnage, feeding upon its victim's entrails.

Then the wizard flexed his hands, and the bird and its demonic fellows disappeared instantly. But the bloody remnants of the soldier did not. He had died, rent into fragments by a creature out of nightmares. The master wizard gestured and wiped all memory of what had happened from the Emperor's feeble mind.

The warlords, however, could not forget, though much they wished to do so. They avoided looking upon the mangled flesh and bone of the dead guard and fought their nausea.

Coldly, the wizard smiled at them. "A small demonstration, to persuade you that not force of arms alone will strike these Lands Across the Sea. Once those aliens have met my little pets, they shall carry the tale with them as they flee, spreading confusion and fear. They will fall easily to your forces, and there will be much, much treasure for the Emperor, slaves for his realm, new territories for his glory."

"Oh, I should like to have treasure!" the Emperor wheedled, like a boy craving a sweetmeat.

"So you shall, Most Perfect Highness. All is in readiness. It needs but a few more ships and the fleet is assembled. Further, we have provisions to fulfill the needs of our soldiery until we have conquered enough of the alien lands to begin to satisfy us there. The attack will begin within the season, at the coming of the Soft Wind. We will deal first with the island kingdom and hold the northerners and the little brown people at bay then while we take the land of mines. I have plans for those peculiar metals and gems . . ."

He tapped a forefinger against his cheek, his eyes very bright. "You see, I do not expect much of you, my generals—only your swords and courage and the strong arms of your vassals. Your soldiery will be potioned and will become an invincible army, incapable

of pain or retreat. The might of Markuand will conquer, in the name of His Most Perfect Highness."

The prospect of conquest and plunder attracted the
warlords. But doubts remained, driving the boldest
among them to speak now. His lineage was nearly the
equal of the Emperor's own, and pride bade him ask,
"Master Wizard, have not the enemy their wizards?
Can they not conjure? Shall they not call up demons
to match your demons, sorcery to counter Markuand's
sorcery?"

"None can rival my arts! I am incomparable!"

His anger made them draw closer together, fearing
a reprisal for such audacity. As his fury seemed to
abate, they sought to mollify him. "We . . . we only
feared that we might be sore beset, once we are at a
distance from your mighty enchantments, O Master
Wizard. Then we will be beyond your protection."

He took pity upon them and actually laughed, a
growling, bestial sound that gave no encouragement.
"But you will never be beyond my protection. I will
accompany you, my generals, and guard you against
the enemy's magics." He saw their mute wonder and
dismay and laughed louder. "It is true they have wizards of their own. But they are frail, weak things. Like
the Lands Across the Sea, they are much divided
among themselves; they do not dance to the single,
masterly command that the wizardry of Markuand
must."

He leaned back in the gold-covered chair, more
regal than his emperor could ever hope to be.
"Markuand shall fall upon the poor fools like a storm.
And if you need further assurances, my generals, be
promised that not all of the enemy's wizards are loyal.
We shall be able to strike from without, and from
within. The Lands Across the Sea will be ours, their
people as midges, to be crushed as I strike my hands
together thus!"

The loud clapping sound rang along the pillared
hall. The master wizard did not deign to turn to the
emperor, but that empty-headed beauty jerked upright on his throne. In a toneless voice he said, "So

I command it, my generals. It will be done. Markuand will have the Lands Across the Sea."

It was a pathetic aping of his late sire's imperial manner, but the warlords responded courteously, assenting. Seduced by lust for booty, chillingly aware of the dark powers ready to obey the wizards, they accepted this yoke.

"Within the season," the master repeated. One of his apprentices conjured a cup of wine, wafting it through the air to his lord's hand, that he might toast the coming victory. "We will begin, and bring all who abide there under the white mantle of Markuand, forever."

II

NYALD ZSED

IN THE CHILL DARKNESS BEFORE DAWN, THE TORCHES were sputtering. Danaer's breath came out in a frosty stream as he left the stone fortress and walked toward the palisades. The sentries at the gate were shivering, and Danaer noticed that they had propped their lances carelessly against the posts. He considered reprimanding them, then shrugged. It would be unfortunate, though, for those sleepy soldiers should Captain Yistar find them drowsing on duty. Danaer smiled wryly, remembering his own early experiences with the commandant.

On the drill field beyond the palisades a teamless caravan awaited its drivers and horses. Both carts and men were ghostly forms in the dim light, the soldiers' cloaks stirring in the rising breeze. Danaer wended his way through a clutter of baggage, now and then startling one of the sentries into full wakefulness.

The fortress had been created in living rock, part of the southernmost ridge of the mountains of The

Interior. This was the last bastion between The Interior and the rolling expanse of the Vrastre Plains. Below, and to Danaer's left, stretching to the horizon, was the grassland. Nestled in the curve of foothills, well sheltered by the fortress, lay Nyald town. Already the torches of both fortress and town were becoming lost in the growing brilliance of the sun's first rays. A golden wave touched the peak of the smoking mountain which loomed above the landscape.

The contrast of that sun-washed crest against the black shadows below would have given many men's eyes trouble. But Danaer's sight was unusually sharp. He walked without hesitation across the drill field and toward the corrals, vaulting the low stone fence. There a familiar voice stopped him.

"La! Danaer!" Troop Leader Shaartre had been overseeing a detail and gathering teams and escort mounts for the caravan. Now the veteran rode apart from his soldiers and came to greet his comrade. "What do you here, youngling? I thought you were free of early watch this morn. You ought to be abed."

For a heartbeat, Danaer was tempted to speak the truth, but prudence held his tongue. He heard himself saying, "I have an errand."

Shaartre leaned forward in the saddle, taking a friendly, confidential tone. "Remember that the Captain has ordered muster for the first candle-mark."

"No fear. I will be back by then." Unwillingly, Danaer recalled waking from a sound sleep, driven forth from his unit mates by a summons he dared not name, not even to Shaartre.

"They say it is a long journey to Siank, and you know Yistar's temper as well as I, youngling." Shaartre's kindly concern touched Danaer, and he was about to reply when the older man added, "Of course, the Captain would not refuse you the chance to bid farewell to your Destre friends in the Zsed . . ."

"I have no friends in the Zsed." Danaer had spoken sharply, too curtly. Indeed, there was none of his tribesfolk he wished to see. Yet he must do this thing. To allay Shaartre's curiosity, he said, "Rest easy.

When Straedanfi calls muster, you will have the unit's full complement, including this scout."

Shaartre's broken-toothed grin flashed when Danaer referred to the commandant by that epithet. "Long-Fang he is! And Yistar will sink his fangs in you, youngling, if you keep him waiting. Well, then, about this errand of yours. But quickly now." He wheeled his mount and bellowed orders to the detail to rouse them from their laziness.

An ominous mood clung to Danaer despite that parting jest. Moving more quickly now, as if he could outrun the chill in his bones, he hurried down the pasture slope.

Only a few times in his life had he been so wakened, and each time the divine will had seized him, just as it did now. He must obey, though he be tense with apprehension and pious wonder.

The smoking mountain grumbled and the earth shifted slightly beneath him. Danaer did not break pace, reflexively compensating for the quaking sensation. He glanced up at the plume of vapor trailing from the peak and muttered a prayer. "Bind Bogotana fast in his deep realms of fire, Argan—goddess, grant it." After a few moments, the shaking stopped.

Now and then he slapped rumps or flipped the trailing hem of his narrow mantle to shoo horses from his path. He regarded these animals with mild contempt, for they were the army's preferred stock. These sturdy, sleek-coated black horses were prized by the people of The Interior. No doubt they were useful for pulling mine carts and plows. But in Danaer's judgment, the black was ill-suited for duty on the Vrastre Plains, the territory the soldiers of Fort Nyald must patrol.

At the far end of the pasture stood two quite different horses, and Danaer headed straight for them, chirruping and speaking the Destre tongue these animals knew best. These were his scout roans—shaggy, big-headed brutes his fellow soldiers scorned and called half wild.

Lulled by Danaer's voice, the skittish beasts permitted him to draw close, though the roans watched

him warily, their stubby little ears moving constantly
and their eyes following his every step. Danaer
grasped the larger horse's nose and slipped a leather
loop over the lower jaw, then swung up onto the bare
back. The roan bucked and reared, sending the other
animals shying away. Danaer clung to his mount without difficulty, and when the roan had vented the worst
of its friskiness, it bore his weight without further complaint, obeying the guidance of his knees and the
single-rein.

The sentries at the outer perimeter of the fort gave
Danaer no more challenge than had those at the palisades or caravan. He had barely passed the gates before they lapsed back into dozing. These men, like all
the others, took their duty lightly, and with reason.
All serious threat of attack lay in the past. The Nyald
Destre-Y who once raided this town and fortress were
a broken people, their power crushed, perhaps never
to be restored to former vigor.

Danaer soon turned aside onto a steep trail crawling along the face of the mountain. This path circled
below the fortress rock, descending to the backwater
of the town's river, the Bhid.

It was a watercourse originating high in the mountains of The Interior, amid snow and ice and fiery
volcanoes. For countless generations the melt had fed
rivulets and waterfalls and rushed down to slake the
thirst of Nyald and the mighty Vrastre Plains beyond.
Then, some twenty springs ago, that flow had ebbed.
The horses of the Destre-Y and the motge herds which
grazed the plains died of thirst, and then the Destre-Y
themselves thirsted and starved, their land becoming
dust between their hands. When plague had struck, a
weakened people were its easy prey.

Now the snows had returned and the Bhid ran full
again with life-giving water. But the Vrastre was slow
to recover from the drought.

Danaer's roan picked its way cautiously down the
precipitous trail. Cliff-crawlers and bats returned from
their nightly hunts chittered at him from the crevices
amid the rocks. An ecar kit, busy robbing eggs from
a mossy nest, hissed and spat as the horse's hooves

made pebbles rattle along the slope. As the roan reached the sparse copses at the base of the cliff and emerged onto the marshy flats, Danaer looked toward the sunrise and inhaled a fresh wind. Bitterness for the ruin of his people was an acrid taste on his tongue. Wind and water and game had all returned too late.

With a sigh, he nudged the roan across the boggy backwater area. Here and there tiny fissures, birthings of the volcano, let boil through sulfurous smokes, a stench that mingled foully with the stagnant pools left by the river floods. It was not a good place to camp, but those who dwelt here had little choice. Nyald tribe must now be beggars at the feet of the army of The Interior.

Here was all that remained of Nyald Zsed. Zsed? Danaer winced to think that such a term could be applied to a ragged cluster of lean-tos and bony roans and listless people. When he was a babe, this zsed had been a strong nomadic community, ever ranging across the face of the Vrastre grassland in pursuit of wild herds and rich caravans. Nyald Zsed had been the heart of a people famed as the scourge of the southern plains. Now only a few hunters were able to track the motge herds, doggedly following a weak Siirn. These people were too plague- and hunger-ravaged to accompany those few hunters on the quest and must camp here, waiting, existing on the army's charity, utterly dependent upon that soldiery which once had fled from Destre lances.

Grain was heaped at the edge of the Zsed, with a few torn sacks nearby branded with the fort's mark. Sad-eyed women and big-bellied children picked through the kernels, gathering their day's ration. They were too spiritless even to look up as Danaer passed them. But a warrior, dragging about on the stumps of his legs, let grain dribble through his hands and stared hard at the soldier. Captain Yistar permitted Danaer to wear his Destre mantle. He set his belt knife aslant, in Destre fashion, and the thongs of his tribesman's sling were hanging visibly near that sheath. But these few marks of his origins could not blot out the rest of his army garb.

He did not meet the crippled warrior's eyes. Soon the man's empty belly made him drop his glaring and return to pawing through the grain. The food had been Yistar's idea, a gift coaxed from the King's begrudging ministers. Yistar was no nobleman, but a townsman's son; and he knew the grim realities of survival on the Vrastre. He had convinced the ministers that food would buy continued peace on the southern frontier. It was a tactic that had worked well. Bit by bit, the pitiful remnants of a bandit horde had become like the fort's herds of blacks and woolbacks—property.

Try though he might, Danaer could not avoid seeing some of the misery and contrasted it against his own life in the fort, with pain. Why had he come here? What did the goddess demand of him? She had roused him with a dream and bade him return to the Zsed ere he left Nyald with his comrades in arms. Was there some penance he must make, some sacrifice to perform?

Noxious smoke, tinged with the fire-god's breath, curled about his roan's ears, making man and horse choke. Trees were bent and gnarled and leafless, and would remain so despite the warming of the season, for the fumes of the fissures had destroyed them. In this place of misery and reeking smoke, the Zsed seemed but little apart from tales of the realm below, prisoners of the fire-god himself, forever cursed.

At last the invisible goad which had driven him here made Danaer draw on the single-rein, stopping at one of the meanest of the tents. An old woman sat beside a fire, and another woman, not quite so elderly, sat a short pace away, watching the first. That crone by the fire raised her head and peered at Danaer, though her eyes were covered with a milky film that shut out the world. In a quavering voice she said, "Welcome, Danaer, kin of my sister's blood. Step down and attend me at my dying."

When last he had seen her, shortly before winter's storms had come, Danaer had not thought the old woman could live till spring. Now she was totally blind and appeared not to have stirred from this spot for days. Yet Keth at the portal of the gods had not claimed her aged body, though she had known eighty full turns of the year's seasons.

Danaer threw a leg over the roan's withers and dropped to the muddy earth. He glanced at the woman to one side, his kinswoman's companion. She shook her head mutely, her expression morose.

"Welcome," the blind crone said once more.

"Osyta," he said with careful respect, "how did you know it was I?"

She smacked her lips, drooling senilely. Then she seemed to puzzle over his question, much disturbed. "I . . . I do not know. Perhaps . . . ai! It is the will of Argan, kinsman. The goddess sent you to me." Her wrinkled features twisted into a tired smile. "It is her doing. I must die soon, and I would give you my blessing, you who are the last of my kindred. I must give it now, and Argan knows this, for she fathoms the way of all Azsed."

"Kant, prodra Argan," Danaer whispered, echoed by the second old woman. Again they looked at one another, awed. Truly Osyta spoke aright, for it was so that those on the threshold of death often were gifted by the goddess and would bequeath some special foretelling to their inheritors.

"Argan, Argan, most mighty goddess . . ." Osyta crooned, rocking back and forth. Her healing skills had availed little against the terrible plagues which had wracked her tribe. Companions of her childhood were all gone, save the one woman who now cared for her needs, gently trying to tidy her disarrayed garments.

Danaer watched with mingled fear and pity. Those blank eyes seemed to be glistening with new wisdom, a final touching of Osyta's spirit by the goddess, ere death took her.

Despite her venerable years, the herb-healer wore the fawn-colored breeches and shirt and leather vest of a warrior woman. She had ridden on caravan raids with the boldest of Nyald Zsed, tending wounds and drawing the enemy's blood, as need be. No half-skirt marked her garb, for she had never bound herself to a man nor borne a child. Her eiphren, that faith-jewel she had received as a girl, dangled from a frayed raw-hide thong and rested between her scraggly gray eye-brows.

Quite abruptly, she reached out, seeking to explore Danaer's face. Her skinny hands groped across his tunic and at the hilts of his belt knife and his army sword. With surprising strength, she clawed down along his left arm until she touched his eiphren, the simple gemstone he wore on his mid-finger. More boldly, she probed ribs and biceps and patted at his belly. At last she sat back on her heels and said, "There is more flesh on you than I remember, kins-man. You begin to resemble your sire in the fullness of his years, when he fought in the Kakyein wars, fought for the honor of Nyald Zsed."

"He died for that honor," Danaer said somberly. "But my honor is pledged to the army of The Interior. I am a warrior of Nyald Zsed no longer, Osyta."

"And soon you will journey to Siank, to join the great battle that is to come." The herb-healer pointed toward a sunrise she could not see, and Danaer shud-dered. Perhaps her mention of Siank had been only a shrewd guess, a copying of some gossip she had over-heard, for the army caravan's destination was no se-cret. But her speaking of a great battle . . . Whence came those words?

"Siank," she repeated in a wistful voice. "I shall never know Siank now. But you will, blood of my blood. You shall ride out Nyald and unto Siank."

Without warning, Osyta began to keen a death prayer. Danaer pulled his mantle more tightly about his shoulders to shut out a cold far deeper than that of the fading night. The herb-healer's friend wept qui-etly as Danaer's kinswoman sang, readying her path to Keth's holy portals.

At long last, the sound trickled away on the sulfur-ous air and Osyta's lips slackened. Visibly, she brought herself back to the earth of the living. "Ai, warrior, you carry the pride of Nyald Zsed with you to Siank."

Danaer grimaced and said with studied patience,

"Search your mind, old one. Remember that I am now Captain Yistar's scout."

"Ai! He is your Siirn, since you rode into his fort and took oath unto our fire-haired enemy, that Straedanfi." Osyta's leathery face creased in a cryptic smile. "Straedanfi, who never takes his fangs from our throats until we surrender, then feeds us from his hand, like his pets. A most worthy Siirn, this Straedanfi, my kinsman. You were wise to follow him, in the time of death."

Against his will, led by her words, Danaer's thoughts turned back through the cruel seasons.

Choose.

Eight years had gone by since he had made the fateful decision. Then he had been but a youth, mounted on a staggering and half-dead roan. Danaer's belly had been empty, his tongue parched, and his heart had been drained of hope. In his mind's eye he saw himself approaching Captain Yistar, dropping his weapons, lifting his hands in supplication, seeking the officer's mercy. What honor was it to die to no point in the clan wars or to starve or suffer the torments of disease when plague struck less severely in the town and fort and there was food aplenty? Better far for a young Azsed to offer his meager talents to Yistar, to that Straedanfi, who had been a brave and respected foe and had so often bested the bloodiest warriors of Nyald Zsed.

Choose.

Danaer was not the only youth who had submitted himself to Yistar and begged mercy. The Zsed had not known whether to spit on the weakness of those who surrendered or to praise their courage—for it had taken much courage to ride willingly into the stronghold of the army of The Interior. Of all those who had taken the risk, only Danaer had survived the test of Yistar's discipline and learned to accept the strange new ways of the unbelievers who now claimed his loyalty.

Choose.

He had chosen, and he had become a man between two worlds and belonging to neither.

Osyta had brooded, as if sensing what troubled Danaer and at one with his hurt and regret. But at last she spoke, without accusation. "Now you serve the King of the Iit."

"I cannot deny it. King Tobentis rules from his place in Kirvii, in the mountains of The Interior. The army moves by his command, and Captain Yistar must obey him."

"Yet you keep your honor, kinsman." All else was of no matter to Osyta, as was proper for a daughter of Azsed. Truly, a Destre-Y *was* honor, no matter if the Siirn be an unbeliever.

Danaer forced a wan smile. "It is so. I keep my honor. Aejzad was a most worthy Siirn, in the days of my father. But my father and Aejzad are dead. Whom shall I follow now? Chikaron? He would claim to be Siirn, but no priest has judged him so. The Zsed is scattered and ruined like grass before a storm. The goddess alone knows if we will regain our strength again."

"Nyald Zsed will be renewed," Osyta announced with a sharp jerk of her little chin. "All of Destre-Y will be made powerful as it never has been. More! Destre-Y shall be one with the Iit. Hear me! It will be Andaru! Andaru!"

"Andaru?" Danaer said softly. "Long have the priests spoken of Andaru, for generations—telling of the coming of a new birth for all Azsed and all Destre-Y."

"It is close upon us, kinsman! Hear me! Andaru! The Siirn Rena who rules all the tribes shall become Te Rena Azsed—lord of all Krantin from Deki on the River to the Tradyan Plains. Destre-Y and unbeliever shall be as one, shall be Krantin!" Osyta's shrill intensity made Danaer lean back, awed by the death vision that had taken possession of the hag. "Andaru! Soon! Kinsman, it will be soon, and you are to be part of it!"

As any honest warrior must, Danaer respected the prophecy, yet wished nothing to do with the thing. The darkness Osyta had penetrated unmanned him as no enemy's sword or lance could. He stammered as he had not since he was a boy. "How . . . how can this be, ancient one? Long has the Zsed yearned for the army of The Interior to give up the fort and vanish back into the Mountains of the Mare. But it will never happen. Every year The Interior grows stronger, and the hatred of the tribes does not abate. How can Destre-Y and Iit be as one . . . ?"

"Andaru will change all that has been and will be," Osyta said. She traced patterns in the air, recounting a history Danaer had learned in childhood.

"Andaru will change us. We have changed before. Again our feet will be set on a new path, even as our ancestors set forth from Ryerdon to cross the broad Irico River and the unknown Plains of Vrastre. Generations past, we were one people—Ryerdon, dwelling where the sun rises. Ryerdon vied against great Traecheus, the empire of empires, and there was in Ryerdon neither Azsed nor Iit, for we worshipped false gods then. As one people, we spanned the Irico and raised the walls of Deki, the entrance to life, forever to guard against the invasion of Traecheus, should it come."

Danaer wanted to take up the tale, reciting as he had heard it so many times from his elders' lips. Osyta nodded approval as he continued. "And beyond Deki the people encountered many testings. They journeyed through the wasteland of Bogotana's Sink and the flaming waters of the Vrastre. In the testing the holy ones separated Ryerdon and gave us unto our destiny. Those of Azsed learned the rule of Argan, and she gave unto us all the Vrastre."

"Ai! Ai! No more was there Ryerdon. There was Iit, the unbelievers who bowed to Peluva and Desin, and Azsed, the Destre-Y, the people," Osyta said, eagerly resuming the narrative. "We came to hate, as Ryerdon had once hated Traecheus and rivaled her through ancient generations. Now those who dwelt in the mountains and valleys prayed to Peluva's golden orb and to the jewels and bright metal of Desin's wealth in the earth. For those who roamed the plains, the goddess of wills and fire was holy. Many seasons and years have turned, and still we hate, ever at dag-

ger and lance. We are Krantin—two peoples, two
lands. . . ."

She paused, and Danaer was held by the spell of the
words, thinking of his own life, suspended in the midst
of that unending rivalry.

"It is so, by the will of the divine ones—until
Andaru," Osyta finished. In a peculiar singsong, she
cried out in the far-seeing, the prophecy most rare.
"Andaru, and you will witness it, my kinsman. Ai!
Do not doubt me! You shall sit at the feet of the
mighty, and new legends shall be borne. Andaru
comes upon us swiftly, upon wings of fire and blood!
Much, much blood! Ah! And there is evil, kinsman!
Forces powerful beyond all dreaming, a great and ter-
rible evil."

Danaer could not move. His stare was locked on
Osyta's ecstatic old face. Her milky eyes swam with
the visions, and she stabbed a finger toward the smoking mountain. *"There* lie the weapons to be found
against this evil, kinsman, weapons forged together
by all Krantin's gods. Iit and Destre-Y must be one.
They must use these weapons as one, or the evil will
devour us all! From Krantin must come a strength, a
magic—fire and fierce power and a matchless blow! It
is in the children of the mountain.

"Andaru. Krantin must be bought with blood, kinsman. The blood of Azsed, of ancient Ryerdon. Much,
much blood! Only then shall the people of the plains
and those of The Interior be rejoined as they were in
the old days. Hear me! Traecheus calls out for our
help, and we must heed her. Krantin in its strength,
new-bought with the blood of great sacrifice, must aid
Ryerdon's enemy. And Traecheus will praise our
name . . ."

Surely madness now seized the old woman! Traecheus was no more. The Empire of the Eastern
Islands was buried with the bones of time. Ryerdon
itself was no more than a dimly remembered legend,
preserved only in words and by a namesake city in
the interior of Krantin.

Some whim made Danaer look to the east and wonder. Was not Traecheus the ancestor of Clarique, the

people who now ruled the islands where the sun rose? And though Ryerdon was dead, did it not still live in the seed of Destre-Y and the people of The Interior?

"That was very long ago . . ." he whispered, trying to thrust away unsettling ideas.

"And it is now," Osyta said, hearing him, though he had kept his voice very low. "There will be rewards. I see beauty. It is woman, deeply tangled with your own life thread. Oh, this prophecy is not only of blood and evil—not all of it. Beauty, ai, and death is its companion, kinsman. Evil, and death. All woven finely together, like the most costly mantle. And what is this?" Osyta gasped in shock, then held out her hands to Danaer. "Let me give you my blessing. Quickly! It is very needful!"

Shaken, Danaer cast aside his helmet and knelt before her. Osyta brushed back the Destre mantle from his hair and caressed Danaer's head and face. "The goddess guard you well, you of my sister's blood." An unseen power might have flowed from her old fingers into his being. Osyta's feeble touch tightened almost hurtfully against his temples then. "What? I see it plainly now! Sorkra! The wizard kind! Ai! There is much wizardry in this prophecy, magic both good and evil, most potent and awful. You must beware of such magic, warrior. It is not wise for those of Azsed to traffic in these things. Stay to the rule of the goddess. Ride Argan's sacred path . . ."

He nodded assent willingly, wishing she had not spoken of such matters. A prophecy was the truth of the holy ones. What had she seen? Wizards? Indeed, that was nothing any warrior would treat with.

Above the Zsed, from the rocky face of the fortress, drums rumbled out a call to muster. The summons woke Danaer from a grim mood. The old woman sensed that other loyalties had ended her link with him. Her hands fell away, releasing Danaer from bonds of prophecy and dark visions.

Though she could not see his gesture, he hid his actions from Osyta as he beckoned her aged friend close. Danaer slipped a few of the King's silver coins in the crone's waiting palm and whispered, "For the death-giving. You will chant her to Keth's portals, and favor the priest and the fire-walkers that Osyta shall be well mourned?" The herb-healer's friend wiped tears from rheumy eyes, murmuring promises that all should be fitting, according to the will of the goddess.

Still he hesitated, looking down with pity at his dying kinswoman. She seemed to be sinking back into a senile crooning once more, her power of foretelling gone. But as he took up the rein of his horse, she suddenly woke from uncaring and cried, "I have told you the truth, only the truth. I shall not see you again on this earth, warrior, for when the sun dies, so will I. Remember, you of my sister's blood, you will be part of Andaru. You go into danger, Destre-Y . . . much, much danger, and perhaps glory as well, if the goddess smiles."

Had Osyta given him a blessing or a curse? Danaer made a brusque farewell, receiving only a disinterested muttering for an answer. Duty satisfied, he vaulted onto the roan's back and drove his boots hard into its flanks, riding hard through the sulfurous miasma, leaving the Zsed behind.

Osyta's words chased him toward the cliff trail, making him urge the horse up at a risky pace through the narrow twists and turns. Not until he was well beyond the outer perimeter and approaching the drill field did Danaer begin to shrug off Osyta's spell. He was grateful to set himself to plain tasks, falling in beside Shaartre as they marshaled the sleepy troopmen and checked equipment for the long journey.

Captain Yistar was on the prowl, alert for any laxness. His square jaw, pocked with the marks of plague, was set, his lips thinned under his bristly red mustaches. There was a touch of gray in his hair now, but he had not weakened. He had survived the plague and many a campaign, assuming command of the fort when no highborn officer of The Interior would leave the capital and take the post. They had lacked the courage to risk disease and hardship.

His successor, a pale-faced nobleman recently ordered to Nyald by royal decree, muffled his yawns and tensed whenever Yistar's attention swung his way.

Yistar was busy with last-moment instructions, disliking to leave his fort in the hands of such an inexperienced steward. But like all who swore the oath, he must obey the King.

He halted before the cavalry escort, nodding to Troop Leaders Shaartre and Danaer. "It will do," he said by way of compliment. The Captain sighed heavily and cast a sidelong glance at the new commandant, then winced.

Near the palisades, a gathering of veterans waited to see their comrades off. Each man bore a wound that lamed him for arduous service, and in the muster they had been commanded to stay and defend Nyald. They waved and flung several last jibes at those who were leaving, a parting of warriors who had shared grief and joy.

Yistar saluted them with pride, a gesture they returned with pleasure, for he had made it plain he entrusted the fort, and the city, to them—not to the raw courtier who now wore the cloak of commandant.

Trumpets were sounded, a gaudy courtesy Yistar would have scorned, but which the young officer insisted upon. Those who now manned the fort stood watch as the caravan began to move. There were shouts and good wishes which Yistar did not quiet.

Shaartre and Danaer tidied the straggling lines, hurrying laggards along in smart order. As they passed the outer barricades, Shaartre loped up alongside Danaer's roan and said with surprise, "It is first candle-mark, and we are well away. Yistar is ever prompt, in war or peace, eh? Which is it to be this time, I wonder?"

Like Shaartre, Danaer mulled those rumors of some distant conflict, tales only partly believed, carried from a place so far away the story had no menace. Yet a royal decree sent Yistar and the best of his troops trekking from the southern fort Yistar had used to tame the Destre-Y. Surely the army did not set such things in motion lest they had good reason to suspect trouble, even from a place beyond the sunrise.

"Did you accomplish your errand, youngling?"

Shaartre must ask that twice before Danaer came to awareness.

"Ai. It was . . . the attending of an old kinswoman near death. I paid for her pyre and the priest's chants, and she gave me her blessing."

"That is good. They say the dying ones have the ears of the gods and can offer a man good fortune because of it."

To Danaer's relief, Yistar bellowed an order and he was forced to leave Shaartre unanswered, spurring to take the point of the caravan. They did not go to war yet, and the highway had been free of banditry for many a season, thanks to Yistar's vigilance. But he never rested on the past, trusting nothing. As scout, Danaer preceded the snaking line of wagons and foot troops and cavalry.

The route wound past the river flats where the Zsed camped. Against a backdrop of the fortress cliffs, the Destre-Y gathered to stare. There were no cheers, not even of hope now that Straedanfi, victor over the plains people, was leaving. Sullenly, tribal mantles drawn to hide plague-scarred faces and broken pride, they followed the caravan with their eyes.

Danaer was riding well ahead of the train, now and then turning to look back and gauge its speed. Once he gazed toward the Zsed, his keen sight picking Osyta's tent from among the other tattered hovels. He could see two thin female forms huddled by an almost dead fire. He would never see the herb-healer again. Indeed, it might be that he would never see the Zsed of his birth again, either.

Unbidden, Osyta's prophecy filled his mind.

Andaru—the terrible sacrifice which would buy a new destiny for all Krantin and all the Destre-Y. Wizardry—both good and evil. Danger and beauty— closely mixed with glory, blood, and death.

Danaer sucked in a deep breath and turned his face to the east, toward Siank of the White Walls and the fort that was to be Captain Yistar's new garrison. The old woman's words could not be escaped. Whatever lay ahead, this prophecy spoke the will of the goddess and fate. He must confront it with courage, as befitted a warrior.

III

THE WIZARD WEB OF ULODOVOL

IT WAS LATE WHEN DANAER RODE AT A LOPE UP THE western road from Siank back to the fort. The evening in the town had been a disappointment, but that was the way of it and nothing could be done. This ride of his had been intended as a small jaunt. But a pious attendance at Siank's temple and a bowl of Destre fare had not been worth the risks involved.

It was common knowledge—marked by orders of the fort's commandant—that Siank's older sections were forbidden to the soldiers. Danaer had thought his Destre blood would keep him safe there, and had been shown his mistake. At least Shaartre and Danaer's unit mates might enjoy the tale of his adventure.

The night air was not so cool as at Nyald, and his horse was puffing a bit as Danaer turned into the stony outer defenses of the fort. He slacked the reins, letting the animal walk through the tortuous staked barricades and pitfall-strewn field leading to the palisades. Like Nyald Fort, this stronghold was built upon the rock of the foothills, girt well in man-made defenses of wood and stone and earth. Danaer had ridden over its length two days past, when first he had arrived at Siank garrison. He had been impressed with the height of the palisades beyond the compound and the bastions which overlooked the highway from The Interior. Great heaps of deadly boulders could be dropped across the road, the better to guard from any incursion by the Destre tribes. General Nurdanth was as cautious in his practices as Captain Yistar had been when he commanded Nyald Fort. As a Destre-Y, Danaer would have been discouraged to learn of such clever fortifications. As a troop leader sworn to Yistar's service, he admired their building and the General who had ordered them.

Torches marked the watchtowers along the palisades, but Danaer did not need their faint light to guide him. Absently, he touched his roan with knee and rein, avoiding traps and stakes.

"Stand and call!"

Danaer jerked his mount to a sudden stop. He swallowed the retort he wished to fling back at the sentries lining the catwalks. Archers would be behind the loopholes, and Danaer knew their arrows were aimed at him and his horse.

"Scout Danaer, in the service of Captain Yistar!" Danaer shouted.

Wood scraped heavily against wood, and the gate opened enough to permit the exit of a mounted sentry and an infantryman carrying a lantern. They moved slowly away from the fort, the one man holding the lantern high and the other riding alongside, his lance at the ready.

As the soldiers came near enough for the lantern to shine on Danaer's face, his horse tossed its head nervously and shied. He curbed the animal sharply, cursing, while the sentries peered at him. Then they seemed disappointed at being cheated of prey. "It *is* only the scout. You had best take off that Destre cloak, Troop Leader. Less careful men might have filled you with arrows before they challenged you . . ."

"I served at Nyald Fort full eight years," Danaer said irritably. "The sentries there learned to know me well enough."

"This is not Nyald Fort. The Destre tribes here are not so well tamed as those dust-lickers back where you came from."

Swallowing his resentment, Danaer followed inside. It was the first time he had ventured outside Siank Fort after sunset, but not the only distrust and taunting he had endured. When the train from Nyald had arrived two days ago, the regular troops had been welcomed as brothers in arms. However, despite Danaer's badges of rank and his acceptance among his own units, the soldiers of this garrison had viewed him with suspicion and had muttered a few insults. Danaer thought he was hardened against such scorn, for he had suffered it long ago when he first entered Yistar's service. Here the animosity of soldiers from The Interior was intact. In this region the Destre-Y were still a most formidable enemy.

The massive gate bars groaned shut and the sentries returned to their watch posts. Danaer rode toward the stabling pens. Several large fires burned cheerily, lighting the compound, offering the greeting the sentries had not.

Shaartre and a few idlers from Danaer's units had been sitting near the quartermaster's cave and gossiping. But now the Troop Leader left the others and ran toward Danaer, waving. "La! You took your time getting back here."

When Danaer stopped, the horse protested the delay, wanting to get to the grain of the stabling pens. Danaer knocked the brute's head away and made a protest of his own to Shaartre. "My pass was clear, was it not? I could have stayed the night, if I wished."

"Dallying in the old section," Shaartre said with a low laugh. "I knew it was a mistake to bring you along. Down in Siank those pretty women of ease will no doubt sell their favors readily to a Destre like you, even if they disdain the rest of us . . ."

"No, not that." Danaer was forced to smile, though ruefully. "I did find a good inn, and no small problem getting there. The innkeeper liked my money, but not my uniform. I had barely settled to enjoy myself when a threesome of drunken recruits staggered in, ripe for fighting. I escaped that only by the hem of my mantle. Then I met a pair of Destre warriors even more eager for battle. I bought my way clear with a bottle I had planned to save for myself . . . and when I reached the fort, the sentries saw my colors and took me for a Destre-Y."

"Enough!" Shaartre's gray eyes had twinkled as Danaer ticked off the evening on his fingers. "Why not put aside that Destre mantle whenever you approach this fort?"

"Why not cut out my heart as well?" Danaer countered.

Shaartre snapped his fingers, remembering what had first spurred him to accost Danaer. "The commandant wants you."

"Yistar?"

"No, no, General Nurdanth. And now. There is no time to go to barracks and seek better dress. The summons was most urgent, some candle-marks past."

Danaer dismounted and made an effort to straighten his dusty uniform. He was accustomed to being summoned by Captain Yistar on little prior warning; but until now he had only seen the commandant of Siank garrison in parade, when the Nyald caravan had arrived.

"You had best hurry," Shaartre said, buffing Danaer's helmet along his sleeve, then clapping it down over Danaer's ears. He roared at a passing troopman, "You, take the scout's horse to the pens. Move lively!"

Danaer himself made haste, heading for the headquarters building, a timbered, two-storeyed structure reared close against the rocky overhang which dominated the fort. As he entered the lamplit interior, a soft, feminine laugh greeted him. After a moment, when his vision had adjusted to the light, Danaer saw that the only person in the entryway was the woman from Sarlos. She had been sorting through some parchments and drawings scattered on a table. Now she looked at him and said with a teasing smile, "You are much of the night, Scout Danaer."

Her voice had a Sarli lilt, very charming, and well suited to her appearance. Like all the women of Sarlos, she was tiny, though nicely fleshed, much to Danaer's taste. Her complexion was not so brown as many of her people; her face was pert and attractive, with rather rounded cheeks and lips. A yellow scarf the same color as her simple gown was bound about her curly dark hair.

"How do you know my name, my lady?" Danaer asked.

"Oh, you are quite worth remembering." Her eyes were unusually large and a warm brown shade, and now they sparkled with promises of mischief.

Yet those were promises Danaer dared not respond to. When he had first seen her, he had watched her with much interest, as had many another soldier in his units. There had been speculation that perhaps she was the commandant's mistress. But the soldiers who had been longer at the fort told them the truth, one which cooled desires and made the newcomers awed. The lovely Sarli was the companion of a white-bearded elder, a man who wore the dark robes of a sorkra. It was apparent the woman was his apprentice, an attendant to magic.

Osyta's prophecies were strong in Danaer's memory, and he had no wish to become better acquainted with any sorkra. He tried to avoid admiring the curve of her breasts and the enticing flow of the soft gown molding against small waist and thighs. "My fellow Troop Leader informed me that I am wanted by Lord General Nurdanth, and I have come to report."

She studied him, and there was an unnerving coquetry in her expression. Then she sighed and led the way through cramped halls to the officers' sector. At the indicated door, Danaer hesitated briefly before he rapped on the wood. But his knuckles had barely struck when Yistar's familiar bellow ordered, "In! Plague! Come in, and be quick about it!"

Yistar continued to grumble as Danaer and the woman entered. At the first break in his superior's tirade, Danaer said, "Your pardon, Captain. I have only just returned . . ."

"Of no moment, no moment. Here we are, General; my scout, as I promised you."

General Nurdanth was of noble birth, and his quarters reflected his station. Expensive tapers burned in a brazen fixture suspended from ceiling rafters. The golden illumination fell over several artfully carved chairs and a cluttering of documents on shelves and tables lining the walls. A curtain in a far corner shielded the General's bed from rude stares. A table was placed in the center of the room, surrounded by

cushions in the fashion of the plains people. Two men
sat there, poring over some dispatches. Neither of
them seemed to take notice of the new arrivals.

Yistar shook back his shaggy red forelock, disgrun-
tled at being ignored. Then General Nurdanth glanced
up and came to his feet. He nodded most courteously
and bade them welcome.

Reflexively, Danaer's arm snapped back stiffly at his
side in salute. "Maen Gra Siirn," he began, then
caught himself before he lapsed further into the Azsed
tongue. The woman cocked her head and looked at
him thoughtfully, adding to his embarrassment.

Nurdanth was unoffended, nodding understandingly.
He was a man of middle years and common height,
with iron-gray hair. His features were sharp and intelligent, and his eyes were those of a healer. In a
gentle tone he said, "Come, Troop Leader, take wine
with us. And you also, Lira, my child."

Danaer glanced uncertainly at Yistar, but the Captain was already seated and was pouring a cup brim
full. The Sarli woman demurely took her place beside
her mentor, the gaunt wizard who had so far made no
acknowledgment of her presence. Feeling awkward
and out of his element, Danaer accepted a cup of
wine from the General's own hand.

"To Krantin," Nurdanth said solemnly, lifting his
goblet as a priest might at a holy ceremony. "To all
Krantin, to our beautiful land. May her peoples be as
one."

Danaer nearly spilled his wine. A different voice,
the cultured language of the lords of The Interior, not
the Destre tongue of old Osyta—but the meaning was
the same. The commandant of Siank garrison echoed
the prophecy of the herb-healer!

Across the table, the arrow-thin old sorkra whispered to himself, an eerie sound like the stirring of a
cold wind among dead leaves. Lira leaned toward him
and asked, "What is it, Master Ulodovol?" She
twisted at the sash of her gown, kneading the cloth
between her delicate fingers. A sorkra woman—
afraid?

Yistar had grunted approval of the General's toast

and quaffed his drink. Danaer joined him, thinking on the words of Nurdanth, and of Osyta. Krantin—her peoples as one. What could unite the hate-torn factions which set clan against clan and Destre-Y against the lords of The Interior and their king?

The wine was warming Danaer's throat and belly almost too quickly. He paused to gulp and clear his head; when he received a gesture from Yistar, he took off his helmet and mantle.

"May I examine your colors, Scout?" Nurdanth inquired. Surprised, Danaer handed the narrow cloak to him, wishing the thing were not so shabby. The General traced the bright stripes. "Mm, Nyald Zsed, of course. And let me see, is this not the clan of Aejzad's consort?"

Danaer's mouth gaped. He had heard much barracks gossip to suggest General Nurdanth was no ordinary officer. Here was proof of the tales. Never had Danaer imagined that an Iit of such noble breeding would be able to read the mantle colors which spelled out the intricate relationships within a Destre clan.

"Indeed, my lord, it is so. She was the most honored of my kindred."

"You have had a long ride from Nyald Zsed." Nurdanth stroked the folded mantle and looked intently at Danaer. "But here at Siank you are still among the Destre-Y, among your own."

"I have been among my own when I ride with my troopmen, my lord. I took oath to the Krantin army . . ."

"To Krantin," Nurdanth corrected him politely. "And that designation includes the plains people. I would that the Destre-Y but realized they are a part of Krantin."

"Some of them do," Yistar said. "Here is a Destre, General, and one most devoted to his goddess, I promise you. But my scout is devoted to our service as well as to Argan's. Ai! I would trust him far more than I would many a worshipper of Desin or Peluva— especially some of these green recruits we get fresh from Kirvii."

"Well understood." Nurdanth sighed tiredly. He

again fastened his gaze on Danaer. "Have you been to Siank Zsed since your arrival here?"

A trifle uneasy at the question, Danaer said, "No, my lord, not to the Zsed. That . . . ah . . . would not be wise, not while I wear this uniform. And regulations . . ."

"Yes, I understand that, too. Siank begrudges us the land this fort is built upon, though we guard the caravans which feed their city's coffers. Our sovereignty ends at Siank's walls; Siank is the jewel of Destre-Y in every wise. Yet . . . you *have* been to Siank, have you not?"

"Ai, my lord. Her citizens will take the army's coin in exchange for food and drink."

"And what is the nature of that acceptance currently? I mean, how fares a common soldier such as yourself who seeks the diversions of Siank's markets and inns?"

"Best called knife-edge, my lord." Danaer glanced at Yistar and then said, "In fact, I barely escaped being drawn into a brawl involving three other soldiers at one of the old sector's inns."

"Soldiers? Who were they?"

"I do not know their names, my lord. Their insignia marked them as part of the new units from Kirvii, the ones which arrived today."

Captain Yistar slammed his hand down hard on the table, rattling the cups. Nurdanth drank the remainder of his wine and shook his head. "And they were strongly adjured to keep clear of the old town. Only such troopmen as have a clear pass, such as yourself . . . We shall be fortunate at this pace if we have any troops left to do battle!"

Cautiously, Danaer felt out the General's final remark. "We go to battle then, my lord?"

"Perhaps. No, I take that again. You deserve an honest answer. We *will* do battle, and the outcome is much in doubt."

Slowly the General regained his composure. "Let me make known certain things to you, Scout. In addition to my couriers, I employ the services of the sorkra—such as Wizard Ulodovol and Lady Lira

Nalu. They in turn contact other sorkra of their . . . their web. Even so distant as Clarique of the Eastern Islands. You may have heard tales of an invasion of Clarique by some strange, white-clad people. By using the skills of the sorkra, we are better informed of all the news of that distant conflict—"

"We had contact, Lord General," the white-bearded wizard interrupted him. It was the first time Ulodovol had spoken in Danaer's hearing. Lira Nalu was shivering, and tears glistened in her large dark eyes. At this moment, she seemed very much a young and frightened woman, in need of protection.

Sorkra. Wizards. Dealers in magic—the prophecy, again!

Ulodovol must have been snowy-haired even in his youth, for he had the extreme height and paleness of the northern people, the Irico. Age had made him gaunt and whitened the more his flesh and beard until he had taken on a living cadaver's form, shrouded in his rough brown robe. He was a man who touched matters no mortal should, daring death and the divine ones' jealousy.

"Jlandla Hill has fallen, my Lord General." Ulodovol brought with his words the frigid winds of his homeland. "He of our Web who dwelt in Clarique —Wizard Orlait—is dead. With him have gone tens upon tens upon tens of Clarique soldiers and seamen, broken and slain by the weapons of the invader, they who call themselves Markuand."

Danaer had felt the touch of the goddess, and he did not shrink from such holy prophecies, for that was what must be. There was no piety in Ulodovol, however. He spoke not out of sacred visions but with the arts of magic.

"When? When has this happened?" Yistar demanded, the first among the others to find his voice.

"Orlait died but moments ago, Captain. But the battle has gone ill for the Clarique for many candle-marks. All hope has now vanished for the beaten Clarique. Sorkra Orlait did not die quickly, I fear. There is wizardry among these Markuand, a most potent wizardry. It sought to draw all the knowledge of

our Web from Orlait. He resisted them courageously
to the very end. A most valiant sorkra. I regret his
loss to the Web."

Nothing in Ulodovol's lean face confirmed that he
felt that loss or grieved for his dead comrade in sorcery. He spoke of the defeat of arms and the hideous
death of a fellow wizard with no more inflection than
a merchant might use to assess broken pots. Danaer's
respect for the man's calling was becoming mingled
with profound distaste.

In the same emotionless tone, Ulodovol told
Nurdanth, "The Markuand have quite overrun the
isle of Tor-Nali. On the morrow, they will plan to
launch further attacks. The Clarique will not yield
easily, of course. But the main portion of their soldiery is shattered. The invaders have captured many
Clarique ships, many horses and woolbacks and weapons—and they do not encumber themselves with male
prisoners overlong."

General Nurdanth covered his eyes for a heartbeat,
badly shaken. "This afternoon, when . . . when you
touched your Web, the situation in Clarique was said
to be most grave. But this . . . !"

"The Clarique might have suffered less loss, or even
held the island, if they had not been abandoned by
their leader at the height of the battle."

"Thaerl?" Yistar's florid complexion darkened
alarmingly. "Are you saying Lord General Thaerl of
the Clarique deserted his soldiers? It is unthinkable!
Why, the man has been the terror of the island
pirates for seasons. And in the civil war against his
queen he . . . he is no coward!"

"Not cowardice, Captain," Ulodovol said mysteri-
ously. He held out a hand to Lira Nalu, commanding
her to join him. She choked back her tears and
blended her powers with those of her master, visibly
bracing herself for some ordeal. "We will show you,"
Ulodovol announced.

The tapers dimmed, though no one had snuffed
them. The room was swept with an unnatural darkness. Images swam in the air above the table and
Danaer beheld a defensive position, thick with sol-

diers, standing upon the slope of an island peak. Stout warships patrolled the harbor below the citadel.

Danaer had never seen such an expanse of water but had listened to minstrels' tales concerning the sea. He knew he was gazing upon a part of the land of Clarique, a thousand king's-measures or more away from Krantin.

It was day, and Peluva's golden burden shone upon a mighty army and fleet. The Clarique were mighty warriors, the seed of ancient Traecheus. Stronglimbed and yellow-haired, they were proud of their heritage and fierce in defense of their island.

Time sped in blinks of an eye, clouds shifting across the sun as fast as birds. The battle came upon the Clarique as Danaer and the others watched. By tradition, a descendant of Ryerdon, he should have scorned those Clarique, sons of his people's old foe. But he gave the Clarique honest due, admiring their courage.

Over the vast Eastern Sea came the ships of the Markuand, their numbers endless. The ships were white, the sails the color of bleached sand or snow, bellied by a wind that should not have blown in that direction during this season. Expecting a favoring breeze, the Clarique had been unprepared and were thrown into disarray. The Markuand reached the island shore and poured from the boats and up the peak, attacking the citadel in force. Their garments were as white as the ships' sails. And there was something more about them to send horror into a soldier's spirit—these Markuand never cried aloud nor gave any sign of pain. Blood turned white clothes to red, yet not one Markuand screamed or uttered any cry. Such desperate silence unnerved the Clarique, as it did Danaer. No Destre-Y would be so craven as to hearten the enemy with howls of pain, even in his death throes. But the Markuand did not even groan or gnash their teeth. It was as if they could feel nothing.

The truth seized Danaer like hurtful bonds—wizardry! This was some magic, and of incredible potency.

Danaer was one with the Clarique, no longer the son of Ryerdon, enemy of those fair-haired islanders. He shared their battle lust and had it turn to disbelief as the Markuand swarms continued to come, a silent wave of white-clad warriors against which no mortal could stand.

Time again sped forward, a sunset as bloody as the scene falling over island and sea. The wizards' images moved into the citadel itself, into the battle post of Thaerl, leader of Clarique's forces. Danaer seemed to be beside him, as an aide might be, and he saw the man defeated by things beyond mortal comprehension.

General Thaerl stumbled back, his courage faltering. He clawed wildly at his body, fending off . . . what? All around him, chaos reigned as his junior officers begged for new orders and received nothing but gibbers from Thaerl. Reinforcements were not sent to critical bastions, defenses were being overrun, utter rout was beginning.

Images within images! And those around Thaerl saw, at last, the fantastic shapes which tormented the doomed general, smoky forms coalescing into demons!

Thaerl and his attendants were assailed by loathsome beings, creatures out of some nameless pit. Their minds were ripped, though no mark appeared upon the men.

In the end, the mighty general of Clarique fled the devils, taking a boat west, leaving his troops leaderless, ripe for slaughter. Then the Markuand overwhelmed citadel and fleet, a white torrent—killing, killing . . .

A sob cut the air and the images dissolved. Ulodovol released Lira Nalu's hand, and Danaer realized her weeping had been the element which broke the enchantment. She lacked Ulodovol's cold demeanor, and the visions had worked upon her far more strongly. It must have been the second time she had endured the horrors in those images.

It was several long moments before Danaer and the officers could absorb the reality of what the wizards had built in the air. After a few false starts, Nurdanth managed to ask, "Those . . . those creatures General

Thaerl saw . . . were they some madness that took him? Or . . ."

"Came they from the regions below?" Ulodovol's serenity was maddening. "They were real, my lord, for him. I am uncertain if their power to harm was genuine or illusion. Orlait coped with the Markuand wizard's spells to the limit of his talent. But this alien is . . . evil. Beyond Orlait's ability to repel."

Did Danaer but imagine he heard a tinge of condescension in that comment? Was it possible Ulodovol scorned the dead wizard? If that were so, what of the Sarli woman? Would she be as ruthlessly cast out of Ulodovol's wizard web, should her magic prove too weak? Lira stared devotedly at her master, his obedient apprentice.

He did not understand such an attitude. But he was not a sorkra, and these were not affairs he should meddle with. Danaer held his tongue, against instinct.

Yistar and Nurdanth were silent in shock. These alien invaders had conquered Clarique, and everyone knew the great numbers of the Clarique army and fleet. The army of Krantin was smaller, and if Markuand had so easily bested Clarique . . .

Markuand mght strike against Irico, Ulodovol's native province, the cold lands rich in timbers and woolbacks. But there would be no hurry, for Irico was never a country of warriors. Sarlos? It was a fertile place and green even in the winters. But Lira Nalu's home lay beyond a part of the Vrastre, a most inhospitable rocky wasteland in that region, and on the seaward side was guarded by river and thick marshes that had foiled even Traecheus's dreams of empire, long ago.

The Markuand would surely do what anyone of wit would—strike at Krantin. Krantin was the sole remaining power of any consequence and had the only military force left which could offer Markuand a battle. Once Krantin had been crushed, the invaders might take their leisure in subduing Irico and Sarlos.

Danaer needed no visions to see what must happen. They would come. Markuand would gobble the remainder of Clarique's islands, and then they would strike across the river, following the timeworn route of the Ryerdon pilgrimage. If they could, they would sweep Destre-Y before them with weapons and wizardry, stabbing at the heart of Krantin.

Suddenly Danaer's gloomy speculations were thrust aside. General Nurdanth was turning to him once more. "Troop Leader, what the sorkra have shown us makes this evening's undertaking far more vital than I had supposed possible. We require something of you."

"My life is yours to command, Lord General."

It was a mere formal response, but Nurdanth treated it with all seriousness. "Matters may well come to that—though I beg the gods it will not be so." The officer drew a sealed paper from a map case and handed it to Danaer. "You must deliver this."

Some years earlier Captain Yistar had taught Danaer the rudiments of letters, a necessary tool used in deciphering the army's maps. Thus he was able to puzzle out the few words written on the message, repeating them aloud with amazement: "To Gordt te Raa, Sovereign of all the Destre Tribes."

Sovereign—the style a lord of The Interior would employ to describe the ruler of the plains people. Among the Destre-Y, Gordt te Raa was called Siirn Rena, the Azsed Rena, leader of the strongest clans inhabiting the Vrastre, chieftain of chieftains.

And to deliver such a message to such a man, Danaer would be forced to enter Siank Zsed.

General Nurdanth avoided Danaer's stare. "I realize what I ask. Worse, I must command that you act as a courier and travel unaccompanied. It is the king's desire, and it may not be changed, I regret to say."

Yistar could not restrain his anger and growled a blunt obscenity. Then he blushed as Lira Nalu smiled, apparently understanding the raw soldier's term despite her gentle bearing and youthfulness.

Danaer had taken oath, and he was a warrior. He would not dishonor his word, though this be a most grim destiny. Yet the goddess would never scorn a man for using whatever cunning he might to survive. He asked carefully, "Lord General, may I dress as a tribesman? The Zsed's outriders might overlook me the longer, and I should have more chance of success . . ."

The nobleman was shaking his head. With pain, he said, "I would most willingly allow you that favor if I could, Troop Leader. But that, too, is forbidden. You have been chosen as our best hope. You are a Destre by birth and know their language and customs as no outsider could. But you must go as the representative of the King's army."

Nurdanth was still regretting that he must be the instrument of command in this undertaking. "I will give you as much as I can, Troop Leader. Here— there is nothing in the task of courier that prevents your wearing of tribal mantle, and your faith-ring. Perhaps those will help convince the Destre-Y that you are not their enemy." He gave the striped cloak back with an obvious eagerness.

Danaer weighed the precious message in his hand. It was very light, a small thing to cost his life. The ways of the gods were ever unfathomable. "I shall do my best, my lord. If the goddess grants her favor, I vow I will place this in the hands of the Destre Siirn himself."

A stirring entered his spirit, a sensation he had known before, when readying for battle. Ai! He *would* succeed, if possible. And if not, then he would show Siank Zsed that a warrior of Nyald knew how to die well.

General Nurdanth nodded. "This message must be given to none save the Sovereign Gordt te Raa. Oh, and you will impress upon him that the words come in all good faith from myself, from Royal Commander Malol, and from King Tobentis." Yistar snorted derisively, his furry eyebrows arching toward his hairline. The nobleman went on with some irritation. "It is true that the responsibility for that last claim is my own. But by Peluva's heavenly orb, if we do not establish communication, and quickly, with Gordt te Raa, Tobentis will not be King at all. His head will decorate the gates of Kirvii while a Markuand warlord sits on the throne!"

Nurdanth turned to the white-bearded wizard. "Traech Sorkra, perhaps you might give the Troop Leader some sign, to encourage him in this mission, that he will know he acts on behalf of those worthy of such risks?"

Ulodovol was sunk in brooding. His mouth parted and silently formed the word "Web." Then he waved absently at Lira, delegating this minor feat of magic to his apprentice.

She sat up straighter, some of her former animation coming back to her pretty face. When images began to form again in the air above the table, Lira Nalu was smiling, no longer tense. A charming little conjurer, she wove pictures out of nothing, now and then looking at Danaer coyly, hoping that he would be pleased by what she created.

Smoke-that-was-not-smoke swirled and became a mountain highway, and a marker stone proclaimed that this scene was some distance away, westward, not far from Kirvii and the palace. A military party proceeded along the road, heading for Fort Siank. There were royal banners and various smaller flags identifying several lords of The Interior. Danaer leaned forward, and he seemed to hear names spoken within that picture.

At the forefront rode Royal Commander Malol te Eldri. He was the King's own viceroy of the armies. Malol's red cloak was trimmed in gold, and his helmet was crested with the sacred plumes of the snow eagle. His countenance was patrician and lean, his manner cultured and as proper as his dark and neatly trimmed mustache and beard. Malol te Eldri looked the part of a Royal Commander. But besides the keen intelligence and courtesy he must share with Nurdanth, there was also a sense of a core of that strength necessary in any true battle lord.

Another name was heard, and Danaer's belly tightened at the sound. A young officer rode at the stirrup of Malol te Eldri, and the Royal Commander smiled fondly at his protégé, repeating that name which had drawn Danaer's keen interest.

Branraediir! The Destre clans of the west, the

Tradyans, had met this soldier in war, to their great sorrow. Minstrels had carried the laments to all the Zseds and warned: Beware of Branra of the Bloody Sword, the favorite of the Royal Commander! Branra, the man who bows to no god and trusts only the blade which has drunk the blood of many a brave Destre-Y!

The famous sword was there at his side. Its silver hilt caught the sun's rays, and black gems, embedded in the metal, sparkled. Despite that costly adornment, it was a true weapon and one to fear, as Destre-Y had learned to fear the man who wielded it.

Branra was stocky and broad-shouldered, and he was swarthy from seasons spent out on the western Vrastre, not locked away in his castle like so many lords of The Interior. He was younger than Danaer had supposed—of an age with the Troop Leader himself. His features were sharp and broken now and then by a reckless grin which bespoke a courage his reputation confirmed.

The smoke melted and twisted, and for an instant Danaer saw Lira Nalu's face instead of Branraediir's. Then he looked upon an island of Clarique. Not Jlandla Hill—another place not far off, where a motley army had gathered in dismay and rage. The ragged forces had come to help Clarique, but the battle was done, and now they milled about uncertainly and tasted frustration. Some were Clarique peasants and some little curly-headed Sarli brigands. A large number were warrior women who had followed a virago leader here to Clarique, in quest of bloody triumph over Markuand.

That virago now struggled to draw an army out of chaos and rally them to fight the white-clad enemy elsewhere. Jlandla was lost, but the war had only begun. She was now called Ti-Mori, though born to an honored lineage in The Interior of Krantin. Moved by some personal fury, she had burst the bonds of her class and become a warrior, leading a horde of battle priestesses, each intent on slaking her blood lust with the deaths of the Markuand. These wild females had become an army—an army which was still intact and able to wage war, though Jlandla Hill had been overrun and the Markuand seized more and more of the Clarique domain.

The visions evaporated. Malol te Eldri, Branraediir and his bloody sword, Ti-Mori and her women warriors—all were gone. Lira Nalu spoke and shattered her own creations. "You see that we will not face the invader alone. There are still many gallant comrades and those who will champion us, men and women who do not frighten easily, whether the threat be weapon or magic."

Yistar's hand fell on Danaer's shoulder with a hearty slap. "You have your orders. We will need an answer to this message quickly, in order to carry forward the Royal Commander's battle plans." He spoke with bluff confidence, to cheer himself and his subordinate, a tactic Danaer knew of old and appreciated.

The General was getting to his feet, and all the others save Ulodovol copied him. The old sorkra remained seated, staring into nothing, and none dared disturb him, not even his apprentice. Lira Nalu pointedly did not look at her mentor, continuing to force an encouraging smile as Danaer said, "My lord, at least in the Zsed I will not lack someone of Azsed to chant a prayer to the goddess, should I be slain."

It was not what she had expected him to say, and her face mirrored her shock, though she kept silence.

Nurdanth was disturbed also. "You must not be slain! If you do not deliver the message safely to Gordt te Raa, all the prayers and sacrifices to all of Krantin's gods may not spare our land from ruin!"

Danaer was shaken by the force of Nurdanth's words. He did not trust himself to respond, saluting the commandant, then following Yistar and the sorkra woman out to the entry hall. Captain Yistar paused and caught at Danaer's sleeve, then brushed away a heavy layer of dust, wrinkling his nose in distaste.

"Put on a clean uniform before you leave," he instructed. "And guard yourself well in this. Keep out of trouble if you can, of course, but do not falter if it finds you, eh? I know you will not shame Nyald troop."

"I will go as if I rode for the honor of my clans," Danaer said.

"Mm! Yes, that will serve. And there will be a special mount for you, by order of the General. Maybe I can find you a Destre saddle as well, one padded with motge hide, such as you have wheedled at me for these years." With that, Yistar hurried out, barely taking time to give back Danaer's parting salute.

Danaer gazed after the officer a while, then said with bitter amusement, "Now he will agree to give me the saddle. Wrath ve dortu!"

"A Sarli oath?" Lira Nalu asked.

"It is a phrase I learned from a trader from your country, my lady." Danaer drank in the sight of the woman, suddenly aware that he might soon go to Keth's portals and know no more of the pleasures of the world. If time were not so short, he might presume to . . .

But she was a sorkra, one of the wizard kind.

"Troop Leader, your eyes are embarrassing me," she said with a becoming blush.

"Your pardon, my lady." Yet Danaer did not turn away. Tiny things were now worth notice—a coppery chain clasped about her small waist, the curve of her boots along dainty ankles, the folds of yellow flowing over breast and hip. He saw as if for the first time that she knotted her Sarli headband on the left side, which meant she was an initiate of the minstrels. "Lady Lira Nalu, if I die, will you sing my memory in your next telling of the tales? There are none left of my clan to repeat my name. My last kinswoman is dead. If you forget me, I shall be lost in the winds."

Her hands crept to her throat. "I . . . I shall do as you ask. But it shall not be necessary. You shall return to us unharmed."

The words troubled him more than a promise to seek favor of the gods might have. Danaer had learned long ago that when women spoke only of success, they often feared danger was most near.

Danaer sighed and went to his barracks, a long, smoke-filled chamber cut in the rock of the mountain. In his absence, Yistar's orderly had delivered a new uniform to his pallet. Shaartre watched as Danaer dressed, looking ever more worried. They had shared many hard campaigns and knew the dangers of patrol. Danaer put on the stiff new shirt and tunic and breeches, then frowned at the polished footwear he had been provided. Making a sudden decision, he put those aside and kept his well-worn Destre boots, using his blade to cut a necessary slash in the crisp hem of the breeches, the better to afford easy access to his old knife, sheathed snugly against his calf.

"Will not the commandant balk at that?" Shaartre asked.

Danaer settled his Destre sling and belt blade against the heavy leather of the new belt and shrugged. "I do not think so. Not for what I have to do."

"Some risk in it, eh? I thought as much."

With a grunt, Danaer picked up the boots he had scorned. "These should not be wasted. You take them."

"No. Keep the things. They were given to you and look too small for me, anyway. You will need them for muster tomorrow, besides."

"Perhaps they will fit one of the new men. That peasant boy with the sunny nature—Xashe?—he is my size, and a good rider. Give them to him."

The veteran snatched the proffered boots and flung them onto his pallet. "The accursed things will be here when you get back. I will hear no more of it." Without another word, he turned away, walking the length of the room and squatting down amid a circle of gamblers.

Danaer let him go, knowing the rules of this, a ritual he had played with Shaartre in times past, when they both knew what fate might bring. He draped his mantle about his head and shoulders and put on his helmet and sword, then ducked through the low door. A stable groom awaited him outside. The man was holding the reins of a magnificent roan stallion. General Nurdanth was said to be a fancier of the Destre horses and an ardent experimenter in crossbreeding roans with the army's own black stock. This beast was a prize of his efforts. On its back was the saddle Yistar had promised, one of the best Danaer had ever seen. The stallion pawed the dirt and jangled its bits, disliking inaction.

Taking the reins, Danaer swung up, pleased to find the roan did not try to fight him. Though roans were restive and spirited, the blending of the stolid black horses' temperament had cooled the roans' natural wildness. Without conscious thought, Danaer flipped wide his mantle, and the cloak settled gracefully behind the cantle, spreading over the mottled rump. The stallion answered to a faint touch of rein and knee and the shift of Danaer's weight.

Danaer rode out into the compound. As he had expected, the stallion was perfectly gaited in Destre fashion. He felt a true warrior, on a steed a Siirn would envy. Sentries and idlers gawked as Danaer nudged the roan, making it curvet and frisk, scattering a few troopmen who had strayed into its path.

Yistar and the General were standing at the gates, and Danaer hastily quieted the horse, approaching them sedately. As he endured their inspection, both looked him over carefully, staring for a long moment at his boots. Yistar swallowed a smile, saying nothing, and Danaer's attention shifted anxiously to the commandant.

"It is well," Nurdanth said. "Most well. A fine appearance. Excellent! Do not grow too fond of this animal, however. It is to be a gift . . . to our noble adversary, with my compliments."

"I understand, my Lord General."

"Then away with you, and the goddess guard you this night." Yistar bellowed to the gatekeepers, and the men cursed and sweated at the bars. There was a final exchange of salutes and Danaer leaned forward. Alert and responsive, the roan trotted out briskly, leaving the firelit courtyard and moving into the blackness beyond.

IV

Siirn Gordt te Raa

The night engulfed Danaer. Though most men would have been lost in such blackness, he found starlight and the dim glow of fort and city sufficient to show the way. Now and then he touched the reins and avoided barricade or pitfall, finally rounding the last of the stoneworks of the garrison's outer defenses. Siank spread out below him, a vista of painted walls and myriad lamps and lofty towers.

Danaer let the roan canter downhill, lured by Siank, the sacred city of the goddess. At sundown, on a much poorer mount, he had ridden this same road. Then his mood had been far different, as he intended to seek the temple and a good inn. That was before he had encountered those hard reminders of his status here. Since leaving Nyald, he had become more than ever suspended between the two peoples, a target for their distrust.

He tried to imagine Siank's walls broken and her Destre pride shattered, and though she had not welcomed him, the prospect brought him deep pain.

The torchlit towers slid past on his right as the stallion followed a beaten trail. Danaer looked again and again at Siank. Like many a youth of the tribes, he once had yearned to make this pilgrimage. Siank—of the green trees and brush nourished by numerous sweet water springs, the life source of the city's security and wealth. Siank shimmered in the night, the legends painted on her white daubed walls softened by wavering lamp light. Limbs of trees tossed above those walls, and Danaer could see clearly the delicate spire of Argan's holy temple and the dome of the Guild of the Caravan Routes . . .

The city of the Destre-Y, and he was shut away from it by his oath. A chasm yawned between him

46

and Siank—a chasm a thousand king's-lengths wide and eight years deep.

He goaded the roan and it sprang forward like a steed from the hero myths, plunging into the darkness, leaving Siank farther and farther to the rear. Within a few long strides distance blurred torchlight into mist-dimmed rainbows, pale candles against the night.

Danaer had scouted the area thoroughly when he had arrived at the garrison, and now he bore unerringly for the Zsed. It was not entombed in the foothills, like the fort, nor yet behind walls, like the Destre brothers who dwelt in Siank. With the turn of the seasons, Siank Zsed would follow the numberless herds of the Vrastre and stalk those caravans which had not paid for enough escort. But now, in the spring, hard on the heels of the goddess's festival, the Zsed was tented near the wells and streams northeast of the city. There was little pressure for the Destre encampment to move elsewhere. For three moons, General Nurdanth had let the Zsed remain quiet, as he might a sleeping den of ravenous prey-seekers.

Danaer twisted in the saddle again, focusing on a particular star. From his vantage, the Eye of Sarlos hung directly over Siank's mountain gate. Given that guidance, he knew he must begin to turn and head out onto the open Vrastre Plains.

The night thickened perceptibly, and then an eerie fog, seemingly lit from within, rose out of nowhere. Danaer had never encountered its like. The horse felt his uneasiness and snorted and shook its mane. Danaer gentled the animal and rode on, though at a slower gait.

He told himself he was no child, to be frightened of fog and dark. Yet he murmured a prayer to the walkers-of-the-night and damp-breathers, those things of legends. Now Danaer sensed a presence—no; *many* presences, all around him. If he turned and glanced over his shoulder, would he catch a glimpse of some nameless demon hovering there?

The roan stumbled and Danaer tightened the reins, using all his skill to control the nervous animal. Before him, the fog swirled and climbed, filling his sight.

Vapor became grotesque faces and gaping, fanged jaws, and sharp talons raked at Danaer and the horse.

Instinctively, Danaer jerked the roan back violently as one of the fog paws grazed his leg. Icy fire seemed to lance through his bones and sinew, and the roan danced aside in terror.

Danaer's heart thundered as he fought the brute, at war with both these supernatural vapors and the horse's panic.

Wizardry! It could be nothing else!

This was no fog of the plains, nor was it his mind playing tricks. The well-trained horse lunged and grew wild-eyed, as it never would be confronting mortal predators, no matter how fearsome.

Now Danaer knew the same horror that must have seized the hapless general of the Clarique. Magic—again working to the Markuand will!

Danaer set his jaw, vowing not to succumb to sorcery. He had sworn to deliver the General's message, and he would not be bested by creatures of the mist. With a snarled warning, he drew sword, though wondering if the army's steel would pierce his foes. Knotting the reins in his right fist, he held the roan against its urge to bolt. "Steady, Sure-Foot, and show them no weakness, lest they take strength from it! Steady! Argan banish you, demons!"

He slashed at the nearest of the fog apparitions, dividing the ugly form in halves, sending the vapor spinning to either side. Another rose to take its place and Danaer struck with desperation, severing slavering muzzle from the head, cutting off the clawed feet.

Other melting and re-forming demons appeared, closing in behind and around and above Danaer while he continued to fight. There could be no parrying and a shield would not avail him much, even had he brought one.

A new presence came upon this unreal battle, an invisible but very palpable force. Had Danaer wished for a shield? A shield was in his hand, not a thing he could touch but as potent as this unseen ally who had joined his cause, setting itself between Danaer and the abominations in the fog.

"Argan hurl you to Bogotana's Realm!" Danaer roared, taking heart and wielding the sword savagely. This time the demon he slashed dissolved away completely. The roan's antics were lessened, as if the brute also sensed that help was with them.

Leaves rustled, though there were no trees close by, and a warm wind swept across the scene, overwhelming the cold fog. Yet more demons broke, bursting into air. Did Danaer imagine a faint howling, a disappointed gibbering boiling from the departing mist? He could not be certain, but knew the creatures were being bested—were gone!

"Kant, prodra Argan," he said with gratitude, giving the goddess her due. As he gulped for breath, that sound of leaves came once more and with it a tantalizing jingle, like jewels and coins brushing one against another. With that, the last of the evil fog disappeared. He was in familiar darkness.

Danaer gazed around, quieting the roan, listening intently. The rustling leaves and the jewel-music were stilled. But he had not dreamed them. He had been well supported in the struggle, and those sweet sounds had been some manifestation of his unseen ally.

Wizardry! More wizardry to counter the magical evil that had barred his way to the Zsed!

Ulodovol had said the Markuand wizard was mighty, and Danaer had felt the proof.

He had dealt with it, through no choice of his own. No, not alone. He was a warrior, but no fit adversary for creatures made of mist. Danaer did not enjoy owing a debt to magic, but he acknowledged what had happened. "The goddess I thank—and I thank you, my mysterious companion."

For a heartbeat, he captured a sensation of sparkling, large, dark eyes and triumphant, feminine laughter. There was no reply from the darkness, nor had he expected one.

Danaer chirruped to the stallion and coaxed it to take up the trail again. With each minute the awful fight with demons lessened its hold upon him. Soon he was on the fringes of the Zsed, and a more straightforward menace claimed his attention. Rolling grassland brushed against his stirrups as the roan trotted down a knoll, then splashed through one of the many streams which fed Siank's springs and wells.

Others were traveling this same path, the inhabitants of the Zsed returning from Siank or journeying on the Vrastre. These could be a danger, but one Danaer knew well and could accept. When the roan nickered to other horses in the Zsed's herds, he leaned on its neck and pinched its nostrils to shut off the exchange. Once he entered the heart of the Zsed, he must be the undisguised representative of Krantin's King. Until then he would act as a scout, penetrating the encampment with stealth.

There would have been Destre spies, watching the fort. But they were guarding against a large body of troops, moving to attack the Zsed. They would take little note of a single rider. The Zsed's outriders had not challenged him, either, thinking that one who wore a tribal mantle was a member of the camp.

The guard line was tenuous, and he slipped cautiously between each outpost. Now and then a challenge was called, but Danaer knew the tongue and gave proper answer, arousing no alarm. As he rode ever deeper into the Zsed, he began to wonder if Nurdanth was correct: a single unescorted courier was the only hope of success in this mission.

Close ahead now were clan fires, casting shadows on gaily striped tent walls and canopies. The women had taken down their looms for the night, and children slept or drowsed on their mothers' laps while the elders regaled any who would hear with Destre legends. Warrior men and women talked of weapons and roans and the movements of the Vrastre game, and they boasted of the raids they would make against the summer's caravans out of Siank.

It was a rich Zsed, well fed and well sheltered, and the contrast with Danaer's home encampment was great. Even the camp dogs were fat. Plainly the Zsed had not suffered in the season just ending. Clans fed on roast haunch of motge or woolback and dipped from steaming pots of simo grain. These were no beggars, and their spirits had never been chastened by defeat.

"Smile, goddess, for all our peoples," Danaer said, sending the words winging to the holy ones.

He must not hesitate from this point forward. At a slow walk, he rode into the clan camp. It would be madness to move quickly. Tribesmen would think it an attack and rope him from the horse at once. He must convince them he was not hostile, and show them no fear.

Danaer drew a few careless glances which soon became hard stares as he passed the first line of tents. A dog barked, then lost interest, though his masters did not. The murmurings began among the people. Before anyone could react, Danaer was beyond them, heading for the next cluster of dwellings. He did not look back, but he knew most, if not all, of the clan he had just left were standing in the path and gawking after him.

He passed two more main camps, using the same method, not hurrying the roan. Word was running before him now, and on either side Danaer sensed the scurryings as people followed his progress. They darted between the tents and picketed animals as they carried the news of Danaer's coming to fellow tribesfolk.

When he rode into the glow of the fourth communal fire, the people were ready for him. A profound silence gripped them, even the youngest babe. If a dog yapped, it was kicked away, its tail between its legs. Rows of eyes watched Danaer. Warriors and dotards, women with sucklings at the breast, big-eyed children, lesser priests and priestesses and herb-healers stared at Danaer in fascination. As he moved by, the stillness broke at last into sharp whispers and angry growling.

At the next fire, a tribe leader waited out ahead of the circle of people. Arms akimbo and feet planted wide, he blocked Danaer's way. Danaer drew rein. The expression on the man's face was one of smothered fury. The cloak he wore proclaimed him a chieftain of a strong clan.

Danaer hoped they would give him a chance to be heard. Careful to use his heaviest Azsed dialect, he said, "Maen gra siray, ae may not ask so great a tribesman to step aside. But ae would beg your people move back that ae can ride through . . ."

"The speech is Destre, but that uniform is much hate to all of the plains." The Siank accent was very thick. "What do you here, Destre? If Destre you be."

"Destre-Y I am, and I bring message to Siirn Gordt te Raa."

"All the way from Nyald, and in that uniform?" Ugly laughter rang through the crowd and children clapped with glee, wanting to witness excitement.

"The message is from Nurdanth, the Iit who keeps his vow, te Fael." Danaer gave the General the title the Destre would know. Words could be weapons as much as steel and lance and sling stone, now.

"An Iit! As are you! You speak the tongue and wear the eiphren, but . . ."

"I will recite Argan's own sacred law if it will prove me a true Azsed," Danaer said. Too much doubt from too many sides was wearing thin his patience, and warning crept into his voice.

This time there was no laughter, and the chieftain glowered at Danaer's challenging tone. "Get down from there! We will learn if you are a Destre-Y. Put off that Iit sword and draw knife!"

Danaer threw his leg over the roan's withers and dropped to the ground. His boot knife was already in his hand, and he kept the chieftain at bay while he unbuckled his sword. Then he took the message from his tunic and put it into the cheek strap of the bridle. "That is to be given to Siirn Gordt te Raa, whether I live or die . . ."

"Let us see if your knife is as bright as your tongue, Iit!"

They circled cautiously, blades pointing. Danaer jabbed an elbow into his horse's flank and it shied into the crowd, buying him room to maneuver. This contest must have a quick ending. On every side rose cries of derision, aimed at him. A wave of hatred washed over Danaer.

Abruptly, he swung his mantle hem wide, into the chieftain's face, then put his foot behind the man's knee. It was a gamble on his greater height and weight, a successful one. They tumbled to the dust and struggled furiously for the advantage.

As they fell, the tribesman's knife slashed open Danaer's arm but did not hinder him. In the next minute he gained the position he sought, sitting astride his opponent's chest, his blade against the other's throat. "A second? Or is this besting enough, warrior?"

"Harshaa!" The crowd's hostility changed to a roar of delight in such fighting skill. "He is no Iit, not and handle a knife so!"

"Let him up, soldier." This was a new voice, very deep and masculine and quite close.

Boots straddled the fallen chieftain's head, and Danaer lifted his gaze to look into the craggy face of a man more than a half-arm taller than he. The giant was breathing heavily, swelling the barrel chest beneath Destre shirt and a black and gold vest and mantle.

Black and gold, and a man of such a size—this could only be Gordyan, the notorious personal bodyguard of Gordt te Raa.

Slowly Danaer stood up. The newcomer appeared no smaller from that angle, and Danaer noted that the people had become very still. The tribal chieftain leaped up, panting, his knife out for another attack. Before he could strike, Gordyan seized him by the nape and threw him back to the dust. It was as though he had chastened an unruly boy.

"They say you have a message for the Rena?" Gordyan asked coldly. "The Siirn Rena is most interested in this message from Nurdanth. Bring your paper, and that fair roan." With that, the big man turned and waded into the mass of onlookers.

After a bit of open-mouthed wonder, Danaer hastily retrieved his helmet and caught up his reins, running in Gordyan's wake. The man plowed through the mob of people, parting them with his immense bulk and daunting presence. Taking double steps to keep up with the man's long stride, Danaer ripped a tag of cloth

from his mantle and with his teeth and good hand
bound the crude bandage around his wound to staunch
the blood. Now and then he tripped on rough ground,
threading his way through tents and camps and trying to remain within escort distance of Gordyan.

He had known, in theory, the expanse of Siank
Zsed. But now he began to comprehend the folly of his
mission. It had been only the will of the goddess that
had allowed him to get this far. If Gordyan had not
come to fetch him, he would not have come out alive.

The Zsed was made up not only of clan tents but of
tribal councils of awesome size. Household pavilions
and fattening pens and makeshift warehouses held the
Zsed's vast properties. Danaer was overwhelmed by
the extent of it all. Now he saw Siank Zsed in the
flower of its strength and himself as a midge thinking
to plague this monster. Not courage but rashness had
guided him, as desperation had made the General send
him on the errand.

The tents increased in grandeur as Gordyan proceeded to the center of the Zsed, the area reserved for
the Siirn. Here were the best water and grazing for
the Siirn's people and herds. The ground rose gradually, and Danaer followed Gordyan toward the highest
point of the encampment. They approached a veritable
palace of a tent, with golden hangings marking the
many entryways. More warriors guarded the pavilion.
Here odors of food and the warm scents of earth and
grass and clean water overcame the common stench of
human and animal offal and dung-chip smoke which
filled the lower Zsed. Somewhere close by there was
music and singing and happy voices.

The guards glanced at Danaer, gauging him, as befit
warriors protecting their Siirn. Just as Gordyan reached
the curtain at the main tent, he stopped so short that
Danaer nearly collided with him. "Now, this message."
He grasped for the paper wedged in the roan's bridle.

Danaer was faster, holding the General's letter
tightly. It had become his safe conduct. "Your pardon
and your favor, but I have sworn to deliver it only
into the hands of the Siirn."

The big man glared down at him, his jaw thrust out

belligerently. At last Gordyan grunted assent, gestured for Danaer to wait, then ducked out of sight behind the golden hangings.

Gordyan reappeared, to bid him enter the tent. As Danaer brushed past him, the giant growled, "That message should be of much importance, Iit."

The pavilion was lit by costly oil lamps and tapers, and the luxury of its furnishings—caravan booty of the best—made Danaer blink. The interior tent walls were tapestries; cushions and tables and chests were of the finest make, fit for a lord's castle. Yet this was but an entranceway, not the quarters of the Siirn and his people.

More guards attended curtained doorways. Like those outside the tent, they were heavily armed against any invasion of the Siirn's privacy. And like those of Gordyan, their garments were vivid with the black and gold colors of the Siirn Rena, the leader of all Destre-Y.

"Here, soldier." Gordyan pulled aside drapes. Each compartment was more dazzling than the one before, and more brightly lit. At a final portal, curtained in silver threads, Gordyan slowed his pace, pausing, some of his rough manner replaced with subdued respect. He indicated that Danaer should precede him, then thrust back the drape and a raven-hued gauze beyond it.

They had arrived at the Zsed's heart. Rich fabric peaked into a high roof, and red and green joined the black and gold among the furnishings' colors. There were many plump cushions and booty chests and a number of carven tables inlaid with gems. One of these was set with wine and meat, and a darkly handsome man sat at the table, enjoying a late meal.

He had laid aside his mantle, baring his black hair. His sleeves were turned back that he might better rub the power-giving fat of his eating on his flesh. The man did not deign to look up when Danaer and Gordyan entered.

A woman sat beside him; not so forbidding as her companion, she smiled and rose to greet the Siirn's bodyguard and the soldier. "Ah! This is the messenger you promised us, Gordyan?"

"True it is, and I grant him that he fights well, army though he be."

Danaer watched the big man sidelong, intrigued by the change in Gordyan. The deep voice had softened and the brute strength was caged. There was even a slight stammer in his words, more than warranted by uncertainty of phrasing. Gordyan's gaze did not stray from the woman but devoured her as a man might the sight of the goddess's image.

"So, you fight well, soldier?" she asked teasingly. "What else do you do?"

"My lady, I have a paper from the hand of General Nurdanth, for Sovereign Gordt te Raa."

"That is a most charming accent, soldier," the woman said. "Now I have placed it—Nyald. We have not heard good news of Nyald Zsed these past years, I fear. What is your name?"

"Danaer, of the clan of Tlusai."

He was trying not to stare boldly at her. The woman's dialect was as outland as Danaer's own, though of northern, not southern, extraction. Her silken brown hair was tied back simply from a fine-boned face, and her eyes were cave-dark, as black as a moonless night. A warrior woman, she wore shirt and breeches and vest, but those emphasized her slender body. A half-skirt and bejeweled tola-belt about her hips marked her bound to a man, and of high caste among the Destre. Despite that, she looked over Danaer frankly, from helmet to sword to boots, then shook her head, bewildered by the contradictions in his dress. As she did, the eiphren suspended upon her high brow sparked with green fire in the light of the tapers. This was a woman out of the ancient tales, one who seemed to radiate a sexuality as old as humanity, and she was most adept at using her femaleness as a weapon.

A servant rushed into the tented chamber and set down a tray of confections. The woman gawked ingenuously at Danaer. "Why, he *is* a soldier! Gordyan did not joke about that, Lasiirnte."

Lasiirnte? Princess of the Azsed?

Danaer's emotions reeled. Had he been talking so casually with Lasiirnte Kandra, ruler of the Ve-Nya tribes, consort of the Siirn Rena?

"Bring wine, for later, Esbeti," Kandra said.

With a sigh, the man at the table pushed away the remnants of his meal and at last regarded Danaer. His face was a mask that revealed nothing, but his dark eyes cut holes through Danaer's hard-bought confidence. This was Gordt te Raa, chieftain of the Vrastre from Deki on the River to the Plains-of-No-Ending beyond Barjokt. He could command the death of an army scout—or an army—by no more than a nod and a word.

"Gordyan tells me that you bring a letter from Nurdanth," Gordt te Raa said. There was little patience in his manner and voice. Reluctantly, Danaer delivered the now somewhat soiled paper, then stepped back to his place and waited apprehensively.

Danaer was impressed to see that Gordt te Raa needed no scribe to translate the scrawling. This was a rare Destre who could read, and he pored over Nurdanth's message thoughtfully. "Your General speaks well, on paper. But dare a Destre trust a lord of The Interior?"

Uncomfortable in this new role of emissary, Danaer said, "Siirn, the General is a worshipper of Peluva, but his honor is that of a tribesman, by all accounts. He is not one who will lie. And I am instructed to assure you that his message comes in good faith as well from Royal Commander Malol te Eldri and from King Tobentis."

A nasty laugh answered him, echoed by a loud guffaw from Gordyan. Only Kandra restrained her bitterness, glancing sympathetically at Danaer. Gordt te Raa lost his momentary amusement. "I can believe in the honor of Nurdanth, for it is fabled. And perhaps we may trust this other lord, this Malol. But King Tobentis? Never! And I see you share our opinion, though your oath to the army makes you hold your tongue."

Danaer squirmed inwardly, fairly struck. Tobentis

was the sovereign who claimed his service, but courtiers and palace politics were poor guides to governing the vast diversity of Krantin.

The Siirn was staring at the message paper, drumming his fingers along the broken seal. "According to this, I must meet this Royal Commander Malol, and soon."

Involuntarily, Danaer gasped. How very important had been the message, and his mission! He had supposed Nurdanth was sending a truce proposal or begging a safe conduct for an army caravan. But this . . . ! Gordt te Raa, scourge of the Vrastre, and Malol, commander of the armies which had so long fought the Destre-Y and their Siirn—meeting in conference! There was no precedent, not since the times before Ryerdon crossed the river.

"Malol will come to a council of the tribes, at a place of our choosing, and he will bring an entourage of no more than three." Gordyan listened attentively, gauging the interest of his chieftain. The Siirn went on with grudging admiration. "He has much courage, this Malol, to put his life in my hands thus."

Danaer seized the opportunity to praise one of the army's best. "Ai, it is said Malol fears only his gods and will not quake even before the King."

"And you imitate him, do you not?" Gordt te Raa's eyes now shone with good humor.

"He does that, Rena," Gordyan agreed. "I saw this troopman teach one of our hot-bloods a lesson in knifing. He could have carved the man's gullet, had he the will to do so."

"Indeed? Perhaps the besting will sharpen the chastened warrior's alertness," Gordt te Raa said. "Soldier, it speaks well for this Malol to offer to come to a Destre council. But it took far more heart to ride into my Zsed alone, at night, and in that uniform."

"I was ordered to . . ."

"We both know that there are soldiers who desert the army's ranks, given such an order."

Danaer did not clutch at honors beyond his due. "I was chosen because I am Destre-Y. The General

and my Captain hoped I might be able to reach you
the easier than . . . than an unbeliever."

"And the goddess has smiled on you, Azsed,"
Lasiirnte Kandra reminded them. She wove the divine symbol of Argan in the air, and the men murmured piously.

Gordt te Raa leaned back, examining Danaer once
more. His expression was less grim than earlier, but
still made the scout most wary. "Argan uses us all, and
she has brought you here. A strange warrior, this, a
rider of Nyald Zsed—in the army of Krantin. Have
you ever pursued your tribesfolk to their deaths, soldier?"

It was a question Danaer dreaded. "At times I *have*
fought Destre-Y, but rarely. Nyald Zsed was ruined by
plague and war before I came to manhood. There
were not many left to kill. I have killed far more Iit
brigands, those who eluded the justice of the lords of
The Interior. That has been my duty for some seasons."

Gordt te Raa nodded, seemingly satisfied. Gordyan's
hand had been resting upon his belt knife, ready to
strike down the soldier if his answer had displeased
the Siirn. Now a grin split the big man's craggy face.
"La ben da, warrior! Well it would be to see an Iit
brigand trapped by the likes of you, and you wearing the army's badges!"

"This news of war in the east," Gordt te Raa cut in.
"What do you know of that?"

"General Nurdanth is consulting with his sorkra, and
they keep him informed on the battles—"

"Sorkra? Nurdanth has wizards at his command?
La! Sorkra! And what say these sorkra-y? What of
these rumors of some foreigners in white garb who
seek to overthrow the islands?"

"The news is most bad; the sorkra tell us that
Jlandla Hill, an important Clarique fortress, has fall-
en to these invaders. They call themselves Markuand,
and they do not cry out in pain or death. They overcame the Clarique through black sorcery as well as
by numbers and arms . . ."

Appalled, as Danaer had been when he first learned

of the horror, the three stared at him wordlessly for
several long moments. Then Gordt te Raa stood up and
went to one of the treasure boxes cluttering the chamber. He took out a map and a writing stick, then
beckoned Danaer close. Kandra and Gordyan followed
him as the Destre leader spread out the chart on a
table. "I have not heard of this Jlandla Hill. Show
me where it is."

The map was caravan booty. The symbols were in
Clarique, but Yistar had taught Danaer a bit of that
language as well as Krantin. He pointed to a central
island in the distant country. "Jlandla is marked here
upon the large map in the General's quarters."

Frowning, Gordt te Raa touched the indicated place
with the writing stick, then traced the line westward,
toward Krantin. The border city of Deki was the first
target. "Patkin!" Kandra whispered fearfully. Her consort gently touched her arm, concerned by her sudden
pallor.

Gordyan had looked anxious, and he explained
gruffly to Danaer, "The Lasiirnte's brother dwells in
Deki on the River."

Danaer nodded understanding, but Kandra would
be a warrior woman, not succumbing to any further
public display. Gordt te Raa turned back to the map.
"Nurdanth says these Markuand will strike first at the
Clarique capital of Laril-Quil, and at the mighty port
that was ancient Ryerdon, now called Alensal. Then
Deki must be taken, if they are to control the river
and cross over into Krantin." He eyed Danaer calcu-
latingly. "Your General speaks of reinforcing the
army's garrison there. What say you?"

The Destre ruler's talent in war had given him his
name: he who cuts. Now he had slashed aside small
details and gone to the core of the crisis. Danaer was
uneasy acting as a consultant to this man who was
the army's most deadly foe. But General Nurdanth was
seeking a truce and a council, and his courier must
speak on that behalf. "Deki's garrison is very small, as
well you must know. The Destre-Y have long harried
the army's supply lines there. I do not think the General can hope to send many troops to their aid, though

undoubtedly he will try. He does not abandon his men."

Gordt te Raa threw down the writing stick and glared at the map. "I would that I had sorkra-y in my service, as Nurdanth does. Ai! I fear them as any Azsed should. But, by Argan, if I could pay one of those wizards to work magic for *me* . . ." A grim thought struck him. "Do these Markuand also have wizards?"

"Yes. Most powerful sorkra-y." Danaer did not go on, but his listeners read the ominous meaning in his words, believing it.

"I like it not," Gordt te Raa said. "The sorkra ways are not for us. Witchcraft! Yet we must deal with these wizards, and with the Markuand. Perhaps if I meet with Malol . . ."

Danaer remembered Nurdanth's parting comment and hoped to help seal the Destre's decision. "To seal this pact, the General has sent you a gift."

Those dark eyes focused intently upon Danaer. Gordt te Raa was an eager audience as Danaer said, "It is a roan stallion from his own stables. He asks that you will favor him by accepting . . ."

"Let us see."

With no more discussion, Gordt te Raa walked through the tent. Danaer trailed him, aware that Gordyan and several of the ubiquitous guards were bringing up the rear. Kandra came also. When they reached the outermost tent flap, she waited in the entryway while Gordt te Raa inspected the scout's roan.

With some anxiety, Danaer watched also, admiring the Destre's sure touch and thorough probing of the roan's best points, even to the saddle Yistar had granted. Finally Gordt te Raa straightened and said, "Gordyan."

Danaer tensed. It was well known throughout the Zseds that Gordyan disposed of the Siirn Rena's enemies, and Gordt te Raa had spoken curtly, as if about to give such an order.

"Provide an escort for the soldier, back to his fort."

Gordyan was a large, wide-eyed child, hearing that

which he could not comprehend. "To the fort, Rena?"

Lasiirnte Kandra smiled at them, as a woman might at the petty confusions of rowdy youths. In the shadows of the tent, Kandra was more than ever a living statue of superb female beauty, a woman whose being glorified the goddess.

"Not into the fort," Gordt te Raa said impatiently. "Just close enough to let Troop Leader Danaer ride in with honor."

"With all honor," and Gordyan grinned in wolfish anticipation.

His master cut his bloodthirsty joy short. "With all honor, alive and conscious and in full possession of his weapons and uniform."

Chastened, Gordyan said in a surprisingly meek voice, "Exactly to your orders, Rena."

"And fetch another roan for the scout." Gordt te Raa ran a hand down the stallion's flank, gloating over his new property. Absently, he told Danaer, "Your General Nurdanth will have my reply within the day. I will give him the meeting place then."

"Most well . . . Siirn."

The Destre chieftain glanced at him with sudden sharpness. "You will not call me Rena?"

Rena, lord of a Destre-Y's loyalty. Danaer's oath to the army bound him away from that loyalty. Yet Osyta's prophecy stirred in his mind. "It is not possible. But someday, perhaps I shall be able to call a Destre the Rena—for he shall rule all Krantin."

Gordt te Raa's stern manner broke. He looked for a moment at Kandra, exchanging some personal feeling. Then he said, "Andaru. So all Azsed prays. May the time come soon."

Leaving the Zsed was far easier than entering it. Gordyan and four of his guards gathered around Danaer, and a replacement mount was brought for the scout. The Siirn and his woman disappeared inside the tent while a servant led away Nurdanth's magnificent stallion. It was all the dismissal Danaer was to receive. He shrugged and took the horse he was given, riding with Gordyan and his men through the encampment. The fires dimmed behind them and they cantered beyond the Zsed's outposts, swinging northwestward. Gordyan was setting the course, and plainly he planned to use the Ve-Nya trail, moving in a long arc to arrive at the fort by a more guarded route. The six loped along a mist-soaked grassland, aiming for the shadowy bulk of the mountains.

They turned south, snaking along the foothills. There was no conversation save for an occasional noting of landmarks, signs Danaer read as readily as his escorts. The velvety night flowed past for many minutes. Then torchlight gleamed ahead, over the mountain road. Siank's walls lay below and to the left. Gordyan slowed the pace and his men moved apart, melting into the rocks, hunting for traps and army pickets, even this far from the fort.

Gordyan continued to ride beside Danaer. Was this an honor, or a precaution against treachery?

"Soldier, are you truly Destre-Y? I thought it were a disguise, but to see you move a roan and handle a knife so well, I doubt it." Gordyan's question was blunt, like the man.

"I was birthed in Nyald Zsed and bowed to Azsed and took eiphren when I was a youth. The army does not command which god a man fears, only that he swear to follow his superior," Danaer said tiredly.

"Ai! And the Nyald tribe lost much when you joined that army." The torches showed Gordyan's grin, broad and without a trace of guile. "Were you not promised to Nurdanth, I should want you to ride with my men."

Surprised, Danaer tried to reject the offer politely. "No, the army has fed and clothed me. The fortunes of Nyald Zsed were in the dust when Yistar took me in. I would have starved with many of my kinfolk elsewise."

"But they breed them brave in Nyald," Gordyan insisted.

One of his riders spurred back toward them, warning, "Your pickets are drawing bow, soldier."

"Stand and call!" roared from the knoll ahead. The sentries had lost none of their sharpness since the last time Danaer had come this way.

He stood in the stirrups and shouted, "In the name of the General, hold your arrows. This is an escort from the Destre sovereign. If they die, you will taste the anger of both the General and Gordt te Raa!"

"Advance, then . . ."

"We leave you here," Gordyan said. His men had already vanished into the darkness. Just before he too rode away, Gordyan turned and added in parting, "The goddess guard your path, warrior."

"And Argan's favor on you."

When he reached the gates, he was startled to find Nurdanth and Yistar awaiting him. He knew they must have come here only minutes earlier, answering the gatekeepers' announcements. Yistar came forward and grasped the bridle and exclaimed, "Back in one piece, by the Black Mare's Mane!"

Nurdanth touched the ragged bandage on Danaer's arm, a thing the scout had nearly forgotten. "Is this a gift from Sovereign Gordt te Raa? Is this how he treats my courier?"

"No, my lord. I received a cut in a fight with a tribesman, a small matter, before I reached the Siirn's pavilion. The Siirn promises that you will have his answer tomorrow. But I gather it will be as you wish —concerning the naming of a meeting place for a Destre council."

"Excellent! Excellent!" Nurdanth briskly rubbed his pale hands together.

"Well done! You did proud by Nyald's units," Yistar said with a nod. "Now get you to the surgeon and have that cut dressed. And turn to sleep. You have merited it."

Danaer returned Yistar's triumphant smile, then rode toward the stables. A flash of yellow caught his eye. Danaer halted, then turned to the headquarters. He had not been mistaken. The yellow was the flutter of a Sarli's headband ribbons. Lira Nalu stood on a porchway of the officers' wing, and Danaer was drawn to her. Only when they were face to face did he realize that there was no wind to flutter her ribbons. Then what had pulled his attention?

The sorkra lingered in shadow, a dark shawl thrown

over her gown. She should have been nearly invisible, from the point where Danaer had first glimpsed her. Yet he had known she waited. She moved forward a bit, the dim light catching her mischievous expression and sparkling eyes.

"Lady, have I you to thank for my life?"

The wavering torchlight gleamed highlights from her tangle of curls as she cocked her head. "Why, I have remained here at the fort, Troop Leader Danaer. What could I do but pray for the success of your mission? And it *was* successful, was it not?"

"How do you know that, my lady? I have only this minute reported to the General and Yistar."

Lira Nalu chuckled softly. "I am the pupil of the Traech Sorkra. His web hears all the things that *he* hears and knows."

There was truth in that. She did not wink and turn her shoulder as a woman of ease might, nor come boldly toward him and speak her will as a Destre would if she favored a man. Danaer had never dealt at length with a woman of Sarlos before, and he was mystified, though not unpleasantly, by her ways. Was such coquetry her country's custom, or was it some nature of her sorkra arts?

She *was* a sorkra, and he had felt the cold touch of wizardry this night. He should have shunned her gifts.

But a stronger urge held him, one he had known before, though never to this degree. It was more than the lust a warrior would feel for a woman of ease. He had no words for the spell this sorkra was working, but he was not entirely certain that wizardry was involved.

"Do you only hear these messages of your . . . your web, my lady, or do you deliver them as well? Say, to a soldier beset by demons in the fog?"

She had no chance to answer. The gaunt wizard came to the arch behind her and called her, his temper obvious. The mischief left her face and she said hurriedly, "I must go now, Troop Leader. I am glad that you returned safely." In a whirl of shawl and bright ribbons, she was gone.

Yet she had spoken to him as woman, not sorkra,

and he suspected she *was* the source of his help in the fog. Magic it might be, but of a friendly sort, gentle and whimsical, as she seemed to be. Danaer smiled and turned once more toward the stables, anticipating pleasurable sleep and perhaps dreams filled with dark eyes and warm laughter.

V

THE SQUARE OF THE CLARIQUE TRADER

"THEY ARE COMING!" THAT WHISPER RAN THROUGH the assembled troops even before the posted lookouts could bray their formal news. The banners and pennants of the Royal Commander's company left the mountain road and came across the field toward the gates. Barricades had been moved aside and pitfalls were guarded to ease progress. The gates swung open and Siank garrison's flags dipped in obeisance to the royal standard. The soldiers lifted swords and spears and a cheer of greeting, pledging their fealty.

Danaer felt privileged, for he had seen these personages before, though only in the wizards' visions. The magic had not lied. Malol te Eldri was in every measure the nobleman he had appeared in the smoke pictures. As he reviewed the troops and accepted the welcome of Nurdanth and his aides, the Royal Commander missed nothing. He was the King's close kin and patrician by birth, but a soldier most practiced.

Close beside Malol te Eldri rode Branraediir. He lacked Malol's elegance but made an even deeper impact upon the garrison. The soldiers watched him with awe, marveling that he was so young but so famous. He gazed upon the lines of troops with a sharp manner, patently assessing if they would serve him well in battle. They must strive to equal his demands, for he need give way to few in his warrior's skill. Now, at this short remove, Danaer could see Branra's notorious sword clearly. It was no ceremonial weapon, and he wore it ready at hand, despite the peaceful nature of this review. Those black gems within the silver were obsidian, Danaer now realized. Save for his sword hilt, Branra's appearance was plain and workmanlike, no richer than Captain Yistar's.

The Royal Commander and his protégé were the chief interest of the onlookers, but there were others in the company to attract comment. One of the aides in particular made his audience gasp; his pennants and trappings marked him a prince, and his cloak and badges were brilliant. This Prince reflected no glory on his royal cousin, though, nor upon the Royal Commander, who must include him in the train. The man weaved dangerously in his saddle, wobbly from drink. His attendants supported him on either side. Malol and Branra had only their orderlies, but the Prince apparently had brought with him from Kirvii a numerous household, all flaunting his colors, and a woman who must be the Prince's mistress. She was dressed in stunning fashion, covered with jewels, her black hair coiled in the style of The Interior. Heedless of the occasion, she teased at the Prince and coquetted with passersby, making no secret of her wantonness.

While Malol and his other aides stood to review, the drunken Prince and his woman ignored the proprieties, laughing at some ribaldry. Like the other soldiers, Danaer viewed them with contempt. It was a poor beginning for Malol's arrival at Siank, to drag with him such hangers-on. Surely politics lay at the root of it, the machinations of the lords of The Interior and affairs of the palace.

As the day wore on, Danaer's suspicions were confirmed. Troopmen grumbled openly about the situation. They had not remarked on the accommodations made for the Royal Commander and Branra and the others, for those were surprisingly modest. Malol had no patience to waste on frippery. His drunken kinsman was more conscious of his rank, and de-

manded courtesies not only for himself but for all his
people. To its disgust, the garrison soon learned that
he was Prince Diilbok, a blood relation of Tobentis,
and one who expected to be served as well as the
King.

By the second candle-mark past midday, the newcomers were safely housed in the stonework headquarters, and all but the Prince's lackeys were content with
lodgings near the regular barracks. The garrison began
to return to its routine.

Quite by accident, Danaer discovered that the problems were far from over. He had finished supervising
recruits in weapons drill and was going back to his
units when he heard a loud argument issuing from the
officers' stables. The voices were feminine, and one of
them sounded much like Lira Nalu's.

Danaer pulled aside the door and went in to see to
this matter, then came to an abrupt stop, suddenly
wary. Several stableboys were off to one side, their
mouths agape while the women harangued each other.
Lira Nalu was indeed one of the squabblers, and her
opponent was the Prince's woman, that raven-haired
beauty who had disrupted the review.

"My mare is accustomed to this stall, and I will not
have her removed on *your* whim!" Lira said shrilly.
She clutched the halter of her mount and defiantly
blocked the other woman's path.

Obviously Diilbok's mistress had ordered Lira's
horse set aside for the convenience of her own animal.
A hapless lackey held the lead rope of the gelding in
question; the boy shifted from one foot to another,
fearful of bringing either woman's anger upon himself.

"Sarli, guard your words. No one insults me without
regret. I am Chorii of the Valley of the Hawk, and I
am Prince Diilbok's ward. Now step aside with that
bony nag." Lady Chorii turned to the groom and said,
"Well? Do as I ordered you! Are you deaf?"

"Act at your peril," Lira warned, halting the groom
in midstep. As the little sorkra's fury increased, her
voice softened to an ominous note. The soldiers well
knew her calling and treated her carefully, not wanting

her to turn her magic upon them. Thus the groom was frozen in place.

"Do you dare to—"

"I dare much, as you will find to *your* regret if you press the point. You are neither lady nor the Prince's 'ward,' and do not presume upon titles here." Lira was much shorter than the voluptuous Chorii. The sorkra's simple homespun gown was embroidered in bright blue, but it was no rival for the purple silks and feathers of Chorii's riding costume.

The Prince's mistress had the classic, sharp-featured beauty of women of The Interior, and her garment was cut very low across her full breasts and cinched in narrowly about her waist. Now her body strained against the cloth as her breath rushed into her lungs, her rage building with her color.

The Prince's woman and the sorkra stared balefully at one another. Though neither moved from her spot, Danaer was reminded of two circling she-ecars. The women wore daggers, a common thing among noblewomen, or on the frontier. Danaer had seen many a fight between women of the Zsed, fights that drew blood as readily as men's quarrels. Like it or not, he must act to end the conflict before matters worsened further.

"My Lady Lira Nalu, your favor—may I be of aid?" he said with extreme correctness.

The women swung to face him, and for an instant Danaer was battered by an onslaught of their emotions. Then, as if they deemed him a neutral, or perhaps unworthy of their spleen, Lira and Chorii mutually shielded their anger. Lira took Danaer's polite offer for an honest one. "You may assign a stall for her gelding, Troop Leader." She gave her opponent no name or title, a rudeness most noticeable.

Chorii eyed her but said nothing. Instead she preened at her clothes and sleek dark hair, tightening sashes until her breasts were exposed provocatively above the purple silk. Lira's own breast was modestly covered, and a small black medallion lay upon it. Now her agitation was revealed by the rise and fall of that little talisman, though she kept her face serene.

Danaer nodded to the Sarli. "It shall be done, my lady. The General has commanded that his sorkra will be obeyed as he would be." He glanced anxiously at Chorii, waiting for a reaction.

To his relief, she surrendered, though with ill grace. Chorii shrugged a bared shoulder and said with disdain, "We must not go against the orders of the General, at least not until my Prince has spoken to him. Another stall will do, for now."

The groom sighed and at a gesture from Danaer quickly led away the woman's gelding to a stall at the far end of the stables.

Chorii jerked around and left the stables, sauntering, putting one foot directly before the other to make her hips sway invitingly. Now and then she tossed her head to make her thick black hair catch the air. She walked like a woman of ease, a creature who would sell her body, though not for the glory of the goddess.

Lira did not look away from her until Chorii was outside the stable door. Then the sorkra shook herself, saying with a smile, "I give you thanks, Troop Leader."

"I spoke the truth, my lady. It *is* the General's order."

"So it is, and shall be," Lira agreed emphatically. She went to the door and opened it a crack, watching Chorii. Guards at their posts and troopmen drilling stopped their work to admire the Prince's woman, and wherever Chorii went, she caused disruption. With disgust, Lira said, "The garrison soon must deal with an enemy which is evil and strong beyond measuring. She is an unconscionable burden to the Royal Commander . . ."

Then she broke off, unwilling to say more in the presence of the grooms. Danaer approved her discretion, though it came late.

Lira calmed herself, picking up a shawl she had dropped and plucking out loose straws. Chastely, she drew the wrap about her dun-colored dress. So modest did she seem now, she might have been mistaken for the daughter of some simple Sarli merchant. But Danaer remembered her anger, and her sorkra calling.

"You behaved wisely a minute ago," she said. Her voice was sweet and soft, without any trace of the fury she had hurled at Chorii. "I shall commend you to the Commander."

Danaer had thought Lira's lure had been a trick of the night, a beauty lent her by dimness and mystery. But now by sun's light, in these homely surroundings, the Sarli was not a disappointment. The strange attraction Danaer had felt two nights past remained. He had reminded himself that she was one of the wizard kind, no woman for him. Yet the spell would not go away, though magic was not in it.

"I . . . I must be about my duties," he said, sounding inane in his own ears. A trifle awkwardly, he made his leave, wondering if she would giggle if he stumbled over the threshold. Fortunately, he did not give her that excuse.

For the rest of the day and night, he took care to avoid the headquarters building and any other place where the women would be found. Danaer busied himself with routine, hoping he could drop back into the anonymity of the barracks.

The grumblings about the overcrowding continued, for every day more soldiers arrived in units of tens. Most were raw and unused to the army and must be taught the simplest detail. More feed must be supplied to the crowded stables and pens, and more weapons must be taken from the arsenal and their work shown to the newcomers.

Troop Leaders such as Shaartre and Danaer had been much occupied taking tally of recruits and making certain each man had sufficient gear. The Royal Commander's power had been felt; there was no shortage of weaponry or clothes, as had too often been the case at Nyald.

Two days had passed since the Royal Commander had arrived, and four since Danaer had traveled to the Zsed and back. The tale-carriers had been busier than any, and many a recruit began to question when this invader would be met. As was typical, the untried men, those who had never tasted battle, complained of inaction and boasted of the deeds they would perform, given a chance to fight.

On the fifth day, shortly after morning drill, Danaer had finished putting off one more questioner when a troopman called, "There are people riding in the gates!"

Excitement ran through the barracks. "Is it more of the Royal Commander's staff?" Shaartre asked of no one in particular. "Hai, you there, Rorluk—climb up in the window and tell us: *is* it more officers?"

"No, Troop Leader. This time it is civilians."

"What?" Both Shaartre and Danaer hurried to the defense door of the rock-bound chamber. Near the headquarters, Captain Yistar was surrounded by merchants, all of them shouting and waving their arms and creating an uproar. The merchants' distinctive, long-sleeved robes and cropped hair looked very out of place in the military setting. Men held their breath as Captain Yistar stamped into the room.

"Of all the cursed times for the Destre-Y to—a fine omen for the Royal Commander's conference! A fine omen!" Yistar roared, then rounded on the Troop Leaders. "Get units four and five ready. Cavalry only, with lances and full gear, at once!"

Yistar paced the courtyard outside the stables while the men were saddling their mounts. He fumed and growled, pounding fist into palm. Danaer and Shaartre were not gentle with the new conscripts among their units. Most were peasants fresh from The Interior, unused to such crises. They dropped tack and startled horses and tripped over one another. Fortunately, many of the men were veterans brought from Nyald and gave the Troop Leaders little worry.

"Step it up! Move, there!"

"No, get the beasts in the second row of stalls. It is speed we will want, not cart horses."

Yistar had been too impatient to send a subordinate with the orders, and now he could not endure waiting in the courtyard. He came to the doors and glared at the confusion within the stables. "Danaer! Fetch three officer blacks, good horses. That white-footed brute will do for me. Lieutenant Branraediir and Prince Diilbok will accompany our units, so choose mounts accordingly. And make sure those wet-ears get their cinches properly tightened! We have a Destre riot in Siank to put down. I will have no loose saddles in the middle of a skirmish!"

The Troop Leaders rolled their eyes. Branraediir should be capable and a help, not a hindrance, to them, but Prince Diilbok might prove quite the opposite, they feared. With grim efficiency, they rechecked details and got the units out into the compound, watching the headquarters building.

"Eyes front now," Shaartre bellowed, and then Malol te Eldri emerged from the cavelike fortification. He stood near the heavy doors and talked to Captain Yistar and two other officers.

Then Yistar and Branra strolled toward the waiting horses. Their heads were together, as if they were planning a method of attack, comparing past campaigns on the frontiers. Both men were stocky and muscular and bandy-legged from long riding. Both had the manner and faces of warriors weathered by battle, a thing which seemed to make the merchant's son and the Royal Commander's highborn protégé close comrades.

No one could mistake Prince Diilbok for a warrior, though. His handsome features were soft to the point of effeminacy, and set in petulance. He looked like a spoiled child forced to obey his elders and resisting an excursion. Unsteadily, he wended his way toward the troop units.

From the corner of his mouth, Shaartre muttered, "Well is he called Diilbok the Drunk. We have our burden set on our backs—him." Then he and Danaer saluted smartly as Yistar and Branra surveyed the men.

"A good stand of soldiery, Captain," Branra complimented Yistar. Then he moved to the officers' blacks.

"Let us get this done," Diilbok said loudly, with courage born of wine. Yistar and Branra were already mounted when he began fumbling at the stirrup of his horse. A stable groom had to brace beast and man to get the Prince safely in the saddle.

Danaer swung away from the unit and presented himself before Yistar. He was aware that Branra was looking him over with intense scrutiny. "Take the point," Yistar said curtly. "Make sure we do not get ambushed. Head for the Square of the Clarique Trader. One of the Merchants' League people will show us the way, once we reach Siank's gates."

Leather squeaked and metal clinked and tens of hooves thudded dully on trampled earth. This was a routine Danaer had known ever since he entered Yistar's service, one he performed without conscious thought. The double column snaked out through the gates and defenses and onto the mountain highway, trotting down to Siank. When he had ridden to the Zsed, the road had been nearly deserted. Now carts and beasts of burden and people on foot clogged the artery. One of the merchants ran before the soldiers, screaming to clear a way. Other merchants, as Yistar had promised, fidgeted while they waited at the gates. As the column neared them, they kicked up their thin little ponies and shunted aside the teeming civilian traffic. "Way! Make way! On decree of the Merchants' League, make way!"

The merchants who led the troops were frantic, constantly waving and exhorting Yistar to hurry. Their comical scramblings worried Danaer. A Destre riot, it was said—in this city of the Destre-Y? Mayhap the merchants could find none among their guards who would dare raise weapons against their own kind, if the rioters were plains people.

But why would Destre-Y attack Siank, the jewel of the goddess?

The column clopped along stone pavements, following the twisting route the merchants traced. The crowds were thick on every side, gawking, barely moving aside enough for the soldiers. Danaer had never seen such a rich mingling of peoples, for Nyald was a smaller and far less sophisticated city. There were the tall, silver-haired men and women of Ulodovol's province, Irico; their native garments of pale blue and gray seemed a flowing extension of their white hair. Of course Sarli were everywhere, busy little folk, the men clad in loincloths and the women in simple gowns such as Lira affected; the rainbow colors of their headbands brightened the dark streets. Siank's own citizenry either wore a wide-sleeved demicloak, like the merchants, or dressed very like the Destre-Y. There were even a few Clarique, their height and yellow hair a magnet for the eyes.

As Yistar's units pressed deeper into Siank, the crowds lessened. The people they passed were running, in the opposite direction from that taken by the soldiers. The citizens' eyes were bright with panic, and they fell often in the slop-strewn alleyways, their fear a mute promise of what lay behind them.

In the better parts of the city, the avenues had been comparatively wide and easy for the troops to cross. Now, as they approached the eastern sector, the streets narrowed and the walls were crumbling and ancient. Dwellings loomed closely above the filthy streets. Danaer scouted every alleyway and portal in this warren, fearing attack from the side. Foul water puddles in the pavement cracks and the reek of offal offended his nostrils. Grimy, pinched faces peeked from slitted windows and shadowed doorways. They reminded Danaer of nightwalkers, so unnaturally pale and furtive were these people, not like an honest dweller in Zsed or Argan's city ought to look.

The eastern sector of Siank boasted an unsavory reputation despite its famous market, or perhaps because of it. Traffic in contraband flourished in the district, drawing much trade. Apparently such a hotbed of thievery had finally burst out of control.

Why had Siank's merchants not turned to Gordt te Raa, though? Attacked by Destre-Y, they no longer trusted their protector in Siank Zsed, perhaps. Was it possible the Siirn Rena's own men were the attackers, assaulting the merchants?

Now Danaer heard cries of men and beasts and loud, smashing noises. They were drawing very near the Square of the Clarique Trader, and a peculiar quiet gripped all the streets radiating from the market. Even the merchants who had been leading the troops had vanished.

Danaer spurred forward to a place where he could look into the square while still shielded by dwellings. The angle of view was narrow, but he could assess the chaos within quite well. Traders struggled frantically to save their wares, while a few of the ineffectual private police fought a band of shouting, charging horsemen. Here and there a peasant crawled from beneath a wagon or a pile of baskets and tried to run to safety, often to be cut down by lance or trampled in the melee.

The riders *were* Destre-Y. Every horse was a roan, and each warrior hid his face behind his mantle.

Why such an outrage against Siank at such a time? Siank and the Zsed had worked glove to glove for generations, and now this conference with the Royal Commander was so near . . .

Danaer signaled a halt, then rode back to Yistar. The officer squirmed in the saddle and demanded, "Well? Well?"

"I make it forty or fifty warriors, Captain. All mounted and armed with lances . . . a few cudgels and knives, though I saw no slings."

Yistar nodded grimly. "Then we must work close in —surround the square and—"

"Surely we can depend upon support from the locals?" That was Prince Diilbok. Now he did not look quite so much the foolish drunk. There was an odd glitter in his eyes, not the same fire for battle a warrior like Branraediir would exhibit, but something else, not quite rational. Branra glanced warily at his fellow officer, reflecting Danaer's own distrust of Diilbok's new zeal. The Prince said hotly, "Why do we wait?"

"I saw very few of the merchants' police, my lord," Danaer said with careful courtesy, not wanting to antagonize this nobleman.

"Nonsense! You are too cautious, Troop Leader." Diilbok stared at the scout with suspicion. "Or *is* it caution? Perhaps it is treachery! You hope to keep us dallying here while your Destre companions have their will with the populace—"

Yistar cut him off. "My Troop Leader's loyalty is

not in question, Prince. Now, as for settling this riot, we will—"

With a roar, Diilbok drew sword. The gleam in his eyes was now awful. Danaer and Shaartre both moved to protect Yistar from possible assault.

But Diilbok goaded his black ahead of the column and shouted a command: "Forward! Attack the bandits at once!"

He spurred his steed so violently that the animal nearly bowled over the two riders blocking his path— Danaer and Yistar. Stupefied by his behavior and fighting for control of their mounts, they did not counter his orders. Obeying the nobleman, the column galloped after Diilbok, heading into the square. Branra had drawn aside, keeping masterful control of his excited horse. As Yistar and the Troop Leaders regained their senses, he smiled slightly and asked, "Do we follow him, or shall we wait a while and enter the fray after he has been disposed of?"

"And after he gets my soldiers killed, too!" Yistar thundered. "No hope that *he* shall be killed, to judge by his reputation!"

"True," Branra said with a sigh, though he was still smiling, as if all this were a game. "Never has he been harmed. Pity. The gods favor those strong in drink . . ."

Yistar grimaced at the impiety. "We must move, my lord, and quickly!"

The screams and the din of smashing wood and pottery nearly deafened them as they rode into the Square of the Clarique Trader. Almost at once Danaer was forced to dodge a barrage of cobblestones, missiles pried up from the street and flung wildly by the besieged merchants. In his mantle, riding a roan, Danaer was a target for them as well as for the attackers, who would see his uniform and deem him their enemy. It was not a new problem for Danaer.

He avoided more stones, then rode toward the rioter closest to him. Two merchants flailed at the man with sticks and tent poles, their wide sleeves flapping. The horseman who harassed them was unusually inept at handling weapon and horse, which made Danaer wonder. A clumsy warrior?

"Harshaa, Azsed!" he challenged in the tongue of the plains people. The masked figure gave no sign he had heard the soldier, and Danaer shouted more loudly.

Still there was no reaction. Rushing in upon the man, Danaer seized the rioter's boot and upended the poorly seated horseman into the waiting arms of the merchants. As the traders fell on him vengefully, the man shrieked in terror, and Danaer's senses wrenched with astonishment.

A scream? From a Destre warrior? Destre-Y was not Markuand, and there was no magic here such as stilled the tongues of those white-clad invaders against pain of wound or death. But a Destre warrior did not cry out in midst of battle, save to strike fear into his enemy. Never would he reveal his agony and give the foe heart by that sound.

Deeply troubled, Danaer looked about, seeking prey. He saw Branra in the thickest of the fighting, busy cutting down rebels. The young nobleman had cast aside his helmet, as if it were an encumbrance. He used his sword with skill and relish, befitting his fame.

Then Danaer noticed an ambusher to Branra's rear. Reflexively, he snatched sling from belt and let the stone fly with an accuracy he had learned in childhood.

La! In the eye! The attacker screeched and clutched his face and toppled from his horse, sprawling on blood-slippery pavement. Branra turned and took in what had occurred, then searched the square for his unknown ally. His gaze met Danaer's as the scout reloaded his sling. The Lieutenant grinned his gratitude like a common soldier ere he moved to engage another opponent.

In glaring contrast, Prince Diilbok struck no one, though, like Branra, he was amid the worst of the battle. Diilbok keened defiance at his would-be attackers, but none seemed able to harm him. All manner of weapons were in use—lance and rock and dagger and swords taken from soldiers who had fallen. Blade and spear and stone dropped harmlessly to either side while the prince rode among them, unhurt.

A glamour of some magician might surround him; or perhaps it was what Branra had said—the good fortune of the sot. For with all his display, he struck the rioters no more than they him.

Contemptuous, Danaer turned his back on the shameful scene. Despite the soldiers, the rioters seemed in no mood to break off the assault. Angry shouts and cries of the wounded rose all around, and many sounds of pain came from the masked riders. Danaer's doubts were reborn. He cut down one of the rioters, and again there was a scream. Danaer sheathed his sword and leaned far from the saddle, scooping up a lance some soldier had dropped. The rioters also used the lance, but awkwardly, and Danaer set to grim work with a will to teach them how to fight with this Destre tool.

A man fell, and there was fear in his eyes and a loud, anguished plea for mercy as he went down. Danaer had again called the Azsed challenge, and again his enemy had given no answer.

This riddle must be solved, this elusive quarry run to ground. He was careful in selecting his next opponent. There! The man's height and weight was near Danaer's own, and the fellow was at least competent with lance, if not adept. A fair challenge this would be—by every tribal law.

The rioter was menacing a shopkeeper and his wife, about to ride them down. Danaer threw aside his lance and gathered himself, springing onto the brigand's back, bearing them off their horses and down to the street. He made certain the rioter landed underneath him, taking the brunt of the fall.

Danaer recovered his breath as the merchant and his woman ran away to hide. For the moment, Danaer and the rioter were alone in a pocket of stillness, as he had wished. The rioter was gasping and rubbing his bruised head and chest, regaining his wits at last. Danaer kicked the man over on his back and drew his sword. With one stroke he cut away the mantle dust mask concealing the rider's identity. Such a face might well be a tribesman's, or that of any man of Krantin; it was ordinary, telling him little.

Danaer pressed the sword against that dirty throat and barked the challenge, words unintelligible to all but a Destre sworn to the goddess during ritual at Argan's sacred fire altar. "Harshaa! Speak, yaen! Speak of her fall to rise again in flames! Ain ae will spare thee!"

The rioter shuddered, staring at the sword in fear and hatred.

Danaer was suddenly aware of a repugnant odor which offended even amid the general stink of the city. Laidil root. To eat the accursed spice was an unthinkable thing to one sworn to Argan. No longer could Danaer believe this cowering dog was a Destre.

The goddess herself filled his being, commanding him to seek out answers before the fatal blow.

"Call out, yaen, your clan, your tribe—call!" Danaer bent close, and fear won over hate in the rioter's countenance. The man understood nothing. Danaer's words were as alien to him as the Markuand language would be.

"Let me up . . . let me go . . ."

"Call, yaen, and I shall gift the goddess for your soul and chant you to Keth's portals, save your name to eternity!"

"I have money, see? Much gold? It is yours." The man fumbled in his shirt—for a pouch of coins, or for a dagger?

Danaer cared little which, his probing at an end. He ran the sword home ruthlessly. This time there was no scream of pain, for the slashed throat was voiceless, the blade wet with blood.

In times past, at Nyald, Danaer had killed Destre-Y in honorable combat under Yistar's command. He had felt regret, though oath bade him act. Now there was no trace of pity in him. This lump of carrion had never been a Destre-Y, never made vow to Argan's flame. This was a cowardly thief in Destre clothes, no more.

Were all the rioters imposters? He caught up the reins of his horse and walked over to another body. As Danaer examined the corpse, he snorted in derision. More scent of laidil root, and the man did not even wear a faith-ring. His boots were those of a plowboy, not a warrior.

The battle was dying away in a few last, flurrying encounters. Groans faded and citizens were creeping back into the square to reclaim their stalls and wares. Danaer swung up on his roan and loped to where Yistar and Branra were dispatching the last of their opponents. Yistar, as Danaer had seen many a time before, laid about him with officer's sword in workmanlike fashion, caring only that his target went down. Branra's enthusiasm shone in his face, and his combat was a joyous art. He seemed disappointed when his antagonist died.

The Captain ordered Danaer, "Get Shaartre and take tally. Let us see what we have from this."

The Troop Leaders shepherded and bullied and helped the wounded, gradually reassembling the column. Danaer was angered to see much needless slaughter, for the ranks were broken. Many of their dead had fallen during the first moments of that blind, senseless rush in Prince Diilbok's wake. Once the shock was over, veterans had used old training, and the newer men had sometimes discovered their ability to kill, often to their dismay. One of Danaer's youngest troopmen, a youth named Rorluk, had saved the life of his comrade Xashe, then had been sickened when he saw what his lance had done. With some effort, Danaer and Xashe got the young man back on his feet and led him, still retching and sick, to his horse and back to the units.

Shaartre was leading several horses laden with bodies as Danaer rejoined him. They made an assessment and turned to Yistar. "Six dead, fourteen wounded—three of the wounded unable to ride; we are rigging litters, Captain."

Branra whistled and shook his head, commiserating with Yistar. The Lieutenant was splattered with much blood, but there was no wound on him. "That is a very heavy toll for such a brief encounter."

"Lucky it was not more." Yistar directed a glare at Prince Diilbok. That worthy slouched in the saddle and cleaned his sword. Danaer wondered why that was necessary; certainly Diilbok had never struck any man who could defend himself! Danaer remembered the strange way nothing could touch the Prince, even in the midst of lances and knives. He put the thought aside as Yistar added, "At least we took down a-many of those cursed Destre-Y . . ."

Danaer nudged his roan forward and interrupted with, "Your favor, Captain."

"Yes?" Yistar eyed him with interest, knowing his scout's tone from long association in their campaigns.

"These rioters were not Destre-Y."

"What?" The Captain arched his shaggy eyebrows. "How can you say this?"

Danaer was feeling curious stares from his comrades and the citizens on every side. What demon had made him open his mouth at such a time? The Azsed tongue of faith was not a thing to reveal in the presence of an Iit. Yistar might have guessed such a secret language existed, but Danaer was bound by oath to keep silence on the matter. "Of how I know, Captain, I may not say. But I swear on my honor that it is so."

"Ridiculous!" Prince Diilbok, red-faced and puffing, exclaimed. "I told you that this man was a traitor, but you would not heed me. No doubt the murderous scoundrel had a part in planning this riot. Now he tries to mislead us with these insane stories."

"Captain, on my oath—" Danaer began.

"Silence! You devil worshipper!" Diilbok came close, his wine-strong breath making the scout recoil. "Give me your sword at once, you cur! You are my prisoner. I will have you executed on the spot, here at the site of your treachery!"

For a heartbeat, Danaer gathered himself to fight clear and flee to the Zsed, seeking sanctuary among the plains people, his own. But who *were* his own? And how many comrades would he have to kill? Shaartre? The men of his unit? Yistar, who had given Danaer his life ten times over in the Kakyein Wars and the southern campaigns?

Danaer let his hand rest on his sword hilt, studying Yistar, prudence ruling him. But Yistar was transfixed,

staring dumbly at Prince Diilbok, disbelieving what
he heard and saw.

"Remove those badges and that helmet!" Diilbok
demanded. "You befoul them!"

Branra said, "And have you already conducted the
Troop Leader's trial, cousin?" His voice was decep-
tively soft, though there was steel under the words.
"You would be judge and executioner in one, I see.
But consider: we have no evidence against the man.
You had best save your accusations for a surer target."

Prince Diilbok sputtered, incoherent with rage.
Branra went on amiably, "I submit that we *may* hold
Troop Leader Danaer for questioning, if you insist.
We will bring this situation before his garrison's commandant, General Nurdanth. The King's articles are
clear in such matters. Surely you remember that small
detail, cousin. Search your mind. I feel it will return to
you, in time."

For a while, Diilbok continued to rant and wave
his arms. But under Branra's serenity, the prince
subsided finally into furious glowering at Danaer and
his fellow officer. Branra was unbothered by that,
nodding to Danaer. "I owe you my life, Troop Leader.
If I may repay you with a bit of justice amid insanity,
well enough."

Then he turned to Yistar and said most pleasantly,
"Have we else to do here, Captain, or do we go back
to the fort?"

Yistar stayed clear of any conflict between the highborn officers. Though he outranked Branra in badges,
Yistar was ever conscious of his humble origins. Now
he seized on Branra's suggestion. "Ai, and at once.
Since you have taken my Troop Leader's case into
your hands, will you also take him into your custody?"

"Willingly," Branra said. "But I do not think he will
need restraint. The man is a Destre, and has sworn to
serve you. Fortunate we are that he keeps his honor,
for he has been left his weapons." Again Branra
grinned at Diilbok.

The fop puffed out his chest and cried, "I demand
that . . . rights . . . the articles . . ."

"Of course." Branra wedged his black in between

Diilbok's and Danaer's horses, nose to tail with Danaer's roan. "Ai, we will play this wager fairly, will we not, warrior? I require your sword, and that sling you wielded to save me. Ah! And your boot knife and belt blade."

Branra was no stranger to Destre arms. He had forgotten nothing. It seemed less shame to surrender them all to Branra. The officer ran a thumb along the well-worn boot knife, saying with admiration, "I learned some time ago that a Destre is ever dangerous, particularly so long as he has this, ready to strike."

Yistar ordered that the bodies of the rioters and their horses be brought along as spoils. There was new confusion, and then the column untangled itself. It moved very slowly now, burdened with litters for the wounded and bodies tied on horses. No longer scouting, Danaer was forced to ride beside Lieutenant Branra, directly behind Diilbok and Yistar. Shaartre led the troops, and Danaer could feel his old friend's sympathetic and puzzled stare burning into his back.

How had he come to this? Bogotana's deviltry—or some evil wizard? Had it been a magical trap, well laid to thrust him into this cage and make him bind himself with his own honest and ill-advised words?

Argan, do not let me die with dishonor!

How was he to convince General Nurdanth that he spoke the truth? It were less abomination to spit on the altar than to reveal the goddess's rituals. Yet he could not expect the General to believe him unless he spoke reasons.

The dilemma tormented him as they left Siank and wound up the foothills toward the fort.

Far better to have fallen in battle. Stripped of weapons, forced to ride bareheaded, he was Branra's prisoner. It needed only chains to complete his black shame.

A sudden horror came upon him. Would they hang him, like a common cutpurse or thiever of woolbacks? Would no one call to Argan for his soul? He would wander the earth below forever, never reaching the goddess or new life. Would Lira Nalu speak in his favor to the General? The pretty little Sarli wizard had

acted kindly toward him. It might be she would not
scorn him . . .

Yet she was a sorkra, and had not some wizardry
had a part in all the things that had befallen him
since he had come to Siank?

As they entered the fort, he lifted his head, hiding
his heart behind a warrior's unrevealing expression.
He had taken oath, and a Destre who broke oath was
less than dust. If he must die, it was Argan's will. All
was in the hands of the goddess now—and in the
judgment of General Nurdanth.

VI

TREACHERY AMONG THE IIT

THE STONE CELL WAS STIFLING AND HUMID AND
proof against tool or weapon. Little matter, for Branra
had pulled Danaer's fangs. Danaer smiled ruefully. To
think that such a courtier would be so familiar with
Destre-Y. Bloody Branra had confiscated all those
weapons with an easy air, as he had disarmed many
another Destre warrior.

Danaer's momentary amusement was buried in
hurt. It was not merely the waste of soldiery in the
riot or Diilbok's accusations. There was Shaartre's
shaken attitude when Danaer had been taken away
to this prison. And worse—Lira Nalu had witnessed
this thing, for the sorkra had passed him and Branra
in the hall of headquarters as the officer was conveying him to the cell. She had known what his empty
scabbard and missing helmet signified, and her distress
was obvious. Once she had helped him with her wizardry. But then she had known that he rode into peril
and had prepared for it. If sorcery lay behind this
shame of Danaer's, she had not been forewarned, and
now it was too late for her countering white magic.

Branra had bolted the door and left him alone what seemed a very long time. It had given him space to think, not always a good thing. There was no pallet or cushion or bucket. The only air came through a tiny barred slit in the rocky ceiling. Rats had scurried in the straw, but kept hidden, wary of Danaer's boots. He knew that by now he presented a woeful appearance —shorn of weapons and insignia, sweaty, his beard stubble uncut, his uniform stained from the battle.

Then there was a muffled thump of footsteps, a bolt was pulled, and the door creaked open. Branra stood before him, gesturing. "Come with me, Troop Leader."

The cooler air of the corridor refreshed Danaer a bit. He came to full wakefulness as he followed the shorter man through the wandering passageways of the fortress. The officer had come alone, without soldiers, a concession Danaer appreciated. The fewer men who saw his condition, the less shame. As they came abreast a junction in the halls, they met Prince Diilbok's mistress.

The woman was angered, her color very high. Her costly gown was emerald-green, and like all her garments, cut low as a common hussy's. As always, she dripped gems and gold. Branra and Danaer stepped aside to let Chorii pass, and she paused, eyeing them intently. She began to flutter her lashes and flirt her head, a seductive smile aimed at Branra. It was a palace game Branra would not play. He treated her as he treated her man, summing his derision with a bow that was too deep to be convincing. Chorii was not fooled, and she flounced her skirts, rushing past him, deliberately bumping the nobleman's arm.

Branra looked at Danaer and said, loud enough for the departing woman to hear him clearly, "We should be grateful Diilbok did not bring his lap dogs as well, I suppose."

Chorii looked back at them, fury in her dark eyes, her lips drawn back in a snarl. She slammed through a door and made the thing shake on its hinges.

Branra chuckled softly, then sighed. "Well, to what must be done, Troop Leader." He moved toward a set of double doors guarded by sentries. They opened the portal for him and Danaer, then shut them carefully at their backs. Danaer had gone by this room several times while on business for Yistar. Never had he expected to find himself within, for this was the officers' conference chamber.

He braced to see General Nurdanth, Yistar, the Prince, and the Royal Commander himself awaiting him. Ulodovol and Lira Nalu were standing before Malol te Eldri; apparently they had just dealt with him on some sorkra affairs, for now they turned to leave as Branra and Danaer arrived. It seemed that for a moment Lira looked directly at Danaer and wished him good fortune with her eyes. Then the sorkra were gone, and once more the sentinels shut fast the doors.

Malol te Eldri was shuffling through some papers, and General Nurdanth, who sat at his side, said politely, "My friend, your aide has returned."

"Ah! This is the accused Troop Leader, Branra?" The Royal Commander pointed to a bench before the officers' table, and Danaer perched gingerly on its edge. His helmet and weapons lay to one side, placed in a neat pile, treated with respect.

Particulars were recited for archives, and Malol's scribe scratched the notations on clay. If the hearing were judged worthy of record, he would transfer proceedings to parchment. Danaer hoped matters would not reach such a pass. The formalities done, Prince Diilbok began a rambling account of the events, from his opinion. Though vague, he was at pains to heap blame on Danaer at every turn. The nobleman seemed less in his cups than usual, and Danaer listened closely.

"And when he was asked to defend his statement, this traitorous—"

"The unadorned facts will do for now," General Nurdanth said mildly.

"With your permission, Lord General, I would add my testimony." Captain Yistar, with an occasional confirming remark from Branra, supplied quite a different version of the riot and its aftermath. The Royal Commander and Nurdanth first stared with surprise and then with growing outrage at Diilbok.

"Is this the way of it, cousin?" Malol te Eldri said when Yistar finished.

Yistar had described the ill-planned assault on the Square of the Clarique Trader, and the Prince hastened to answer the criticism. "I deemed that speed was the best tactic in—"

"Enough!"

"But you have not heard—"

"I have already heard more than I wish to bear!" Malol exclaimed. "We came to Siank garrison to help, not to sacrifice our troops in street brawls. There is a war at hand, and we will need every soldier. The scribe is instructed to remove all references to charges that Troop Leader Danaer was negligent during the defense of the square."

"But I claim justice!" Prince Diilbok would not let the matter drop, even at the risk of angering his kinsman.

"Be still, cousin, or you will have far more justice than you would like." When he had first seen Malol, Danaer had thought the partician had a rather gentle manner and a face most unstern. Now his fair complexion had whitened and his fists were clenched. This cultured nobleman was also a soldier, and he had learned that his troops had been senselessly slain by his relative's stupidity.

Diilbok leaped to his feet. Danaer, though loathing the man, reacted to rank and started to rise. Branra jerked his hand, ordering him to remain seated. "The King will hear of this!" Diilbok wailed, like a pampered child.

"Sit down." Malol's voice was as soft as a firesnake's, but it cut through Diilbok's pettish temper. "May I remind you that Tobentis is in Kirvii and we are in Siank. Do not think to use our uncle's authority here, on *me*. Accidents may happen to those who do not understand the country they travel."

Diilbok peered at him owlishly. Then his manner changed. He did not appear a foolish drunk, but a sly schemer who had changed his tactics. "I . . . I do see. My rude behavior shames me, cousin. Yet these charges—"

"We will consider the rest of them, once you take your chair." When Diilbok, with ill grace, had done so, Malol said, "Now, Troop Leader, on this matter of the identity of the rioters—can you explain yourself?"

"I did come forward, my lord, to say that the men were not Destre-Y. But it was not because they were known to me."

Malol rested his chin on the heel of his hand, meeting Danaer's gaze levelly. "What then, soldier?"

His manner was encouraging, but Danaer replied, "Of that I may not speak, Royal Commander. It . . . it is a rule of . . . of my goddess. But there is this— and Captain Yistar will confirm it—that a true Destre would never plead for his life in battle, as these dogs did."

"He is right," Yistar put in.

"So the plains bandits feel no pain?" Diilbok sneered.

"They feel pain," the red-haired officer retorted hotly. "But they are proud, and they will never beg for mercy or cry out."

"Is there more evidence, Troop Leader?" Nurdanth asked. He had said very little so far in the inquiry. Now he pressed Danaer. "Will you tell more of what you know?"

Caught on the lance point of his goddess, Danaer heaved a sigh and shook his head. Nurdanth laced his slender fingers together. "You called challenge?" Danaer gaped at him, and the General went on. "And they gave you no proper response? Then indeed they were not true Destre-Y. I am not sworn to your goddess, soldier. I worship Peluva, not Argan. Therefore, will it cost your honor if *I* am the one who tells of the Azsed challenge?"

Nonplused, Danaer said, "I . . . I think not, my lord. I have never heard the priests deal with this. Such a thing has not been known."

The General smiled, speaking with quiet pride. "I believe I may clarify the problem. Gentlemen, attend me. Quite beyond the Destre dialect we all have acquaintance with, there is a secret religious language among the plains people. The Destre are taught the ritual when they are but children. They are forever bound to conceal it from outsiders. Challenge may be called to one of the faithful, and that one must answer in the true tongue of Argan. It is proof of Azsed, and information most jealously guarded, is it not, Troop Leader?"

"So I thought, until this moment, my lord."

Yistar pursed his lips, then said, "I had heard tales of such, but I assumed it was another myth spread about the Destre-Y—with no basis."

"You are too famous a foe, Captain Yistar. Most of all, they would hide their secrets from you, and from such as Lieutenant Branraediir. I have made a lifelong study of the customs of Destre-Y—not as a soldier, but for my own knowledge and curiosity. Once I was a hidden observer when two Destre warriors fought to the death. It was then I learned of the challenge, and later I gathered scraps to tell me of its secret and holy nature. And," Nurdanth's tone grew guarded when he concluded, "I have other methods."

Danaer remembered the sorkra. Truly, the General had sources, closed to men who did not treat with the wizards, things most people would avoid. It was not evil, but it was a trick of spying that served him admirably.

Malol and Nurdanth put their heads together, whispering. Yistar leaned back, his burly arms crossed. Prince Diilbok twisted about on his chair, trying to overhear what his royal cousin and the General were saying. Branra showed no interest, waiting patiently.

At last Nurdanth said, "We judge this matter closed. If challenge was given and not answered, then Troop Leader Danaer was correct in his accusations. The rioters were not Destre-Y. He committed no treachery, but a profound service in reporting this to his Captain."

"I protest." That, of course, was Diilbok. "We do not know the whole of it."

"Perhaps we do not," Malol said ominously.

"I . . . I meant that the Destre-Y are not to be trusted—*any* of them. Perhaps the rioters were of a different clan than the Troop Leader's own, and knew some alien tongue. Perhaps . . ."

Malol te Eldri regarded his kinsman with wonderment. "The matter is closed, cousin," he said. "Have done with it."

To Danaer's amazement, Diilbok took a wheedling note. "It is only that I am concerned for your welfare, Malol. Here, so far from the palace, we are prey for the devil worshippers. And now you plan to deal with them personally. It may well be that those such as Nurdanth and Yistar here have grown careless from too long association with the Destre. They do not see the dangers we do."

"Your advice is taken under consideration, cousin, and we thank you for your loving anxiety on our behalf. Nevertheless, we will stand by this decision. The inquiry is at an end."

Diilbok opened his mouth, thought better of what he had been about to say, and gritted his teeth in frustration. Then he rose and bowed to Malol and the General, seeking permission to withdraw. As he hurried from the room, a nod from Malol te Eldri sent Branra in Diilbok's wake, though following at a discreet distance.

Nurdanth indicated Danaer's helmet and weapons. "You are to take up your rank. We have no time to waste on these events just past. Come with us."

Mystified, Danaer obeyed, trailing the three officers as they went out into the corridor. He sheathed his sword and put knives back in proper places and his sling into his belt. Nurdanth led the way. He stopped briefly at the kitchens, pointing to the cook's table. Danaer gratefully scooped up a handful of grain cakes left from the officers' meal, far better fare than the gruel he got in barracks. He wolfed down the cakes, Destre fashion, as the four continued to the end of a rocky corridor and out into the night.

They had exited at General Nurdanth's private stables. Malol te Eldri sent away grooms and orderlies, then took a lantern from a peg and held it high. Light fell across a row of blanket-draped bodies.

"Who are they?" the Royal Commander asked.

Danaer pulled away one of the blankets. In the warmth of spring damp, the corpse had already begun to stink. Danaer had smelled the like before, and heeded it little, examining the body. The face told him nothing, and the clothes were ordinary Destre shirt and breeches and vest, undistinguished by markings. Then Danaer grasped the man's left hand, turning the eiphren he wore. "This, my lord . . ."

"Let me see," Nurdanth said. Danaer took off the ring and the officers crowded about him. The scout turned the stone to catch the lantern's pale light.

"What is it?" Malol shifted from foot to foot in his impatience.

Nurdanth snorted, taking the ring from Danaer. "Observe the cut of the gem. All Destre-Y eiphrens are triangular or circular in shape. This is square. It was never blessed by Azsed priest, you can be certain. Most likely it was purchased at some market in The Interior."

"*Where* in The Interior? And they did not get those clothes in the mountains."

"*Some* of them wore true eiphrens, my lord," Danaer volunteered. "I killed such a one. Perhaps they had more clothes to steal than rings they could find."

"Are there any other clues to their origins?"

"Where are the roans they were riding, my lord?"

"This way." Nurdanth led them to nearby stalls. Danaer looked over the sleepy-eyed horses, running hands along hides and hooves, seeking a tribe brand. Discouraged to find none, he was about to confess failure, then noticed the discarded saddles stacked to one side. Yistar knelt beside him as they picked over motge leather, fur, and cloth. Both men tugged at the saddle's undersurface and the fabric gave, revealing a striped inner lining they read instantly. Nurdanth, too, recognized the pattern, and in one voice they exclaimed, "Rierdon-ne!"

"But how is this?" Danaer murmured, dusting his

hands. "Rierdon-ne is the tribe of Jatri, and he is kin to Gordt te Raa. He would never sell Destre gear to those Iit disguised as rioters . . ."

"There are other ways than purchase," Yistar said.

Danaer winced. "Theft from Destre-Y! It would have cost much blood, for these were not easily come by."

"Blood, and money." Malol held the eiphren ring close to the lantern. "And it may be there was also evil sorcery. There are those in The Interior who would go to any length to prevent an alliance with the Destre-Y."

"From The Interior? But surely they knew the need for this alliance?" Nurdanth was distraught that any could deny it. "How can anyone imagine the army alone could hold back these Markuand, now that they have overrun Clarique's islands?"

"Their hatred is all-consuming, my friend. Some work for greed or power. And some because they fear any union with the Destre-Y far more than they dread the invader." Malol put the false ring in his tunic and said, "It has been done. Now we know how far they will go to stop us. Troop Leader . . ."

"My Lord Commander?"

"These are your people, the Destre-Y, and your sacred language. I want you to act as liaison when I ride to meet with Gordt te Raa and his council of tribal chieftains. He said it would take him a seven-day to gather them, and the time will soon be upon us. I want you with me." Danaer nodded obediently, and the Royal Commander went on. "I must speak no ill at this council, nor do anything to offend them. You are to warn me if I say anything to prejudice myself with the devil worshippers. Always speak freely. It is my order."

"Then . . ."

"Yes?"

Danaer took a deep breath. "As a beginning, my lord, never call them 'devil worshippers.' At least not where they might overhear you."

Malol laughed. "Very good! Exactly the sort of advice I must have. Now, I must select the others who will accompany me. Yourself, General Nurdanth . . . what of Lieutenant Branraediir?" Danaer's hesitancy was obvious, and Malol said again, "Speak freely and honestly."

"I have much cause to respect the Lieutenant, and I owe him thanks for his fair treatment of me this day. But it is not wise that he meet with Gordt te Raa, not yet. His reputation runs ahead of him, Royal Commander. Even I had some trouble in seeing the man behind the bloody name. It was my people he killed in his famous campaigns in the Tradyan prairies."

"Then we shall save his introduction to the Destre-Y leader, for a while." Malol considered a substitute and put forward the former commandant of Nyald fort.

"No." Yistar was startled to be rejected by Danaer, but the scout explained, "The Destre call him Straedanfi—Long-Fang. And like Lieutanant Branraediir, he is respected and hated. It is too soon for the Destre to embrace old enemies. And Captain Yistar was the renowned victor in the Kakyein Wars. They know him too well."

Malol sighed at having another choice turned away. He thought several minutes, then said, "Of course—a sorkra. What does Sovereign Gordt te Raa think of the sorkra?"

"All the Destre revere wizards, and fear them mightily. They dread calling any magic down upon themselves."

"This time the wizards will be their allies, not enemies," Malol promised.

"But Wizard Ulodovol is . . ." Nurdanth said, then let his voice trail off. He sighed and added, "His age is an infirmity. If we would let be his contacts with his wizard Web at this critical time in far Clarique, he cannot be distracted."

"Plague!" The Royal Commander was much disappointed. "Truly, we dare not tax his feeble body. Well, then, we shall have to employ his apprentice."

"I am sure the lady Lira Nalu would be most agreeable," Nurdanth said. "It might be an even more useful choice. Many women rank high among the

Destre-Y. Lira Nalu's presence in your entourage should make a good impression. A woman sorkra. They will not have met her like before."

"Then the list is complete. Tomorrow we set forward our preparations for the council. There is much left to do." Malol blew out the lantern and hung it on its peg, a tacit adjournment of the inquiry and the investigation of the rioters' identities.

Danaer's head was spinning. Lira Nalu—riding with him and the Royal Commander and General Nurdanth! Two lords of The Interior, a Destre turned soldier, and a big-eyed Sarli woman who knew the frightening secrets of wizardry.

You will sit at the feet of the mighty . . .

Osyta's prophecies of Andaru rang in his memory. He would indeed sit with the mighty, Destre and Iit gathered in council—a reunion that had not taken place since the peoples of Ryerdon had divided themselves during their terrible journey across the Vrastre.

Had he wanted Lira Nalu to sing his name in memory when it seemed possible he would not survive his errand to the Zsed? Now the minstrels might sing all their names, and taletellers would chant this council's gathering to children yet unborn, to generations of Krantin—where Andaru might at last become real.

VII

VRENTRU

"HERE IS THE ESCORT!"

The lookouts and sentinels had their instructions. Arrows stayed in quivers and no one rushed to bar the gate. Bitter at the turnabout in all the way of things, the soldiers watched as eight well-armed Destre-Y rode into the fort. Gordyan led them, and Danaer went to meet him.

"It is the Destre soldier," Gordyan said cheerfully to his warriors. "And where are these Iit lords of yours?"

"They will be ready soon. Why have you come so early? We were informed the council would not begin till the sun reaches center-stand."

Gordyan spread wide his hands in mock surprise. "We wished to take you there early, for this will be a vrentru remembered for many a season."

"Vrentru?" At that voice, Danaer turned and saluted General Nurdanth, who was crossing the compound toward them. "You spoke of festival, warrior?"

"Ai, with skills and contests."

"And who is to be tested at this vrentru? Destre, or unbeliever?" the General asked. He cocked his head and surveyed the group, then remarked, "I believe you must be Gordyan. I have heard of you."

"And I of you, Nurdanth Who Keeps Faith." Gordyan eyed the older man with thoughtful respect, then nodded at Danaer, approving his commandant.

Then a soldier's warning cry of "Pre-sent!" told them the Royal Commander was leaving the headquarters building. Danaer glanced around eagerly. Lira Nalu walked by Malol's side, her small hand resting lightly on his arm. Her gown was flame bright, her brown wizard's cloak thrown back from her shoulders, not hiding her. Junior officers and staff had crowded to windows and porches, and some lined the yard outside the building, standing at attention to see the Commander on his way. Prince Diilbok should have been most prominent in that group, but instead he viewed the scene from a window high in the rocky wall of the fortress. His mistress was beside him, her silver dress catching the sun and hurting the eyes. Since Prince Diilbok had been chastened at Danaer's hearing, he had sulked in his quarters like a punished child, let his woman and his many lackeys comfort him. Now as the pair looked down at Malol and Lira, Danaer felt a strange disquiet, wishing they had remained hidden, and out of his thoughts.

Branraediir and Yistar and a few aides left the lines and followed behind the Royal Commander, offering last-moment good hopes for the success of his conference. Malol said, "Have no fear. Gordt te Raa is a man of honor, and we have his sworn pledge."

"So great a risk," Yistar complained. "Both you and General Nurdanth . . ."

Malol smiled at the compliment. "If we fall, there are those as brave and some far younger and hardier to take our places . . ."

Gordyan leaned from his saddle and whispered to Danaer, "Who is the woman in red? Does she come with the Royal Commander?"

"The Lady Lira Nalu. She is General Nurdanth's sorkra. She will advise Malol te Eldri on matters of wizardry." Gordyan did not care for the answer, but he treated it as of no moment, feigning disdain of Lira's sorkra calling.

Yistar veered away from the Commander and came to Danaer, flicking imaginary dust from a uniform Shaartre had already brushed vigorously. Gruffly Yistar said, "See you do me proud, for Nyald and the old days, eh?"

Danaer muttered an embarrassed assurance, then Lira Nalu said, "Will you help me to mount, Troop Leader?" She was standing by her mare. Danaer hurried to her side and cupped his hands. As she stepped up, he saw that beneath her long red gown and wizard's cloak she wore soft Destre boots rather than Sarli sandals. Her weight hardly bore down his hands at all, and she settled gracefully onto a noble-woman's sidesaddle, chastely gathering the folds of her cloak over her legs as she did so. Danaer had heard that the women of Sarlos were modest to the point of prudery, but her action seemed more that of good breeding than of excessive primness. She smiled down at him. "My thanks. I have never mounted so swiftly."

Shaartre and many of Danaer's barracks mates scrambled to the walls to see the spectacle as the Royal Commander's party set forth—three soldiers and the woman sorkra, with two Destre warriors to guard each of them. Soon the little group was well past the gates and outer fortifications, entirely at

the mercy of Gordyan's whim. He took the same trail
Danaer had that other night, heading down toward
Siank and then turning northward. Malol te Eldri and
General Nurdanth rode together, often talking softly
as the scene changed. Danaer and Lira Nalu were
behind the officers. Before them and behind them and
on either side were Gordyan's riders.

"You move a roan well, Troop Leader," the lady
said. Danaer raised an eyebrow at her easy use of a
common Destre phrase. "I marvel that you have never
been wounded by your fellow soldiers, dressed as you
are in that mantle."

"I am known to them, my lady. And then I often
ride one of the army's blacks; this roan is my own
beast, used for scouting and special occasions."

"He is most handsome." But she was not looking at
his animal, but at him. "Perhaps I might try him
sometime. Is he gentle?"

"For you, I would make him so, my lady."

"My name is Lira. Call me so."

For a while Danaer let his mount have its head,
trusting it to follow the tail of the officer's black ahead.
The Sarli woman continued to fascinate him. In her
frankness she was not wanton. Nor was her manner
quite like that of any woman of the plains people.
Her alien modesty and the faint lilt of Sarlos in her
speech added to her intriguing charm.

"I . . . am honored that you give me that permission, Lira," Danaer said at last. "You know much of
me, and I so little of you."

"Oh?"

"When first I came to Siank garrison, I did not
know you were a sorkra. You are so young and . . .
you rarely wear the wizard's cloak. None of the men
knew, at the beginning, that you were one of
Ulodovol's sorkra Web."

"What did the soldiers think I might be?" Apparently Lira read the answer in Danaer's expression.
"The General's woman?" She threw back her head
and laughed, her full lips parted, her dark curly hair
tossing, and the red ribbons of her headband streaming in a hot breeze. She composed herself and said,

"All the wizard Web may not wear the brown robe—only those who are nearest the Traech Sorkra in learning. I do not yet have that right."

As suddenly as a dust viper would strike, an alarming thought hit Danaer. "Lady, can you see into my mind?"

She laughed again, more softly, a chuckle pitched low in her throat, like an ecar's purring. "Have no worry. Sorkra *do* speak with the mind as well as perform magic. But we do not intrude on the privacy of good people. In fact, in most ways, we are quite ordinary."

"Not at all, Lira, or else we all could make pictures of smoke . . . and chase demons with our spell casting." Danaer wanted to abet her cheeriness, but not if it meant talk of wizardry. He turned words to things inconsequential, such as amusing gossip of the fort—pleasant matters to pass time between man and woman on a long ride. It was a sounding out of each other, a mutually enjoyable adventure, Danaer hoped. All too soon the tents of the Zsed came into view, and the journey was coming to an end.

Gordyan led them at an easy amble around the Zsed and beyond, onto the extension of Siank Plains which lay north. They passed many gaily striped tents with the markings of Siank Zsed. Then began other tribal communities, in miniature, clustered on an open meadow. There were billowing, dun-brown canopies from the eastern clans, the green and gold of the north Vrastre, and even a few woad-blue tents belonging to representatives from the western plains. At the far end of the Zsed lay a field of contest, stretching out from the rolling meadow into the Vrastre. On a rise facing the field a gigantic pavilion had been set up to shelter the chieftains from the sun.

Malol te Eldri beckoned to Danaer. "That is the council tent? Do you see Sovereign Gordt te Raa? You have met him, Troop Leader. We know him only by name and reputation."

"There he is, my lord, speaking to that tall, brown-haired woman."

The officer had been trying to count the assemblage

beneath the canopy. "Surely not all those people are
tribal leaders."

"No, my lord. Some are Siirn-Y, and others are
their seconds of command or priests. It is the custom
among the plains people, even as you have brought
with you General Nurdanth and the Lady Lira Nalu."

Gordyan halted abruptly, and those following him
were hard put to avoid overrunning his animal's rump.
"We are here," Gordyan said simply.

The Siirn Rena's servants took charge of the
mounts, and Gordyan led the Royal Commander and
his party to the pavilion. Gordt te Raa and Lasiirnte
Kandra did not sit on thrones, but upon cushions, like
all the other Destre. However, from the elevation of
this knoll, these powers among their tribes had a fine
view of the field of contest. The visitors from the fort
were led to a place directly before Gordt te Raa. This
was an honor, and it also put them handy to the knives
of his bodyguard, should there be any sign of treachery.

Before sitting down, Malol faced the Destre chieftain and recited the formal greetings he had memorized with the help of Nurdanth and Danaer. As the
four took their assigned places, the General and
Danaer whispered to Malol the names of the various
dignitaries of the plains people who were gathered all
around them. The Royal Commander scribbled these
on a piece of parchment he had brought. Lira Nalu
wrote nothing, but her manner told Danaer she would
forget none of what she heard.

"Thiirt of Ve-Nya, second in command of the home
tribe of Lasiirnte Kandra, the Destre sovereign's
woman," Nurdanth said softly, identifying particular
leaders by their distinctive mantles.

"And there, my lord," Danaer added, "is Handri-
Shaal of Kalisarik . . ."

"That is Vandrei, who led the Kakyein rebellion."

"Vandrei was sorely bested by Captain Yistar in
that war," Danaer put in. "Well it is that they did not
meet here today . . ."

"Jatri of Rierdon-Ne . . ."

"Now you shall see true skill, soldier." Gordyan

broke in upon Danaer's efforts to brief the Royal Commander. The Destre sat close beside the guests. He struck a playful fist against Danaer's bicep, nearly knocking the scout from his cushions. On the field, targets were being set up for the first contest: archery. The row of contestants was small, for the bow was not a favorite weapon among the eastern Destre-Y.

"Troop Leader," Malol began, eyeing the archers thoughtfully.

Danaer knew what interested the Royal Commander. "The shorter men are most likely Sarli half-breeds, my lord. There are always a few of those traveling the Zseds. The big fellows are Tradyans, from the far plains. Lieutenant Branraediir would know them well. When Gordt te Raa was named ruler of the tribes, Stethoj of the West gifted him with a troop of his Tradyan archers, with other warriors to replace those at each Summer's Height. It is a form of tribute most welcome . . ."

"Stethoj? Is he here?"

"No, my lord. It is more than a ten-days' ride to his tribe. He could not have been summoned on such short notice."

A shout went up from the spectators and Malol exclaimed, "Look at the shot that Tradyan made! We must have such archers, cousin." General Nurdanth nodded, as intent on the contest as his fellow officer.

The range was comparatively short when the archery contest began. Then it was increased to eliminate the lesser entrants. Eventually, only two men were left—a Sarli, wearing only knee breeches and sandals and one Tradyan, who went bareheaded in the western fashion and wore an unbelted surcoat rather than a vest. The Sarli knelt to the mark and released his arrows after much calculation for wind and distance. The Tradyan remained standing, aiming with a seemingly careless air. His bow was enormous, and his shafts nearly the length of a man's arm. At last the Sarli missed and resignedly unstrung his little bow.

"Harshaa, Azsed!" rose from a thousand throats. The call could be a challenge or a cheer. In its present inflection it was an accolade. The Tradyan accepted the plaudits, shaking his bow triumphantly above his head.

A big foot nudged Danaer. Gordyan was grinning and pointing to another part of the field. "You would not dare ride to *that*." Workmen were finishing a lance course. It was the most intricate contest Danaer had ever seen. Tiny circlets of bone hung from hairs attached to willow wood frames. These were set at all heights and angles, some appearing impossible for a horseman to spear.

"The army, too, uses the lance."

"Not like this. The Iit merely toy with the weapon," Gordyan said loudly.

Danaer knew he was being baited. The big Destre's grin burned at him.

"Do you think you could compete with these tribesfolk, Troop Leader?" Malol te Eldri asked. "Would your competition in this event harm the conference to come?"

Surprised by the Royal Commander's attitude, Danaer said, "If I show badly, my lord, it will not enlarge your standing among the chieftains." In the back of his mind, Danaer was also most aware of Lira's presence.

"Would you show badly?" There was a twinkle in General Nurdanth's pale eyes. "I doubt not that your scouting roan is well versed in these lancing tricks, and he is used to your touch."

Danaer seemed to feel a lance in his hand already. Gordyan slapped his shoulder. "You handle a roan like a true warrior. Can you handle anything else?" Then his expression sobered and he stared at Lira Nalu. "But there must be no sorkra dealing to help you."

Lira's mouth twitched with amusement. "I vow there will be no magic. The Troop Leader will have only bone and blood and heart to sustain him."

Gordyan was satisfied, and Danaer made up his mind. "With your permission, my lords?"

"You have it," Nurdanth said.

Gordyan could move most silently and swiftly for a

giant. He was halfway down the slope leading from the pavilion knoll before Danaer could get to his feet. Lengthening his stride, Danaer caught up with the Destre by the time the lancing contestants had assembled. A covered pail was handed around the circle, and each rider took out a colored pebble to set his order. Danaer was several turns along, directly following Gordyan. He squatted beside the Siirn's guard, and together they commented on the technique of the first warriors riding the course. The targets were many—at the height of a charging foe, far to one side, far overhead, and one placed at near ground level to simulate an enemy hidden in plains grass. Most of the men and warrior women rode adequately, but without art. They struck the targets squarely with their lances, but bumped obstacles or swung too wide on turns or touched reins too often. It was good enough for warfare, but not for vrentru, where judges and crowds were most exacting.

"My turn!" Gordyan swung up on his horse, a huge, ugly blue roan. "Now you shall see how to handle a lance, friend. Watch!"

Gordyan moved with astonishing lightness and grace. Danaer cheered with the rest of the onlookers as the point of Gordyan's lance stabbed every little circlet cleanly. Pride swelled the man's barrel chest as he rode back to the line of contestants and grinned at Danaer. "Does that meet with the army's standards?"

He was like a youth seeking praise, open and blunt. Danaer liked the man, despite Gordyan's fearsome reputation and their divided loyalties. "It was most well . . ."

The place caller pointed to Danaer and spoke coldly. "You are next, Iit. Unless you come to your senses and withdraw now."

"Care!" Gordyan growled. "He is Azsed, and an honored guest at this vrentru."

"Then ae know not of your colors, stander." The caller, skeptical and contemptuous, lapsed into a rich Destre accent.

"Out Nyald." Danaer enjoyed matching the challenge with his own dialect. "Ain mae of the Siredri ve Aejzad."

Gordyan smiled maliciously at the place caller's stupefaction. Then he took Danaer's sword and helmet. "Warrior, you cannot lance while you carry these. I will hold them in my honor."

"My blood one with yours, Azsed," Danaer answered formally. He was touched that Gordyan volunteered to act as his second.

"Then at it! Let us see how your lance arm fares after the army's tampering."

Danaer mounted at a run, a heady exhilaration seizing him. Vrentru! Lancing contest! Nyald Zsed had known no such festival since Danaer was a boy, and never had they staged one so grand as this. Danaer felt himself newly sworn to manhood again, meeting his first testings—a good roan between his knees and the weapons keeper waiting ahead. The weapons keeper handed up one of the slender contest spears; no man was allowed to use a favorite lance to his advantage. The starter dropped his hand.

The roan broke into an easy lope, and Danaer smoothed a hand along the mottled neck and rough mane. "Calm, now. Let us prove it, Sure-Foot." He let fall the reins and they dangled from the animal's shoulders. Shift of weight and press of knee guided the roan through the targets. The Destre lance was shorter and thinner than the army's weapon. But the moment the wood touched his palm, it was as if Danaer had never handled anything else.

Man and animal must act as one. All the old turns and tricks were still his, and Danaer had taught them to his mount—for these arts were as useful in war as in contests. No sudden breaks, no awkward movements. The lance must strike true, whether it be target or deadly enemy. One by one, Danaer speared the little trophies. His mount could not have been better behaved. Only the sharpest eye could catch the slight dip when the animal changed leads.

"Harshaa! Har-shaa!"

Elated, Danaer trotted back to the waiting line. In the pavilion, the officers were nodding approval, and

Lira waved the long ribbons of her headband to celebrate Danaer's success. That last was far more reward than the cheers of the crowd, and Danaer was smiling slyly to himself as he dismounted and squatted once more beside Gordyan. He did not crow yet, for this was but the first testing.

Gordyan took him by the nape and shook him, though not hurtfully. "Harshaa, indeed! How did Nyald Zsed ever lose you to the soldiers? You are none of them, Azsed. Come to my lances and be my man."

"My Siirn is Straedanfi, and General Nurdanth." Then Danaer softened his refusal. "Then this was but the first challenge. Perhaps I will not last long in the contest."

"You will stand to it," Gordyan said with confidence. "At least until you match with me. School that roan of yours well, then, warrior."

Side by side, they watched the others compete, trading remarks and jests as if they were blood friends of long acquaintance. And one by one, the others were ruled out. Twice more Danaer and Gordyan each passed the judges' demanding eyes. Now stamina counted as much as skill. Danaer thanked Yistar's drill training, which had kept him taut over the years.

And then there were but two left. The onlookers were intently silent as Gordyan rode forth.

One on the ground—done. Another three, far to the sides—done, just when it seemed man and rangy blue roan must overtopple. Mistakes could be fatal when a rider moved at such speed and in such awkward positions. Again and again the lance struck. Even as Gordyan speared the last circlet, Danaer gauged that the big man had been off balance. The giant's gracefulness had failed him in that critical instant. As the Siirn Rena's bodyguard returned to the line, it was obvious he shared Danaer's judgment and was much displeased with his own performance. "A bad lunge, that last one," Gordyan said with an unhappy grunt.

"You struck it fairly." Danaer sensed this was a

man who needed such an assurance, and he did not begrudge it. But as he again took up lance, Yistar's words rang in Danaer's memory: *When you ride to the target, put all else from your mind. Strike to kill.* Whatever the cost, he would not do less than his best. If defeat rankled Gordyan, Argan would determine the price of victory.

For the most part, the targets came easy now, practice and art blending to put the circlets on the spear point. Danaer dipped the lance as he passed each position, by the rules, dropping his trophies one by one, then going on to the next target. At last he was crossing the space before the final and most difficult of the goals. His roan shaved the entrance poles, but none fell.

Danaer matched his balance to that of the horse as they came at the run. His lance was ready and he called, "Ka-saa!" The responsive roan increased his pace, dipping, bringing his rider into direct line with the target. Done! Danaer quickly lifted the lance and circlet and braced for the jump over the water barrier beyond the last position. The roan sprang across and landed cleanly on the grassy flat.

A deafening ovation erupted as Danaer delivered up his last precious circlet of bone and turned toward the contest line. For a heartbeat, Gordyan glared at him, his craggy countenance dark and threatening. Then a reluctant smile broke. "Warrior, you won honestly. Where did you learn that trick of setting the roan at the charge just as you hit home?"

"Spearing sand lizards at Nyald Zsed," Danaer said, only partly joking. "I had a further advantage; my roan is smaller than yours, and more of a level with the targets."

Gordyan cocked his head, weighing that placating comment. Then he said gruffly, "Get to the judges, or they may still award me the honor by default."

Danaer's name was announced, and then the judges stepped back to leave him alone, facing the pavilion. Malol and the General and Lira Nalu were gazing down at him with pride. But Gordt te Raa's face was unfathomable, as were the expressions of many other Destre chieftains.

It was the custom for a victor in contest to dedicate his triumph. That simple ritual was now heavy with peril. Danaer knew he must guard every word lest he give offense.

"All praise to Argan, the praiseworthy, and to Gordt te Raa, Siirn of Siank Zsed . . ."

That much could be said safely. But more was expected, and the crowd hushed, waiting. Danaer steeled himself and said, "My soul to Argan, my honor to my word, and my victory to Krantin."

Murmurs, and sighs of relief, spread among the onlookers. It was obvious they had feared some alien Iit dedication which would spoil the vrentru. Even the chieftains under the pavilion seemed easier for Danaer's dedication, one acceptable to any Destre-Y. Most turned to their companions and chatted on the fine points of the contests just concluded.

One of the dignitaries continued to stare at Danaer. Gordt te Raa studied the soldier until Danaer began to feel a deep uncertainty. The Siirn Rena was inscrutable, unmoving—and he was the final arbiter of what would be the outcome of this fateful council.

VIII

THE STORM MAGIC OF MARKUAND

OTHER, LESS IMPORTANT CONTESTS WERE BEGINNING on the field. But Gordt te Raa gave a barely perceptible signal, and all around the canopy servants began working ropes. In minutes the immense sunshade was converted to a tent, enclosing the council. The chieftains and their attendants rearranged themselves into a rough circle, with Commander Malol's party now seated at the Siirn Rena's left. More servants hurried in and out, bringing roasted meat and larded grain cakes and leathern bottles of wine for each dignitary and attendant.

Malol and Lira were disturbed by the unseemly haste of Destre eating habits. General Nurdanth, with his deep knowledge of the plains people, was not surprised. Nor, of course, was Danaer. Ill at ease, the Royal Commander and the sorkra tried to copy the manners of their neighbors, refraining from conversation and gobbling their food. Destre-Y ate as if they knew not when they might eat again. The last crumbs were licked from fingers, then servants bore away the remnants.

Warrior chieftains picked at their teeth with knives and wiped greasy hands on forearms and their richly stained vests. All around the circle intent and none too friendly stares were shifting toward the four strangers. When all the amenities of belchings and compliments had been done, Gordt te Raa ceremoniously removed his mantle, folding it and placing it on the bare earth before his cushion. His hair was still covered by a plain dust cowl, in the manner of Destre-Y on formal occasions. The Siirn Rena stood and stepped out into the circle, standing beside his mantle. He raised high his eiphren ring and invoked the goddess. "Argan, guide our wills."

Tribal mantles were taken off and laid before their owners, a massive proclaiming of the assembled clans and callings. Gordt te Raa returned to his position of honor beside his consort. "Speak, Royal Commander."

It was all the introduction Malol te Eldri was to receive. Kandra glanced at the visitors, her eyes shining with sympathy. For a moment Danaer thought she might plead with her lord and beg more welcome for these people of the army. Danaer was not the only one who noticed Kandra's reaction. Gordyan was hunkering against a tent pole near his master and mistress. Now he rubbed a hand over his chin, looking torn. He would second the desire of the Lasiirnte, even if it might run counter to that of his sovereign. Yet the Siirn's bodyguard dared not open his mouth. He hulked and seemed miserable to be caught in the dilemma. At length Kandra sighed, deciding not to argue or to defend the guests.

If Malol te Eldri was daunted, he concealed it well. He spoke without apology or preamble, as Nurdanth had advised him. Danaer listened with great interest as the Commander told of Markuand's invasion and victories, and what was likely to come. That done, he broached the possibility of an alliance, a thing unheard of between Destre and the army, a united force to hurl back the awesome might of Markuand.

Nurdanth had tutored his kinsman and fellow officer well. Malol's manners were nearly impeccable. Though an Iit and gently born and reared, he adapted himself readily to this audience. The Royal Commander wisely did not attempt the difficult Destre dialect, speaking only Krantin, with an occasional reference in a plains tongue common among traders and caravan leaders.

When he came to the end, there was a long, brooding silence in the tent. At last, it was broken. "You speak of the survival of Krantin, Army." The curt statement came from a tribal chieftain at the far side of the circle. Danaer eyed his mantle, remembering the man as Handri-Shaal of Kalisarik. "All Krantin, then?"

"All Krantin," Malol te Eldri insisted. "In this defense of our land, we must be as one."

There was another thoughtful silence until Gordt te Raa urged, "You must reply to this, Siirn-Y. The tribes, and the spilled blood, will be yours."

A woman got to her feet, and Lira plucked at Danaer's sleeve and leaned close, whispering, "Wyaela te Fihar, the second in command of Vidik Zsed?"

"Most correct." Danaer marveled that she had heard the woman's name but once, in passing, yet had forgotten neither title nor tribe.

"What of these invaders, these Markuand?" Wyaela demanded. She was not beauteous, nor did she wear the half-skirt of wedlock, as did Kandra. "How great is this threat? What manner of warfare may we anticipate from this new enemy?"

"The sorkra can tell you." Malol te Eldri gestured to Lira. "The Lady Nalu is part of the Web of Wizards. She will give you what we have learned through that Web of far-seeing . . ."

Lira, even standing, looked small and fragile amid the Krantin-Y on every side. But everyone attended her with awe and respect. Like Danaer, they all feared and honored the sorkra, and like him, had been glad to avoid dealings with wizards until now.

Dramatically, Lira pressed her fingertips against her temples and said, "Know you that for those of my calling the mind may see just as the eyes may. With the Web, a sorkra may see across a journey of a candle-mark, or across a ten-days' distance. My Web has seen terrible slaughter and conquest in the land of the Clarique. These alien Markuand have overrun the outer islands. The Markuand dress all in white. They are ever silent. They chant no war cries and, like the Destre-Y, never show pain during battle. They do not beg for mercy, nor do they give mercy. No man survives their victories—only women and children they capture as slaves. They butcher their captives and mutilate the bodies savagely. Quick death is the most desired gift of their bested foes. And the women . . ."

Lira faltered, her tiny figure swaying as if she were about to faint. Danaer got to one knee, his hands out to break the sorkra's fall. But gradually Lira came to herself and steadied, swallowing, forcing herself to go on.

The tent seemed cold. Even with Peluva's sacred burden shining brightly and gilding the grass beyond the pavilion, a great grim shadow fell over the council as they listened. Could it be the wings of the beast-bird, Nidil, the omen of terror and death? Men and women chafed limbs to bring back warmth to flesh prickling with chill.

"The women," Lira said, her voice trembling, "endure brutality beyond imagining, a using by beasts and demons, not men—a degradation past bearing. Women pray to find a weapon to strike back at their new masters, or failing that, one to kill themselves with. The regions of the Evil God are preferable to their lives now . . ."

Gasps of outrage shook her audience. Among the plains people, the will of the goddess was supreme, and the delights of the flesh were worship of Argan. If a man were worthy and took warrior woman in honest battle, she might deem him her true conqueror and accept him. If she resisted, he must relish the challenge of proving his valor until she was persuaded. In time of content, a freeborn Destre woman bestowed her favors as she chose, or perhaps pledged herself to that man who won her loyalty. The goddess blessed those who took joy in her, and rape was a crime associated with the Iit, not with the easy favors and lusty customs of the Zseds. This story of the Clarique women, and what they had suffered at the hands of the Markuand, shocked the council. Unthinkable!

Kandra found the courage to ask, "And where are these . . . these monsters now?"

In answer, Malol te Eldri unrolled a map he had brought. "They advance on Laril-Quil, the greatest city of Clarique, that place that once was Traecheus. It is not hoped Laril-Quil can withstand Markuand long."

Gordt te Raa mentioned the news received in his original message from General Nurdanth. "You say the best soldier of the Clarique was defeated by magic . . ."

Lira nodded. Danaer watched her worriedly, alarmed by her pallor. "That is true. General Thaerl was enchanted by evil spells. He ran witless from the field of battle, bested by the sorcery of Markuand."

"He had somewhere to run," Malol said. "Krantin does not. Beyond the Plains of Barjokt lies the end of the world. If we survive, we must deny Markuand our country—*all* of Krantin."

Gordt te Raa glanced at Lira. "Wise little sorkra, what of that woman warrior, that she-devil Ti-Mori?" The Royal Commander stiffened at this insulting reference to the heroine, the daughter of a lord of The

Interior. Danaer shook his head, warning him to contain his anger.

"Ti-Mori?" Lira blinked several times, seeming disoriented. The folds of her gown stirred, but no breath of breeze had come through the tent. Visibly, she shivered away the phenomenon. "Ti-Mori gathers her scattered forces. South, south of Jlandla, southward of the Markuand advance. She intends to march around them and rejoin the army of Krantin, and her warriors are still many in number. We may count on her aid . . ."

"And the Markuand? What of their numbers?"

"To our Web they appeared past counting—twenty legions, thirty, or forty. Row upon row of white-clad hordes, and more arriving daily over the Great Sea Beyond the Islands . . ."

Gordt te Raa and his Destre-Y winced at this recital. One of the chieftains stood up, and the mutterings around the circle hushed. The Siirn was of paler complexion than most Destre-Y and his hair was streaked with gold. Plainly there was much of Clarique in his ancestry. "I would add my words to those of the sorkra."

"Lorzosh-Fila," Danaer prompted Malol as the Royal Commander furtively searched his parchment for the man's name. "He is Siirn of Deki on the River."

"This army leader speaks truth," Lorzosh-Fila said. "The Markuand face us squarely. My spies bring me bad news every candle-mark now. Many of the Clarique are crossing the river to us, seeking sanctuary. We take them in if we can, but our food supplies are dwindling. Deki and her granaries cannot continue this charity for long. The Markuand are beginning to press hard, to north and south, and against the coast of Clarique. Few boats now come down our river, and no ships come up from the Clarique seas. I plead for all your help. I would, on my faith, that I had both an Iit army and a band of Destre warriors to guard Deki's walls. Deki is a fortress, but it will fall to Markuand if you do not come to our aid. We will starve, and then we will die."

Often Destre-Y would hide their innermost thoughts at council. But the faces of the chieftains revealed their dismay, so shocked were they. Questions came at Lira and Malol te Eldri, and at General Nurdanth, who was well known among the Siank clans. The voices were less and less belligerent with each new answer. Many of the chieftains knew only the Azsed tongue, and often Danaer had to translate for Lira and the officers. Some questions were repeated again and again, a probing of details in search for truth, no longer doubting the greater story.

Danaer detected the altered attitude and exulted. Malol's gamble was winning. Danaer had sat on the fringes of smaller gatherings such as this, when he was a youth in Nyald Zsed. He knew the directions questions would take, and when the shift in the wind would mark growing agreement. Success was surely very near.

At that moment, alarm spread over Lira's round face. Her garments were stirring again, but now the cold wind that assaulted her could be felt by everyone in the tent. Winter's ice, stinging the skin, slicing into marrow, came without warning, carried on a howling wind.

Buffeted cruelly by the worst of the sleet, Lira raised her arms. Her voice was shrill as she chanted a magical phrase. In sudden horror, Danaer understood. Wizardry! Attacking the sorkra—and the council!

Even as that comprehension rushed upon him, the wind strengthened to a fierce roaring, ripping at the canopy and shredding it, exposing the council to the open sky and fields. And a new astonishment fell upon the gathering.

The storm existed only in this spot! On the field of contest and among the dwellings of the Zsed there was calm. The chieftains and Malol's party were cut off from the rest of the world, caged in by witchcraft!

Warriors cowered and some left their places, trying to flee this magical storm—only to be knocked to the earth by that merciless, alien wind. The priests among them mouthed prayers, invoking Argan's protection. Their words were torn from their lips, lost in the roaring sleet. Hair and beards thickened with icy coatings, fingers turned blue with cold, and men and women choked on fear.

A blinding sheet of lightning broke overhead. Every face was lit brilliantly, and when vision cleared, all saw that they were bathed in blue-white radiance. They braced for the deafening thunderclap which must follow—but it did not. Lightnings walked the tent poles, those which had stood against the wind. The eerie glow danced through the rags of the pavilion, and never a crack of thunder. Warriors who could confront the most murderous human foe had no stomach for this terrible wizardry.

Amid the chaos, Lira fought to keep her position, her arms still lifted in some countersorcery. It seemed the little Sarli must be picked up and devoured by the storm wind. Danaer gulped down his dread, concentrating on Lira, realizing the sorkra was their one hope against this thing. Her lips moved, forming the name "Ulodovol." She was summoning her Web to help her! Indeed, one tiny woman should not wage such a battle alone.

Till her fellow wizards came to her aid, Danaer must champion Lira. Crawling against the sleet, he groped toward her. Another figure approached from the opposite direction with the same intent. Danaer and Lasiirnte Kandra reached the sorkra simultaneously. Resisting the furious wind, they rose to their knees, locking their hands about Lira Nalu. Army scout and Destre princess supported the pretty Sarli wizard. When her strength failed, they helped her lift her hands skyward once more—for only her spellcasting held off the evil storm from slaying them all.

"Power . . . you of the Web . . . to me!" Lira was screaming, very close to Danaer's ear, or he would not have heard her. Kandra's exquisite face was contorted by the wind and her honest fear. But she maintained her grip on the sorkra, as did Danaer. If Lira did not win, this Markuand magic might strike them all, destroying the council!

Their alliance bolstered Lira as she continued to chant. Ulodovol must be at Siank garrison, some distance away. And the other wizards of this Web? If they could reach out to far Clarique, surely they could rally to Lira's aid . . .

But they had not been able to save their fellow wizard in Clarique.

Kandra bent her sleek head, bracing Lira's with her own, steadying the smaller woman. Danaer felt a man's hands upon his, adding to the ring of bodies protecting Lira. It was Gordt te Raa, side by side with his consort, fathoming her purpose and Danaer's. They sheltered the wizard woman all around, giving Lira space to breathe—and to weave magic—amid the raging storm.

All at once, as suddenly as it had fallen upon them, the wind died. A cloud beast might have sucked up the darkness and silent lightning into itself, then melted away as mist in the sunlight.

And there *was* sunlight. Peluva's golden burden poured warmth and comfort down on the shattered ruins. Men and women picked themselves out of the rubble. They had braved death in clan wars and caravan raids, but now many edged away, as if to flee the knoll where wizardry had seized them.

"Destre! Do you forget? We are a council." Gordt te Raa proved his right to be Siirn Rena, his courage, and that of his woman, an example to his chieftains. "Resume your places. We are not done."

Gordyan was wide-eyed, but unlike many others, he had made no attempt to escape the knoll. He came to Lasiirnte Kandra, anxiously asking after her welfare, then, belatedly, after the sorkra's. Encouraged by their replies, he looked at Danaer and said fervently, "The goddess will honor you for your courage, warrior."

"Not that," Danaer said, aware of a shuddering in his belly, now that what had happened came full upon his mind. "It was only that she had to complete *her* magic." Lira was extremely pale, now and then a sob catching in her throat. At the moment she seemed very delicate and most ill-suited for her wizard profession. Danaer put an arm about Lira and slowly led her back to her place. She sat on the cushions, very erect as she smoothed her sleet-torn gown and broke melting ice from her ribbons. Her pallor was fading, but Danaer continued to watch her. She must not be taxed, for the magic storm might come again—and again she would have to seek the distant powers of her wizard Web.

Gordyan bellowed at his guards and the servants, setting them to repairing the canopy. Not all of it could be found, but enough was roped together to form a roofless tent.

The contests on the meadows had stopped, for now the people of the Zsed at last could see that something had struck the pavilion. Much confused, they rushed toward the knoll, full of questions. Gordyan's guards held them back. "Tell them all is well in hand," Gordt te Raa commanded. He glanced at Lira and added, "Ai, it is well in hand, for now Azsed has enjoyed the power of the sorkra. Thanks to that, we still will have council."

A semblance of order was restored. Uneasily, warriors and priests and attendants formed a circle again. Gordt te Raa remained standing until all the mantles were properly in place. Then he addressed Malol and Nurdanth. "For this war against Markuand and its evil wizardry you will need Destre warriors, you say?"

There was a stirring around the council circle, but none challenged the Siirn Rena. He behaved as if nothing had happened; an alliance was already struck.

"Indeed we shall," Malol said quickly. "Not merely the army needs your warriors, but all of Krantin, to guard our borders. Think not that the Markuand will spare the tribes of Destre-Y."

Gordt te Raa surveyed the flimsy makeshift canopy, his face darkening with anger. "As we have seen. They dare to strike at a council of Azsed, these Markuand! They have come against Destre-Y—and they shall pay a cost they have not prepared for."

Malol pressed his arguments. "The Clarique army is larger than that of Krantin—yet the Clarique were broken. There was treachery and evil magic, it is true. But in time the numbers of the Markuand alone might well have won victory, for they are most strong. I must be frank. The army of The Interior cannot hold back Markuand, not unaided. Lorzosh-Fila is right, and the sorkra is right. We need warriors, Destre warriors, and we need them desperately. Without them, Krantin will fall to Markuand, and to the terrible wizards who guide them and plague us with magic storms."

"And you ask our help. I warn you, Commander, lancers we have aplenty, but few swordsmen," Gordt te Raa said.

"Excellent!" Malol exclaimed. "We need lancers, and we have seen how superb the Destre are at such arts—if we had any doubts after so long meeting your warriors in battle."

Gordt te Raa grinned nastily. "And we do not fight afoot."

"That is understood. The army will supply the necessary infantry."

The Siirn Rena conferred with his consort with his eyes. Kandra nodded encouragingly. Obviously the beautiful Lasiirnte had a profound influence over her lord. "Lancers . . . and archers?"

Nurdanth was delighted to find the army's new ally so astute. "By all means!"

Gordt te Raa and Kandra and several of the more powerful chieftains studied the map Malol had brought. Gordyan used his height to see over their shoulders, curiously peering at the chart and his Siirn's gestures across the marked territories.

"How much time have we?" the Destre leader asked Malol.

"None at all! We have lost too much already."

"It is more than a ten-days' ride to the western clans, if my messengers go by the plains route. The Tradyans are widely scattered. It is the time of their great hunts. If you wish Tradyan archers for this war, how may I summon such quickly?"

"Perhaps we might use a special messenger," Lasiirnte Kandra suggested. Her dulcet voice made the men attend her instantly. "It may be that a Destre courier could cross the Mountains of the Mare in a few days—with your safe conduct, Royal Commander."

Malol was tempted, but he sighed and said, "That would not be wise, I fear. There are those in The Interior who oppose this alliance between our peoples. A Destre would be a target for their assassins. I propose that summoning the Tradyans to our battle ranks shall be the army's risk."

"But who of the army could ever reach Stethoj of the West?" Gordt te Raa wondered. "He abhors helmet and sword. He would never welcome the army's messenger, nor *any* representative of The Interior."

"I will send one of my officers who is well known to Stethoj—a man hated by the Tradyans, but one they trust, a man who keeps his vows to them. They respect him, even though he has slain many of their tribesmen." Malol took a heavy breath and spoke one word: "Branra."

Kandra blinked in amazement and Gordyan spat an oath. Only Gordt te Raa seemed unperturbed. Around the circle there were growlings, and one chieftain leaped to his feet to protest.

"Hablit, Siirn of Vidik," Danaer murmured to Malol and Nurdanth. Vidik lay on the direct route to Deki and the eastern border. Any relief column must have the cooperation of Vidik's chieftain, and plainly Hablit was in no mood to offer that cooperation.

"And you call yourselves Azsed!" Hablit was shouting. "Now these Iit talk of Branra, that slayer of hope, that bloody-handed devil who comes straight from Bogotana's Realm! Dirt eaters! will you abide this? I marvel that you have not all sold yourselves to the Iit, just as that young bejit with them has . . ."

The obscene insult made Danaer snatch at his sword, but Nurdanth dug hard fingers into his arm and whispered sharply. Seething with frustration, Danaer obeyed.

"It is easy to give insult to those who may not challenge, and that should be beneath the honor of a true warrior." The taunt came, surprisingly, from Wyaela te Fihar, Hablit's own second in command. The virago sneered openly at her Siirn, not hiding her contempt.

"Then I speak in appeal. Siirn Rena?"

"You seem to be talking more than enough for us both," Gordt te Raa said dryly. "I thought perhaps you scorned to let me voice an opinion."

"We began our reigns together, Rena. We saw then as one in all things."

"Too much as one. And now we see the same things, but for different motives." Gordt te Raa eyed his fellow chieftain narrowly. "You saw the Markuand wizard work his magic storm upon us. Do you deny it was aimed at this alliance?"

"I care naught for any magic—only for the pride of Azsed." Hablit waved his arms as if to chase off midges. "It may be this magic is not so evil, not if it conspires to save Destre-Y from a shameful slavery under the yoke of the lords of The Interior. We give them everything, and they give nothing . . ."

Kandra raised a slender eyebrow, and Gordt te Raa smiled thinly. "In that at least you may speak truth. Royal Commander, Siirn Hablit thinks of the future, when the army has used our best warriors to bleed the Markuand. Then will they turn upon us and conquer the tribes at last? You ask us to stand at the side of a sword-drawn Iit army. This is well, for now. But what of in time to come? What will we gain from the alliance?"

"Your land! And it *is* your land, this Krantin. Already you own it and control it and nurture it, whether you realize it or not," Malol said with passion. "Siirn Handri-Shaal, for all purposes the caravan routes south of Kalisarik are yours to command. You do not need to send your warriors to bandit them, for you own their riches and their profit. You others, is it not the same with many of you?"

"This may be," Gordt te Raa admitted. "But might not this newfound power end if our chieftains die buying your victory over Markuand?"

"*Our* victory, but . . . what do you wish?"

"Amnesty, to the time of this war. Beyond that, every Destre-Y may look to himself. But let no tribesfolk be accused for deeds committed before now," Gordt te Raa said. Gordyan smiled and several chieftains nodded vigorously. An amnesty would let go free many notorious brigands and killers.

Malol took a paper from his tunic and gave it to the Destre leader. "There is my authority, with King Tobentis's seal. I am the King's proclaimed heir, and the army's commander. And the army is the only weapon the lords of The Interior have against Destre-Y—or Markuand. You have my word of honor and my bond on this matter of amnesty. But only until the war is won. After that, I will hold you to *your* honor, Sovereign Gordt."

"You parry the lance well, Royal Commander—"

Before Gordt te Raa could finish, Hablit interrupted. "It is not yet enough."

"Agreed. We also want a temple on the most sacred ground, in the hills above Siank. It is Argan's holy spring, and an Iit possesses it."

"That is my realm," Nurdanth said. "I am sure I can secure for you the Spring of the White Flame. You shall have your temple where Jiish Fiin first evoked Argan."

"Not enough." Hablit, again.

"It is my turn to agree," Malol te Eldri said. "I would require a pledge for Inner Krantin, for The Interior, to bind our peoples together as one for all time to be."

A new coldness, from within, twisted at Danaer. Prophecy now spoke in Malol's voice, not in that of a dying herb-healer.

"How may that be done?" Gordt te Raa asked. "Paper may be burned and words lost from hearing."

"Your successor has been selected by your priests, Nurdanth tells me. I understand she is a young girl named Sha-Lei."

The Destre leader was suspicious. "Ai. It has been done according to Azsed, Argan's omens read by the priests. The child will be reared by our precepts, and she will become Rena upon my death or abdication. That will not be for many, many seasons. She is but a child."

"As is my son."

A profound stillness held the audience. Arranged

marriages between children were nothing strange to either plains people or those of The Interior. But never had such a thing been known *between* their cultures. Malol was, as he had said, the king's own heir. The seed of ancient Ryerdon was his, and his blood was pure beyond questioning. His son would be destined to wed with a princess royal, and in the fullness of years the boy would most likely assume the throne of Krantin. The proffered sacrifice stunned even Hablit, for the moment.

Gordt te Raa consulted with the priests among the group. As one, they judged that the goddess would not forbid such a union. Yet the Siirn Rena hesitated, turning to his consort. "What say you, Maen?"

Kandra had been gazing steadily at Malol te Eldri. Like Lira, she seemed deeply moved by the officer's proposal. Gently, she asked, "What is the age of your son, Royal Commander?"

"Nine." The nobleman's voice was constricted and husky. He was putting forth his most precious gift, his final weapon to save his beloved country.

"That would be well," Kandra said. "Our Sha-Lei is a pretty child of nearly eight summers. This union should bind our peoples and promise peace for long times to come . . ."

Danaer felt as if the earth had dropped away beneath him. Andaru! When the Azsed Rena would become the Rena Azsed, lord of all Krantin. And if this marriage came to pass, would not the girl child who was Destre indeed unite all the land? A new birth of Ryerdon, a coming together again of the scattered peoples, and the ruler would be Azsed, strong in the faith of Argan.

Osyta had foretold most well. The veil of the future had been parted and the dying crone had seen what would come to pass—and its beginning was here, at this Destre council. But Andaru was no free gift. It must be bought, in blood and in sacrifice. Where was the blood? Who would die, whose life be severed to gain the victory so long promised?

Gordt te Raa was about to answer Malol's generous offer when Hablit exclaimed angrily, "You would enslave our future Rena to an Iit husband?"

Her black eyes sparkled as Kandra retorted, "I do not call it enslavement to be wed, Hablit, and had you ever taken wife—"

He would not listen. Red with fury, he pointed a shaking finger at the Siirn Rena. "You may not permit this, on your oath to Azsed!"

"That is for me to choose," Gordt te Raa said frostily. "The decision is always made by the Siirn of the female's tribe, with the consent of the Siirn Rena —and I own both titles. I accept the Royal Commander's pledge, and the betrothal. I deem it binding on our peoples, pending final judgment from the gathering of Azsed's priests."

"And you control the head priest. His faith is as false as your own, to sell his people so." There was a concerted gasp from the audience as Hablit hurled those accusations.

Gordt te Raa did not deign to reply. Kandra looked around the circle and said sweetly, "May we render our agreement, Siirn-Y? Whoever would join with the Siirn of Vidik, stand with him." Hablit waited, sputtering, but no one seconded him, not even his own delegation. A few chieftains appeared to have reservations about the alliance, but they would not challenge the Siirn Rena and his consort. Kandra chained their loyalties with her presence. "Then it is done, my lord Rena."

Nodding, Gordt te Raa started to intone the solemn oath. "In the name of Azsed, kant, prodra—"

"Not in my name!" Hablit thundered.

"Resume your place, Siirn. You may cling to your stubborn opinion, but the alliance has been agreed upon, and we will be one in this—"

"None of my warriors will ever take lance, save to kill the bejits from The Interior," the chieftain of Vidik vowed.

With amazing patience, Gordt te Raa said, "You will send your warriors to me, and I will lead them as the Royal Commander and I choose. You will accept the judgment of your fellow Siirn-Y."

"My fellow Siirn-Y are easily swayed by a power-greedy Iit who pretends to be a true Destre—a Rena who uses his woman of ease to force agreement from us. She gives promises with her eyes and body that no woman wived could keep, with honor!"

The air within the ragged walls tingled, though in a far different way than it had during the lightnings of the storm. An awesome expression spread over Gordyan's hard face. This insult had been given not only to the Siirn Rena but to his woman as well, and Gordyan's abject devotion to Lasiirnte Kandra became ever more evident as his rage heated.

Hablit ignored the menace in Gordyan's manner, and Danaer wondered if the man had utterly lost his wits. Did he not realize what he had said?

Gordyan stepped away from a splintered tent pole where he had been leaning. Lightly, like a great predator stalking its next meal, one hand on his knife, Gordyan approached the Siirn of Vidik. Kandra noticed what was happening, and she held up a dainty hand, arresting Gordyan's ominous prowling in mid-stride. A leashed killer, he awaited her pleasure, his expression terrible.

Gordt te Raa had been wrestling with his own considerable anger, and now he said softly, "Beware, Hablit. I am no youthful warrior bound by oaths of honor and on guarded behavior. I will not be forced to swallow your insults."

Malol and Nurdanth and Lira understood but a fraction of what was occurring. But they were not blind or deaf. Like Danaer, they held their breath, sensing a conflict coming to a climax. Danaer was rigid with anticipation as blood words were flung. This was a thing out of hero tales, when tribe friends fell out, and insults might well lead to a clan war such as had wracked Nyald Zsed so bitterly.

"You are not fit Rena to serve Argan!" Hablit's rage fed upon itself and would not be slaked.

"I am Rena, and you will obey my commands." Gordt te Raa's tone would brook no further defiance. Gordyan was still held by the invisible reins Kandra had drawn. But now the big man's glance shifted to his master, eager for a word that would release him.

Hablit snatched out his dagger, and Gordyan, not waiting for permission, began to lunge for him. Before he could close with Vidik's chieftain, though, Hablit struck his weapon hilt deep into the soft ground, a mute gesture changing everything. Gordyan slammed to a stop, balancing on the balls of his feet.

In another snake-quick movement, Hablit yanked his knife from the dirt and flung his tribal mantle over his shoulder. "No need to loose your golhi-wolf to slay me, Gordt. I will leave of my own will, and the Zsed of Vidik goes with me."

"Your personal guard goes with you. The Zsed of Vidik stays." Wyaela te Fihar did not turn to address Hablit, scorning him with her back. She looked at Gordt te Raa and Kandra. "Vidik Zsed does not endorse rebellion against the will of the Siirn Rena. We ride with you."

Hablit spat like a cornered beast, gripping his knife hilt again, this time intending to murder his former second in command.

"Gordyan," the Siirn Rena said, and the big man started forward once more, a delighted and bloodthirsty grin splitting his face.

"Argan's rule protects me here at council!" Hablit reminded them all. The old ritual merely slowed Gordyan's pace a trifle. Hablit was walking backward, stumbling over debris left by the storm. Suddenly he shook his knife at the clouds. "You Markuand wizards! Heed me! I am your tool henceforth! Use me to slaughter these blasphemers and devils! You wizards from over the sea, I am your minion, sworn to blot out this outrage upon the face of Azsed . . ."

Gordyan was almost upon him, and Hablit's personal guards closed about their chieftain protectively.

"You will hear of me on the plains wind," Hablit said loftily, though a bit shrill. "And you, Royal Commander, you will curse the day you first met Hablit—"

"And bless the day he last saw your face—which shall be now," Gordyan warned. His own men were moving in upon Hablit's flanks, and they far outnumbered the rebel's guards.

Hablit waited no longer. The erstwhile Destre chieftain plunged through the remnants of the pavilion wall and down the slope toward the picketed roans of the council. Gordyan and his guards pursued. But Hablit was quick, once his flight began, and he reached the safety of his horses. Headlong, the now realmless Siirn rode through the vrentru and out of sight. Gordyan sent several of his men to follow and be sure there was no turning back. Hablit's life had been spared, but he was outcast, and if he tried to return to Siank Zsed, he would be slain without pity.

Wyaela te Fihar picked up her mantle and moved it into the spot vacated by Hablit. Then she sat on the cushion he had left. None questioned her right. Vidik's Siirn had abandoned his oath—and now Vidik Zsed would follow a new Siirn.

Now Gordt te Raa took out his ceremonial dagger and held it crosswise on his palm. All conversation ceased, save for Danaer's hurried instructions to Malol. He had not hoped that affairs would move so swiftly, and now he must guide the Royal Commander with little forewarning. Malol laid his hand upon the knife, pressing Gordt's palm, binding himself in sacred pledge to the goddess of the Destre-Y.

"All we vow, then Argan witness," the Siirn Rena said solemnly. In unison with him, the chieftains and priests and all their servants chorused those words. "Her fire will shrivel our minds and souls if we break this faith or shame Azsed. Honor upon honor, Argan, ruler of wills. Witness! Blood by blood, stirrup by stirrup, now—we are one!"

Malol te Eldri stumbled along in recitation of the oath, and no one laughed as he dealt with the Destre tongue.

When it was done, Gordt te Raa flashed a rare wide smile, a warrior scenting battle. He added his own pledge then, with joy. "Argan, taste the blood of a Markuand army."

IX

BOGOTANA'S FURIES

"THEY ARE SO FEW, AND MOST OF THEM HAVE NEVER known war," Lira said sadly. She stood beside Danaer on the fort's banquette, looking down on the drill field outside the gates. A confusing array of men rushed about, trying to follow the orders they were given. Dust rose in a gritty cloud, but fortunately the wind was kind and carried the worst of it away from the sweating soldiers.

"Older and wiser heads command them, Lira." Danaer straddled the crenel rail and pointed out particular details as the conscripts were trained in lancework. "These troops will form part of the units the Royal Commander will send to Deki ...."

"Under your Captain Yistar."

"He is much honored to be chosen. Straedanfi is experienced in battle," Danaer assured her. "While Nurdanth and Malol and Gordt te Raa assemble our main forces, Yistar will do them proud at the siege of Deki."

Lira caught his arm, begging Danaer to step back to safety on the banquette. Amused by her concern, he agreed. She had asked him to help her climb the ladder to the lookouts' post, and he had been more than willing to serve as her escort. Since the Destre council, a six-day ago, she had spoken to him often.

She toyed with the streamers of her headband as she walked back along the catwalk to the ladder. Danaer followed her closely, though he did not dare to behave as boldly as he might with a woman of his own people. If he were not so intrigued by the Sarli's attractiveness and nature, he would not have presumed this far—not with a wizard's apprentice! That still troubled him, yet he continued to seek her company.

126

"Deki will be a brutal encounter," Lira said, half to herself. "The Royal Commander admits he has little hope the city can be saved. The forces of Markuand are already too solidly entrenched on the Clarique banks across the river from Deki."

"But Yistar's reinforcements will give Malol and Gordt the time they need."

Lira smiled, and Danaer guessed she knew all these things. She would know many things he did not, perhaps military secrets not even the officers had learned, till Ulodovol's wizard web deigned to reveal them. Then Lira grew morose. "You will go with Captain Yistar's caravan?"

"Ai. Shaartre and I and some of our units are already assigned. Most of the men will be these new, unblooded conscripts fresh from Kirvii, though. When we cross the Vrastre, they will have need of my scouting; Gordyan and some of his men will accompany us, but..."

Lira nodded, aware of that part of the alliance's workings. The Siirn Rena was sending his most trustworthy minion and a number of warriors to guarantee the safe passage of the supply wagons through to besieged Deki.

Shouts from the gate interrupted their conversation. "Pre-sent!" rang out, but it was too late for such formalities. Five dusty soldiers on lathered, staggering horses galloped past the palisades and into the courtyard. Danaer and Lira peered down and said with one voice, "Branra!"

Branraediir indeed was with the small band; it was obvious he had ridden twenty times the distance his companions had journeyed. Bareheaded and begrimed, Branra spurred his black for the rocky fortress which housed headquarters. Startled soldiers gawked, snapped to attention, then broke into spontaneous cheers as Branra passed them. All knew of Branra's mission, and many had thought they would never see him alive again.

"He *said* he would come back in time to go with Captain Yistar," Danaer said, then whistled admiringly at the nobleman's feat.

"I must go," Lira exclaimed, hurrying to the ladder. Danaer sprang to steady the thing till she touched boot to earth. Together they walked across the yard. But Danaer was brought up short by a hail from Yistar. Lira went on, favoring him with a parting smile.

"You saw the Lord Lieutenant? Good! We will go and see what he has to report, and make preparations to begin our trek," Yistar said. "That is, assuming you are still alive when the journey starts." Danaer blinked and tried to frame a reply. But the Captain went on. "I quite appreciate the joys of lusty young manhood and the charms of a pretty woman, especially the sort a sorkra must possess. But you will kindly take some care, and quit perching on rickety railings, Troop Leader. That is a four-length drop to the drill field. I have spent too much time and effort on your training to see you break your neck impressing women."

"It . . . it will not happen again," Danaer promised with a sheepish grin. Yard idlers and grooms and camp followers had overheard the lecture and were smirking at officer and scout.

"See it does not." Yistar ignored the onlookers, leading the way rapidly into the headquarters building. Danaer found the rooms and halls crowded with what seemed to be all the combined staff of Nurdanth and Malol. Like Yistar, all were hurrying to the main chamber. There Branra was the center of a commotion. Everyone was talking at once. Danaer looked about curiously, but neither Lira nor her wizard master was present. The absence of those two on such an occasion puzzled him.

Branra was speaking excitedly to Malol, pulling papers from a scuffed leather pouch, pointing out passages in the writings. Someone gave him a cup of wine and the young nobleman tossed it down, totally without the delicacy expected of a courtier. He was amazingly enthusiastic for a man who had ridden half the land and back.

As Branra paused to ask that his cup be refilled, he spotted Danaer. "Azsed! To me!" Aides and junior officers edged aside to give the soldier room to come close to Branra. The Royal Commander's protégé flung an arm familiarly about the taller man's shoulder. "Hai! Have you ever met Stethoj of the Killing Arrows? No? Now *there* is a true warrior, an admirably bloody man. Trust him, but never fight him, if you have a choice. And the range of those Tradyan arrows! You must see them at the hunt—or in battle!"

"We hope we shall," Malol said gently, nodding to General Nurdanth. "But not aimed against us."

"They will cut down the Markuand like weeds! He is sending ten tens of his archers to us—to Gordt te Raa, to take part in our alliance," Branra exulted. He gulped more wine, choking in his haste.

Danaer now understood that Branra suffered the near hysteria of exhaustion. Considering the vast territory he had spanned in his epic ride, and the dangers involved, how could he not know weariness?

"The . . . interference we dreaded?" Nurdanth asked softly. Few of the aides could have heard him, but Branra did, and so did Danaer. He remembered the masquerading rioters and the finding that spies within The Interior plotted to destroy this alliance of army and Destre.

Branra dismissed the General's worry lightly. "Nothing of consequence. We were ready for them." In his dark blue eyes there was that same glow of blood fever Danaer had seen during the riot. If there had been assassins, they must have been bested, perhaps slain by Branra's famous sword.

"My Lord Commander," an aide called. The man was at the door, and he glanced behind him uncertainly.

"What is it?" Malol said, intent on Branra.

"It is . . ."

"Another messenger." Lasiirnte Kandra brushed by the flustered aide and all sound died. Kandra entered like the Destre royalty she was, her kirtle bright with jewels, her green demiskirt a lush velvet, and the tolabelt slung around her hips, a priceless tapestry picturing her rank. Further, she wore her weapons—a glittering bronze-bladed dagger and a ceremonial sword that must have been made for a wealthy lord, who sheathed it in gold and emeralds. Slowly, very conscious of her power, Kandra moved through the room.

Some of the staff surreptitiously tidied their uniforms or struck poses. Alone, of the officers who had not met her, Branra did not play the mooncalf. As a foe of the Destre-Y, he had heard of Kandra's ability to spellbind with her beauty, and he was forearmed. Kandra smiled graciously as she paraded among the aides, stunning them the more.

"Are you accustomed to serve as your lord's courier, my lady Kandra?" Malol seemed astonished that the Lasiirnte had come alone, and so richly garbed, as for festival.

"When I choose to do so. We always spy upon the fort. We know who leaves, and who returns—if it be of great importance." She looked narrowly at Branra. "You did in truth counsel with Stethoj?"

"Yes, Lasiirnte. He will come. He sends a hundred archers before him, and he gathers more of his hunters even now."

"Ah! Then I will match your good news with some of my own. Your route to Deki lies open and clear. The army column may travel at all speed." Kandra patently enjoyed the stir her announcement created.

"Vidik's chieftain will not hinder us?" Nurdanth wondered. "Hablit swore to traffic with the enemy wizard . . ."

"One slinking cur cannot maim an entire herd. Azsed is law, and Hablit forfeited his honor. He hides out on the Vrastre, a hunted beast. We will run him to ground and sever his brutish existence soon. Do not fear him." Kandra's scorn was tangible, the worse that Hablit had dared insult her in his parting oaths. "Under Wyaela's chieftainship, Vidik will welcome the army bloodlessly."

One of the junior officers expressed his fellows' disbelief. "It is true, then? A woman rules Vidik and all its tribes?"

Kandra laughed at him. "Does this astound you? But we have heard that Iit hold women in low regard. Even your Ti-Mori must go to the island kingdom to prove her worth as a warrior."

"Wyaela will be a splendid ally, I am sure," Malol te Eldri said judiciously, making amends for his aide's foolishness.

Danaer felt strangely apart from the others, at one with Branra in this regard. He could not say what left Branra unmoved. For himself, there was some aura about Kandra which would not let him worship her as others did. What was it? He should not be immune to that heat that most men knew whenever Kandra was present. Perhaps it was her rank, for he was Destre, and was awed to be so close to the famed Lasiirnte. Yet men of the Destre were also entranced by Kandra's beauty, as he had witnessed. Hablit had slandered her, but there had been some truth in his words. For such beauty, used in such a way, *was* a promise of sexuality —a sexuality Kandra had no intention of offering to any man but her wedded lord. But the promise was there, nevertheless, a weapon far more potent than her little dagger or pretty sword.

He looked at her with odd disinterest, his mind drifting to . . . Lira. Danaer tried to hide his surprise at that thought. Was the sorkra's unique charm a shield against Kandra's power? If Kandra worked magic upon men's hearts and lusts, was not Lira also a worker of magic?

Danaer did not relish that idea, wanting to remain his own man. Then, as he continued to watch Kandra's game with the smitten officers, a new sensation filled his being. He felt a terrible sadness, a tinge of awful grief.

He shook his head and the moment was gone. But he remembered the sadness most vividly and was deeply troubled.

Kandra had been enjoying the attentions and compliments, but now she turned to Malol and said, "I must bring you other news, not so happily. From Deki."

"My wizards inform me of—"

"Deki is our city, my lord, and perhaps our riders are a match for your Branraediir," Kandra said with some pique. Like all Destre, she did not like to believe that wizards could hear things ordinary mortals could

not, outracing the swiftest roans and the best horsemen.
"Laril-Quil is about to fall. Lorzosh-Fila says a flood
of Clarique come into Deki now, and burn their boats
behind them. Soon the Markuand need waste no forces
against the cities of Clarique; they may turn full to
assault upon Deki."

"Inform the quartermaster to double the provisions
the caravan will take," Malol instructed his aides. "Assign extra wagons to the column. Lady Kandra, your
news is most disheartening. But we thank you."

"I am your ally, Siirn. And we have sworn to deal
honestly with you."

Quite abruptly, Kandra left. Her soft Destre boots
were noiseless on the stone floor. The rustling of her
mantle and the tiny clink of the chains which held her
dagger and sword were her only sounds of departure.
Her leaving sucked life from the room.

"Such unseemly haste," Malol marveled.

"Azsed protocol, partly," Branra said dryly. He finished his wine, then went on. "They leave before the
welcome sours. I assure you I did not linger over my
going, once my mission to Stethoj was completed. My
reception in his Zsed was stiff at best, gained only
through Gordt te Raa's safe conduct. One does not
challenge a truce to the breaking point by overstay-
ing . . ."

"Of course. And now I have another duty for you
to perform, Lieutenant." Bewildered by Malol's commanding tone, Branra at once set aside his cup and
stood to attention. "You will retire to your quarters and
sleep. If I see you before sundown, you will trade ranks
with the Troop Leader here."

Branra relaxed, grinning. Then Malol announced
he wished a private conference with Nurdanth and
Yistar, and the others were quick to take their leave.
In a few minutes Danaer was back outside the building, blinking in the sunlight. He had taken a few steps
toward his barracks when his name was called. This
time the voice was feminine, and much more welcome
than Yistar's gruff hail.

Lira was standing on the steps of a little balcony outside the room she shared with Ulodovol. Danaer met

her there, responding to her tug on his arm. Together they sat on the topmost step. "I will hear of this from Shaartre," he said with a smile. "Here on a sorkra's very doorstep."

She was pensive, and Danaer quickly dropped his attempt to amuse her. Lira traced patterns in the dust on the step. "Kandra brought you news of the battle at Laril-Quil?"

Taken aback, Danaer said, "But Malol said his wizards had not yet informed him of that."

"We will, soon." Behind her, the drape of the door was open a trifle, and Danaer could see Ulodovol bending over a bluish flame. The old wizard rocked to and fro, his eyes closed, his white hair wild and unkempt. His lips moved, but Danaer could not hear what he was saying, for which he was grateful.

"And we had hoped not to become deeply involved," Lira said with a bitter little laugh.

"In the war against Markuand? But I thought your Web was of white wizards, who ever worked for good."

"And is war good? At first we agreed to advise the King and the Royal Commander, no more. But these Markuand, the wizard genius who guides them—" She broke off, clasping her hands at her breast, her large eyes filling with tears.

"Lira?" Danaer put his arms about her, wanting to ease this agony which seemed to be torturing her. She began to moan, speaking alien words in a sibilant speech. It was not Sarli, but perhaps some wizard language. Danaer resisted the urge to flee, refusing to leave the woman in such anguish. Gradually Lira's pain eased, and she ceased mumbling those eerie phrases.

Danaer felt cold, though they sat in bright sun. He guessed at what had happened. "You have seen to Deki? To Laril-Quil?"

"Hunger and death, Danaer. Oh, to see children dying of hunger! We must help them." She sighed and smoothed her gown over her knees. "At least Branra achieved his goal . . ."

"With your protection?" Danaer studied her face. "Did you guard him against magic? Did he confront

both assassins and the evil sorcery of Markuand—as
I did?" Lira did not answer, but there was a gleam in
her eyes that suggested he touched the truth. "And did
Branra also hear leaves and jewels where there were
none?"

Lira was startled by those questions. But before she
could say anything, a frantic scream cut the air.
Ulodovol, crying for help!

"To me! To me! My Web—aid me!"

Danaer and Lira raced toward the little room. But
a single stride across the threshold was all that Danaer
could make. He froze in place, his hand on his sword,
his jaw dropping.

The chamber swarmed with monsters!

Clawed hands appeared out of nothing—disembod-
ied. Fangs and venomous horns and bulging eyes . . .
monsters and demons whole and in pieces, and evil beyond comprehension.

Everywhere at once!

Ulodovol was in their midst, the brazier overturned
and blue flame licking at the stone floor and his feet,
like a many-headed snake. The elderly wizard gesticulated wildly and flung words of conjury at the slavering
things surrounding him, holding them at bay for heartbeat by heartbeat—countermanding this magic.

Bravely, Lira ran to him, kicking aside blazing embers, stamping on the smoldering cloth of her master's
hem. Without hesitation, she placed herself back to
back with Ulodovol, her own sorcery echoing his as the
demons ringed them both.

Danaer's blood pounded with superstitious terror.
Then he read Lira's own fear, despite her courageous
defiance. He cast away his natural dread, finding
strength he did not know he owned.

Drawing, Danaer began to strike out at the gibbering abominations, slashing right and left with all his
sinew.

These were no fog demons! The sword struck, and
to Danaer's shock, he felt a resistance—though not
flesh and bone. Howls battered his ears. A filthy gray-
purple spurt of . . . blood? . . . splashed his tunic and
hands and the walls of the chamber.

The thing fell, flopping obscenely, a severed limb spewing unnatural gore. For a heart-stopped moment Danaer was rooted, unable to move.

Other creatures renewed the attack. More of them were forming out of thin air, circling the three mortals. They closed particularly upon Ulodovol. The old wizard sank to his knees, barely coherent, fighting back their magic. Lira wept but maintained her precarious balance, desperately chanting spells through her sobbing.

A great hairy dog-thing materialized, jaws carmine and dripping, and leaped at Danaer. He had no time to stab or slash, but quickly raised the sword to protect his throat. A tremendous force hit the blade, knocking Danaer backward into a table.

The furniture broke under him, the dog-thing scrabbling and snarling and trying for his throat as it bore him down. Danaer tightened his grip on the sword hilt and twisted it aside, then thrust up into the creature's belly.

Fangs sank into Danaer's forearm as the demon-dog collapsed. Its stench was suffocating, and Danaer struggled to get free of its crushing weight. The animal that never was contorted in its death throes—if such a thing could die! Danaer was drenched in the beast's vitals and ichor, and his own blood welled from its vicious bite.

Through the confusion of monsters and a rising smoke of illusion formed by Ulodovol and Lira in their magic, Danaer saw the Royal Commander and Nurdanth and Yistar. They stared incredulously from the doorway as Danaer had done.

The distraction proved a new weapon for the sorkra. The attacking demons were suddenly swept by an enveloping smoke, and from the smoke were coming other beasts—true and natural animals, obeying the will of Ulodovol and Lira. Ecar and golhi and woods wolf and eagle formed in smoke and fell upon the demon things.

There were other things in the smoke: people. Danaer gazed into castles and villages of The Interior, into Krantin's palace and the King's own court. In each scene there was a wizard of Ulodovol's Web. And each fought this same battle against the beasts of nether regions.

The visions enlarged to include the snows of Irico and the marshes of Sarlos—and here too were members of the Web, and here too were the attacking demons of Markuand's wizard!

Malol te Eldri and his fellow officers were steeling themselves to enter the fray, drawing swords, moving forward bravely. Even as they did so, Ulodovol came back to his feet, raising himself to his full, impressive height.

"Away!" he shrieked, his bony hands clutching the air and flexing in warning. Lira duplicated his cry, flinging her own counterspells.

And the creatures of Bogotana were banished, all the furies melting instantly—as did the animals and the visions in the smoke.

The small chamber was left to the humans, and the four soldiers gawked at one another, stunned by what they had seen. Then Ulodovol toppled toward Lira and she called in alarm, "Traech Sorkra!" For a moment she bore all his weight. At once the men moved to help, finding the old wizard an easy weight. His physical strength seemed utterly spent, but his mind was clear, and he continued to mutter incantations to insure that the demons could not return.

They laid the wizard on a cot, but Ulodovol waved a hand weakly, indicating he wished to be propped into a sitting position against the wall. Lira knelt by her mentor. Tears wet her cheeks and his garment as she said, "Traech Sorkra, you defeated him! You defeated him and his minions!" Her reverence came through her shaking voice.

Ulodovol managed to raise a blue-veined hand and touch Lira's curly hair. "It was the Web, my dear. I could not have succeeded without the Web, and without your courage, young man. My blessings on you . . ."

Danaer had been sucking at the bloody bite on his arm. The officers reacted to Ulodovol's praise with approving nods of their own. Danaer hoped his apprehension did not show in his manner; but what would these compliments serve if the bite had been filled with poison? Would he die, writhing in agony as the creature had?

Where *was* the beast he had slain? No entrails were on the floor, nor was there trace of the purplish blood. The only mark of the demon thing was the oozing wound on Danaer's arm.

"They attacked the King," Malol said, aghast, the memory of the smoke images coming home to him. "The King!"

"Yes, it was a most fearsome testing of our Krantin, Royal Commander." Ulodovol spoke weakly, pausing often. "You cannot know its vehemence. How . . . how powerful he is, this Markuand wizard, to conjure such illusions . . ."

"Hardly illusions," Yistar murmured, anxiously looking at Danaer's arm. "Not to draw blood. Get to the surgeon . . ."

Danaer did not move, fearing that the hurt would have no healing by mortal medicines. "Master Ulodovol, I thought . . . I thought you saw through the powers of other sorkra of your Web. Yet there were no Markuand wizards among us . . ."

Lira gasped, her eyes meeting Ulodovol's, their mutual dismay obvious. With great reluctance, she said, "That is so, Danaer."

"We have suspected, since you rode to Siank Zsed, that the Markuand wizard has his allies even in Krantin, among us," the old man muttered. His head dropped back against the wall and his rheumy eyes closed. "Sorkra, our own people—helping the enemy. All around us, as those beasts came into being all around us, through the help of Markuand's minions."

"Treachery, in our midst," Nurdanth whispered. "At our backs . . ."

"And how to protect the King?" Ulodovol shuddered violently. "I must remain here, close to Kirvii and the palace. But . . . but I was to accompany the trek to Deki, to guard against the magic of the enemy wizard."

"We will deal with the Markuand, be he soldier or sorcerer," Yistar said proudly. But the Captain's ruddy complexion was unusually pale, and there was a crack in his voice Danaer had never heard before.

A curious group of soldiers had clustered around the door, and Yistar vented his rattled composure by bellowing at them and chasing them away. As he did, Malol was saying, "We cannot spare you, Traech Sorkra. The King must be kept safe. And you are not fit for such an arduous journey. The caravan—and Deki—will have to do without your skills."

Ulodovol sighed and patted Lira's shoulder. "I fear there is wisdom in that. Age and infirmity are my burdens. I must not tax my body, or my powers. There may be much evil yet unknown to be dealt with in the future. I will send Lira Nalu in my place. Our Web will help her, and me, while I ferret out these traitors. We must find the Krantin-Y who would give us to the enemy, find them, crush them and their magic . . ."

"You shall, Master," Lira assured him. But Danaer sensed her dismay. She accepted the awful responsibility Ulodovol had put upon her, and without question. Yet there was doubt in her face, which she hid poorly.

The old wizard beckoned the officers close, wanting to talk of strategy and protection for King Tobentis. Lira spread a robe over the thin legs, then drew back. Though still much worried about her master, she took Danaer's arm and led him aside. She examined his wound intently, then began passing her talisman over the bleeding punctures. The obsidian pendant felt oddly cool on the fang marks, and to Danaer's surprise, the swelling subsided at once. Blood clotted and scabbed and fell away before his amazed eyes, the arm healing—whole!

A wound of black wizardry, cured by Lira's own magic!

"Sorkra, I . . . I give you thanks again. I thought I would die from that brute's ravaging."

"It could have happened." Lira gazed up at him, as concerned for his hurt as she had been for Ulodovol's frailty. "It was sorcery most powerful, and it might well poison you. Not now. You have courage beyond most men, for few would have risked those demons' teeth and claws. And had you not distracted them at the height of the Markuand wizard's attack, I do not know if Master Ulodovol could have defeated him. You turned the battle for us, Danaer."

He chuckled nervously, probing his arm. "It was my battle as well. But because of your arts, now I will ride with the captain, not languish in some healer's tent, dying of venom."

"And I will go to Deki with you." That was not a happy statement.

"It is too hard a journey," Danaer said. A Destre warrior woman was bred for war from girlhood. But Lira was made for more tender existence. "You are gently born—"

She cut him off with some pique. "I am *not*. I am a commoner, a tanner's child. The Web makes no distinctions of age or sex or birth. A sorkra serves where needed, and where the Traech Sorkra bids. I am needed on the trek to Deki. I will go willingly."

Her retort was too fierce. Danaer remembered his first caravan raid, when he was but an unblooded youth—and he knew that Lira quaked inwardly. Pride would not let her admit her fright, though.

Suddenly Lira favored him with a warm smile. "You fear for me? You must not, my Sharp Eyes. No sorkra is ever alone; my Web will go wherever I go. Others will comfort me and guide me, our minds speaking together."

"It was not only your mind which interested me," Danaer said, indulging in a grin.

Lira's full, throaty laugh made the officers glance at them both for a moment before they returned to their whispered conference with Ulodovol. In her easy acceptance of his remark, Lira was indeed like a Destre woman—unafraid of life's pleasures. "Then how dare I fear for the safety of my body when I have your sword to protect me?"

"On my faith, I *will* protect you—from swords or magic."

Her smile faded, and Lira caught at the thong about her neck. She pulled off the talisman, then lifted aside Danaer's helmet. He saw what she wished and bent his head, letting her slip the shiny black stone down to rest upon his chest. The medallion was carved with the head of a man. "Is this your god?" he wondered, touching it carefully. "You must keep a holy thing for your own sake. . . ."

"No, it is not my god," Lira said. "And wearing it will offer no offense to your Argan, I promise. Rasven is . . . not divine. But I want you to wear his image always. Give me your oath on it."

She was most determined, and Danaer did not refuse. Perhaps the talisman meant more magic, but after what he had felt of Markuand's wizardry, he would take Lira's black stone as a help against worse evil. It was not a man's adornment, and Danaer began to feel embarrassed by the trinket. Lira did not object when he slid it inside his shirt, against his skin. She led him outside to the porch.

Breeze played at Lira's long gown, whipping her white ribbons and tousling her hair. Sweat beaded her brow, the aftereffect of her struggle against demons. Danaer looked at her steadily, relishing the sight, even that honest sweat. Kandra had touched him but little, despite her sexuality. He had been roused to delight by many a woman of ease and her carnal offerings. Yet Lira's power over him was different.

Lira might have read his thoughts. She stood on tiptoe and kissed his lips. Even the kiss was not what he expected. She did not give him moist promises with her laughter. This was a kiss of sweet longing and modest uncertainty, bound into one heady moment. Before he could embrace her, Lira was gone, back into Ulodovol's room.

If only she were not a sorkra. . . .

The talisman was pleasantly warm, lying on his heart. Lira's gift to him, to guard him against enemy sorkra. And like Lira, the carved stone that should be cold and lifeless seemed to throb with spirit, past fathoming. Lira was whims and surprises never-ending, a mystery that tangled Danaer closer each time they met.

He braced himself to take a ribald teasing when he returned to the barracks. Shaartre and many of his unit mates would have seen that kiss, and they would be quick to draw lewd conclusions. No matter. There were dangers ahead, and much of it dark magic—but he had a wizard's talisman now, and Lira was coming with the caravan. Ulodovol and the officers were making plans, and so would he. He would not be greedy or think in such grand terms as the Traech Sorkra and the Royal Commander. Danaer would be content with a small conquest—only one small part of Sarlos, in the person of a woman, a lady artful in magic.

X

ALL SHALL BELONG TO MARKUAND

THE ISLAND OF TOR-NALI WAS BATHED IN MOONLIGHT, the rays reflecting on the harbor waters, rivaling the bright array of torches ringing the Markuand encampment. Darkness veiled scenes of warfare and butchery, now ended. Tor-Nali's men were dead, their bodies flung into pits and burned without ceremony. A few of her women, those sufficiently beautiful to please the conquerors' tastes, had been taken in slavery. Their laments floated from the castles of the slain princes of their island, a wail of shame and sorrow.

The warlords had established a command post overlooking the bay. From here they had dispatched supply fleets and troop barges against the Clarique mainland, and all had gone well. But the generals were uneasy as they entered the tower where their cruel viceroy strolled among cauldrons and consulted arcane tomes.

The wizard's assistants stirred frothing decoctions and mixed powders to his directions. They never questioned or uttered a sound he did not command. After a long hesitation, the most famed among the warlords spoke to the master. "Our spies tell us their chief magician repelled your magic, and that this Krantin alliance is holding fast."

Priceless kash fur robes swirled as Markuand's

mightiest sorcerer spun on his heel, confronting the committee. "You doubt me—still?"

"No, Master. We . . . we are balancing the odds for the coming battle. The emperor bade us complete our victory ere the snow flies again . . ."

"So you shall." He seized air, symbolically clutching the sprawling land that lay before Markuand's armies. "Before snow falls on our homeland, we shall climb the mountains of this Krantin. And we shall rule the northern forests of this place they call Irico, and the fens and meadows of their Sarlos. All shall belong to Markuand . . ."

"Their wizards, though? Our spies speak of a thing termed a sorkra, and a web of these magicians."

"Your spies," he said with withering pity. "I have my own, far cleverer than those dogs you employ. *My* spies can be sorkra, too, or a serpent who knows the heart of our prey, and where to strike to cause the most pain."

The hero among them would not be put off. "But your magic did not crush them, they say . . ."

"Silence!" Tongues cleaved to roofs of mouths, and for an instant even his minions gulped and forgot their tasks. "It was a bad casting of the lots. I play them, to tire the game and make its taking the sweeter. They think they have bested me. Ah! This adds savor to the hunt." He licked his lips.

"Yes, they have their alliance—and so have we, one they do not know. We begin to strike on every hand. Soon they will have no wits to withstand us. They will confuse reality with . . . nightmare!" His laugh was dreadful.

The spokesman for the warlords must clear his dry throat ere he could blurt the rest of their worries. "You promised they would be crushed before now, swept away like smoke. Yet they still stand and grow ever stronger, joining with those who were their enemies . . ."

"An alliance like a goblet of thin crystal, and as easily broken." He pointed at a shelf of delicate Clarique wine vessels, shattering the contents mercilessly. The warlords jumped at the sound. "As easily as that, my generals."

They waited long, eyeing one another, not daring to question further. In the end, he condescended to ask, "And what else disturbs you?"

"Great One, these . . . these soldiers—this weird silence you give them with your potions. Must it be so in all our battles?"

"Each man will fight until he dies. You have seen its results in your conquests."

"But . . . but they do not act like . . . like men."

No one uttered the fear that ruled them all—that these silent warriors were in truth the wizard's soldiery, no longer the followers of the warlords. Bit by bit, their power slipped through their hands and was taken into his. And they had no weapon to wield against his awful force.

"So they do not act like men. They may be beasts, if I choose. I permit them to sate themselves on drink and women and strip bare the larders of these Clarique. And you—have you not enjoyed those same spoils? On the morrow, your soldiers will drink *my* wine, and then they will once more go into battle, feeling no wound, fighting and conquering for Markuand."

They bowed their heads. He gestured, and a map glowed on the tile floor where a simple design had been. "Now you will disperse your troops as I have instructed you. To the north and to the south. Seek out the remnants of the Clarique and the soldiers of that bitch from Krantin, Ti-Mori. And find that Sarli who plagues us from those fetid marshes near the river. I want his head. Keep the Irico locked above their falls; it is Krantin I want, now that this Clarique is ours. I have found fellow wizards to serve me, in Krantin's own fortress. Tomorrow we close the noose forever around Laril-Quil and move to take that city on the river. When we breach her walls, their alliance—and their wizard Web—will be in shambles! I vow this! Hear me, and obey!"

They fled him, and the sorcerer went to peer out a window, across the water. His minions faithfully stirred the potion that made Markuand's armies invincible, and their master contemplated his triumph-to-be.

"Yes, you on the mainland, you in Krantin—struggle like insects. I shall toy with you, and treachery shall taunt you from the rear." He clenched his fists and nodded. "In the end, you will all die. And I alone will reign, the monarch of New Markuand."

XI

MIRAGES OF THE VRASTRE

"THEN CAN WE REACH *here?*" YISTAR JABBED AT A mark on the map a bit farther west than he had first selected. Wagon breakdowns, inexperienced troops, bad weather, and a steady plague of mirages had taken a toll of Yistar's already fragile temper. Even Lieutenant Branra, who stood to one side talking to other staff aides, made no attempt to interrupt. But he glanced sympathetically at the scout.

Danaer clutched the map as a nagging plains wind fluttered the cloth. "We can manage it, Captain, if there are no more delays or misturns."

"'Bog' take those mirages which guided us amiss! And there will be no more delays. Do you need this?" Yistar asked, indicating the map. Danaer tapped a finger against his temple to assure the officer he had the chart memorized, and Yistar rolled the cloth with savage haste. "Then take the point again and get us moving. Lieutenant . . ."

Glad to escape, Danaer mounted at a run and spurred toward the head of the caravan. Two recruits had been assigned to him to learn the art of scouting. Xashe and Rorluk sat on a grassy slope, passing time while they waited in bragging and barracks gossip. Danaer dropped down from his roan and quickly drew a crude copy of the map in the dust. The young soldiers leaned over his shoulder to watch. They were apt pupils, luckily. In days to come, they might well fall heir to Danaer's post and be forced to guide a part of the army back along this path. Keen memories would be needed, and sharp eyes. At least these novices were anxious to learn.

When they had time to look over the map, Danaer scraped it away with his boot. "Xashe?"

The youth had been a peasant herdsman in a mountain valley, and he knew horses and how to find his way even in strange country. He closed his eyes the better to recall the chart and recited, "Two candlemarks' travel through the lee grass of this dry lake. We take Zaetre Canyon, angling north. Then we cross another waterway at Many Rocks and then must look for the blazes on the willows. We take the main route thence to Jsersotka Springs."

"Good!"

"When do I get a turn?" Rorluk asked. Rorluk was younger than his peasant friend. The son of a merchant, he had hopes of emulating Captain Yistar and someday rising to be an aide or junior officer. Danaer had not discouraged such dreaming, out of kindness.

"The next time we stop," he promised. "Which had best not be soon. Yistar is much fretted by too many delays already."

They led off the caravan as it started forward once more at a groaning pace. During his years at Nyald Fort Danaer had escorted many a pack train, and he did not expect heavily laden wagons to make much time. But the supply caravan for Deki was as slow as mud seeping from a geyser pool. Little wonder the Captain chafed and cursed their creeping progress.

Before another mark had passed, the watercourse appeared, too soon. Even as Xashe and Rorluk expressed their own doubts, remembering the map, Danaer twisted in the saddle, looking back the way they had come.

Dust thrown up by the caravan obscured most of the horizon, but he could pick out enough landmarks to place them on the trail. When Danaer swung around again, he realized the watercourse was a hundred king's-measures west of where it should be.

But the illusion was magnificent! Without the map and alertness, he would have been fooled—again. Danaer caressed Lira's amulet absently, as he had often done under mounting problems.

"Troop Leader?" Rorluk asked uneasily. "Is it . . . ?"

"Another mirage? Yes."

The youths whistled and slapped their thighs, and their blacks jangled at the bits. "At then," Xashe said in quaint mountain accent, "we saw this one ere we led the caravan awrong."

"Thanks for that, or Yistar would have our hides. Ignore the illusion. Our horses scent no water, you notice. When we *do* near the springs, the drivers will have their hands full, keeping the brutes from bolting to drink."

They proceeded on the true route, muttering over the strangeness of these things. It was the fifth such trick of the eyes they had met in less than two-days' journeying. Though Danaer had never ridden the eastern Vrastre, he knew well the ways of the grassland from the taletellers and minstrels. His companions put his own worries into words. "We thought mirages only happened when it was hot and Peluva shone brightly. Today it is cloudy and the heat not so great . . ."

Danaer nodded, giving no answer. Lira had not elaborated on the powers of the talisman, but plainly some magic lurked in the obsidian. Thrice he had been deluded by mirages, and to his shame he had turned Yistar into dead-end paths, where they must retreat and find the correction after much difficulty. The fourth time he had felt an eerie, invisible touch, one he had first sensed when he encountered the fog creatures. He had responded and caressed the amulet, and suddenly he had been able to see through the mirage and know it as false.

His apprentices had voiced it—these were no ordinary mirages. But the less they knew of wizardry, the safer they would be. Danaer himself had tasted more of these secret things than he ever would have wished.

Once safely past the illusion, the landmarks were clear and where they should be. After many a quarter-period's riding, Xashe stood in his stirrups and pointed to a cloud of dust ahead. Danaer tested the young soldier. "Name me the riders, if you can. How good are your eyes?"

"I think . . . they are roans, Troop Leader. Destre-Y? The leader appears to be a giant of a man. Is it . . . Gordyan?"

"Ai! None else!"

Since the caravan had left Siank, the Siirn Rena's bodyguard and his warriors had paralleled the army's path. Usually they remained just out of range of the train's outriders, causing little alarm. Now and then Gordyan would veer in and meet with Yistar. But for the most part, the two groups kept separate.

Now Gordyan rode directly toward the three scouts, drawing rein at the last moment to challenge the soldiers' courage, throwing up much dirt. Xashe and Rorluk spat out the dust and glowered, but handled their blacks well.

Gordyan brayed cheerfully, "Is this all the faster your wagons can move?"

Danaer had not let his roan break stride, bumping through the other horses and leading his apprentices straight ahead. Gordyan grinned and swung around, matching his animal's pace to that of Danaer's. Danaer returned that smile and said, "They hope to make better time on this leg. Yistar plans to camp at Jsersotka tonight."

"We will travel by starlight, then. It is good you have my warriors to defend you against any brigands who do not honor the truce. You are like helpless babes crawling on your hands and knees."

Danaer chuckled sourly. "You have not seen the troop muster. That would make you smack your lips and myself desert to join those brigands."

"You? Not you," Gordyan said. "I hope you will not be so unwise as to die for that army of yours, though."

One of Gordyan's men spoke up. "I think I know

you, soldier. Did you not win the lancing contest at the vrentru?"

"He did." Gordyan cut off further questions with a glare. Then his expression warmed. "And how does your infantry handle itself under this steady marching?"

The abrupt change of topic made Danaer eye the big man thoughtfully. Gordyan seemed easy enough, so long as his besting in the contest was not mentioned. Danaer shrugged. "The infantry has sore feet to match the cavalry's sore thighs and buttocks. A ten-day trek will toughen all the newcomers nicely."

"That is good. Deki needs this food, but it needs fighting men as well."

Gordyan rode by Danaer's side for the rest of the morning. He reminisced at length over his past adventures, regaling Danaer's young companions. They drank in his stories with awe, though Danaer reserved judgment. It was possible all these tales were true; with such a giant, heroic deeds seemed very believable.

Shortly before center-stand, Gordyan and his men left. Danaer watched his going with regret. Gordyan's company had protected them from any outcasts who would not honor the truce, and his diverting tales had passed the time most entertainingly.

The wagons creaked to a stop and sentries went out to take their posts, passing the three scouts coming in to report. Yistar fretted about the lead wagons, establishing a temporary command post for this needed halt. Danaer noted that the cart-horse blacks were foaming with sweat. The rest period would likely be a long one. Yistar growled at him, "Poor time, poor time. Even the Destre-Y are sneering at us."

The scout followed Yistar's frowning stare and saw some of Gordyan's men quartering just beyond the army lines. They were stringing rope corrals between scrub brushes and tsyoda stumps, as if they planned to be here for days and set up a Zsed. It was a patent display of their contempt for the caravan's sand-lizard pace.

"And some of that bandit's warriors have been riding too close upon our rear, trying to shame us into more speed," the Captain complained. "It makes for bad order. You know the tongue. Go over and tell Gordyan I would speak with him, at his convenience, of course." Yistar walked away, muttering, not bothering to answer Danaer's perfunctory salute.

Danaer did not obey the order at once. For a while he wandered about the forefront of the caravan, pretending to cool his horse. Finally he caught sight of Lira. She was perched on one of the high wagon seats, nibbling some of the crumbly grain cakes that were the army's staple. She nodded at him and rewarded his search with a smile. She had not been as delicate as she seemed; on a trek like this she did not ride her mare, but bounced about on the boards like any hard-bitten driver. She wore a boy's uniform, her hair tied back. The garment was too large for her, and she might well have been taken for a youth of exceptionally feminine features and tender years, one ill-suited to rough living.

There were too many men all around. Danaer knew the evening would offer more privacy. Then he would ask her further about the power of the talisman, and perhaps about other things as well.

He rode toward the Destre-Y corral on the nearby hill. Warriors squatted about a hastily built fire. Gordyan had joined them, saying as Danaer dismounted, "Hai! Have you decided to come to my lances at last?"

"I should call *you* Long-Fang, rather than Yistar; you never quit worrying an idea," Danaer greeted him. "No, I came to tell you the Captain wishes to speak with you, after your meal."

"Oh? Then eat with us, Destre. We offer far better fare than those baked rocks the army calls food. First, help me pen these." Gordyan went to a pair of ground-hitched roans, one of them his big blue horse and the other a rangy, skittish red. He swung up on the blue and dug in his heels, riding into the makeshift corral. Danaer thought nothing of the request, or of riding those few short paces. No Destre would go afoot unless his mount needed rest. He seized the second roan's mane and leaped up on the bare back.

He had made a mistake.

Gordyan most certainly had not forgiven his besting in the lancing contest.

The roan seemed to explode beneath Danaer. He gripped desperately with hands and legs. The twists and turns and rearings were those of a fractious brute anticipating its rider's every move. Danaer tried to out-guess the animal, clinging to the heaving back with all his considerable skill.

Just when he thought he would prove its master, the roan made a charge at one of the stumps support-ing the corral ropes. Danaer tried to turn its head, but the beast was past control. Man and roan crashed in-to the stump and went down, thrashing in the dust.

Danaer threw himself clear, but as he did he landed off balance. His right ankle gave agonizingly and he rolled, biting back a cry of pain. Then he looked about sharply, expecting the half-wild roans to tram-ple him as they broke from the corral. But Gordyan, still atop his blue roan, blocked the opening. One of his men was quickly restringing the ropes to keep the herd penned.

The big man grinned at Danaer and jumped down. Danaer managed to get to his feet, carefully favoring his screaming ankle. Gordyan's warriors howled at this spectacle—a Destre and an army scout, thrown like the greenest boy. Danaer himself saw the humor in the prank, a typical Destre jest. He started to laugh along with them.

Then he was startled to hear his name called. A woman's voice—Lira's! She was hurrying up toward the camp. It could only mean he had seen him thrown so ignominiously. Danaer's pride easily tolerated the good-natured gibes of Gordyan and his men, but this!

His laughter faded, and Gordyan's grin was as salt on a fresh wound. Danaer snarled, "If you were of a size a normal man might challenge, I would lesson you, stander."

He hobbled away along the ropes, around a small slope, trying not to limp. After forcing that stride as

long as he could bear, Danaer half fell against brush
and the corral. With a grunt, he sat down and tugged
off his boot. There was no bruising or heat yet, but he
knew the joint would stiffen badly if not tended. He
began rubbing his ankle to combat a growing tight-
ness.

The initial rage at Gordyan was spent, and now he
felt emptiness. How would Lira look at him? He knew
so little of her ways. This would have been no more
than friendly roughhouse, if she had not witnessed it.
Danaer cursed and chafed his foot painfully.

Suddenly, large hands pushed his away and began a
massage much firmer and more useful than Danaer
was capable of. Gordyan bent over him, sincere concern in his manner. Unnerved to be caught off guard,
Danaer glanced around, ashamed that he had not
heard the man approach. Gordyan must move like a
dust-crawler, to come so silently.

For long moments neither of them spoke. Gordyan
concentrated on his work and Danaer on swallowing
any sound of distress. Finally Gordyan said gruffly,
"How comes it now?"

"It begins to warm and loosen."

Gordyan nodded and rubbed even more vigorously.
"I should not have given you that roan."

Touched by the clumsy apology, Danaer hurried to
take his own guilt in hand. "I should have been able
to handle it."

"La! That one answers only to my weight. You are
not the first one he has thrown, nor will be the last."
Gordyan's leathery features were taut with remorse.
"I had not counted on that stump. This ankle was
none of my intention. You might have been crippled,
and the maiming my doing."

He was so ingenuously earnest, Danaer bore no
grudge. "It is even. We are paid equally—lancing for
horse handling."

"Ah! I knew you would taking a throwing well. But
I am sorry to have timed it poorly. I would not have
used that trick had I known your qedra watched.
That is unfair, especially for a man who has an Iit
woman . . ."

"Lira Nalu is not . . . not so strong a word as 'qedra' . . ."

Gordyan cocked his head. "You would not tell me so had you heard her. I did not understand half the insults, so learned were they." Gordyan looked at Danaer with respect. "A sorkra, and you her qedra."

"Not qedra. Not . . . yet."

Gordyan chuckled and said, "She was convinced I had killed you and hidden away your broken body. It took no small talking to change her mind on that, I swear. She wished to come looking for you, but I thought perhaps . . ."

"Thank you for that."

Gordyan sat back and said, "Try it now, warrior."

Danaer caught the proffered hand and let Gordyan help him to his feet. Gingerly, he tried his weight on the bad ankle. "It pounds with blood. I think it will serve."

"Will you be able to ride?" Speechless with surprise, Danaer gawked at him until Gordyan said, "I forgot. In that uniform you look so much like an Iit that . . . of *course* you can ride, Destre." He picked up the discarded boot and slipped it on Danaer's foot. The scout steadied himself against Gordyan's shoulder, marveling to feel the muscle rippling under the Destre vest. Could such a man ever be defeated in battle by any ordinary foe? He could imagine a lance striking that big chest cleanly and being plucked out and cast away as disdainfully as if it were a splinter.

Together they returned to the campfire. One of Gordyan's guards lifted a bird from the spit and tossed it across the flames. Danaer came up with his boot knife fast enough to spare himself burned fingers, and won applause.

Lira was nowhere about. Danaer bit into the fowl and complimented their fare. "Sling game? This is fine xorlya."

One man twirled a sling strap around his fingers. "It is the season in this area. We have bagged quite a few so far."

"Gordyan, could you lend me two slings?"

"You already have a sling, warrior. Have you grown extra hands?"

"No, but I have two novice scouts," Danaer explained. "I have a mind to make sling handlers of them."

Gordyan's men whooped at this outrageous plan, sure that no Iit could master the weapon. When they had done eating, they tossed a leathern bottle to Danaer, and he took a healthy swig before he learned the wine was uncut. He brought it down choking and grinned, then finished more cautiously, to more laughter. Shortly after, Yistar beckoned him back to the wagons and he made a hasty farewell, praising the Destre hospitality.

The Captain was again poring over a map when Danaer knelt beside him, balancing on his left foot to ease his sore ankle. Yistar said sternly, "We must push faster these next few periods."

"I believe, with the goddess to help us, we still may make the Springs when you hoped . . ."

"We will, then. I do not want to arrive at Deki with exhausted troops, but these supplies will do the city no good out here on the plains." The officer sighed and mopped his forehead with his sleeve.

"This map is not army issue, Captain. Where comes it?"

Yistar paused in the act of rolling up the chart. He opened it once more and eyed it with suspicion. "It was given to the Royal Commander by Gordt te Raa. Why? Is it inaccurate?"

"Much the other way. It is Azsed, and might have been designed for my use."

"As some horses are not?" Yistar said wryly. Then he asked, "Were you hurt in that spill?"

"A twisted ankle. No more. Gordyan loosened it well."

"Gordyan? But the Lady Nalu said . . ."

"Has she mentioned to everyone what happened?" Danaer said with irritation.

"Only to me, and only because I inquired. If you were badly injured, I should need to find a replacement."

Danaer was not deluded by the offhanded tone, and he appreciated the Captain's concern. He put off any further discussion curtly and rode back to the point. The caravan moved forward again under a hazy sky and through rising temperatures. Several times there were hints of mirages. But now that Danaer knew he could penetrate the illusion with the aid of the talisman, he kept to the trail with no trouble.

Despite Yistar's urgings to speed, the pace remained very slow, slow enough to give Danaer much leisure to introduce his two unit mates to the art of sling handling. The youths were doubtful, as Gordyan had been. But once the slings' tricks were demonstrated, they showed interest and learned swiftly. By a period later, when they scattered a covey of xorlya, the novice scouts actually brought down a few birds. They were much helped by the close winging of the creatures as they panicked and flew. Nevertheless, the beginning hunters had game to show. Xashe and Rorluk strung their catch from their saddles and rode on jauntily.

The long afternoon passed more quickly for occasional game taking. Danaer let his students hunt landmarks as well as birds, pleased to see they were becoming adept at both. They had much to master, but they displayed early talent.

When the order came to halt, the sun rested on the horizon. The willows and bubbling springs of the camp lay close, and the weary men and horses gathered wagons and baggage near the best water and grass. Danaer again passed outgoing sentries and rode to Yistar's command area. The Captain was acting more cheerful now. "We did make better time, ai?" Yistar fingered the birds dangling from Danaer's pommel. "Getting a little sling game along the way, are you?"

"Only while pursuing our course, Captain. We stumbled across a few and thought to provide you with some fresh meat for your mess."

Yistar snickered and tugged at his mustache. "I wager you thought that." He took a few of the squabs and tossed them to his orderly. "But I will take my bandit toll all the same. Enough. Get you to your units and your own mess, and some sleep. We make an early start on the morrow."

Xashe and Rorluk chattered all the way to their unit camp, basking in the envious stares that followed them. As they reached the picket lines and dismounted, a wave of pain swept up from Danaer's ankle. He clung to his roan, gritting his teeth and choking on a rush of nausea.

"Troop Leader . . . ?"

"It is nothing. Away. See to your mounts and go show off your catch." Hearing the strong warning in that, they obeyed, though they looked back at him anxiously several times. Danaer bit down any shameful outcry, slowly recovering from shock. Then he swore an oath at his own stupidity—to ride so long with his foot out of the stirrup!

"Danaer?" That came softly, and sweetly, out of the twilight. But at that instant he felt not at all like confronting Lira. She persisted, seeking him along the pickets until she found him. "Danaer, what is it?"

He sighed and slumped against a post, pulling off his boot with difficulty and a gasp. "I twisted my ankle earlier . . ."

"Warrior? Where are you, Destre?" That voice was deep and not made for whispering, though the speaker attempted it.

"Then! At it! Wrath ve Dortu! There are more here than at Yistar's staff tents," Danaer muttered. "Over here, Gordyan."

The big man came up to them as Lira was saying aggrievedly, "Why did you not tell me he was hurt?"

"Because he would not have wanted me to." Danaer had slithered down the post until he sat on the grass. Gordyan fumbled in the pocket of his vest and took out a small hide flask. For a while Danaer was lost to anything save the cold fire of the liquid Gordyan swabbed on his bruises. "You knew this would happen. Why did you not step down from your roan more often, soldier?"

Stung to hear his self-reproaches put against him, Danaer flared, "We are in a haste to reach Deki, or have you so soon forgotten the plea of Siirn Lorzosh-Fila?"

Gordyan looked fiercely at him, then abruptly knocked off Danaer's helmet. Too stunned to move, Danaer sat dumbly as Gordyan also shoved aside his mantle. Then he lifted the scout bodily, carrying him past amazed picketmen and recruits, into the glow of a nearby campfire. Some of Danaer's unit mates were gathered there, and they gawked at the gigantic apparition lumbering into their midst. Lira ran along behind Gordyan, upbraiding him for this manhandling.

Danaer was set down beside the fire. His ankle bumped sharply on the ground, and while he sucked in his breath a moment, Gordyan swept an arm around and commanded, "Send them away!"

Whatever was to happen, Danaer sensed Gordyan would not be denied. The soldiers scattered with little argument. Just as suddenly, Gordyan himself vanished into the night. In a short while he returned, carrying Danaer's helmet and mantle and the string of birds. He tossed the helmet aside scornfully and folded the mantle, setting it beside Danaer. Then he asked, "Can you cook these, sorkra lady? I always burn them."

Lira blinked, a slow smile brightening her face. "Yes, if you will rig me a spit."

Gordyan set to work with brushwood and knife. Once, as he was constructing the spit, he glanced at Danaer and commented, "That helmet bothered me. Without it you are a true Destre, as you ought to be."

When the gutted birds were roasting, Gordyan took off his headcloth and mantle and the dustcloth draped about his throat. He crossed his arms over his knees and hungrily watched the sizzling game. Danaer eyed Lira, but she did not understand the significance in Gordyan's baring his head this way. The big man's hair was wiry and peaked at his brow, like the images in Argan's temple which depicted Bogotana. Lira tested the birds and plucked one off the spit, offering it to Gordyan. But he leaned forward and snatched out Danaer's boot knife, spearing the food and handing it to the scout. "Let me lesson you in an old Destre custom, sorkra lady—the hunter always feeds first on his catch."

Danaer stared at the empty sheath in the one boot he still wore, then at the knife it had held, now resting in his own hand. "Gordyan, be assured *I* have been lessoned; I will *never* dare challenge you."

"Eat!" Gordyan said. He was already biting into a second bird Lira had taken off the spit. Through a mouthful he added, "Find out what a good cook your qedra is."

"I told you that word was too strong."

"I do not mind it," Lira said. Danaer was unsure if she grasped the full meaning of the Destre term, but she must know it in part; her smile was sly.

"See? Your woman does not object. I would she would call *me* so. But she prefers to call me other things." Gordyan chuckled.

"I . . . I am sorry for that," Lira stammered. "I did not know of these rough games you play. Forgive me."

"Forgive? I would think far less of a woman if she did not defend her man.'" Gordyan regarded them both fondly, his attitude embracing them.

"You do us honor." Danaer finished his bird and sucked the juice from his hand, then said, "On such a night it is easy to forget past injuries. This *is* honor, and I give you thanks."

"I would ask honor of you in return." Gordyan's rumbling voice dropped into a still deeper register. "Call me hyidu. Swear blood friend."

Danaer was grateful that Lira did not break the brief silence. This was a time when a man must probe his heart and seek out the goddess and her will. After much considering, he said, "To no man have I . . ."

"Nor have I. Many of my men call me friend, but to none of them have I felt this loyalty, Danaer. It is touched by Argan, a blessing she puts on my spirit. Perhaps there is wizardry in it, too, your qedra touching my mind as the goddess touches my soul." That last was a weak joke which barely caressed the tension holding them. Gordyan's inner feelings shone in his dark eyes, and there was no jesting there.

"It is true. I had not studied my heart until now."

"Much has passed between us, and most suddenly."
Once more Gordyan's words reflected Danaer's
thoughts. "It can be only the will of Argan. She gov-
erns mortals whatever ill we may do to each other. If
she judges us of kindred blood, it is so."

Danaer accepted. This was not a matter of reason,
but of a man's being. It might speak to man or woman
but once in a lifetime, or never. And it could not be
refused.

Both men drew their belt knives. Gordyan's was
steel, the plunder of his raidings. Danaer's was bronze,
the issue given Troop Leaders by the parsimonious
suppliers who quartermastered Siank garrison. They
took the blades awkwardly in right hands and put the
points to the base of their eiphren fingers. The small
bleeding slit gave Danaer almost no hurt.

"Kant, prodra Argan . . ."

They prayed in unison, clasping hands above the
fire, letting mingled blood drip into the flames according to the ritual. At first Danaer could do little but
wonder at the immensity of Gordyan's hand. Then
the power of this pledge engulfed his senses.

Hyidu. Blood friend until death. A vow of the
heart, sacred to Argan above all things. The solemnity
he had felt was torn away and replaced by an intense,
unreserved joy.

Gordyan and Danaer repeated the oath, gripping
forearms, sealing a pact that could never be broken.
As Gordyan would guard, so would Danaer. Should
the necessity come, he would willingly die that this
man could live. Or he would bloodily avenge
Gordyan's death if his friend was called too soon to
Keth's portals.

The cut, and his ankle, gave him no pain at all
now.

"Danaer," Lira said very carefully, as if afraid to
break the spell. He and Gordyan smiled at her.

"It will be well," Danaer explained. "It is *most* well.
Argan binds us forever, henceforth."

They sat around the fire, talking into the night.
Once more Gordyan applied the stinging liniment to
soothe Danaer's ankle. Lira proved her minstrel's

headband by singing tales of Sarlos and Krantin. Her voice was vibrant, sending a pleasant shiver down Danaer's back, as intriguing as that husky laugh he so liked to hear. Gordyan had unsaddled Danaer's roan and fetched his pack, making excuses to his unit when Shaartre had come looking for his fellow Troop Leader. At Gordyan's insistence, all Danaer's mates were kept at bay, and the little camp was theirs alone. Danaer lay back on his blankets and folded mantle, listening to Lira's songs of lovers, enemies, blood friends; her music lulled him into deep contentment.

Half asleep, he heard Lira and Gordyan conversing in Sarli. Where had Gordyan learned the southern language so well? Danaer knew a few words of Lira's homeland, but his blood friend was fluent; he could not follow the things Gordyan was saying. Without any jealousy, delighting in the contrast of powerful man and pretty little woman sitting close and speaking on good terms, Danaer drowsed.

Lira's face seemed to shimmer, perhaps distorted by the heat rising from the fire. And in her place he saw . . . a green jewel between winged brows and black eyes, pale brown hair of silken brightness, not Lira's dark curls.

Kandra? The Lasiirnte seemed to sit gazing at him, as Lira was doing. And with the same expression, far more than the sensuous half-promise Hablit had noted.

How could Kandra be here? She was with her lord, Gordt te Raa. She was the Siirn Rena's woman, and those promises could not be made to such as Danaer.

He tried to call out to Lira and Gordyan and ask if there was sorcery afoot. Danaer could not speak or move, trapped in the waking dream. Then he stared at Gordyan, watching his blood friend. This was a man in easy, relaxed conversation with his hyidu's woman. His words and manner were without any sexual overtones. Indeed, now Gordyan would protect Lira as furiously against any insult or attack as he would act to aid Danaer.

And his manner was not the way Gordyan would

address Lasiirnte Kandra. He would not sit so close
nor speak so familiarly.

Danaer did not want to look upon the illusion. His
mind grew restless, silently searching for Lira. The vision shimmered once more and disappeared, and
Danaer sighed happily. Lira was there, and the image
of Kandra was gone. All was as it should be again.

He was too sleepy to wonder on this. Mirage or
magic? What matter? His hands, like his eyelids,
seemed borne down by heaviness. He could not reach
to touch Lira's obsidian talisman.

For a heartbeat or two, he dimly remembered that
he had intended to speak to Lira concerning the talisman. Even that eluded him, drifting away. The Sarli
tongue was lilting and musical of itself. Danaer yielded
to its comfort, dreaming of cool waters and good company by a cheering fire.

XII

VIDIK

"THERE!" XASHE POINTED TO A MASS OF BRICK ON
the flatland ahead to the east. He and Rorluk asked
together, "Vidik?"

Danaer laughed at their hopeful tone. "And you
have been looking forward to Vidik's women, with
their reputation, ai?"

"Is it true, Troop Leader? You are a Destre. You
would know."

"You will discover for yourselves, soon. Now hold
us straight to this route while I notify the Captain."
Danaer galloped back to where Yistar and Branra
headed the column, wheeling his roan to fall in beside
them. "Your favor—Vidik close before us."

"You know the proper fork to take," Yistar said by

way of grumpy acknowledgment. "Get us camped by good water north of the city."

"Out of the city, Captain?" It was one of Yistar's aides who asked that, and Branra looked over his shoulder at the man, grinning wickedly. The staff were like boys wanting a treat who had been told their father would not linger at the sweetmeat booth. "We . . . we thought, sir, that we might camp in Vidik . . . for provisions."

"You think too much, sir," Yistar growled. "We will have trouble enough from Vidik's cutthroat merchants and women of ease, even if we camp well out from the walls." His aides reddened and Branra's grin widened into a leer. "We will not enter Vidik and invite such trouble."

But as the serpent of wagons crawled in a long arc to the north of the city, it quickly became plain they could not avoid contact with Vidik's people. Rising clouds of dirt marked the approach of riders and carts. It was the women and merchants Yistar had sought to avoid. They were rushing out to meet the caravan at its campground. Tradesmen wanted to hawk wines and gewgaws, and the women would sell their favors for the glory of the goddess.

The column passed huge herds of grazing roans and shaggy motge and fat little woolbacks. Danaer sympathized when his companions cast longing glances at the motge; the kine were a walking feast to men weary of the army's dry fare, and the game birds had been scarce this day. Xashe and Rorluk teased at the risk of lancing down a heifer or calf and butchering it. Danaer let them make banquets with daydreams, knowing they but wished, having no courage to attempt it. The young men would be soured once they learned that some of those brutes *would* be butchered and sold to the army, but at prices only officers could afford.

Fading sunlight reflected from a particularly tall structure in Vidik. Danaer knew that would be the temple. Vidik's Zsed honored Argan in humble brick, but it was said the temple's interior was of surprising richness. In happier times, Danaer might have made a pilgrimage there. But he knew Yistar would be in no mood to grant any man leave from the camp tonight.

Like a living thing, the caravan spilled through the grassy hills and eddied around wells and groves. This was the last good campsite for such a large body until they should reach Deki. Troop Leaders cast lots with one another to find the best placement of their units.

"Now, then, no grumbling," Shaartre warned the greener men. "Get busy, or I will have you transferred to infantry. Then you can dig latrines rather than tend to your horses."

Danaer was unsaddling his scout roan when Shaartre came over and ran a hand down the beast's steaming side. "By Des', Yistar ran us all hard, even you scouts, eh? Some of these blacks are nearly foundered . . ."

Loud quarreling came from the banks of a nearby spring-fed creek. One voice was Rorluk's, but the other man spoke with a pure Destre accent. "I will see to that," Danaer said. Grateful, Shaartre nodded.

A small crowd had collected at the creek, hoping for diversion. There were both soldiers and Destre present, and Danaer saw that with very little friction this might erupt into a serious brawl. Rorluk was glowering at a Destre a good deal older and taller than he, and their argument was worsening and becoming ugly.

"Out, you carrion!"

"Iit . . . back! Before I wear your hide for a cloak!"

Danaer thrust aside spectators and caught Rorluk's arm, pulling the young soldier back roughly. The object of contention stood to one side of the disturbance, smiling archly. Vidik's women of ease had lost no time in finding the army camp. This one's green skirt, the badge of her calling, was slit to her waist. Gaudy gems pinned her gown together, but it revealed far more than it hid. She played with her elaborately coiled and braided hair and fluttered her lashes seductively at the circle of soldiers around Danaer.

"She was sworn to me," the Destre said furiously. "And while I looked to my roan, she crawled off to this Iit warren."

Danaer eyed him with suspicion. "Since when is a woman of ease sworn to any one man?"

"She is Azsed! She has no place here."

"That is her choice. You will not fight with my men —or did you not hear Gordyan's orders? You were commanded to pitch your Zsed well away from the army's tents."

At that, a wariness entered the Destre's expression. But it was not a sort Danaer liked. There was no fear in this warrior, not even sensible caution. Danaer could put no reason to his feeling, yet he knew there was some unusual danger here.

The Destre was not alone. Four of his comrades waited on the opposite bank of the stream. Soldiers leaned close to Danaer and Rorluk, hoping for excitement, eager for a brawl. The woman of ease was merely an excuse. The leader of the Destre-Y stared at Danaer, then said, "Let her have the Iit, though why she should want to play with *children* . . ."

Rorluk lunged at him, spitting oaths most barbed for one so young. "No man calls me—"

Danaer threw out an arm, stopping him. "This one shall, or you will stand double watch tonight, soldier." Chastened, Rorluk mumbled unhappily but stepped back.

"Ai! You bejit traitor to your own kind, call back that lizard spawn—"

Danaer whirled to face the Destre. "He's a quarter less your weight and the same of your age. Do you always challenge a safe contest, warrior?"

"You take me, then, you false-eiphrened dog!" The man whipped out his boot knife, and his cronies grinned in anticipation.

Danaer was more exasperated than angered. He had rarely seen a tribesman so Bog' determined for conflict. "Save it for the Markuand," he said, turning away to show his contempt. There was a touch on his sleeve, and Danaer knew before he looked down that the man's blade had ripped through the cloth. No blood was drawn, for the blow was precisely aimed— a dare.

"What be your mother's name? I will tell her she

bore a coward, and her an Iit's slave to the bargain, no doubt!"

By now Danaer's mood had turned cold. He was annoyed by the naive boy and the woman who had put this affair in motion. The Destre, however, was a matter that could not be shunted aside. Danaer spat at his feet. "I will not wager my life over a woman of ease. There are better things the goddess means for me."

"An Azsed woman?"

"None of your kind." As the man puzzled the remark, Danaer rasped. "Har-shaa!" and simultaneously kicked him in the belly. The Destre doubled over, gasping, his knife spinning away. Still choking, he tried to scramble toward it, but Danaer stepped on the blade. With another kick he drove his opponent away from the weapon, then tossed the knife far up the rise on the other side of the stream. The man brought his hand away bloody from a cut lip, glaring his hatred.

"I draw no knife on a man not seeking honest challenge," Danaer said. "Get out of here. The woman is free to stay, if she wishes."

The woman studied both groups, then slipped her bejeweled arm around Rorluk's waist. With a snarl, the defeated Destre staggered to his feet and edged away.

"Well to decide that!" Gordyan was striding purposefully down the slope. He ignored all but the fight-bent warrior. The man attempted to sidle past him, with no success. "Know what your witlessness nearly cost you—I call this man hyidu. Now I will call you challenge, since you seem to wish it so much."

The Rena's bodyguard struck with a stunning back-hand, knocking the Destre several paces back and sprawling to the ground. Clutching a bloody nose to match his lip, the would-be challenger grunted on his pain as his companions helped him to his feet.

Gordyan said heavily, "If it is women of ease you want, there are many more of them at the Zsed. Argan will readily accept your gifts from their hands. But if you want to fight, come to me. I will oblige you all, to your grief." They scurried away, their bruised and bloodied leader throwing Gordyan a look smoldering with hate.

"And you, to your work. The entertainment is over," Danaer ordered, and with dragging feet the soldiers moved off, gossiping on what they had seen. When he and Gordyan were alone, Danaer smiled at Gordyan and said, "You time your entrances well, maen hyidu."

"I was watching from those willows up there, to see how far that sand-crawler would test you. This is more than hot blood over a woman, I fear." Danaer nodded. "This is Hablit's realm, or it *was* his. And I have seen that bejit we just lessoned before, wearing Hablit's colors."

"Has Hablit been found?"

Gordyan was vexed. "He has seemed to disappear. There is no explaining it." He shook his head. "That warrior might claim to follow Lasiirnte Wyaela, yet I think he is still Hablit's man. This disturbance was much worse than it seems."

"Hablit swore he would destroy the alliance, and would join with the Markuand and their magicians to do so." Danaer knelt by the creek and dabbled his hands in the cool water, splashing it over his sweaty face. Gordyan hunkered beside him, worriedly mulling the problem. "If he is a spy for Hablit, was that blow you dealt him wise? Now he will waste no opportunity to kill you, Gordyan."

"Him? He could not handle lance or knife well enough to reach me in one strike, and he would not get a second."

"Perhaps he will not seek open challenge but strike at your back."

"No Azsed warrior would come at a man's back."

"He came at mine," Danaer said. "The motives can be Hablit's. The stakes are high, and there could be wizardry involved." They stood up, and Gordyan's concern worsened. He had a pious dread of such things, as did Danaer. "I have coped with mirages where there should be none, hyidu. I thought my eyes were past deceiving, but some evil power deluded me."

The big man was unwontedly solemn, much impressed. "Ai! Lira warned us that there are traitor wizards, some even within Krantin. They too may strike at our backs. But we will win this game, for the Siirn Rena and for your Royal Commander. The goddess will make it so." Heartened by that vow, Gordyan slapped Danaer's bicep, then left to check on his Zsed.

The conversation lingered in Danaer's mind through evening mess and into the night. But before long the revelry began. Gradually his grim thoughts were put by. Few men of spirit could resist the gaiety spreading through the encampment. Women of ease were everywhere. Their ornaments and bright garments among the drab uniforms were like a scattering of stars brought to the dust. The women were young and old, fresh beauties and jades past their best years. But the invitation was always the same. Men who feared what might await them on the walls of Deki were not overly discriminating. Drunk with wine and the darkness, they kept even the plainest wenches busy.

With the women had come the merchants, hawking wine and baubles and confections for the army's gold and silver. Most were Azsed, wearing the traditional wide-sleeved merchants' cloaks over their Destre shirts and breeches. But a few were Sarli or Irico. Some of the latter were clad in somber blues and were white-haired, reminding Danaer unwillingly of Lira's wizard master, Ulodovol.

"Hssst! Danaer." Shaartre and his fellow troop leader had been watching the festivities from the sidelines, exchanging ribaldries on the scene. Now Shaartre pointed to newcomers, a group of Sarli. Unlike Lira's people, these stocky little folk wore heavy tunics and knee breeches, and ribbons at waist and shoulder and anywhere else they could.

"Nortea," Danaer said. "From the high desert of Sarlos. They are most likely minstrels and tumblers. Commonly found in the Destre Zseds."

"Ah! Then there will be a show."

One of the Sarli set a small drum throbbing and another began a wail on some tamsang reeds. Drawn by the music, the women approached, their men following like curs greedy for food. The eldest of the minstrels marked off a pattern in the dirt around the campfire close by, and one of the women of ease danced into the circle. Her feet pattered in rhythm to drum and fife, her bangles jingling accompaniment. She swayed with animal abandon in a dance well calculated to arouse the soldiers and make them bid for her favors and those of her friends.

Danaer, too, moved a bit in time with the infectious music, then shook off the temptation.

Then, as he surveyed the area beyond the dance circle, Danaer was delighted to see Lira perched up on one of the wagons. He threw a quick farewell to Shaartre and started to work his way through the crowd toward her.

"Troop Leader . . ." Yistar was also wending through the press. "Watch for trouble. I am having all the officers and Troop Leaders put on alert. Enjoy yourself, but stay wary. We have had several close brushes."

Danaer had not bothered to report his own encounter by the stream. Apparently such stillborn brawls had happened elsewhere in the camp. "Ai. I will do my best, Captain."

Yistar glanced around and noticed Lira, then grinned understandingly at Danaer. "Behave yourself. See you do not tire the lady. She has much sorkra dealings under way, and more on the morrow."

When the officer had gone, Danaer squirmed past dancers until he got to the wheel of Lira's wagon. Nimbly he swung up and sat beside her. She was gazing after Yistar. "It is strange. I think he wants very much to send away all these women, but he does not."

"It was the same in the southern campaigns and the Kakyein wars," Danaer told her. "Yistar always allows his men license on the eve of battle, even though he disapproves wantonness . . ."

"Harshaa, Azsed!" Gordyan plowed through the twisting bodies and grinned up at Danaer and Lira. "A good vrentru this, eh?"

"Hardly a vrentru, but Peluva will be well on the

journey across the sky ere we get this drunken rabble on their feet and moving," Danaer said.

"And what heads they will have!"

"Hai! Troop Leader!" An example of Gordyan's prophecy reeled close to the wagon. Rorluk and his unit mate Xashe were flanking the woman of ease who had caused the argument at the stream. Rorluk had one arm about the female, and with the other he embraced a bottle. It was plain most of its contents already filled his belly. He was clinging to the woman as much for support as out of lust. Xashe also reeled, but seemed in better condition. He snatched the bottle from his friend and held it out to Danaer. "Here! For that scrape by the water. You saved Rorluk's salt."

"You had best keep it yourself, soldier," Danaer said tolerantly.

"There is plenty. Plenty." Rorluk owlishly wagged a finger. "Many wine merchants here. Many."

Gordyan shrugged and said, "He is right. The same merchants visited the Zsed earlier, and most of my warriors are drunk, too. The ones who are still conscious are riding into Vidik to try to drink *it* dry."

"Well, at it then, you two," Danaer said with a sigh. He wondered how much longer the young conscripts could stay on their feet, or if their virility would survive the wine. The woman might earn her fee for doing nothing. "Keep away from the wagerers, though. You will lose both your weapons and your horses to those quick-fingers."

"Ah, no fear, Troop Leader. We like our mount and will keep her." Rorluk winked lewdly and the woman giggled. Danaer nervously eyed Lira. Sarli women were reputed to be prissy in such matters. Lira seemed unoffended, however.

"The fool," Gordyan remarked, holding up the bottle the threesome had left. "It is half full. That boy had best pinch his money."

"Rorluk has enough to waste. His family is wealthy."

"And the conscripters got him?" Gordyan laughed at this irony.

"Malol te Eldri obtained a royal decree that could

touch even a merchant's son. But I understand Rorluk wished to join. He has listened to hero tales and wants to do great deeds."

"He may get his stomach of deeds at Deki," Gordyan said, then took out the cork with his teeth and swilled at the wine. He and Danaer traded turns at the bottle. Lira daintily rejected their offer to share. Instead she tapped her feet and sang softly with the minstrels.

The dances grew ever wilder. Men linked arms and performed athletic leaps to display their strength. Women formed twining serpents, gamboling like Argan's imps, lifting high their knees to send their gowns flaring and advertise their trade shamelessly. Again Danaer studied Lira. She remained undisturbed. She did not appear to approve all these gross posturings, but she was not shocked, either.

Suddenly one of Gordyan's men was there. Gordyan cut off his cheerful whistling and leaned down to receive a message. His face darkened ominously. "Trouble has found me, friend. There is a fight near the army's horse pens—some Destre again. Your pardon, Lira . . ."

"Gordyan, wait! Lira, I will only be a short while . . ."

Gordyan had surely drunk far more than he, but the big man had sobered quickly. Danaer stumbled trying to catch up with him, running along in the Destre's wake. He was still a number of strides behind when Gordyan reached the corrals.

It was hardly the riot Danaer had feared it would be. Most of the men were content to be spectators, cheering on five or six soldiers and Destre-Y who rolled about in the dirt, pummeling and kicking. Bets were changing hands, but no one else wished to join the fray. Wine and women had mellowed them too much.

Wading into the brawl, Gordyan seized arms, legs, or clothing and heaved first one man, then another, out of the thrashing mass. All the while he roared oaths and kicked at those he had not yet reached.

One of the men Gordyan had tossed aside got to

his feet with knife in hand. At once he charged back toward the fight, his blade aimed at Gordyan's broad back.

Danaer flung himself at the man, grasping his arm. They both went down hard, wrestling furiously. Danaer fended the knife off his throat, then a boot smashed into his shin. A moment later a knee came close to ending all his will to continue.

No quarter was ever the rule in such a Destre fight, and as a last resort, half blinded by dust and knowing he was outweighed, Danaer sank his teeth into the knife hand pressing close to his face.

"Shaa!" His opponent's face screwed up, but the cry was one of self-encouragement, as Danaer would expect from a Destre warrior. Staring up, Danaer suddenly recognized the man—it was the combative warrior from the squabble by the stream.

Then his head snapped back as a fist struck his jaw. The knife was coming again, dimly seen through the lights sparkling in Danaer's vision.

Suddenly he was no longer pinned. Danaer sat up, wiping dirt from his face as Gordyan held the would-be assassin—lifting the man over his head.

"Fair challenge!" the warrior yelled.

Effortlessly, Gordyan set him on his feet, then waited, arms akimbo.

"Fair challenge," Danaer's erstwhile foe demanded, less loudly.

"No man who comes at my back deserves a fair challenge. But I will give you one," Gordyan answered.

Paling, the man exclaimed, "Not you! I will fight him." His knife was clutched in a tooth-marked, bleeding hand, and he used it to point at Danaer, who started to draw his boot knife. Gordyan stopped him with a curt gesture.

"This is a Destre challenge. So my size bothers you, eh? But only when I face you." Gordyan took out his belt knife and his attacker shrank in dismay. "Hyidu," Gordyan said, tossing the dagger, and Danaer deftly caught first that, then his friend's boot knife. "Now. Does that even it sufficiently for you, devil spawn?"

Danaer dared not protest such rashness; that would insult Gordyan's courage. He waved back gawking soldiers as the assassin rushed at the big man. Gordyan avoided the murderous slash, laughed, and delivered a blow on the neck as his challenger lunged past. Stumbling and shaking his head, the man regained his balance just short of a headlong fall.

He eyed Gordyan with new caution. He had assumed, as many did, that Gordyan's size would make him awkward, easy prey. The truth was a distinct surprise.

There was a flurry of feints, a rapid shuffling to one side, then the other. This time the attacker parried Gordyan's large hands well enough to cut the giant's thigh.

"Two!" Gordyan's lips drew back in an awful grin. "You get one more."

Cocky after his little victory, the man struck at Gordyan's belly. But those powerful hands shot out with astonishing quickness, seizing wrist and throat. The challenger fought to free himself, beating at Gordyan with his free hand. He attempted to reach over to his knife, held uselessly in his left, but could not.

Gordyan's grin was terrifying. His fingers tightened and the bloodied knife fell to the dust. A gray pallor covered the man's features, and Gordyan's eyes narrowed.

His opponent went limp, and Gordyan let the body fall. "I should save your carcass and throw it in Hablit's face, once I run him to earth. You were a poor Azsed, but an Azsed still. I will sing you to the gates, and you may hope Keth does not remember your name. Kant, prodra Argan, ai, te prodra graat . . . receive his soul, goddess, and judge him as he deserves."

Danaer chased away the soldiers and their women, then handed back Gordyan's weapons. As his friend sheathed the knives, he bellowed at the Destre-Y who had lingered. "Out, all of you. If another warrior starts a fight this night, you may expect the same as this bejit got. Make this carrion's pyre far from my

tent. I will not abide his stench polluting my nostrils."
Several men bundled the body into a blanket and toted
it off while the others melted into the darkness, glad
to escape Gordyan's anger.

"Best tie that up," Danaer suggested, indicating the
dripping cut along Gordyan's thigh.

"Bah! It is not deep. He could not possibly have
done more than scratch me, coming in at that angle."

Two more of Gordyan's guards hurried up to join
the man who had summoned their leader. "You should
not have troubled yourself, Gordyan. We could settle
filth like that while you enjoyed . . ."

"You cannot be everywhere." Gordyan patted their
shoulders, brushing aside their words. "I have something else for you to do now. Get to Lasiirnte Wyaela,
in Vidik. Take this with you." Danaer was startled to
see Gordyan give them a fragment of the dead man's
mantle. Not even his keen eyes had observed the taking of the trophy. "Tell her I shall meet with her
later and we will talk of this, and of Hablit."

As they left on their errand, Gordyan turned to
Danaer and asked, "Did that cur hurt you much?"

Danaer gingerly pressed his groin, deciding he had
been fortunate. "Nothing of concern."

"Then get you back to your qedra. I must attend
to other matters."

Danaer studied him anxiously. "Hablit meant to
kill, through that assassin. Stay here in the camp,
where I can continue to guard your back."

Gordyan smiled, touched by Danaer's worrying. "I
will be cautious, no fear. And I must warn Wyaela
so that she too can take measures against Hablit's
treachery. The man must be mad, a victim of the lash
of Kidu."

"And probably there are other conspirators, some
traitors within The Interior, Lira has said."

They commiserated over the shame of this thing.
Then Gordyan nodded and gave Danaer a gentle
nudge. "Go now. Do not keep Lira waiting. And be
certain you guard *your* back, hyidu, while I am not
here to defend it."

By the time Danaer returned to the wagon, the

crowd had become even more boisterous. He could barely make himself heard when he replied to Lira's questions, explaining briefly what had happened at the pens. He brushed over much of the danger, presenting the deadly encounter as no more than a rough argument. Reassured, Lira relaxed, and she and Danaer again enjoyed the dancing and music.

Two of the minstrels performed in the circle, wheeling and jumping dramatically, acting out a story. Both wielded the peculiarly curved Nortea swords, swinging the blades about wildly. It was a dance done to the glitter of hammered steel, a mock battle scene, in rhythm to the drum. Their fellow minstrels chanted a disonant tale which carried the listeners far away to the barren Nortean high desert.

Swords tore the air mere fingers'-breadths from bodies. The song became one of sexual conquest, veiled in terms of warfare. The onlookers cheered and offered suggestions to the dancers.

With a cry of pretended defeat, the woman let her sword be struck out of her hand. Her partner capered victoriously and then swung her up to his shoulder, bearing her out of the circle amid drunken, congratulatory shouts.

Couples moved into the circle again as the music grew less violent. Lira sighed and said with regret, "I wish I could stay the night, but I must go."

Danaer helped her down from the wagon and escorted her toward Yistar's staff area. Many times he was forced to step to one side or another to fend off the weavings of some sotted soldier or junior officer. Now and then Danaer saw an Azsed warrior. But wine had been working on these, too, and they had become too befuddled to be a menace.

Women were never alone. The carnal sisterhood indulged little in drink, too intent on plying their calling with as many men as possible. They lay with one, left him to drunken sleep, then sought out another. As they went by such scenes, Danaer again and again glanced at Lira. But she said nothing.

Near the officers' tents the crowds began to thin a trifle. From here Danaer could see beyond the oasis.

Twinkling watch fires studded the night beyond. Were some of those torches in Gordyan's Zsed? His warriors, unlike most, seemed fairly sober. They would be on the prowl, seeking out Hablit's minions lest there be more trouble.

Lira had a tiny private tent in the corner of the command section, close to Yistar's own, but at one side, nearly at the edge of the camp. Campfires cast an unsteady glow and threw shadows along the tent walls. In such soft light, Lira took on an alien loveliness that held Danaer's gaze.

Then he was aware her mood had become very morose. She had been happy, watching the dancers. "Lira?" he asked tentatively, scarcely knowing what he intended to say when she responded.

"Ah!" Was she in pain? A frown tightened her high forehead. Danaer tried to enfold her in an embrace, but Lira pulled away from him, her eyes very wide in sudden fright.

She was cold to the touch.

Cold!

Her body might have been encased in snow brought from Irico and farther north, from the region of Eternal Night.

"No, you must . . . must . . ." Lira's hands were icy, and she whimpered. "You must control . . . Hablit . . . cannot locate him . . . somewhere! Find him!"

She looked at him, but did not see Danaer. He had hoped, once she left Siank and Ulodovol's daunting influence, this Web would not bind her, torturing a lovely young woman made for joy and a man's love. Angered, Danaer longed to deal directly with Ulodovol's magic and end Lira's servitude.

And then he too was cold—cold beyond bearing. An awful spasm shook him, worse than any shiver in winter's blasts.

The torches were growing dim! Their light faded, and though the night had seemed black a moment earlier, now it was pitch, the inside of a demon's maw. Utter darkness, raging with the terrifying cold.

A wind was rushing upon them—a bitter storm from the bowels of Bogotana's realm, stinking with the very breath of sorcery. But there was nothing there! No ice, no wind! The pennants at the officers' tents hung limp in the hot spring night. He should not have been able to see them in the icy blackness—yet he could!

He was being swallowed, though he could look out at life, at the world that was. All about him and Lira was a rustling, a murmuring, as from a number of presences, gathering close, shutting him off from warmth.

Hablit's face swam before him—or was it only an illusion? Danaer saw a lust for vengeance in Hablit's eyes, saw his lips moving soundlessly, as if he were speaking of that vengeance to someone.

The vision enlarged, and there was another figure, hidden in shadow, form and face concealed by a cloak. About this second person there was an aura of wizardry and evil. A small, gloved hand cast down a pouch before Hablit, and much gold spilled forth. Gold—to buy death and betrayal, to keep Hablit safe from his pursuers while he carried out the will of his conspirators. There was a seal on the pouch, and though Danaer did not know its specifics, he marked it well as one belonging to some lord of The Interior.

Cold! Too much cold for mortal form to endure! It covered Danaer and searched along his veins and sinews.

Somehow he found will to speak, trying to shout, though he could only whisper. "Lira . . . Lira . . ." It seemed to break away some of the ice, and he grabbed the sorkra and shook her, driven by fear for them both.

Lira shuddered, and more of the ice vanished. Danaer released her, at last able to raise his hand and clutch the obsidian talisman. As he did, cold and darkness fled. Slowly, Lira's abstract gaze focused squarely upon him, losing that wild fixation. "Oh, Danaer! I did not mean to involve you!" She wept, clinging to him.

"Argan protect us! What *was* that?"

Superstitious terror raked at him, but in honor he could not run away. He had sworn to protect her, and now Danaer looked down at Lira in fear and pity. She was trembling like a woman taken deathly ill, only bit by bit calming herself. She said between chattering teeth, "Qedra, you must not stay with me—near me. These things . . . they are . . ."

"I will guard you, as I told you I would." Danaer spoke with more courage, by far, than he felt. "You are in danger."

"Danger?" Lira's trembling grew less and she managed a bitter smile. "No, no danger, not as *you* think of it. No swords, no knives, no blood is shed in these undertakings. This is something far worse."

"I will lend you my strength," he said in grim determination.

Lira brushed his cheek with cool fingers. Cool, not that supernatural cold which had imprisoned them earlier. She was trying to dismiss him, like a beloved but unknowing child. Resentment flared, wiping out ardor.

Then that too was gone. He remembered his panic, and its cause, and that Lira, for all her desirability, was a sorkra.

Wizardry seemed to be a path that led in many directions. Lira could reach out with her enchantments, touching her Web in distant places. And in return, she could be reached, and not always by wizards friendly to her kind.

He had been near her, and that hostile magic had made him its target as well, forcing him to share what she experienced. Though he wanted to flee, murmuring prayers, invoking Argan's protection, Danaer said, "I will stay. I will guard your sleep."

Lira's pretty face was upturned, and for a delicious minute her lips were warm and inviting beneath his. Then she was gone, with no further word. Frustrated and confused, Danaer stood rooted. The flap of her tent was shut tightly, and a lamp was being lighted within.

Danaer stared at the tent. If she were Azsed, there would have been teasing banter between them and more kisses filled with promises, some veiled in sweet phrases, some most frank. And if he had pleased an

Azsed woman, she would bid him enter the tent and take joy with her, worshipping the goddess in that ritual as ancient as earth and fire.

But a sorkra? If he acted so with Lira, would her fire, like a tenderly nursed ember, burst into ardent flame? Or would her alien nature be repelled, affection become loathing, not love? He could not tell.

Her lissome form was outlined against the cloth by the lamplight. Lira was bent as if in prayer. Then she straightened, her head thrown back, her body rigid. He heard a mewling as she called to her Web across space a man could not ride in a three-day or more.

She must contact them, he knew, for Ulodovol must be informed of Hablit's activities, that the conspiracy was wider than they had known. Danaer's own fire was quenched by that sight. He could not leave and keep honor. So he loosened his knife and sat beside the tent. The blast of cold evil had robbed him of both lust and sleepiness.

Lira said she was not in danger from ordinary weapons, but she might have spoken in womanly innocence. The cloaked traitor in the vision and Markuand's wizards dealt in incantations and icy winds from nether regions. Hablit would prefer a more direct method. Lira had not broken that spell until Danaer had cried out to her and touched the talisman, he remembered. She had needed him. Perhaps her powers were somewhat diminished here, so far from her master.

Very well, he would guard her with steel and bronze, companioning her magic with his soldier's skills. Danaer sat, ignoring the dewing grass and the raucous shouts and music from elsewhere in the camp. Within her tent, Lira communicated with those unseen —Ulodovol and other wizards called by strange names and dwelling in stranger places. Danaer had not heard them before, nor did he wish to now.

Gradually the revelry died, and the early morning was punctuated only occasionally by an annoyed complaint as someone stepped on another's foot or hand or interrupted lovers in their blankets. Picketing blacks nickered to the rest of their herd and to the roans tethered near Gordyan's Zsed.

Still Lira's chanting continued, and Danaer held sleep at bay. He would pay a hard price, once day arrived. And with little to show for it save a dark memory! Not even the pleasure of being drunk. Ruefully, amused by his dilemma, he grinned. While his troops sported with women, he sat guard, chaste and all too sober, keeping watch over a sorkra.

Osyta had prophesied he should be part of things undreamed of by most Destre-Y. Again the crone had foreseen rightly. He sighed and acknowledged his dead kinswoman had told him the truth.

Then he tensed, hand on knife, peering into the approaching dawn. Seeing would have been easier had it still been full night. But his scout's vision probed movement where none should have been, past the pickets, coming toward Lira's tent.

Quietly he got to his feet, cocking his head. There was a moving shadow out there, and he would know how it was shod. Boots? Sandals? It was no animal, and it was not a thing of magic, but had weight and substance.

He kept his back to the tent, letting the flickering torchlight fall over his shoulder and catch the glint of his blade. As he did, the movement in the darkness stopped, frozen.

For many minutes Danaer waited patiently, watching. The unknown stalker waited also. Then, as furtively as the light seeping through purpling clouds in the east, the figure withdrew. Danaer did not lessen his vigilance until it was gone. The horses stamped nervously and whinnied, apparently reacting as the stranger crept by their pickets. Whoever he was, he had successfully evaded sentries of both army and Destre.

Daring at last to lower his guard, Danaer eased himself down beside Lira's tent once more. He scanned the area, looking for other forms lurking in the twilight, finding none.

Had it been one of Hablit's men? Or was this an

agent of that mysterious cloaked figure, the traitor from The Interior?

No matter. It was too late. They did not like the day, and now the sun was Lira's ally, forestalling the enemy. The sky was coloring to pink and gold. Soon the trumpets would blare the call to muster. Lira's web was safe, and so was she, and Danaer prided himself that his diligence had served her well.

XIII

BOGOTANA'S SINK

THERE HAD BEEN LITTLE CONVERSATION AMONG THE troops this day. At first that had been the result of too much merriment and drunkenness the night before; and Danaer too had been silent, held by memories of magic and lurking assassins, though he had not shared his unit mates' revelry. The caravan moved deep into the blasted wasteland east of Vidik. Dullness left by drink and lack of sleep were forgotten, for now the column entered Bogotana's Sink.

Since midmorning they had been passing bleached bones of humans and animals and the wreckage of countless carts and wagons. Sulfurous pits boiled and bubbled, emitting a poisonous stench which made men choke and sickened the horses that strayed into the fumes. The scant vegetation was encrusted with a peculiar white exudation. If man or beast touched that material by accident, skin burned and seeped agonizingly, and after a few such occurrences, all took great care to avoid the stuff. The trail grew serpentine, winding around great rifts and fissures torn through the earth. Some ancient cataclysm had rent this place, and the legends said it was then that Bogotana climbed from his realm and took possession of the Sink. The tortured waste stretched far to north and south, nearly

to the borders of Krantin. There was no swifter way
to Deki than through its fiery width.

Not only the land assaulted the caravan, but the
sky as well. The heavens were leaden, and a sun
which had seemed comfortingly warm at Siank and
Vidik now shone with merciless fury. The sandy
ground gave the heat back again, redoubled. Men
trudged listlessly and the animals' tongues began to
loll. At Vidik, Gordyan and Yistar had taken good
care to see that every water wagon and vessel was
filled to the brim. Now they exhorted their commands
to hurry through the worst of the Sink, fearing to lose
both time and lives.

But trouble afresh had come from a quarter no one
could have expected. The sky lowered and filled with
terrible black clouds. Men had only moments to appreciate the blotting out of the burning sun. Then rain
poured down in long, sleeting streamers, a dark loom
set against the horizon, the warp threads thundering
down on the column.

No rain had fallen in this part of Bogotana's Sink
in generations. Yet it fell now, in torrents that tore
away the trail and made the road a sodden trap. Dry
sand sucked up the rain, and wheels sank axle-deep.
Cart horses mired and bleated piteously as they tried
to get free. Drivers flogged their brutes; soldiers,
soaked to the skin, put shoulders to the wheel, pushing the wagons out of the new-made ruts. Some animals burst their hearts in the struggle; a few men
slipped and were crushed under the wheels when the
wagons came free too suddenly for them to step out
of the way. Curses and wails rose into the steaming
air, and many prayed to any god who would succor
them.

Then, almost in an instant, the rain vanished. In its
place was the normal climate of Bogotana's Sink—
the cloudless sky and a sun so brilliant it leeched
juice from man and beast. Damp fairly boiled from
clothes and hair as the caravan doggedly staggered
forward again. Yistar set his jaw and ordered the advance, no matter what supernatural form the weather
would take. Far on the fringes of the army column,

Gordyan's warriors suffered the same astonishments and discomfort. And like Yistar, Gordyan would not be bested by these strange events.

Within a thousand lengths, the rains closed in upon them again. No! Upon *part* of the caravan. This time some drivers baked while four wagons ahead men were drenched and their teams floundered.

Once more, as quickly as it had begun, the storm dissipated, moving to strike at another section of the afflicted column.

Uneasy whispers ran through the lines. Men spoke of witchcraft, when they had wit and strength to speak at all. Danaer felt the same dread, and he knew his young apprentices must share his fear of magic. Xashe and Rorluk made no complaint, though. Perhaps they were too wearied after their night's carousal. If they spoke at all, it was a terse comment on landmarks, a question about the route.

That was a sore point, and an embarrassing one, for Danaer. Twice he had led the caravan a hundred lengths astray, for the mirages had come back in full force. These were so real he had not doubted them.

Once Gordyan, more familiar with the trail, had ridden close and warned Danaer before the caravan had gone too far in the wrong direction. The second time he caught the mistake before Gordyan had to come to advise him. But his chagrin was growing. He was a Destre, a scout, and he should not let himself be tricked by the overheated air and lying images in the sand.

Even as Danaer had sought to steel his resolve and be fooled no more, the accursed rain had rushed over him once more. He thought of Lira, remembering how she had turned back the magical storm which had attacked the Destre council. Was she even now waging a similar war against this furious torrent? That was her calling, and she would try to combat that sorcery with her own. But she was so far from Ulodovol, and she was so young. Had she sufficient art? It was a heavy responsibility, worse than Danaer had first realized.

He ignored regulations and took off his helmet. He

shook out his mantle and used the cloak against the sun, kicking up his tired roan. Gordyan and his warriors had likewise taken out their full cloaks, and Danaer wished he still owned that Destre garment. But the army traveled these sun-baked regions seldom, and they had brought little equipment to cope with Peluva's blazing orb.

Burned and drenched in rapid succession, the column crawled through the miasmic wasteland. In the distance, tantalizing, a dark line seemed to dance above the dry plains. It was the Dekan ridge, marking the end of the Sink. But Danaer knew the landmark was farther away than it appeared.

For now, he wanted only to reach the Wells of Ylami, the only safe campsite between Vidik and Deki, the only water that would not be tainted with sulfur and poison. With Gordyan's help and the Destre map Yistar possessed, Danaer would guide the column safely there. He forced himself to sit up in the saddle, pretending an energy he no longer owned. His eyes burned both from sand and sleeplessness, but he concentrated on the route ahead, beyond the mirages and noxious pits.

Shortly after center-stand—which Yistar had not allowed for rest, fearing they would never reach the wells if they tarried in the Sink a moment too long— Rorluk fell from his horse. Danaer hurriedly dismounted and examined the young soldier, finding no broken bones. He and Xashe rolled Rorluk onto his back. An unhealthy flush suffused his face. His breathing was rapid and shallow, and he did not react to Xashe's voice or fussing over him. The peasant herdsman stood between his friend and the sun, hoping a bit of shadow would give Rorluk ease. Danaer fanned his stuporous apprentice with his helmet.

Thirty lengths behind them, the caravan again was at a stop, but not because the scouts had halted. Rain again lashed at the wagons, and the foremost drivers had bogged down completely. Officers shouted and troopmen swore; even as Danaer looked, wind and water closed about the column like a dark curtain.

Eerily, the very world seemed to still. He heard his

own blood coursing. The streamers of rain parted a fraction, and Lasiirnte Kandra rode out of the storm, coming toward Danaer.

He stepped away from Xashe and Rorluk, staring incredulously. The Destre princess was untouched by the rain. Exquisite, flawless, her hair and mantle gently stirred by a kind breeze, she drew rein and looked down at him. "Yaen, stander, Danaer of the clan of Aejzad's woman, I seek your favor, Azsed." Her accent was pure, dulcet, seductive.

"Lasiirnte?" He had not thought he could find his voice, so parched was his throat and so rattled his wits. "I . . . I give you greeting, Lasiirnte."

"The priests say you will die in Bogotana's Sink, you and this army which fights a war it cannot win." The heavy scent of musk radiated from Kandra, overcoming the wasteland's odors. Her green eiphren sparkled in the sun, and golden chains softly clashed their links together at her waist as she moved in the saddle.

Somewhere, a thousand king's-measures away, Xashe was speaking his name. Danaer could not take his eyes from Kandra. She was the Lasiirnte, the most beauteous woman of the plains people, the adored consort of the Siirn Rena. She *was* Destre-Y. The language of the tribes came sweetly from her lips.

"Why should you die to no purpose? In days to come we will need every Azsed. It is a sin to throw away your life and leave your bones to bleach in the Sink."

She was breathtakingly lovely, sitting the roan like a true Destre princess. Even the animal befitted her. Its costly saddle was studded in gold and green gems, mates for Kandra's eiphren.

"Troop Leader . . . ?"

Faintly Danaer heard his apprentice and tried to reply. A frown creased Lasiirnte Kandra's brow. "Hear me, warrior, Azsed needs you. *I* need you. I will give you everything that you desire. Leave this place. Come with me . . ."

"Gordyan?" Danaer said at last, shakily, puzzlement

beginning. "Does Gordyan know you are here? He will want to see you."

"It is of no matter," Kandra said impatiently. At her back, the black storm clouds ravaged the column. *His* column. And his duty was to guide it to safety. Danaer's head was spinning. The beautiful vision said, "Come with me. Mount your roan and come with me. The wells are not far away. These Iit will not hinder us. We will leave them to wander about blindly. Are they not the enemy? Why should we share Destre waterholes with the likes of these unbelievers?"

"The alliance," Danaer said, and resistance rose within him. It was reversal of that peculiar sensation he had known when he drowsed beside the fire and saw Kandra's face superimposed upon Lira's. For a space, Lira's younger, more rounded features formed where Kandra's had been. Confusion ripped at Danaer. But before he could react to Lira's dimly glimpsed image, the image shifted again. Kandra's sharp cheekbones and fine nose and arched brows melted in the air, like a mirage, and in their place was . . . a cloak!

A hooded cloak, shrouding the face and body inside. A hand was bared and a brightly painted fingernail stabbed at him; a shrill voice commanded, "Come with me! At once! Ask no more questions!"

As if he moved against that drenched sand which bogged the wagons, Danaer reached for the talisman.

Kandra's form mingled with the traitor's. The voice, though still feminine, lost its allure, becoming menacing. "Ride, or you will rot here and the leather-wings will pick your flesh and gnaw your bones! You will die, warrior, unhonored and unsung, forever lost to your goddess . . ."

Suddenly Danaer broke free of the spell, staggering back from this thing which was not Kandra. He clutched the obsidian charm and cried, "Begone! You were never Kandra! She would not flaunt the alliance and break her lord's pledge!"

And then she was gone—woman and bright jewels and horse and the heady scent of musk, gone!

Gone with her was the rain which plagued the

caravan. Officers and men gaped at the sky. Clouds shattered like pots and dribbled into nothing. The heavens were clear, almost in the blinking of an eye. Sodden puddles seeped into the thirsty sand. This time, the whole caravan was left under the sun. Not a spot of storm remained.

"Troop Leader!" Xashe grasped Danaer's arm and shook him hard.

Danaer swayed, closing his eyes, trying to shake off the evil spell. When he looked at Xashe, he saw that the young soldier was as worried about him as he had been for his heat-stricken friend.

"You spoke to the air, Troop Leader. I feared the heat had addled your mind."

"Perhaps it has." Danaer gazed around the horizon. There was no trace of storm clouds, or of the beautiful illusion the rain had birthed. Despite the sun, Danaer shivered, and Xashe took his arm more firmly, as if to prevent a fall. "No, it is all right, soldier. Let us tend Rorluk."

Xashe raised his eyebrows but did not argue. He helped Danaer pick up the merchant's son, and together they wrestled him onto Danaer's roan, the steadiest of their three mounts. While Xashe held his friend to keep him from toppling off, Danaer swung up behind his apprentice. "I will take him to the surgeons. Keep to the trail. If you have any suspicion that a mirage lies before you—stop. I will be back as soon as I can."

Nodding, Xashe offered him the reins of Rorluk's black. Danaer and Xashe looked at one another intently, then Xashe accepted that his Troop Leader was once more himself, and was reassured.

As Danaer rode back toward the wagons, Branra met him at the halfway point. "Another sunstroke?"

Danaer nodded, glancing over his shoulder to where Xashe slowly moved on into the Sink. The false Kandra was gone. She had never been here, in truth.

Branra felt Rorluk's reddened forehead and asked solicitously, "Is it bad?"

"I pray not, my lord. But few of the men are used to this heat."

"Or to these storms." Branra had discarded his helmet, as was his habit. Wisely, he had adopted a Destre custom, wearing part of an old cloak to ward off the sun's rays. He rode beside Danaer. He made no reference to magic, though every man in the caravan now suspected the source of the rain and mirages.

At the surgeons' wagons, Danaer gave his apprentice into the physicians' care. Gentle hands bore the unconscious young soldier into the shade of a canvas and laved his burning face with precious water. Danaer peered into the wagon for a while, encouraged when Rorluk began to wake and beg for a drink. He had begun to feel some affection for his scouting companions and hoped the goddess would make this only a light blow of the sun for Rorluk, not a fatal one.

Branra had followed him, and now he cupped his hands over his brow and looked northward. A rising dust cloud marked the progress of Gordyan's men. Their billowing mantles flapped in the breeze. "Would that the army issued such cloaks," Branra muttered. "Rorluk is one of the first cavalrymen to drop. But the infantry is falling like slaughtered motge."

Danaer mopped his brow with the hem of his mantle, and brought it away nearly dry. The Sink leeched off a man's sweat before it could bead on his skin! "La! Could the quartermaster not concoct some makeshift to serve us as mantles, my lord? The route was known in advance. The climate of the Sink can be no secret, even in Kirvii."

Branra regarded him with sour amusement. "You have been too long with the army to dream such as that. It would ascribe forethought and intelligence to the king's ministers of war. Kirvii has no such weather as this—therefore *we* shall have none, and that is the end of it, they believe."

Danaer did not know how to reply to such sarcasm. To his surprise, Branra winked, then saluted and rode away. Though Branraediir was the famed killer of many a Destre and a kinsman of royalty, he behaved like a warrior, or a common soldier, knowing their feelings and sharing their disgust with senseless regulations. In spite of the man's record, more and more

Danaer had come to like him, willing to put aside old
hatreds, as the alliance had bid them all to do.

Conditions did not improve much as the caravan
crept toward the nadir of the Vrastre. Myth would
have it that when the world was made, none of the
divine ones would claim this place. Even Argan, born
in fire, scorned to occupy the Sink. The streams
which would have fed grass and slaked thirst had been
stolen for the bowels of the earth, and only Bogótana's
demons enjoyed the waters of the Sink. The water
was far below, whence sulfur and the pits of the cursed
lay. Alone in the wasteland, the Wells of Ylami were
pure and free-running. Ylami was Argan's sole stronghold, her sanctuary here in the midst of her immortal
sire's realm.

Not even sand lizards lived in this part of the Sink.
The only life was the soaring carrion seekers, sailing
the hot wind and hovering above the waste, hoping for
death. Nothing dared the Sink save man and his
beasts, and those could not survive unless they brought
with them water and provender. Yet the ancient
Ryerdon-Y had crossed Bogotana's Sink and given it
its name and reputation first. They had no choice,
fleeing as they did from the might of Traecheus.
Danaer had heard those tales of their epic journey
since he was a babe. Now he fully appreciated the
courage of Ryerdon. They had braved the Sink, not
even sure there would be an ending to the burning
death. How they must have celebrated their arrival
at the oasis of Vidik!

The Sky Lord's burden poured heat over animals
and men. Yistar broke regulations and told the men
they might shed tunics and wear only shirts. His orders
saved many men from collapse. But little could be
done for the teams. Horses dropped in their harness
and were dragged off the trail. There was no time to
butcher the dead brutes. They must be left for carrion
feeders. Only the sick and injured were allowed to
ride in the wagons. Even the surgeons walked alongside, lightening the load for the overburdened horses.
Danaer choked on past pride; he had thought his
background and long years of service in Yistar's cam-

paigns had toughened him sufficiently to any duty. Such boyish beliefs seemed the silly dreams of an age ago.

By evening, Xashe was leaning on his horse's neck unashamedly, and Danaer himself feared that with every step of his roan he might tumble off and give the lie to the tale that a Destre could keep to his mount even when he was dead. A hundred lengths, and a hundred lengths more, and then greenery shone brightly in the dying rays of the sun. Ahead now, very close—grass! And trees!

Horses raised their heads, their nostrils flaring, and drivers sawed at the reins. Weakened though they were, the teams fought to get to the water. Men pitied them, but feared bloat if the beasts stampeded and drank their fill too quickly. Infantrymen helped cavalrymen, roping back the panting brutes, moving slowly toward the long-sought Wells of Ylami. With care, knowing the beasts still must take them far, they let the teams and cavalry mounts drink, and soldiers dropped down beside them, plunging their heads deep into the soothing pool.

Danaer had sent Xashe back to their units and said he would report for them both. He wended his way through the column as it straggled through the groves of sturdy desert trees clustering around the pure wells. If he, a seasoned horseman and campaigner, was so drained as this after a sober and unwenched night at Vidik, how must other men feel? He wondered that so few of them had succumbed to the assaults that nature and wizardry had hurled at them. This was becoming an army in truth, tempered in a forge fiercer than any drill field could offer.

Yistar and Branra and their hardier aides were looking over some royal documents as Danaer neared them. He overheard their conversation. "I cannot comprehend why the Commander tolerates this," Branra was saying. "There are quick, efficient ways of dealing with treachery, if he will only use them."

"But perhaps Diilbok, too, has his acolytes who would—" Yistar broke off whatever he had been about to say and returned Danaer's salute. With his eyes, he begged the scout to say nothing of what he had heard. Then he spoke brusquely, treating only the matters of the route and tomorrow's business. "Good time made, all things considered. We will soon be in Deki, if we press on. Most well."

"Captain? I beg permission to leave camp for a while."

The officer frowned a moment, then understood, his expression softening. "Nine-day? Ai, it must be. I keep not the count of your goddess and her worships, lad. Do you actually think Gordyan's bandits will find a priest out here?"

"He told me it was so, earlier today. They have come out from Deki and awaited the Destre at the farthest wells."

"Of course you have permission. When have I ever denied a man his piety? But be cautious. I need your eyes to lead us safe to Deki."

As the Captain returned to reading his dispatches, Branra stepped close to Danaer and said, "May I ask a favor, Troop Leader?"

"My lord?"

"If you have a devotion to spare, speak to your goddess for me, if you will. If ever a man was destined to fall by Destre lance, it was myself. Now I would strike a truce with Destre-Y, and with their holy lady."

Indeed, Branra was not what he appeared! With much feeling, Danaer said, "My lord, I am Azsed, and I hold you no hatred for performing your sworn duty against my people. I will pray that Argan grant you long life, and that henceforth Destre and Inner Krantin may be as friends."

"Yes, as the Commander hopes. If not, we will die together, at least." Branra's ferocity was oddly mixed with a fatalism that unnerved Danaer. He was glad when the young officer and Yistar went into a just erected staff tent and left him alone.

He walked his lathered roan before letting the animal drink, then went seeking Lira. Weariness made his thoughts a jumble, running this way, then another. Now he envisioned Lira, clad in a silken piece of flimsy cloth, her lips inviting him. Now he remembered what it was to be caught by her wizard web and to be swept by icy cold. And then he wondered if he could find a good remount for the ride to Gordyan's Zsed. His scouting roans would fare better than most, though. How many of the army's blacks, bred for The Interior, would be able to bear a man's weight or pull a wagon come tomorrow?

Nine-day. Argan called the true Azsed. Staggering or not, he must find the strength to make his obeisance. There would be no sleep, not yet.

At last he found Lira, climbing down from a surgeon's wagon, where she had been nursing some of the sick. Her face was smudged with soil, or perhaps with some healing herb. There were dark lines under her pretty eyes, and Danaer saw his own deep fatigue mirrored in Lira. She saw him and drew near, beginning to smile. Then she sighed and chided him. "Danaer, go and get some rest."

"I must seek Gordyan. This night is holy to the goddess . . ."

"But, qedra . . ."

Her endearment drew him, and they stepped into the wagon's shadow, sharing a kiss. Lira's response was that of a weak and flight-worn little bird. Danaer's own fervor was not what he would have wished. Yet even so tired as this, she had the power to stir his blood. But she . . . there might still be evil magic, waiting to pounce. Danaer took one of her soft tresses between his fingers and said absently, "I saw Kandra today." She stared in bewilderment, thinking him mad. "It was an illusion, some sorcery, I think. When I touched your talisman, it vanished. But for a while, it was real. It was during the last of the rainstorms."

Lira sucked in her breath. "I felt it! But I did not know what . . . I was busy, casting spells to chase off the clouds."

"Then you succeeded," Danaer said with a weary smile. "She disappeared and so did the rain."

"We combined our magic." He could not tell if she joked or not. Lira said earnestly, "You are certain it was Kandra?"

"It shifted and became you, and then a figure

hidden in a cloak, and then was banished with the storm."

She nibbled a fingernail, trying to shake off her weariness and study this thing. "I will tell the Traech Sorkra. They seek to seduce you to their will now. Stand fast against them, qedra." Lira laid her hand upon his chest, on the talisman. She seemed much concerned.

"They shall not make me turn traitor. I refused the image when it bade me desert Yistar."

"They are dangerous. All of them. Stay here. I can summon my Web if they try to come at you again."

"I cannot. I must not neglect my faith, not so close to Deki and the battle that will come. Since I left Nyald, I have had no chance to seek out a priest."

Like Yistar, Lira was mystified. "But how can there be a priest here?"

"Lorzosh-Fila promised to send his holy people out from Deki to meet us on Nine-day, for the sake of Gordyan's warriors. I will join with them."

Lira submitted, though she grumbled. She went to the quartermaster's wagons and fetched a small packet of food and a skin of fresh water. These she forced on Danaer. "You are too tired to remember such things. If I did not see to your sustenance, you might forget these necessities, my Sharp Eyes."

"My only necessity is that you call me qedra." Danaer had never been glib with those pretty things women liked to hear. But this time the phrase came unbidden, sounding as it should, with truth behind it. Tonight there was no coldness and no wizardry about Lira. She was woman, not sorkra, and it was hard to part from her.

On a fresh roan, Danaer set out from the army encampment, heading along the line of wells. The moon was rising with the sun now, and the stars were his main light. Here in Bogotana's Sink, when day ended, the wind turned sharp and very cool. Danaer rode into the evening, eating his frugal meal with Destre haste.

He detected the Zsed long before sight warned him. His mount nickered to other horses and there was an

undefinable quickening in the air, as if he sensed tens
of hearts beating in time with his own. It was a feeling he had known often, though never so strongly,
for Nyald Zsed had no such gathering of warriors as
Gordyan commanded.

"Harshaa!" A Destre, leading his roan, came out
of the night. Danaer answered and dismounted. There
was firelight ahead, enough to let the man see Danaer's
eiphren and mantle. He grunted and knew him for an
Azsed, and together they walked toward the glowing
flames.

Soon Danaer was moving along with many others,
Gordyan's men. They left their blankets and tiny tents,
forming a river of humanity. They collected around a
great smoky fire which threw back all night-wings and
sleep-demons. One by one, the warriors loosened
cinches and left their roans behind, without fear of
theft. There would be none, on Nine-day.

A ritual fire had been fueled with scrub wood. This
was altar enough, and a bed of embers had been
raked out on the upwind side. A small pyramid of
stones was heaped up, the symbol of Argan. Destre-Y
surrounded the holy place, welcoming the flames and
their heat.

A priest, clad in robes as bright as the fire, stood
beside the altar. With him were two women. Their
journey from Deki to the Wells of Ylami could not
have been easy, though it would not cover the worst
part of the Sink. Danaer marveled at their dedication
and the kindness of Siirn Lorzosh-Fila in risking his
holy people abroad while his city was besieged.

Like all the others, Danaer cast off his mantle, bar-
ing his head, then kneeling. He glanced around the
gathering and saw Gordyan among them, to his left.
All the murmurings ended as the priest began to chant.
One of the women put by her robe and started to sing.
This delisich was gifted in the divine speech of the
goddess, and her voice sent a thrill through the soul.
Clear and vibrant, it enraptured the listener.

As the song rose to the stars, the priest dropped the
blood of sacrifice on the altar, slashing his own arms
and breast and cheeks to honor Argan. White-faced

with ecstasy, he cried out the reverence that now held them all.

"Goddess, smile on us! Kant, prodra . . . and those who would declare oath, let them be heard . . ."

A number of men got to their feet and broke their silence. Fanatic zeal shone in their countenances. Their oaths were bloody—to avenge the death of a friend or kinsman, to bathe in the gore of the Markuand they intended to kill, to send to Argan the souls of those they would slay, each branded by a marked face or missing limb.

"Goddess, smile, and witness those who bind themselves in your honor . . ."

It was Danaer's turn to stand, and Gordyan's. Danaer would have remained Gordyan's blood friend till death, without the blessing of this ceremony. But now the promise was sealed even beyond the portals of Keth the Dreadful. Now they might know one another in a life reborn, if the goddess chose. Once again they would meet and mingle their blood and call one another hyidu. It was so.

There were other rituals, and then began the chant of the fall to flame and the rise to grandeur. In a sonorous voice which blended well with the pure song of the delisich, the priest gave them Azsed—the Rule, the Will of Argan, she who was ruler of wills. As one, the Destre shouted her praise. "Kant, prodra Argan . . ."

The legend continued in song and speech, whipping their pulses and exciting them still more. When it seemed the mood must break, the second priestess dropped her cloak and walked to the carpet of embers. She was shorter and slimmer than her holy sister of the goddess-voice. But she was beautiful, dark and delicate, rather like Lira in form, though her face was sharper.

The prayer changed and the delisich's song climbed to inhumanly high notes. This was not invocation but evocation. Call Argan, not to witness. Call her to earth, to reenact her fall to the depths, ere she rose again in immortal fire.

The dancer to Argan, the ha-usfaen, pranced gracefully, and her diaphanous orange-colored gown swirled dangerously close to the fire and the glowing coals.

"When shall we call thee goddess? May any of earth call to her? Let who will, speak, and she will live to eternity!"

It was the ritual challenge of the divine ones, as they sought to keep Argan from her sacred place. As one, the assembled warriors roared the answer, embracing the daughter of the evil god, proclaiming her victory over them all.

"Rejoice, yaen of fire-hair! She rules!"

The priest shut his lips and the delisich sang a different melody, rich and trembling. The ha-usfaen danced more quickly, her small bare feet scattering coals, though she evinced no pain. Some worshippers moaned in near delirium. The ha-usfaen was changing —before their eyes! In truth, no man could bear to look anywhere else but at her. The slender dancer grew taller and her body bloomed with voluptuous flesh. Her dark hair lengthened and curled and became as flame, the sacred color of Argan. Her very garments altered and seemed to take on the character of the fire. Not even her face was now her own; it was the face of Argan! The ha-usfaen was bathed in fire, a woman of fire, a goddess of fire. She was possessed, at one with Argan, becoming Argan, for a few incredible moments.

Was there any man who did not lust for her? But a strange sort of lust this was. By taking that perfect body, even in his dreams, a man became as the ha-usfaen, one with the goddess—possessing and possessed. His blood and bone were hers, to work her will. Women, too, professed that they felt allied with Argan in this moment of transformation—that they felt themselves become the goddess, tasting with the ha-usfaen the awesome joy of fire and immortality. Each worshipper became incomparable and invincible as the dancing form changed.

It was a power far overshadowing any herb-healer's potion or wizard's enchantments.

The priestess put her hands into the flames, laughing as they parted harmlessly for her. She threw back her head, tossing her fire-bright hair. She had complete rule over the destroying blaze.

The delisich sang of victory, and of Andaru. Osyta's prophecy seemed to flow and join with the chanted legends. But Danaer felt no fear. He wished he stood at this instant on the walls of Deki, weapon in hand, facing a countless horde of Markuand! He would kill them all. And if he died, his blood would become part of Andaru! Markuand would fall, a sacrifice to Argan. Gordt te Raa had said it: Argan would drink the blood of the Markuand armies, and their wizards as well!

The song stopped on a high, pure note and the hausfaen posed amid the flames, her transformation at its climax.

Then she was gone, leaping free of the fire, wrapping herself in her robe and fleeing into the night before she could change back to mortal form. The worshippers must remember her as she appeared in the ceremony, holding fast to the dedication they had felt then. The singer followed her sister priestess a moment later. The priest intoned once more from the ritual and spoke again of Andaru, sealing all the vows that had been made here. Then he too was gone into the night, leaving a circle of emotionally spent Azsed-Y.

Danaer's knees trembled and he dripped with sweat, not alone from the heat of the fire. It was not only the aftermath of weariness but the weakness of holy ceremony. All felt the same. They would remember this ritual in battle and use it to flog themselves to a frenzy that terrified their foes. The Iit could never know this transport, but they could fear its results. Danaer was glad that now Destre battle fever would be turned against Markuand, not against Yistar and Shaartre and many another good soldier comrade. Even Branraediir of the Bloody Sword was now their ally and would fight beside them.

Branra. Danaer recalled the officer's request, and he wended his way through the warriors, going to Gordyan. They had exchanged friendship with their eyes across the worship circle. Now they spoke together warmly.

"Hyidu! Joy in Argan, joy to call you maen." Gordyan gave Danaer an exuberant hug. His craggy face was full of that same rapture which had touched them all.

"It was a fine ritual . . ."

"Ai! That ha-usfaen is the most glorious Argan I have ever beheld. There will be many more most savage oaths made this night, and many a Markuand will shed blood because of this ritual. Come to my tent, hyidu. We will share wine and make pledges of our own to cut down all the enemies of the Rena."

"I would," Danaer said ruefully, "but I may not stay. Yistar wants an early start, and there are . . . problems." He did not wish to talk of wizardry, nor especially of the illusion of Kandra. Danaer did not wish to ruin Gordyan's delight in the ceremony and the mood it had left. "Are the holy ones still in the Zsed?"

"Ai. They will spend the night in a tent near mine." Gordyan seemed puzzled over Danaer's attitude, but he did not probe its reasons.

"Then would you beg the priest to speak prayers for the continued health and strength of Branraediir? I will pay for the sacrifice." Danaer took coin from his small pouch, then saw Gordyan's expression. "I know Branra has fought most bloodily against us in the past. But now he is our ally. Gordyan, his sword will strike for us, as the Commander and Gordt te Raa would want. He is like the Commander's son—a promise of the future of Krantin, both Azsed and Iit. He has put aside any wish to kill us, wanting only to slay Markuand now."

Slowly Gordyan smiled down at Danaer and again clasped his friend close in a rough hug. "Ai! If you wish it, hyidu. Branra wins your praise. Then he must be worthy. I will see that the priest offers strong chants. May Branraediir's sword kill ten times the Markuand that he ever slew us—and Krantin may need no other warrior!"

The inspiration Danaer had felt at the ritual did not fade quickly. His fatigue was held off by the rich memory as he rode back toward the army's camp.

Again he wished they were already at Deki, on the walls, and that he confronted the Markuand—killing them.

If only he could kill the Markuand wizards as well!

Other memories came to him, crowding his tired mind. Would Lira spend the night treating with her Web again? And would the shadowy assassin stalk her tent? She said she could beat back the evils, and that he must not trouble himself, but he had not told her of the figure in the darkness. Nothing must distract the sorkra from her spell-casting. The caravan depended on her, as did Ulodovol and the Royal Commander.

So much burdening those small shoulders!

He left his roan at the pickets and spoke briefly to Shaartre; the veteran and Gordyan were men of different worlds, and Danaer's comradeship with Shaartre lacked the bond he had sensed at once with Gordyan. But they shared a rough affection, and this time Shaartre made only a few jokes, readily guessing where Danaer would go.

"Well, who would not, if he were on such terms with a woman, out here in this blasted hell?" Shaartre said with a chuckle. "Though after Vidik, I marvel that you—ah! You youngsters!" He slapped dust from Danaer's uniform, then waved him on his way, saying, "But get some sleep, eh?"

That reminder tweaked Danaer's humor, though only a trifle. He was growing weary again, fighting off an aching languor. He strolled through the camp and was startled when Lira came to meet him well away from the staff tents. She seemed much relieved to find him safe. "I . . . I had heard that the Destre are most fervent in their worship, that sometimes they kill each other, or themselves, to please their goddess," she explained timorously.

Danaer laughed softly. "You should not believe foolish rumors. Argan heartens us to slay our enemies, and the enemy is Markuand." He sighed and said, "I wish you could have seen the wonderful ha-usfaen."

"Ha-usfaen? Is that a priest?"

Surprised that her great knowledge did not extend so far, Danaer explained, "She-who-dances-the-goddess. A priestess who may safely enter the ritual fire and become Argan . . ."

"A power over fire? And *how* does she become your goddess?" Lira was obviously deeply interested in the phenomenon.

Danaer spread his hands helplessly. "She . . . she is Argan. Her form and garments change. She becomes the holy one." Lira's eyes were wide and gleaming in the torchlight. "It . . . it is the gift of the ha-usfaen. It is Azsed," he finished simply.

Lira frowned, and he wondered if his faltering description had annoyed her in some way. Then she smiled. "How is this wonderful gift first discovered, Danaer? When does a ha-usfaen first learn that she has been blessed by the goddess in such fashion?"

Ill at ease as she pressed him, Danaer said, "They . . . they are known to the priests of the Zseds. When the girls are young, the priests find them and teach them of the holy rituals. And when a ha-usfaen enters womanhood, then she is able to walk the fire and take on the form of Argan at Nine-day."

Lira clasped her hands to her breast, greatly excited. "Oh, Danaer! We must communicate with them!"

"We?"

"My Web! We did not know about these ha-usfaen, not in all our sorkra searchings. It must be because their gifts are hidden in religion. We had thought there must be sorkra yet unknown to us, and we have found, to our sorrow, that it is so, when the traitors struck from The Interior. But among the Destre-Y? We had not imagined it. How many ha-usfaen may there be? And what shame it is that our Web has never focused upon them. Such a waste! This could mean great things."

"A . . . a ha-usfaen is . . . you say she is a sorkra?" Danaer stammered in amazement.

"She must be! And if the priests are able to seek out these gifted girls, they too must be latent sorkra of some power. They must touch the minds of the children and discover their specialness . . ."

Chilled by that, Danaer reminded her in a hurt

tone, "You said the sorkra did not look into the minds of any but their own Web."

"Danaer, oh, my Sharp Eyes!" Lira caressed his cheek. "Never against their will, never to do harm. Only if invited, not as an invasion. But . . . how shall I explain it? When a child is of the sorkra kind, a potential member of a Web, he or she explores, seeking others who speak across distance and own such powers of illusion and conjury. I did. So do all who have joined us. And your Destre holy people have formed such a Web among themselves, one we did not know existed! I must contact the Traech Sorkra and tell him."

Lira's face was drawn from lack of sleep and her constant need to deal in magic by both day and night. Even in the storm, she had been busy with her spells, holding back the worst of the rain with sorkra arts. She had won, but at fearful cost, the price written in her face and body.

"He demands too much of you," Danaer said sharply. "A ha-usfaen is a holy thing, nothing to do with the sorkra. It is not like that image of Kandra."

"Yes," Lira murmured, anger chasing away tiredness. "That, too, I must speak of. How dare she? This . . . this foul creature who tries to make you believe she is the Lasiirnte! To take the form of a princess of your people, one who might capture your loyalty and . . . you did not tell anyone else of this, Danaer?" she said anxiously.

He was a bit sheepish. "No, my apprentice thought me sun-stricken. He could not see her and assumed that I talked to the air. I did not tell Gordyan, either, because . . . he would be tormented by such a thing. And as helpless as I am to strike back at such wizardry."

"But I am not," Lira said, staring toward her tent.

Danaer caught her arm. "Are you Ulodovol's slave?"

"I am sorkra! I choose my calling freely. Let me go! You do not understand the strength of our enemies, Danaer. You must let me tell Ulodovol, that we may defend ourselves," Lira cried. She had begun her protest with almost angry desperation. Now she seemed distraught and near tears. Would this wizardry never give her peace?

More gently, Danaer said, "You must not tell him about the ha-usfaen. It is a sacred thing, not magic."

Lira gazed up at him intently a long moment, then nodded. She behaved as if she were bending some oath in doing so, and agreed only for his sake. Danaer's fingers relaxed, and instantly she slipped away from him into the darkness. He cursed his weariness that slowed his reactions. Then Danaer ran after her, hoping to catch her before she gained the sanctuary of her tent and her wizard Web.

He was too late. Lira knew the route better than he, and by the time he reached the staff area, the flap of her little dwelling was already closed and tied. Again a lamp was being lit and eerie, alien chants had begun, as on the night before.

The encampment was very quiet. Men had been too worn to eat much, and after slaking their thirst, most had fallen on their blankets, asleep almost at once. A few sentries had been posted, leaning heavily on their lances and trying not to doze on duty. In the officers' tents, there were some lights and soft conversation; Yistar, despite his own exhaustion, would want to plan for the morrow.

Danaer stood in the clearing, listening. Lira sounded like a hurt little creature, moaning those strange phrases in a language of sorcery.

Danaer peered around blearily, wondering if Hablit and his assassins had tracked the caravan through the Sink. They were Destre-Y, familiar with the terrain, not hindered as the army was with wagons and the black horses so ill-bred to this climate. Further, Hablit was an ally of the Markuand wizard. No freakish storms or mirages would be thrown across his path to confuse him. Was he even now lurking nearby, waiting for a chance to strike? The Markuand wizard wished Lira dead, and so did Hablit and the traitors. Her magic had turned back their witchcraft and heartened the caravan, though she was only the apprentice, not the master sorkra they had earlier tried to kill.

Once more he sat down outside her tent, ready to guard her from harm. His limbs ached and his eyes burned. Stars wheeled above the Wells of Ylami. Here in this green haven on the burning desert, night life croaked and slithered near the pool and in the grasses, a softly repetitious murmuring that lulled him. Despite his best efforts, his eyelids were drooping.

Suddenly Danaer came fully awake, his hand on his knife. Someone was standing before him. He came to his feet, ready to parry a blow, then let out his breath. It was Branra who faced him.

The officer looked past Danaer at Lira's tent and the shadow on the cloth. He said quietly, "This is not the first time you have stood sentinel for our sorkra, is it?" Danaer blinked and rubbed his eyes, trying to muffle a yawn. He was too sleepy to deny the accusation. "If you keep to this task, you will be too weary to read landmarks tomorrow. Get to your units, and some sleep. I will stay and guard the sorkra."

Danaer was about to yield, then felt the warmth of the obsidian talisman. Something made him say, "No, I must be close to her. I will get no rest elsewhere. And . . . are you not also tired, my lord?"

"I need less sleep than most men." It did not seem a boast, but simple truth. Branra studied him a moment, then pointed to the spot where Danaer had been sitting. "Very well. Stay. But sleep. If trouble comes, I will wake you."

"Hablit has been stalking the caravan . . ."

"Yes, I have heard, from the Captain. I will be wary. And I think you will allow I have some skill in coping with even the fiercest Destre tribesman."

Danaer smiled feebly and muttered, "Lira . . . the Lady Nalu . . ."

"If she needs you, I will wake you," Branra promised again. He spoke no oath and called on no god, but it was a pledge, one Danaer accepted readily. Too spent to argue, he sank down and drew up his knees, pillowing his head on his crossed arms. From the corner of his eye he saw Branra's feet move this way and then that, patrolling the space before Lira's tent like any common sentry.

Very soon, Danaer's eyes closed. He could not feel the cold touch of the web tonight. He gave himself over to Branra's care, as once he had put himself into Yistar's mercy, sinking into a dreamless sleep.

XIV

DEKI–TE VOND VE EXIS

YISTAR'S TROOPS HAD HOPED TO MAKE BUT ONE DAY'S journey from the Wells of Ylami out of the Sink, but in vain. The worst of the wasteland was behind them, passed in that first terrible leg. The water wagons were refilled at the wells, sufficient to sustain the slow-moving caravan through the following two days and another night's encampment. There had been more magical rainstorms, but of less fury. Danaer heard Yistar saying to Branra that surely now the enemy wizards had learned Lira's counterspells were a match for their assaults, and there would be an end to this weather soon. Danaer had shared that wish, though with less confidence. He did not doubt Lira's powers, but he had felt the force of the Markuand magic and knew it was most awesome.

Bogotana's Sink seemed loath to release the caravan from its clutches. There were many opportunities for Danaer and Xashe to stop and wait while wagons were repaired. On the second day, Rorluk was so much improved he insisted on rejoining his companions and riding point once more. Occasionally Danaer had seen Lira, riding in one of the lead wagons. She had nodded a greeting, but always appeared preoccupied. He did not disturb her, wary of distracting her from some incantation that might be the caravan's protection.

Most of all, Danaer was happy to be a scout, not a

driver. He had ridden by when a loud argument boiled between Yistar and the chief wagoneer, and pitied the hapless teamster. "It is the brakes, Captain," he had been explaining. "We will have them repaired soon."

"Bog' take the whoreson who designed your wagons! And Bog' take this infernal trail, and you!" Branra was grinning appreciation at his captain's stream of profanity. "Bejit, dog-spawn of a . . . storms, heat, mirages . . . wizardry! I declare, by the Black Mare's Mane, I will run through the next man who speaks failure to me! We will reach Deki tonight!"

Flogged by Yistar's temper, the column moved forward again. This time, it was on the descent, though the slope was so gradual that Danaer was uncertain for a while that they truly crept downward. He checked landmarks, seeking signs of change. Yistar was right. Soon they must leave this bone-dry waste of jumbled rocks and merciless sun and bones of those less fortunate.

At last, several candle-marks eastward, Danaer saw what he had been expecting. He made no announcement, waiting for his novices to notice the subtle difference in the landscape. Rorluk was still a trifle unsteady in the saddle and not yet fully recovered. It was Xashe who cried out, "Bushes, Troop Leader! And trees! We have seen nothing growing since . . ."

"The Wells of Ylami," Danaer agreed.

His apprentices grinned at one another, anticipating what lay ahead. There would be grassland and water aplenty. They were winning through to Deki, and the triumph tasted sweet.

But though they were slipping out of the claws of Bogotana, the ordeal had not ended. Only a short time after Danaer had spotted those signs of vegetation, an immense dark cloud built on the horizon, a towering column of churned-up dirt.

Danaer's first thought was that they were menaced by a priuda, the terrible dust storms which sometimes haunted the Vrastre. Priuda could trap hunting or raiding parties, cutting warriors off from their Zseds, strangling their roans with dirt. Entire sections of

Zseds had been swept away in priuda, and if this was such a dust demon, the caravan might be hard hit.

Then, at the base of the onrushing cloud, Danaer discerned life, a rolling movement—motge! A great herd of the bovines, galloping toward the wagons. His panic rose, then was quenched, his senses tingling and the obsidian responding to a supernatural warning. Not motge! Argan guided his will and opened his eyes. He could fathom the truth of it readily now. The tossing heads and pounding hooves and fat bodies, even the swirling dirt, were wavering and shimmering before him. "It is another cursed mirage!"

"The column, Troop Leader? Will they think it is real? The cart horses may bolt and tear their traces . . ."

Danaer nodded, approving his apprentices' concern for their duty. He turned to ride back to the caravan. The wagons had stopped, and all were gazing at the oncoming stampede. The earth seemed to tremble with the weight of the thundering kine; dust appeared to blacken the sky. Lira was standing up on a wagon seat, shouting to Yistar, "It is an enchantment, Captain, no more. Order the men to stand fast and steady the horses."

Without questioning, Yistar obeyed the sorkra, sending his aides loping to carry the command along the column. Danaer saw that many drivers and troops had already reached the same conclusion the young scouts had. The trek had hardened conscripts as well as veterans, and they were learning to brave each new challenge of the journey. Fear changed to angry muttering. Soldiers tightened reins and stared belligerently at the stampede which seemed about to crush them.

Lira's head tilted back and her eyes closed. She could not see the mirage which now filled the horizon, and Danaer knew she called on her Web, and on her own powers. Her Web was very far away from her, and much engaged in other magic, dealing with wizardry on many fronts. Lira was not afraid, though. Had she the strength to deal alone with this latest attack of Markuand sorcery? She chanted into nothing, as officers and their men watched the raging beasts approach. Then, like dew, the vision began to die in the sunlight. By ones, then twos, then tens, the motge winked out of existence, and with them the cloud of dust. A stillness covered the land. The charging animals had never been. No hoof prints marked the earth.

Lira sat down and for a moment buried her face in her hands. Danaer was about to rush to her side, but other men were closer; they offered her water and fanned her with their cloaks. After a while she regained her poise, looking embarrassed that she had come near fainting. "I sensed some abatement of the enemy wizard's magic this time, Captain."

Yistar and his aides grinned. "Well at that, sorkra lady! Now the way to Deki is clear before us!" They doffed their helmets and cheered, then passed the word to set forth once more.

Danaer continued to stare at her anxiously, though Lira forced him a thin little smile. Was her Web involved in this last conjury? He thought not. Danaer suspected she reached out into skills and arts of her wizardry that were beyond her training and experience. She had succeeded, but the strain had been extreme. She lifted her head proudly and tried to look as if nothing had happened, as if the countercharm had not been a terrible effort. He did not shame her by voicing his doubts while others could hear. But Danaer prayed there would be no more assaults on her powers, at least until they reached Deki. Perhaps there she would have time to recuperate from the ordeals of the trek. If the repelling of those demon beasts had taken Ulodovol's strength so severely, how much more must this responsibility weigh upon Lira, who had not his years of wisdom to help her.

He went back to the point, wanting to lead them directly to Deki, to comparative safety. But there continued to be delays, some of them the curse of fate, and some of them part of the Royal Commander's plan. Once, when they had barely started along the downgrade that led to the distant river, a halt was called at a rebuilt ruin. The place was a strange building of stone and brick and timbering. Generations ago, it might have been the castle of some Ryer-

don lord, soon after his people had crossed into Krantin.
It had been laid waste several times since, and now
the workmen of Lorzosh-Fila had come out from Deki
to reconstruct its walls and roof. They were not quite
done when the caravan stopped there, but enough
was completed to shelter against the weather—not men,
but supplies. Quickly, several wagons were wheeled
out of line and their teams unhitched and corralled.
Half a unit was ordered to stay and help the Dekan
workmen thatch the roof. Then they must stand guard,
as long as need be. With that, the caravan rolled on,
toward a second such halt, and then a third, each a
bit farther down the long grade approaching Deki.

The officers did not comment, but there was whispering among the men as they wondered on this
procedure. Danaer and Shaartre and some of the veterans exchanged knowing looks and then took pity on
the greener men. "Caches," Shaartre explained to
them at the third stopping place. "The men we leave
are to guard the supplies for us until we need them."

"When will we need them, Troop Leader?" Rorluk
asked innocently.

Danaer grimaced, knowing the youth had spent an
easy life. "When we are fleeing from the city and must
have the food and water in order to cross the Sink
successfully once more, back to Siank."

Rorluk's wondering stare shifted from Danaer to
Shaartre and to some of the older men. "You are thinking we may not win?"

"The Royal Commander considers all possibilities,"
Shaartre told him as gently as he could. "A good soldier hopes he will not need such caches as these. But
if disaster comes, the Markuand are not likely to let us
take much out of Deki with us—*if* we can get free."

An even younger conscript than Rorluk was round-
eyed with dread, gazing at the wagons being rolled
into the buildings, at the troopmen and Dekan workmen setting barricades to guard the supplies against
intruders. "Have . . . have you ever had to retreat and
use such caches, Troop Leader?"

"I have," Danaer said grimly, and ended the conversation by walking away.

The wagons that went on from those places now faced a new problem. Where once they had struggled through wet sand and obstacles which slowed the caravan, now drivers stood on brakes to retard their descent. Infantry and cavalrymen slung ropes at the back of the wagons and acted as drags to help the teams. Some wagons overturned, and either the supplies were transferred to vehicles that still operated, or the drivers were ordered to make their way back to the cache points and deliver their cargoes there.

Downward, steadily, the column went, and the country changed from dust and sand to soft earth and grassland thick with brush and copses. The trail wound through pasturage and tilled fields. They were entering the Dekan lowlands, rich river country. Small forests dotted the hills, and little valleys and prairies began to be junglelike. Indeed, a bit farther south this terrain *was* jungle, the start of the Sarlos marshes which led to Lira's homeland.

The trail widened into a true road, and there were more and more villages. The path was beaten earth paved with chips of rock and broken brick taken from old farmhouses and the face of the river bluffs not far ahead. The comparatively smooth highway was a relief to many a driver whose wagons were being held together by little more than rope and curses. Now wheels rolled easier and men marched more quickly.

Bogotana and his demons no longer ruled. Here there were spring-planted fields green with new shoots of grain and pastures grazed by woolbacks and tame motge and roans. Youthful herdsmen tended the beasts, and they looked curiously at the army wagons. Danaer returned their scrutiny, recalling the taletellers' stories of Deki. At Nyald there were few tame motge. But Deki was an ancient city, and here the animals had been domesticated for generations. The herdsmen must drive them out to graze each day, then bring them back to pens near the city walls at nightfall, or perhaps into Deki itself, now that the threat of siege was near. The herds seemed smaller than he had expected, as if many animals had been culled already, to feed a city feeling the hunger of diminished trade and approaching war.

There were few tents about, and no Zsed, just thatched huts made of bricks and quiet little farmers' villages. Deki's inhabitants were Destre who lived a life half nomad and half city-bound. Some still roamed out to hunt the Dekan lowlands, yet deemed themselves citizens, dwellers behind walls. Of late, it was doubtful many hunted at all. Markuand would force them ever more tightly within the security of their defenses. Deki's Siirn had long ruled from behind her gates.

The villagers and herdsmen were content to watch the passing caravan from a distance. They waved, not unfriendly, for they had heard of the new alliance. But they did not as yet trust their old enemies. A few young people decided to prove themselves and finally rode out to meet Danaer and his novices. The boys and girls looked over the three scouts rudely, giggling, and one exclaimed, "It is true. The Siirn promised that the army was coming in force to Deki."

"Did you not believe Lorzosh-Fila, young warrior?" Danaer asked with a smile. None of them was above twelve summers, yet they wore weapons, as befit Destre youth; the knives and lances were castoffs, for the most part, but they flaunted them proudly. The lances were sheathed, Destre style, under stirrup straps, and both boys and girls wore belt blade and boot knife and Dekan mantles. Rorluk and Xashe stared at them curiously, but the youths' attention was held by Danaer. They could not understand his uniform and his Destre ring and cloak. Danaer nodded and told them, "When Royal Commander Malol te Eldri says he will ride to the aid of his Destre allies, he will keep that pledge."

Their laughter rang in the moist, heavy air and they chattered in thick Destre slang, further annoying the two soldiers from The Interior. Danaer glanced warningly at them as one of the girls boasted, "It is Argan who has wrought this miracle, through guiding her Siirn Rena. If Gordt te Raa did not permit it, you would never have crossed the Vrastre alive."

Danaer's comrades sulked while he traded banter

with the young ones, and at last they rode back to tend their herds. Despite their boldness, Danaer had noted their pinched faces and that ribs showed through their thin shirts. Hunger and siege had not quenched their spirit, however. Deki was the Zsed of Walls, and the courage of her people was a badge they might wear proudly.

Zsed of Walls, and The Entrance of Life, as the Ryerdon had called it when first they looked west from this place, ere beginning their trek across the Vrastre. In the old language they had styled it *te Vond ve Exis,* and when Destre tribes came to rule the Vrastre, they did not abandon any of Deki's titles.

It was just past center-stand when Danaer saw the famous walls. Far in the distance, a gray expanse seemed to rise, beginning to fill half the horizon. Not too long after, Xashe and Rorluk also spotted the city, and gasped in wonder. Siank's walls were fragile, a glorification of the goddess formed of stone and paint, for Siank was an Azsed city surrounded by loyal Destre. But Deki was very ancient. For generations she had stood on the brink of Krantin and watched against invasion from once-mighty Traecheus. Her walls were no symbols, but the outer fortifications of a strong city. Deki guarded the river and ruled it, and faithfully protected those who had gone on across the Vrastre. Traecheus had crumbled into dust, never breaching Deki's walls, and Clarique had arisen from the chaos and learned to keep peace between the lands, to share the mighty river.

But Deki's walls must still stand firm, for another enemy was coming, one far more merciless and deadly than ever Traecheus had been. Te Vond ve Exis now must repel the invasion of Markuand, an assault of weaponry and wizardry most evil.

"How close are we, Troop Leader?" Xashe asked in awe.

Danaer squinted and held out his hand, measuring his fingers against the distance. "A candle-period. Perhaps a bit more."

"La! And already we must look up at those battlements!"

It was so. The city rose before them, growing, climbing skyward. Deki was their destination, the reason for the arduous journey.

The walls were uniformly gray and hung with gates of tremendous height and thickness. As a boy, Danaer had been enthralled by minstrels' stories of Deki and heard these walls and gates described. It was one thing to hear of walls so wide a wagon could drive atop them; quite another was it to behold those walls with his own eyes. And the gates! The trees which had birthed them must have been floated downriver from Irico, the fruit of the Death God's haven. Krantin in her earliest days had learned of Irico's matchless timber, and the northern axmen had been willing to trade for Krantin's bright new metals pried from the bowels of her mountains. It was fair trade. The trees were magnificent and the wood resisted rot most well; the metal was silver or the dark iron that Krantin's craftsmen forged into axes far harder than bronze, tools that would not blunt when the forest dwellers of Irico felled their towering trees.

Now Markuand wanted Krantin's metal and Irico's timber, and they were prepared to hurl magic and armies of silent, white-clad soldiers in countless numbers against Deki's walls to conquer both peoples.

The humidity of the lowlands diffused sunlight into a deceiving haze, but Danaer thought he saw some sort of official entourage gathering outside Deki's gates. He threw up his arm to signal the column to a halt, then told his apprentices, "Yistar will now pass the command for everyone to look his best. I hope you saved a clean shirt, as I bade you to ere we left Siank."

At the caravan, a great cacophony filled the air. Equipment clattered and horses whinnied and pawed restlessly, leather squeaked—all combining into great confusion. As Danaer had promised, Yistar's orders were running through the column. Wagons wheeled into line more smartly than most had hoped. Units regrouped. Men sought out their kits and splashed water on dusty faces, brushing stained uniforms. They had been frugal with water, but now there would be plenty. Most of the troops had come from the mountains of The Interior. They had spent their lives near castles and walled cities, and while the size of Deki's defenses impressed them, they looked upon this as a familiar thing, a city as it should be, not the anomaly Siank had been.

Order came into being surprisingly soon. Indeed, the command had been strengthened by ordeal. The losses had been hurtful, but Malol had tried to make allowances for such. Stock had died, wagons had been wrecked and abandoned along the way, and some men had sickened, though very few had died of sunstrokes or accidents. Despite natural hazards and wizardry, it was a far stronger force now than when the shambling company had left Siank garrison days ago.

Gordyan and his warriors came in to join the column, acting as honor guard for the entrance into Deki. Danaer was chasing a few scatterbrained conscripts past the head of the column when he heard Yistar bragging to Gordyan, "It may well be we have stolen a march. Lady Nalu says that General Ti-Mori holds fast with her army along the southern river. She has struck an alliance of her own with a Sarli brigand called Qhorda. And she said in her messages to Malol that we would never reach Deki in time to be of help! Ha!"

"A Destre warrior can cross the Vrastre in a five-day, easily," Gordyan said with a loud snort.

"He does not transport with him a wagon train of supplies to relieve the siege of Deki."

Irrepressible, Gordyan grinned and said, "I know that, but still it is a good jest—to see Straedanfi being escort to a line of creaking wagons." He slapped his big thigh and guffawed. "Straedanfi, the terror of Kakyein's tribes—nursemaid to a bunch of carts!"

Yistar's red mustache bristled. "I do not think Lorzosh-Fila will begrudge the wagons' heaviness, though. And he may appreciate that we brought the caravan through nearly intact. Further, I intend to show him this is a fighting group of warriors, not a gaggle of drivers and plowboys."

Gordyan noticed Danaer and his conscripts going by and winked at him merrily. "Ai! Now to your true work. You on the walls and my warriors on the northern bluffs to guard your flank. And I will match you —if my men do not please Siirn Lorzosh-Fila, I will set them to mucking the army's stables instead of fighting with me. Eh?"

"As may be," Yistar said gruffly, only partially mollified. He glanced at Danaer. "And what are you grinning at, you Nyald lizard-chaser?"

With some effort, Danaer swallowed his laughter. "I think a welcoming committee is approaching us, Captain."

"Mm? Very good! Lieutenant . . ."

"We will be ready." Branra's helmet dangled from his saddle, and as yet he made no move to don it. But the rest of his uniform was quite correct. As Yistar fretted among the other aides, Branra nodded to Danaer and said, "Notify Troop Leader Shaartre I will be wanting your units to lead off. You may ride with them now, for your task is well done." The warmth of Branra's tone was that of one soldier to another, a campaigner complimenting a comrade. Danaer gave him a sharp salute, then chased his conscripts where they belonged.

"There you are," Shaartre said when he reached their units. "Enough time gone, I must say." He swung around to bellow last-minute insults at the lines. "You have saddled those blacks like some fop's carriage team! Straighten up, there. And you, put that helmet on right!"

His apprentices had taken their places and Danaer had assumed his ordinary duties, seconding Shaartre in getting the men set at their best. Then he heard admiring whispers, the sounds soldiers made when looking at an attractive woman. Envying looks flicked toward him, and Danaer turned around quickly, sensing what he would see. Lira was riding along the column toward him. She had discarded the youth's uniform; her bright yellow gown was belted with a kirtle Danaer had not seen before, a narrow little band of leather adorned with chips of obsidian and copper. Her apprentice sorkra cloak, a dun color, not

Ulodovol's dark brown, was flung loosely about her shoulders, stirring a bit in the breeze.

Danaer stepped away from the lines to meet her, wishing they had more privacy. She leaned forward a bit and said softly, "I . . . I wanted to see you before we enter the city." She seemed unusually hesitant, uncertain. Danaer noticed she had tried to disguise the pallor caused by her fatigue with touches of woman's paint. Her lips and cheeks were rosy, a false bit of color. Danaer wanted to say she needed no such shams to enhance her beauty.

"I must ride with Captain Yistar," she said. "See? He even brought along a noblewoman's sidesaddle for me to ride, and my little mare, so I can make a grand impression on the chieftains of Deki. He wishes me to represent all my Web." Her gaiety was as false as the paint, and Danaer felt the terrible fear that filled her being. Her voice lowered, barely audible, as she asked, "Do . . . do you still wear the amulet of Rasven?"

He touched his breast and nodded, wishing he could forget the onlookers and speak freely. She was terrified! Of what? More magic?

"Perhaps it would be better if—but no! You must keep it close with you—always." Lira sucked in her breath sharply. "Oh, Danaer, they are so powerful. *He* is so powerful. There is one wizard who rules them all, the Traech Sorkra thinks. He . . . you must promise you will never take the talisman off. Not for a moment."

Again he nodded, much disturbed. Lira said no more, but tugged the reins and loped back toward the head of the column. She left Danaer touched by a taint of dark things, a daunting reminder that in these matters he was helpless to protect her.

Branra approached them, and Shaartre and Danaer sat up straighter, awaiting his orders. The officer's black moved along easily, sure-footed and unlathered, proof of its rider's skill. Shaartre and Danaer jabbed heels in their mounts, edging them apart, leaving a gap into which Branra could ride. He smiled at the veteran's trick, accepting the invitation and stopping between them. "We move up, directly behind the Captain and the Dekan officials. Be grateful. This way we will not be eating wagon dust."

The Troop Leaders grinned at one another. Branra had adopted their units, and made no secret of it. The Lieutenant went on, "We get the chance to awe the citizens with our splendor. The Captain believes the spectators will grow bored and leave long before our more slovenly troops and rickety wagons pass through the gates. And *our* mounts will be the only ones stabled within Deki, rather than pastured out in the villages. Should the occasion arise, we will act as mounted couriers or escorts for dignitaries. It is unlikely that will be needed. However, bear well in mind that having our horses close at hand also means we have a great advantage during a sudden retreat."

"Are we to expect retreat, my lord?" Shaartre asked with guarded politeness.

"Expect everything, and receive fewer surprises." Branra brushed patrician fingers over his sleeve, preening like a courtier. But his hands were soiled with honest dirt and scratched and scarred from labor and battle, like any common soldier's. He smiled benignly at the Troop Leaders and their units. "Look sharp, now. We will show Deki their walls will have fighting men to defend them now."

The caravan wheeled out, Danaer's units first, past infantry and other cavalry lines, forming up at the head of the column. The dignitaries had come out from the walls and Yistar was exchanging courtesies with them. Danaer watched the proceedings sidelong. Lorzosh-Fila looked thinner than he had at the Destre council; his gaudy Clarique-fashioned sleeved cloak all but hung on his gaunt frame. By his side was a younger Destre, a close attendant or some fellow Siirn; that man's hair was a light brown and his eyes were very dark, perhaps black. After studying him surreptitiously a few minutes, Danaer looked at his mantle to identify his tribe: Ve-Nya. Of course; he was Patkin, brother to Lasiirnte Kandra. It was his life she had feared for when first she had heard news of Markuand and the assault of Deki. He was young, but he looked capable. Danaer felt sure he would acquit himself with honor in the battle to come.

The formalities were lengthy. The alliance was very new and must be treated delicately. The proprieties must be observed, on both sides, with much care that no offense was given to customs of Destre or the army.

At last the flags went up, fluttering colorfully, spelling out this combined force in silk and wool. The red, black, and gold crossed lightnings of The Interior and the green half-moon of Deki stood side by side—the flags, and the warriors they represented. Hard-faced Destre galloped in to join Gordyan's men alongside the wagons. The teamsters eyed them uneasily, preferring their own soldiery as escort. But now the wagons had been delivered to Lorzosh-Fila, and Deki's militia of plainsmen would guard their contents henceforth.

"Forward at a walk, Troop Leaders," Branra said calmly as the Captain and his staff and the Dekans rode toward the gates.

It was pleasing to see improved horsemanship and an even pace. Wagons and foot troops and cavalry went smoothly down the gentle incline. No trees obscured the view now, for the wood nearest the walls had been felled generations ago to fuel the cook fires of Deki. The gates had been opened to welcome the caravan. Like some immense gray woman of stone, the walls flung wide their arms to embrace the army of Krantin.

Danaer sought out Lira's form among those of the dignitaries. Now and then he caught a glimpse of her yellow gown and headband. But she and her mare were so small that they were often hidden behind an official or a staff officer.

The gates loomed frighteningly large, and Danaer was gripped by a strange illusion that the walls had begun to lean outward. Presently they must topple down on the puny caravan below! It was only a trick of his eyes, but most vivid. He looked away from the towering heights and concentrated on the gates. Determinedly, he pulled his lips into a firm line, for it would not do to ride into Deki with his jaw agape like some rude peasant.

Pennants and banners waved, then passed under the massive arch. An audience of eager Dekans craned their necks to peer out of the city and see the oncoming parade. They gawked at their Siirn and Captain Yistar and Lira.

Then Danaer was riding under the arch, through the gates, and into Deki. It was like coming out of blinding sunlight into a windowless cell. The buildings soared above him, sometimes touching above the crooked, narrow street. Everything within Deki was constructed of the same heavy gray stone as the outer walls—like a city made out of a hideous dark fungus which had turned to rock.

He felt momentary panic, thinking of entombment, that peculiar custom the Iit used to honor their dead, burying them in their mountains. What if he should never see the sky again?

This was no way to fight battle. A man should ride on the plains, over hills and valleys with space for a roan to run and slopes to give impetus to lance charge or hurtling sling stone. How could a warrior fight here inside these walls, in these cramped and tortuous alleyways? There was no room here for even a small unit of soldiers to maneuver.

Despite his promise to himself, Danaer looked up apprehensively at the looming structures and his mouth opened in dread. The city was dressed in gray, color of death, like some stony corpse. Osyta's prophecy roared in his mind, and Malol's warnings.

You go into danger, Destre-Y . . .

I do not believe we can save Deki, but we must try . . .

Now that he rode through these impossibly close quarters, Danaer's spirits sank. The only hope for victory lay in keeping Markuand safely outside Deki's walls. If they breached the barricade and entered the city, there would be slaughter to equal the carnage at Jlandla Hill, and worse.

Truly, how *could* a man fight in these cold stone streets?

The answer was obvious, and chilling. A man would not be able to fight long here at all. Surrounded by pitiless gray walls, he could die swiftly, and without any hope of vengeance.

XV

MARKUAND WILL COME LIKE A FLOOD

"THEY ARE TAKING OUT THE WAGONS!" ONE OF THE infantrymen shouted, and a ripple of dismay ran through the marching lines.

"Keep moving," Danaer ordered sternly. They obeyed, but continued to watch with anxious eyes as a stream of civilian refugees moved past them toward Deki's western gates.

"Those . . . those are army wagons," the soldiers protested.

"Ai, the ones in worst shape." Danaer was unsympathetic with their fear. "The passengers are women and babes, now that the supplies are all emptied."

"But they are abandoning us here, with no way to get back across the wasteland!"

Shaartre rode back along the line, adding his voice to Danaer's. Both Troop Leaders wanted to forestall malingering and panic. "What is this nonsense?" Shaartre yelled at them. "Why did you think we came to Deki, soldier? To turn and run immediately? Move! Move!"

Mumbling complaints, they trudged on through the darkening streets. These were the last of the troops to be led to makeshift barracks Deki had provided for the army. Danaer was beginning to wish he had left this lot of puling whiners back at the intersection where he and Shaartre had taken them in hand. The infantrymen had been lolling about, tired and confused, their own Troop Leader having wandered off somewhere. His men were ripe targets for any of the less savory locals who coveted their gear and arms.

If Deki was menacing by light of day, it seemed a maze of stone by night. Blackness filled narrow, winding streets, broken only occasionally by the gleam of smoking torches or lamplight escaping from below-streets doorways. Many Dekans were abroad, towing small carts or toting their meager belonging on heads and backs. A great number seemed to be hurrying to escape the city, willing to risk the dangers of the open lowlands and the Sink beyond.

"This way! Lively, now! Move, you sluggards!" Shaartre guided the ragged group into what was once a large stable belonging to a Dekan merchant. When the newcomers saw some of their comrades awaiting them here, some of their uneasiness dissipated. Shaartre craned his neck and looked back down the street. "Is that the last of them?"

"No stragglers," Danaer assured him.

"Bah! I heard some of these same wet-ears bragging that they wanted to go into Vidik. They boasted, then, that they would have Destre women and would kill any Destre who opposed them. Look at them now. I am glad we are quartered on another street, not rubbing elbows with *this* bag of fools." Shaartre sighed. "Well, we have them safely tucked in, at least. I had best report to Yistar. You go get some sleep."

"I think I will come with you, just to see a bit more of Deki."

A gap-toothed grin was Danaer's reward for that. "Huh! And to see the wizard woman, eh?"

"Is the Lady Nalu quartered with the Captain's staff?" Danaer asked innocently, and Shaartre's laughter rang off damp stone walls.

It was not far to the command post. Siirn Lorzosh-Fila had given over for Yistar's use a large inn. Danaer could well imagine the outrage that confiscation had caused in a Destre city long unused to the presence of any large body of army men. But he would cast his wager on the side of Yistar and Deki's Siirn against any merchant's objections, no matter how wealthy the tradesman might be.

When Danaer and Shaartre arrived at the inn, they were almost bowled over by a courier. The soldier ran out the open doors and leaped on his horse, then raced off on a near collision course with the two Troop Leaders. They gazed after him a moment, then at the steady traffic of officers, and orderlies going and coming from the inn. Everyone seemed bent on important errands. "I will report," Shaartre said, "but I suspect the Captain will not have much time to waste hearing of petty details like ours."

There was a babble of conversation in the main room of the commandeered inn. Messages were dispatched and arguments raged between aides and minor officials of Deki's hierarchy. There were army uniforms and those of Deki's militia, marked by vests stitched with the green half-moon symbol of the city. A few Siank Destre were there as well, and Gordyan most definitely was present. His strong voice overbore many of the others'. The big man was regaling younger members of Yistar's staff. Danaer had heard some of the tales before and smiled at the awe in the junior officers' faces and the way they flinched when Gordyan buffeted them to punctuate his stories.

Then Gordyan saw Danaer and greeted him heartily. He left his audience and led his friend aside, speaking low. "Do you remember what occurred that night near Vidik, hyidu?" His mood was quite altered now, very somber.

Danaer shot a wary look around the room. "Is Hablit here?"

"There are rumors of it. Lorzosh-Fila has set agents to seek him out with all diligence. If he or his traitorous minions lurk in Deki, they will find him. I must soon ride out to the bluffs north of here, so guard your back well while I am gone, eh? What do you here at Straedanfi's little fort?"

"My fellow Troop Leader must report . . ."

"Ah! Long-Fang's snarling of late. It seems Yistar did not win the race against Ti-Mori after all," Gordyan said.

Danaer followed Gordyan's nod. Across the room a curtain was being flung back, revealing an alcove where high officers had conferred in private. Now they came out into the room and much of the chatter ceased. Leading the group were a strong-faced young woman and a strutting bantam of a Sarli. The man was Qhorda, the brigand who ruled the river marshes south of Deki. A notorious thief, he was also a patriot who had struck an alliance with those who had been his enemies, the better to fight Markuand. The woman at his side was taller than he, for she was a Krantin of noble blood. Many had called her mad, but none had gainsaid Ti-Mori when she raised an army to go to the aid of beleaguered Clarique. Long ere most in her own land had sensed the danger of Markuand, she had reacted to this holy cause, trading the luxuries of her rank for the skirted knee breeches and close-fitting tunic of Clarique's army—a uniform now frayed and stained with blood and dirt. The clothes did not conceal a woman's body, but she had cropped her hair and put by all else that might mark her for female. Had her father sired a son, he could not have wished for a more valiant one. But because she denied her sex and birthright, her kindred knew shame. The minstrels, though, already proclaimed Ti-Mori a heroine.

Officers bowed respectfully to them both. The Sarli accepted their homage and preened. Ti-Mori ignored it. But her rapid progress through the room came to an abrupt halt as she noticed Danaer and Gordyan. Qhorda looked them over idly, but Ti-Mori's scrutiny was sharp. "You are Destre, but what are *you?*" she demanded of Danaer. It was not a hostile question, though startling in its bluntness.

"Troop Leader Danaer, in the service of Captain Yistar, my lady . . ."

"General. Call me General." Ti-Mori continued to study him. She reminded him of Branra in her method of assessing a man to see if he was worth the food he consumed and what manner of fighter he would be. Indeed, in her own way, her fame approached Branra's. "Yistar's scout. I think he said he owned one. A useful thing, no doubt, scouring the Vrastre clean of bandit tribes."

She made no concessions to her surroundings or to Gordyan's frown. Qhorda smirked and said, "But bandits can sometimes be useful, eh, General? Do not my men clear the route for your army to control the river marshes?" It was her turn to glower at her ally of the moment.

"Come. We must present our findings to the Captain," Ti-Mori said brusquely, losing interest in Danaer, or in anyone else in the room.

As they left, Gordyan said with a snort, "If I must fight beside a warrior woman, I will take Wyaela, who is not afraid to be a female . . ."

"Or Lasiirnte Kandra?" Danaer teased. The big man actually blushed a bit. "Go tell some more lies to those wet-ears. Maybe it will inspire them as much as Ti-Mori does."

Gordyan returned to entertaining the staff, and Danaer wended through the milling crowd. He toured the main room, peeping through curtains and doors left ajar, but failed to find Lira. Two sentries guarded a wide staircase leading to the upper storey. They did not challenge Danaer when he started up the steps. He feared that laxness boded ill for defenses against spies; neither man had seen him before, and he could have been a Markuand in disguise for all they knew.

Upstairs, more orderlies and aides bustled about, and Danaer carefully kept out of their way as he searched more rooms. At the fifth door he stopped. Lira stood within, reading parchments, her expression deeply introspective. She looked careworn far beyond her tender years. Danaer hesitated to intrude, but as he paused on the threshold, she looked up at him. For a frightening instant she seemed to stare through him. Her mind was someplace impossibly distant from her body.

Warily Danaer approached her, glancing at the parchment she had dropped on a table. Most of the writing was a busy scrawl far beyond his learning. But he could read a few names, ones all too familiar: Hablit and Diilbok. The scribbling was enclosed by a strangely drawn tracery, an intricate and magical net of ink. Looking at it made Danaer dizzy. The dread emptiness had left Lira's eyes now, and she managed a wan smile. "Danaer . . . is it . . . is it well with you?"

It was not her normal tone. She seemed to be returning from wherever her mind had been, a place Danaer had no wish to know. "Ai. Shaartre reports to the Captain, and I hoped to steal some time with you while he does."

"I am glad you did." But her face did not reflect that. Her shoulders slumped and Danaer tried to embrace her. Lira pulled away irritably. "It is these . . . these workings of the Markuand wizard. I had not imagined anyone could be so powerful, and so evil!"

"Let me lend you my strength, qedra," Danaer began. She tensed and shook her head. Yet he felt in her a desire to yield to his protection, a desire she dared not submit to.

"Do you guard the walls tonight?" she asked.

"At midwatch. I am to be Branra's lookout."

She allowed him to take her hands, but still refused his embrace. Danaer had feared that her fingers would be cold, but they were warm, unmoving within his own.

"Warn the Lieutenant to be most alert. I have already spoken to him and Yistar, but I fear they do not quite understand just what threatens us. I have warned the officers so frequently, but I know that in the military sometimes such words are lost along the way."

Her womanly phrasing of a Troop Leader's classic complaint made Danaer smile. "I will warn Branra, and I will be your defender against this wicked Markuand sorcerer."

She trembled violently, resisting his devotion. He sensed that in some unfathomed manner she attempted to protect *him*. Visibly she retreated within herself, to a sanctuary he could not reach. "My Web will defend me."

"Here? So far from Ulodovol?"

Fear flared in her countenance. "Yes! Do not be concerned for me. I am a sorkra, and you do not know our arts in these things. I will be all right. Please go now, and . . . and beware of the unexpected, qedra."

Reluctantly he obeyed. In the doorway he looked back and saw Lira again staring down at the magical parchment, her lips moving. Muttering in his anger and helplessness against these things, Danaer went to find Shaartre and get back to their barracks.

His sour humor did not abate, nor did troublesome thoughts leave when he lay down on his pallet. The straw seemed filled with rocks and crawling with vermin. He tossed restlessly, his dreams ominous. When Shaartre began kicking the men awake at mid-watch, Danaer found a bitter taste in his mouth. Shaartre only laughed when he snapped an obscenity at the older Troop Leader. Danaer set himself to what had to be done.

He armed himself and got others to take up weapons, issuing commands and marching in step. He moved by reflex and long practice, too weary to initiate thought. They tramped through torchlit streets and close alleyways and places so steep the steps cut in the stone resembled ladders. Gradually Danaer came to full wakefulness, at about the time they began mounting a long brick ramp. Lances banged clumsily against walls, and men stumbled over broken pieces of brick and cobblestones. One ramp became another moving at right angles, and then a third turned back on itself, a twisting snake of brickwork, always crawling up toward the unseen stars. Ramps ended and became stairs, then wooden ladders.

Men tripped and puffed and dripped sweat, groping for footing in the wavering light of torches bracketed at irregular intervals along the walls. Danaer whispered to Shaartre, "How far up are we going? I thought we were to guard the walls, not the moon."

"We will be there soon. Patience. I learned this route while you were busy with your witch woman, and you must trust me."

As they continued to climb, Danaer wondered if he could memorize all the twists and turns. He was a scout, but not at all used to this sort of territory. If he had to lead his units back this way in a hurry, could he retrace each staircase and ramp?

At long last they emerged from that ascending tunnel. The dank and filth-strewn streets lay far below. Men took positions along a broad stone banquette, flopping down gratefully and panting after their exertions. Danaer queried Shaartre, then went to a small turret at the junction of two stair tops. "My lord?" he said softly. Branra sat in a tiny room, studying maps by the dim light of a candle. A cloak was thrown over the loophole opening toward the river so that no light could escape in that direction. Branra looked up with a more ordinary form of that air of distraction Danaer had witnessed earlier in Lira. The officer oriented himself to react to the man before him. "Units one through fifteen are now at their positions, my lord."

"You look none too alert," Branra said. "That will not do. I need your sharp eyes. Siirn Lorzosh-Fila says the Markuand have sent attack boats to harass the walls each of the last eight nights. Now that we have arrived, probably they will strike the harder."

"I am awake now, my lord. The Lady Nalu says we must expect wizardry as well as a frontal attack. In what form she does not know. It may be that this night is critical."

"Mm, yes, before we have time to lay our defenses more strongly." Branra snuffed the candle with his hand and rose. "I want you serving as lookout here, near me."

Danaer went to the low wall and peered through the narrow horizontal grille. The angle was wide and gave him an excellent vantage clear to the opposite bank. Branra crossed his arms atop the wall and rested his chin on his knuckles. "Is the river larger than you anticipated, Destre?"

"It is not the Bhid," Danaer admitted, awed. The streamlets of Siank and Vidik and the broad, lazy ooze of Nyald's watercourse were trickles compared to this monster dividing Krantin from Clarique. "The Markuand cannot cross without being seen."

"Stopping them after they cross is the problem. But yes, they are easy enough to see."

All along the far bank lay a golden line of twinkling lights, much like a row of brightly glowing insects. To be seen so far away, those fires would have to be of council size. "Perhaps it is a sham, my lord, to frighten us."

"Perhaps," Branra said morosely. "Our spies give us contradictory reports, as spies usually do. I think we may rely on nothing about these Markuand, or about their black wizard Lira Nalu warns us of."

Danaer strained his eyes looking northward, toward the bluffs where Gordyan must be by now. Then he looked south, though he knew he would not be able to see the marshes in the darkness. Did the Markuand also guard Deki's flanks, where Gordyan and Ti-Mori and Qhorda waited an attack? "How far along the river do the campfires go?"

"Not so far as they did formerly, according to the Dekans. The Markuand now seem to be gathering directly opposite the city. Deki controls the only shallow water and good ferry point for many leagues in either direction. North stand the bluffs and the Irico Falls; south lie the marshes and the white water rocks. The odds are worse there than here." Branra was bareheaded, his brow glistening with sweat and his dark hair straggling damply over his forehead. He shooed away midges and spoke calmly of the situation confronting Krantin. "Whoever leads the enemy is canny in both magic and tactics. He will strike here. He must crush Deki first if he hopes to conquer our land."

Danaer gazed at the fires. What had Lira said at the council? *It seemed that their numbers were endless.*

He heard murmuring voices far below and peered over the wall. A few fishermen had anchored their rafts and cast lines, trying to keep to their trade despite the dangers of war. Their cries of satisfaction when they landed fish rose in the muggy air. Danaer's eyes were adjusting rapidly to the night, and he could easily discern their dark forms. He could also see the broken remains of a quay, demolished by the Dekans in order to deny landing to the Markuand. Every wharf and pier along the bank had been razed, converted into rocky barricades to wreck the bottom of craft which came too near. Calculating the drop to that wreckage, Danaer saw that Deki's eastern walls were much higher than the western ramparts, lofty though those were, for these defenses were built on part of the bluffs. Beneath crenels and watchtowers the massive wall dropped smooth and sheer to a rock-strewn landing area many lengths below. The river gate, like the once-proud quays, was battered into uselessness and obstacles heaped before it. Not even the Dekans could now use the gate. The fishermen must have rowed here from somewhere else along the banks, from bluffs or marshland. Deki was locked solidly against any assault from the east.

Danaer studied the broad face of the river and the fires a long while. Sentries patrolled the stairs and ramps, and soldiers hunkered at their posts. Officers took messages and gave orders. Once Captain Yistar and Lorzosh-Fila walked by Branra's position, surveying the condition of the defenses, then returning to a command location elsewhere on the walls.

Well past the middle of the night, Danaer suddenly leaned forward and squinted into the blackness.

"What is it?" Branra came at once to see what had drawn the scout's notice.

"I am not sure, my lord. A boat? Perhaps a swimmer?"

"The fishermen?"

"They have gone. No, this is something that was not there before. See the wake?" Danaer pointed to a shimmering disturbance in the river, an arrow of water aiming at the walls.

"Your eyes are better than mine. I . . . I see nothing."

The vee of that wake was very close now, no more than twenty lengths out. Danaer glanced briefly at the officer, reading his face. Branra did not doubt him, but he truly did not see anything. Nor, it seemed, did any other lookout; no cry of alarm came from other posts along the walls.

Danaer sensed an unpleasant and increasingly familiar coldness stealing through his marrow, radiating from the obsidian talisman. Lira was not with him, but this was very near the same chill he had felt outside her tent. "It *is* a boat's wake," Danaer said decisively.

Branra leaned over the wall and slapped the stones in his frustration. "I still cannot see it. Where do you make it come to berth?"

The mysterious movement in the water was disappearing even now, and Danaer quickly traced it toward the head of the watery arrow, slightly to his left and squarely against the sheerest part of the wall.

"Indeed?" Branra said in a tight voice. "Come." He was angry, but the anger was not directed at Danaer. Puzzled, the scout hurried after him. They raced down ladders and stairs and ramps, taking a different route than the one Shaartre had followed.

Once in the streets, Branra led the way past the huge barred gates, which were protected by sentries even though the outer approaches were thoroughly barricaded. The officer rushed through cluttered, twisting lanes foul with slops. As he passed, guards straightened and dropped their lance butts on the stone pavement, coming to abrupt attention, saluting in surprise, then staring at Branra and the soldier at his heels. Danaer suspected the two of them looked like a hunting wolf trailed by a bewildered cub.

"Are we near the place, would you say, scout?"

"Ai, my lord, I make it very close."

"Sergeant of the Post?" Branra hailed. A squad stood at attention near the end of the little street. Their arms did not move, nor did they blink in response. They seemed frozen.

For a moment Danaer thought they had been slain and propped up in these lifelike attitudes to serve as decoys, a Destre ruse he knew well. Branra was acquainted with the same trick, and they both moved forward cautiously, hands on their swords. Taking a deep breath, Danaer shook the arm of the man commanding the post, a fellow Troop Leader from Siank garrison. Instantly the soldier's eyes opened wide, and he cried out and seized Danaer's tunic. "What? What is this? Why . . . why, my lord. How? Why . . ."

It was plain the fellow was as lost as one yanked out of a deep sleep without any warning. The scent of witchcraft filled the street as the man gaped about in pitiful confusion. Branra pointed to the other sleeping men trapped in a waking nightmare. "Rouse them. Your little sorkra was indeed wise to warn us of magic this night."

As Danaer brought each man back to himself, Branra questioned the stunned Troop Leader. "Did anyone approach your post? Did you see anyone? Was any attempt made to accost you, to cast charms or spells over you?"

"I . . . I swear, my lord, no one! We saw no one. It . . . all at once the two of you were here and . . ."

Branra edged toward a narrow opening beyond the post, peering into the dark space. "What is this?"

"Part of the original walls." Branra put a finger to his lips and the man spoke more softly. "So the Dekans told us." In whispers, Branra bade him fetch reinforcements. Eager to make amends, the man ran off and soon returned with two more squads of unit men and some Dekan militia.

Branra and Danaer had squirmed into the opening and examined the stone crevice. Danaer held a torch while Branra scraped at the dust with his boot, then knelt to probe at a pile of brush against the wall. His eyes met Danaer's. Brush, here in a city of stone?

Keeping Branra's order for silence, the soldiers and militiamen crept into the narrow passage, clustering around Danaer and the officer. Danaer put out the torch and they stood listening in the dark. Behind the brush there was a soft clinking and scrabbling and male voices. Danaer's gut tightened and he slid his sword from its scabbard, as did Branra and all those who had such weapons. Others hefted cudgels and stood ready with lances, their attention focused on the wall.

Something fell within, and there was a momentary hush, as if the unseen workmen feared they might have been overheard. Then they moved again and stone scraped against stone. With much grunting and alien cursing, a part of the wall was being removed. Feebly, filtering through the brush, came the gleam of a lantern.

Steadily the enemy gnawed away at the city's belly, burrowing through a forgotten chink in Deki's armor.

Then the lantern's gleam drew nearer the brush and fingers groped through broken stone, digging at loose pebbles, pushing debris into the alleyway where Branra and his men waited. A white-clad arm, covered with stone dust and dirt, swept aside the last of the loose fill and brush, and a man stepped through the newly created doorway, beckoning out those behind him.

"Now!" Branra roared as the unsuspecting sappers crawled out into his trap. The lantern was with them, behind them, silhouetting them as ready targets for those standing in the darkness.

What Lira had described was true—the Markuand, even when stabbed or battered, did not scream. But they could fear, and seek life, and two of them rushed back into the opening they had just left, as their companions were being killed. Branra and Danaer ran after them, eager in pursuit. The sappers' tunnel became their grave. It was not true swordwork, but more like killing rats with great knives.

Their swords gory, Danaer and the officer stood over the bodies and peered deeper into the man-made cave. "They broke all the way through," Branra said incredulously. Five lengths' distant they could see another opening at the far end of the tunnel, with rippling water lit by the faraway Markuand camp-fires.

How was it possible? How could the Dekans not have detected such extensive tunneling within the very bowels of the walls? Surely this had been the work of many nights, and the sappers' boat would have been seen. . . .

The tunnel air was heavy with the odors of earth and stone, but to Danaer another smell pervaded the place—the reek of wizardry. The tension in his belly became a hurtful knot. He had seen the boat's wake, but he wore Lira's talisman. The Deki lookouts had not. Was this the reason . . . ?

"My lord, I do not think we are alone, nor were these the last of the Markuand to invade the walls."

"What?"

Even as Danaer spoke, a shadowy shape eased away from the side of the tunnel ahead—a man shape, large and powerful. A terrible aura of evil emanated from that form. Branra's further questions were still-born in his throat as the nobleman sensed the same horror now raking Danaer.

"The Markuand wizard!" Danaer realized with a shock he had blurted that aloud, without conscious thought or will.

"We must destroy him!" Branra shouted, charging forward, Danaer right behind him, fury overriding his fear.

The shadow shape retreated toward the opening in the outer wall. He was trapped! If his magical glamour had hid the boat, it would not protect him now. Branra was almost upon him, and if the wizard took to the river, he would shout for archers and burning oil to send the enemy sorcerer to his death in the water.

They roared in triumph, daring to anticipate victory over this awful foe . . .

And then the tunnel filled with sunlike brilliance. Branra and Danaer instinctively flung up their hands to save their eyes. They held out their swords blindly, fending off attack—but attack did not come as the brilliance died.

Danaer and Branra were unhurt—but the wizard was gone. The opening in the wall was empty, and there was no sound of oars or a boat on the water beyond. Branra threw himself down at the edge, peering out. The entrance was barely wide enough to admit his head and shoulders. The sappers must have had to climb in on their bellies.

"Do you see him?" Danaer asked. Even as he spoke, he felt a peculiar emptiness, no longer cold, and knew that they were truly alone once more.

Branra spat a soldier's oath and crawled backward until he reached a spot where he could stand nearly upright. "Nothing!" he snarled. "No sign of him! We saw him—and then he was gone!"

Branra was not the sort who could swallow defeat easily. He paced like a man-eater robbed of his prey, an emotion Danaer well appreciated, suffering his own deep frustration. A few of the soldiers poked their heads through the brush-cluttered opening, staring in wonder. Finally Branra gave up and snapped orders for the bodies to be dragged out of the tunnel. He and Danaer followed and inhaled the comparative freshness of open air.

"A tunnel," the Sergeant of the Post was mumbling. "Must be a cave-in. Some fault in the walls that permitted these sappers to—"

"Use your head, troopman," Branra said. "It was no cave-in. Those stones were moved by labor and stealth while Deki defended her walls above the sappers."

"But . . . how, my lord?"

Branra's glare was fierce, and Danaer spared his fellow Troop Leader the pain of another sharp answer. "It was wizardry." The men shuddered and spoke prayers.

"Get our own sappers, Sergeant," Branra said. "I want this tunnel blocked at once, completely! Now! Have them move from the outside in, and be sure it will withstand any enemy undermining henceforth." As they ran to do his bidding, Branra leaned against the gray stones and looked up at the wall. "It took our ancestors many a long year to build walls so high and so well, when Deki was founded. And now Markuand uses magic to breach them. That wake you saw in the water . . ."

"I *did* see it, my lord," Danaer said defensively.

"Well that you did." For the first time in some minutes Branra smiled. "At any rate, we have now gained precious time and foiled their attempt to strike at our backs."

Dekan sappers arrived and began work on the tunnel, and Branra ordered the Sergeant of the Post to stand close guard until it was done.

"I will, my lord. And this time I will not sleep."

His earnestness softened Branra's irritation. "You

were not asleep. But perhaps the enemy will find itself too busy to trouble us further with these enchantments. Keep alert, and call for help if you suspect someone tries to cast a spell over you."

Danaer and Branra headed back toward the ramps leading to the walls, and Branra shook his head, repeating with consternation, "Enchantments."

"Kant, prodra Argan," Danaer said piously to ward off more magic.

"Your goddess protect us all, here in a city of her Azsed-Y." Branra lifted his hands to the starry skies. "All you immortal ones, lend us your strength against this Markuand. We need your help sorely!" The sight of Branraediir of the Bloody Sword, notorious for his disbelief in anything but the Royal Commander and his weapon, invoking any gods who could hear him, unnerved Danaer almost as much as the wizardry they had confronted.

Respectfully quiet, he accompanied the Lieutenant back to the ramparts. Yistar was informed of the incident, and messengers were sent to the inn to notify Lira, if she did not already know through some sorkra methods.

The Captain would spread the word to be on guard. But he could do little to combat wizardry. Any countermeasures must fall upon Lira and her arts—one more weight added to her tremendous burden.

Danaer took his station again and resumed his staring across the river. There was an empty barge tied below the place where the tunnel had been dug. The wizard had left behind his boat! Danaer did not like to imagine what dark powers the Markuand sorcerer had used to escape—without boat or without need of swimming!

For a long while he gazed at the watch fires. The night had darkened with clouds, and the strain of seeing through this made him close his eyes now and then to ease them. He began to wish for action to break the tedium, though no more magic!

He rested his eyes, then opened them, not quite believing what he saw. He could swear by his eiphren that the opposite bank was closer than it had been before, the watch fires coming toward him. A heartbeat or two later, Danaer realized that something formerly connected with the bank had begun to move away, across the river.

As before, Branra was by his side before Danaer had a chance to call him. Danaer relayed his discovery, whispering, half afraid of some unseen presence overhearing them. Other lookouts at other posts were shouting and summoning their officers. So it was no illusion made only for Danaer's eyes.

Branra gave orders and there was a stir among the men, a tightening of discipline. The banquette and walkways were full of men, but now more came to join them, forming a second row of defense. Men buckled helmets and fussed with the placement of their extra weapons, lances laid ready at their feet.

Branra cautioned and encouraged, every now and then glancing toward the river. Even in the dim light, it was impossible not to see the glitter in his eyes. Plainly he knew far more joy in facing a multitude of enemy warriors than one Markuand wizard.

"This is no feint," he said, surveying the oncoming flotilla. "The Dekans said all previous attacks had been of an uneven nature. Those boats are well massed."

"We blocked their secret passage and thwarted their wizard. It must have taken much of his energy to escape us," Danaer speculated. "Now they must attack us straightforwardly, my lord."

"Ai!" Branra gripped his shoulder tightly in comradeship of arms. "On our terms, and against our strong fortifications!"

The moving "bank" the lookouts had detected was now visible to those with less trained eyes. Boats of diverse sizes and shapes bobbed over the slow current, aiming for the walls. To those awaiting the attack it seemed the moments crept by. Every man now shared part of Branra's eagerness, wanting the suspense to be ended.

Danaer, too, was glad the enemy was coming at last. Yet he thought of Lira and Gordyan and his friends in the troop, the pleasures of good wine and warm fire

. . . the comforts of the flesh. Would he know these things after tonight? Or would Argan beckon him to Keth's portals? He must not dwell on doubt. If his life was forfeit, he would die a warrior, honoring his name and taking many Markuand with him. He heartened himself with the memory of the ha-usfaen. Strange! Her lithe body seemed smaller than he recalled, and she resembled Lira as much as the goddess.

But Argan was all female, all women—and she knew how to touch a warrior's heart with fire, giving him visions he desired; she was priestess and goddess and beloved in one.

Slay the Markuand for me, faithful ones! Send me the souls of the Markuand. Let us revel in your victory!

Danaer caught up the trailing hem of his mantle and tied it across his chest. A loose cloak might tangle his own blade as well as the enemy's.

How long since he had sighted the Markuand boats? A clock-period? Surely not so long. But then time was nothing.

Everyone saw them clearly now. The dark shapes were boats and rafts laden with soldiers. And there were also towers, miniature forts reared on stilts and floated on barges, waddling into shallow water.

Flame lanced out from the towers, arcing toward the walls. Danaer crouched behind the parapet as three waves of fiery arrows sailed in high parabolas above his head. Most struck the ramparts or bounced harmlessly down onto the banquette, where the defenders stamped out the flaming heads. Some soared on into the city, and Danaer hoped those patrolling the streets would be watchful, for there was much thatch to tinder a fire if they did not pluck out the arrows quickly.

On a still higher level of the wall, catapults hurled huge rocks back at the approaching boats. The stones whistled through the air in short, flat trajectories. Danaer waited hopefully for the impacts, then narrowed his eyes, doubting what he saw. The rocks were striking some invisible barrier a length ahead of the towers, then ricocheting off and down into the river. A few missiles broke through, with the loud smack and crunch of stone breaking wood and bone. But most of the defenders' artillery was wasted, never reaching the enemy.

Where had he seen this before?

It came to Danaer in a rush—Prince Diilbok, riding at the edge of a riot, posturing courageously while no arrow or club or rock could strike him, though many were thrown at the drunken fop. It had seemed the whim of some god then. But now Danaer suddenly recognized the similarity. Wizardry! As the Prince had been protected, so were the siege towers and boats—not by gods, but by evil magic!

He must tell Lira about this! She in turn could reach out through her Web and speak to Ulodovol. The Royal Commander must be warned that his sotted kinsman was more than he seemed.

Treachery—everywhere! The accusations Diilbok had laid against Danaer? Not mere drunken meanness, but an attempt to silence the one man who could prove the rioters' true identity. And the riot? To ruin the alliance ere it could begin. How the opposition dreaded the joining of Destre and Iit!

Diilbok was the King's own kinsman, and if he plotted with wizards and assassins . . . !

Danaer could not linger over the worrisome discovery. Death, garbed in white, was fast drawing near.

There were few flame-tipped arrows shot now. But bowstrings still sang and rains of barbed shafts flew in both directions as the Markuand archers and Deki's few bowmen dueled. Whenever one of the arrows or catapult stones broke through the wizard's barrier and struck home, the soldiers and Dekans cheered mightily. However strong his enchantments, it seemed the Markuand wizard could not protect all his forces at once. Some rocks smashed into boats and tipped or sank them. The archers on the walls cut down many a Markuand with their cruel arrows.

They did not die screaming. When a man defending the walls was hit, he might gasp in shock or cry out if he was from The Interior. But as the Markuand went down, there was no sound. The sappers had died silently, too. And unlike the Destre, these Markuand had no battle shouts, no ululating shrieks to terrorize their foes. Did their commanders tear out their tongues to bind them to such muteness? Or . . . was this more evidence of magic?

Danaer had no bow, and the boats were still too far away to waste a lance. But he loosed his sling and risked peeping over the wall and trying for a kill. It took four attempts before he at last struck cleanly. The white uniforms reflected star and torchlight and distant campfire well, and he saw a Markuand officer topple off the edge of his raft. At once another moved to assume his place. There was no moan or plea for help, no confusion.

The deadly, silent Markuand . . . Deki's defenders now sensed why the Clarique had been stunned to meet such a foe, and ripe for the conquest. Krantin had been warned, and though this thing made men shiver, they did not panic and flee.

Boats and tower floats rode above the stony barricade strewn against the walls, and white-clad soldiers debarked, scampering forward. The smack of wood against stone warned those above that ladders were being put in place, ladders of incredible length to scale Deki's mighty walls.

Now the Markuand siege towers used their own catapults, aiming high for their opposing members and for the groups of archers on the lofty parapets. A storm of countering fire raged back and forth as the towers groaned ever closer.

Danaer dared a peek through the lookout's grille, seeing the towers creeping inexorably over the ruins of the quays and wharves. Over broken stone and the bodies of their dead, they came. By morning, the river would be thick with blood and splintered weapons.

"Steady, now!" Branra bellowed, in a voice any Troop Leader would envy.

Arrows hummed like bees, and to Danaer's left a man screamed and clutched an arrow which caught him full in the breast. He lunged upright, then toppled over the wall, smashing down on the rocks. One of his friends wailed in anguish, "He would never keep his head down!"

One tower was now directly in line with Danaer's

section of wall. There was a room built near its top, and Markuand milled about inside. Arrows and rocks continued to bounce away before they could seriously damage the machine.

"Ready, warriors!" Branra again. His voice was like his sword, cutting fear away from them all, steeling them with battle fever.

Like some tremendous wooden demon, the mouth of the tower opened. Running across plankwork and toward the walls, on a new-made bridge, came the Markuand—silent, white-clad, with swords and lances and axes in their hands.

XVI

WIZARDRY MOST PROFOUND

THERE WAS A GAP BETWEEN PLANKING AND WALL, and the foremost Markuand threw down pieces of wood to span the rest of the distance, bracing the device atop an attack ladder. Defenders thrust at the makeshift bridge with pikes and lances, trying to dislodge it. Noise ruled the scene, for though the Markuand did not scream in pain, they could not still their feet or the sounds of their weapons; and Deki's warriors cursed and shouted and cried in triumph or agony as blade or lance or arrow met flesh.

As the first wave of invaders clambered atop the wall, Danaer drove the flat of his sword against a Markuand belly. The man tried to strike with his ax. Sprawled on the parapet, the Markuand was easy prey, and Danaer brought down the blade hard between shoulder and neck. Then he upended the slain Markuand, flinging the body over the wall.

The white-clad foe was everywhere now, weapons in constant play. One Markuand leaped over the crenel to Danaer's left; before he could turn to counter, Branra was there, as swift as a lightning stroke. The invader dropped in a gory heap and Branra immediately attacked another opponent.

A Markuand fell heavily against Markuand as Dekan pikemen dispatched him. Together the Dekans and Danaer heaved the corpse down into other enemies just mounting the wall. In a tangle, living and dead disappeared into the darkness below with a sodden splash.

As each head or body appeared, Danaer struck reflexively, and so did most of the other defenders. Men moved in concert, a ritual of slaughter, a deadly dance.

"Archers!" Branra yelled above the din. "Now! Set the towers afire!"

They strove to obey him. At first the fire-arrows and globbets of balled fire bounced away uselessly, as they had before. But as the barrage kept on, Danaer felt an odd pressure building, a tautness in the air and a crackling.

Lira? Hurling her magic against the mighty Markuand wizard?

She was taxing him, while he must be put to his utmost powers, for the assault of the Markuand pressed forward all along the river, and surely he could not be everywhere at once.

Danaer's talisman was quiet, but he sensed Lira's presence, though he could not see or hear her. The tension in the air grew, like stinging nettles raking along his skin, and an eerie blue glow limned the siege towers—the unseen barrier, becoming solid!

And then it burst! All at once the fire-arrows struck home, and so did the catapults' missiles. Markuand plucked out the blazing shafts embedded in the towers and tried to throw them away before their siege machines caught fire. Their white clothes in flames, they fell like living torches. The towers were now so close that Deki's archers skimmed their shafts barely above the heads of the defenders, a whistling melody accompanying the raging man-to-man battle.

Indeed, it was a battle, true and untainted by wizardry at last! Arms and courage alone would now decide this outcome. The fearful cloud of wizardry which had shielded the Markuand melted away. Every man on the walls seemed to feel the same release Danaer did, an inner knowledge that he could strike and no magic would thwart him.

For long minutes they were all absorbed in the business of keeping alive. Arrows sped toward targets, the Markuand hurled back flaming torches, and men died. Again and again Danaer slashed at the oncoming white wave, a wave of soldiery seemingly without end.

Branra howled elatedly and others took up the cheer. The siege machines were ablaze, and the Markuand were climbing out onto ropes, trying to escape the flames. Silent or not, they feared death. The ropes burned through and many fell to the rocky waters. Others dived off, preferring a quick end to a pyre. The pikemen seized on that confusion, put their shoulders to dislodging the makeshift bridge, and succeeded. The bridge carried with it those Markuand who had been crossing to the walls at that moment. One jumped off and clung to the parapet ledge. A soldier, using a shield against the onslaught of Markuand arrows, leaned over and prodded until the enemy's fingers lost their grip and he too fell.

Branra exhorted his troops to press the counterattack. "This must be their main assault! Get oil on those scaling ladders, quickly!"

In the bright light of the burning towers, the scene below was order being rebuilt of chaos. With superb discipline, the Markuand paddled forward in small landing boats to take the places of the dead and injured. They did not help the wounded but kicked them aside mercilessly or walked over them.

Heavy cauldrons were wheeled out of special bastions and slid out into the machicolations Deki's wise defenders had constructed long ago. Soldiers drew back to permit the sweaty operators to work their contrivances. Ropes were pulled and chains fed through pulleys, and the cauldrons poured their boiling contents of searing oil onto the Markuand below.

Even then, there were no screams. But a chorus of

shocked, strangling noises rose, as if agony caught in tens of throats of the tortured and dying. There was a terrible hiss and a column of steam as hot oil and scalded bodies fell into the cold river.

A second siege machine cast grappling hooks into the flaming wreckage of its predecessor, attempting to pull apart the remains to clear a path for its own approach to the walls. Still other towers vied for attack vantages all along the walls at other points.

"Save the ricochets," Branra commanded, and the word was passed. Troopmen retrieved spent Markuand arrows and returned them to Deki's archers. Soon more fiery shafts were winging toward the second row of towers, setting those ablaze, too.

But some of the Markuand arrows could not be retrieved without the aid of surgeons. At least five men lay near Danaer, writhing and pleading for help as they struggled in their own blood. How many more defenders had been wounded or were dead?

Though their aim was sometimes shaky and the fusillade ragged, the archers succeeded in setting more towers and barges afire. The burning platforms and the accumulation of bodies began to block all further attack at those places. Branra regrouped his units at the vulnerable spots as Markuand swarmed up the ladders not hit by the boiling oil, undeterred by the fate of their comrades.

Danaer parried and thrust and slashed mindlessly now. The Markuand must not cross the wall, and any who did must die. The banquette was slippery with blood and the footing treacherous. It was difficult to move now without treading on the fallen. Markuand and defenders were tangled together. No man had the leisure to discover if those groaning forms were friend or foe.

More oil, more arrows, little feathered lances—blows from the Death God tipped with deadly metal.

No more did Deki's defenders shout defiance. They became almost as silent as the Markuand, too spent to exhaust themselves in speech.

Danaer did not know how long this had gone on. He had never fought so desperately, not in any of

Yistar's campaigns, not in any knife fight in a Zsed. But finally he heard Branra ordering men to hold their arrows and rest on their weapons. Danaer, sore-eyed with weariness, slumped against the wall and stared out at the river, uncaring that he exposed himself to possible return fire. There was no longer a need for such caution.

The river was clogged with tens upon tens of Markuand boats, but most were burning. All the siege towers were in flames or already blazing to the water-line. And everywhere were bodies, crushed or impaled or broken. Piled in bloody heaps on the rocks' broken teeth. Some dangled lifelessly from the towers or across the sides of boats. Some floated in backwaters, the current tugging at them, a few beginning to drift downstream. Dawn was starting to dapple the sky with gold, and showed Deki a vista of unallayed carnage. Redder than the flames ran the mighty Irico River, streaked with the gore of the dead and dying Markuand.

Men lay down where they had fought, heedless of the hard stone bed beneath them or the stench of death or the cries of their fellows. Surgeons came and carried the wounded to their workrooms below, and the dead were shrouded and borne away.

There was no relief. Every warrior who had been able to wield a weapon had gone to the walls this night. In a half doze, Danaer knew that Yistar and and the Siirn were conferring with Branra, speaking in low and worried tones. The Captain's helmet was badly dented, and clotted blood smeared his brow and cheek. He too had waged personal war on the Markuand. Despite his stamina, even Branra looked tired. In disjointed sentences, the officers and Lorzosh-Fila talked of losses and regrouping and how they must withstand other attacks.

Danaer watched them listlessly. There was something he meant to say, to the officers or to Lira—some important thing he had learned amid the battle. But he could not remember what it was. It could not be so important as sleep. Nothing could.

He wanted to go back to his barracks and sink into

his pallet, vermin-riddled or not. But they were commanded to stay where they were. And sleep was difficult to find, even if they were exhausted. Day had come, but that was no respite. The sun was barely above the horizon when a thick fog rolled out from the Clarique bank. The Dekans muttered in superstitious fear and said the fog in these regions never behaved so. The strange mist crept over the river until it reached the destroyed siege towers, and there it hovered. In the fog there were sounds—oars and creaking of boats and noises that might have been men shifting about in craft or clashing weapons together softly as they prepared a foray. One false alarm after another was cried, and weary officers and men stared into the alien mist, unable to penetrate its secrets. If Lira was countering this latest magic, she could not remove it completely. Now and then the fog moved back a pace, only to roll in again, and the sounds came with it.

And while they endured the uncertainty of the fog sounds, a cold sleeting rain began to fall on the defenders. This, too, was unnatural and unseasonal, as had been the mirages and the storm which tore the Destre council tent. Men shivered miserably and crawled beneath whatever shelter they could find, their chance for sleep ripped from them by discomfort and fear. Lookouts like Danaer kept short watches, taking turns trying to see into the fog, until their eyes drooped and they were told to sleep—if they could.

Danaer had cursed bad conditions often during war and campaigns in Yistar's service. But it was patently unfair to suffer the plagues of witchcraft in the form of weather. Silently, he begged Lira to find some measure to give them surcease.

Yet she was alone, days away from her Web, and the Web was busy in other matters they deemed equally important. Lira had to fight this battle alone. She had broken the wizard's barriers and let the arrows reach the towers. But like all the defenders, such terrible exertions must exhaust her. She too needed rest, though she wielded no sword and shed no blood.

Danaer longed to be with her, support her as he had in the council tent when he and Kandra had kept her safe from the buffeting wind. He must stay on the walls, though, and she in her room at the inn, bearing her burden of darkness and sorcery.

The rain was followed by a brief hail, pellets of ice that hurt and drew welts and blood. Men swore and shook their fists helplessly at the sky and endured what they must. Some raged against these unholy things and became hysterical and must be restrained by their comrades. The cost in broken sleep and tenseness was heavy.

When the hail ended, Danaer again felt that gentle ebbing sensation, a touch of Lira, though she was nowhere in sight. After that there were no more unnatural torrents, and in what was left of the day men drowsed in peace.

The second night was much worse than the first. The assault was no greater or more fierce, but now the defenders knew what they must expect. They had hoped Markuand had spent its fury in that massive attack. But another flotilla left the Clarique bank, coming toward the walls. There were more siege towers to replace those lost, more white-clad, silent warriors eager to fight and die, inhuman in their refusal to be thrown back short of death.

Many men doubted they could withstand another such terrible attack, but they found courage in themselves they had not known existed. It was not even a thing of honor, for they could not think that clearly. They fought to survive, lifting weary arms again and again, striking and killing as they must. Citizens with hay forks and other homely implements ill-made for war filled the gaps left by Deki's wounded, standing next to soldiers and militiamen. They fought clumsily but with fervor. Some were well dressed and had obviously never known privation. Others were gutter sweepings of the lowest sort, conscripted by Lorzosh-Fila in an attempt to hold his city. Merchant and peasant and beggar and soldier stood and fought together and died together.

But they held. There was more magic, more

shielding of the Markuand towers. And more counter-magic from Lira, the tingling in Danaer's talisman and that crackling pressure in the air, and a bursting of the Markuand wizard's spells. Like the gently bred Dekan merchants, Lira was engaged in a war much against her nature and against a foe with many times her powers. Yet the combined forces of her dedicated sorkra arts and the valiant defenders of the walls threw back the Markuand once more.

The dead were past counting now. Deki's own losses were severe, but nothing to the carmine harvest of the river. As Deki had protected ancient Ryerdon's people against invasion from Traecheus, now she successfully held off the onslaught of an alien enemy evil beyond comprehension.

Danaer had no spirit to welcome the second dawn breaking over the scene of butchery. Like the rest, he dropped in his tracks, barely able to move. Then came an order he did not believe—he and those who had been there since the first night were to go to their quarters and sleep. Danaer peered over the parapet at the Clarique bank. There were no more boats, no wizard's fog filled with warlike and ominous sounds. The fires were gone, mute proof of the toll of the battle. Uncaring, beyond wondering on this, Danaer staggered down ladders and ramps and followed some kindly citizen who led his surviving unit mates to their shelter within a barn. Men fell on their blankets, asleep before they could stretch their lengths.

Much later, Danaer slowly wakened and sat up, running his tongue over crusted and foul-tasting lips. The candle on the wall indicated that he had dreamed for ten marks. His arm still ached from the swordplay he had put it to, and from the weight of Markuand bodies he had thrown back over the wall.

Had it really happened? The second night of battle was a blur. There had been towers, more arrows, more boiling oil, and many, many bodies. He ground his knuckles into his eyes and cheekbones, yawning back to some semblance of awareness.

It had happened—all of it. And when it was done, Markuand had seemed broken, her fires gone, her boats all smashed, and her army drowned in the bloodied river. Markuand did not know retreat, and neither did Deki, for there was nowhere to go. Every Markuand who crossed the river attempted the walls, and all of them died. Soldiers had tried to take some prisoners, only to lose men as the Markuand stabbed their captors and killed several. After that, the Siirn ordered all to be slain, as they had dealt with the Clarique they had captured at Jlandla Hill. They gave no quarter and asked for none, and died in silence.

Yistar had made some sort of announcement that his sorkra had penetrated the Markuand wizard's plans and found there would be no more frontal attacks. Danaer wondered if he remembered that aright. If so, it was gladsome news. As many men as Deki had lost, Markuand had unquestionably lost more, and perhaps his generals had slain their wizard, deeming him a false sorkra.

Danaer stared down at himself. His helmet had rolled off and lay beside the pallet. He had slept on his sword, not out of diligence but because he was too tired to remove it. His clothing stank. Like any Destre, he did not scorn dirt, but the shirt and breeches were stiff with gore and spittle and chafed him sorely.

"Awake at last?" Danaer blinked at Shaartre as the older man limped toward him. Shaartre was a bit pale. "I have found you another uniform, so give me those rags. Some Dekan laundresses set up their tubs outside and offer to serve the 'brave soldiers.'"

Danaer began to strip, pointing to the leg Shaartre favored. "What happened? I did not know you were wounded."

"Ah, it was not too bad. I lasted both nights. Luckily the Markuand arrow was nearly spent when it struck me. The surgeons wanted to keep me in the infirmary, but I know better than to lie abed while my leg cripples on me." The Troop Leader treated his close escape lightly. "Besides, Yistar needs everyone who can fight. We are off duty for now, but stand ready to assemble should the call come. They say there will be no more attacks, but . . ."

Danaer went to the water barrel and stood in the

catch pan, pouring several dippersful of rainwater over his itching flesh. It washed away the worst grime and left him more awake. As he put on the uniform Shaartre had brought, he noted neatly sewn tears on the tunic's belt line. The man who had suffered that wound must be dead. Danaer asked no questions. The previous owner would not come seeking his uniform, certainly, and Danaer had no compunction about wearing it.

Shaartre snatched up his discarded garments, and Danaer had to jump to rescue his Destre mantle. True, it was also badly dirtied, but he would not risk it to the untender mercies of laundresses' rocks and washing paddles. Shaartre flung the dirty clothes to a passing soldier and ordered him deliver them to the tubs outside. Then he grinned and winked at Danaer. "We will all get new issue when we return to Siank garrison."

"If we ever return to Siank."

"We shall, youngling. You have not heard all the news—your big friend Gordyan had an easy time on the bluffs, killing many Markuand. They never came close to the top. And they say Qhord's cutthroats did for the Markuand by the hundreds, and any who got through the marshes were torn to pieces by Ti-Mori's harpies. We suffered at Deki, ai, but we taught them a lesson."

"How many wounded?" Danaer asked, not wanting an answer. "Well, at least we gave better than we got."

"Come along with me, to an inn called the Green Skirt. We will celebrate the victory. I assure you, both the wine and the women are worth your coin, and they do not scorn even us men of The Interior."

"Perhaps I will join you later."

"You long to see your witch, eh? I hear Yistar has kept her busy with her sorkra dealings," Shaartre said with affection.

Danaer was coming to hate the word "sorkra." "If so, she has earned a respite."

When he left the temporary barracks, night was blackening the streets once more. The nature of the

populace seemed to have changed. There were honest
women like the laundresses and citizens' wives, those
who remained with their men even in a city under
siege. But now Danaer saw many more jades and
women of ease. And there were men who dealt in
human misery and the wages of war. They had
avoided the fighting, but now they looked to reap prof-
its in hawking scarce wares.

Yistar's headquarters buzzed with activity, though
things were less disorderly than the first time Danaer
had been at the commandeered inn. Many junior officers wore bloodied clothes, and their sobered expressions showed their taste of battle had matured them
too quickly. Neither Yistar nor Branra was anywhere
to be seen, and Danaer edged past the other staff
members, heading for the stairs. One of the aides was
saying, "We threw the devils back and drowned
them. That is it, fellows—a good war!"

Danaer's momentary amusement at that boastful tone
faded. A good war? How many brave men had died
in this good war? And the war was not won, despite such bragging. Danaer recalled blades a finger's-
breadth from his neck or chest and the gleam of the
enemies' eyes, bright with a strange fanaticism which
controlled pain and made them silent in the face of
agony and death. Men falling, dying, lances protrud-
ing from their guts or their heads split with ax, their
eyes pierced by arrow—men he had known and ridden beside for years.

It was never easy to feel the Death God's icy breath.
Danaer scorned the aide who spoke so casually of his
first battle.

He was more anxious to see Lira than he had ever
been, mounting the stairs to the upper story three at a
time. She was still within the same room. There was no
magical parchment this time. Lira sat on a low stool, her
hands folded in her lap, ordeal written large on her face.

But she rose to greet him, and Danaer clasped her
hands to his breast. He drank in her presence, reveling
in her daintiness and beauty, the scent of her hair.
Her dark eyes met his and he forgot blood and vomit
and dying men.

She did not resist his embrace, her lips a heady intoxication that warmed Danaer, giving him renewed vigor after the terrible fight and weariness. "Rasven kept you safe, my Sharp Eyes," she was whispering, her voice shaky with awful fatigue.

Danaer was deaf to that note. Strangely, he played the braggart, like the young officer below. "We turned back all their onslaughts . . ."

Lira's expression clouded. "Only for the moment, Danaer. You do not know the strength of their chief wizard, and he rules their warlords."

He led her to a couch and drew her down beside him, heedless of what she was saying, of her mood, kissing her and caressing her. A hunger grew within him, a strong calling of the goddess's summons, male to female. "I thought of you often while I was on the walls, and called your blessing to me, qedra. Markuand will not come past my sword to hurt you, ever. We have dealt death to all of them, and broken their machines."

"Oh, indeed you are brave, but the dark power which threatens us—"

He did not let her continue, silencing her with his mouth. For a moment Lira's response was equally greedy, all Danaer wished, a sensual promise of what would be. He had no care but the joy of this moment, wanting to prolong it and increase its delights to the full. They would leave behind wizardry and blood and feed this ardor into a life-giving flame . . .

Yet when he touched her intimately, to his astonishment Lira jerked away and cried for him to stop. He could not understand. Her hunger was as great as his. Why, then, this prudery that denied her body? Anger grew where desire had been. "How have I displeased you? Is it because I am not a man of your own people? And not one of your sorkra?" Danaer got to his feet, his lust turning to a different sort of heat.

Lira cowered, seeing his rage, shaken. One part of him wanted to beg her forgiveness and take back the hard words. But instead he was saying still more cruel things. "Mayhap there is some young wizard who owns your favor, a man I can never challenge to fair combat—having no magic to counter his."

"No, please, Danaer, do not say this," Lira pleaded, distraught.

A stinging insect plumbed his brain, a harassment he could not put away. *Destre. You are Destre. Serve the goddess. You must not dishonor her law . . .*

"Teach me your ways, then," Danaer said suddenly, struggling against this aberrant urge. "Teach me the customs used by Sarli men to satisfy their women. I can learn. And if I cannot, I will show you that a Destre is as lusty a lover as even a Sarli woman could desire." Boldly, in a fashion that shocked them both, he seized her, starting to pull her to him.

A lancing fire seemed to scorch his hands, and Danaer recoiled, sucking his fingers, his mind whirling. What had he done? What was governing him to make him act and speak so?

"Danaer, listen to me . . ." Lira said, trying to take his hand and soothe his hurts.

"Now you strike at me with your wizardry!" He drew back his arm to deliver a blow, then froze, horrified by what he was doing.

"Nothing! I swear, qedra . . ."

"Upon Rasven? Upon that sorcerer god of yours?"

Tears welled in Lira's dark eyes. "You must listen. There is no lover save you . . ."

"Then share joy with me." For a precious moment the unwonted fury left him, and Danaer felt the warm yearning again. "Be my qedra, my woman, if I am your lover."

"I cannot! Not . . . yet. Please wait a bit longer. I must remain chaste."

"For another man?" The anger returned, double, an overwhelming hot rage that brooked no argument. It bade him take her, crushing her will, like a coarse peasant of an unbeliever . . .

Or like the Markuand who ravaged the women of Clarique!

He shrank from that comparison. He twisted his anger to deal with Lira's rejection, making a knife of words she had struck into his heart. Coldly, not recognizing his own voice, Danaer demanded, "Is it the time of your courses? Is that the reason you deny me?"

"No, no, Danaer . . ."

"I know I am crude and unlettered, not of your birth and breeding."

"Danaer, do not! It is only my wizard oath which keeps us apart."

An invisible hand clutched his vitals. It both intensified his ardor yet turned it oddly off the path. "That is a wall as strong as Deki's, a wall you always will put between us. You were not slow to meet my embrace a minute ago. Now you put me aside. Such a woman has a name among the plains people." Lira wept and tossed her head from side to side in her confusion and desperation. He would not hear her tearful begging. "Hablit was right. Like Kandra, you promise what you will never give. Kandra's wall against men is her rank, and yours is your sorkra calling. You are owned by that wizard Web."

He rushed toward the door and she grasped his shirt, shouting, trying to break through the anger. Roughly, Danaer thrust her aside. "Slake your desire with sorcery, then." He stormed out into the hall and down the stairs. With unnatural satisfaction, he heard Lira running after him and calling to him. The sound touched him, made him want to turn back.

It would be difficult, but he would ask her forgiveness and say he accepted and understood, even if he did not. He would tell her that he would wait. Was he not a man of honor? Had he not sworn . . .

Do not be trapped. She has trapped you again and again and laughs at your torment and foolishness!

Danaer was lashed by conflicting impulses, helpless to stop himself. He ached for Lira—but he could not stop running. He fled the inn and down the street, easily outdistancing Lira's short stride. In a few tens of paces he had left her far behind, the demon which had seized him riding him at its will.

Fury and self-pity fought and faded and were swallowed in the pain of the lash of Kida. A kind of madness took him, and Danaer walked without knowing where he went.

Gradually, after much aimless wandering in Deki's narrow streets, he began to come back to himself and knew profound shame. Why had he been so perverse? It was as if he had no power over his tongue or brain. Something had used him and done these things. He halted, rubbing his temples to chase away a deep aching there.

Yet his hunger remained, seemingly strengthened by that mad storm of anger. Dimly Danaer remembered Shaartre's invitation. The Green Skirt? Had he not seen a sign of such a name over an inn not a few doors back? He retraced his steps, moving like a man already drunk, finding the place of revelry. Light and music and laughter spilled through the door.

Danaer stood on the threshold, trying to see Shaartre amid the crowd. A group of minstrels played raucously and women of ease danced to entertain the patrons. The mood was that of celebration, in victory. There were no dancing couples, for the eastern tribes did not like that custom. But men pulled at the women's skirts, and one lost most of her garment to a quick-fingered patron. Unashamed, she wriggled about lewdly, bringing herself a rain of coins.

Danaer pushed his way through the noisy throng to Shaartre's table, and his friend welcomed him jovially. "You finally did come to us! Here! Wine for my comrade!" Danaer was told that a wealthy wine merchant, grateful to the defenders for saving his city and his wares, was treating every military man in the inn. Danaer gulped down the strong vintage, wanting the forgetfulness it would bring. Soon he joined the ribald singing of Shaartre and the others.

He knew he should be chary with the drink, that they might be recalled to the walls at any time. But the same heedlessness that had made him cruel with Lira governed him now. He drank, tempted to stay just a while longer, until the last bitter moments with Lira were lost in the wine.

A woman of ease sat beside him and refilled his cup. She said to Shaartre, "I see you have brought us another customer, and a handsome young one, too."

"Not him! He waits only for one woman, and her
a—"

"Not tonight," Danaer said sharply. Shaartre raised
an eyebrow but said no more. The woman pursed her
lips and regarded Danaer frankly, then squirmed close
to him, her hip against his. She shared his cup, touching the spot his lips had pressed.

"Are you truly Azsed? I see your eiphren, but . . ."

"I am faithful to Argan, and I would worship her
this night." She smiled and Danaer gazed at her
with growing ardor. Her eyes were very large and
warm brown in color, and her face was full, her dark
hair falling in ringlets. "Does Sarlos sing in your
blood?" he asked.

She was surprised but said lightly, "My father was
Sarli, or so my mother claimed. And my hair proves
it, ai?" She twisted a curl around a small finger and
laughed. It was the same sort of seductive, low sound
Danaer had learned to like in Lira's voice. He called
for another bottle and let the woman draw him into
conversation—the sort of talk women of ease employed to excite their potential customers.

She was neither loud nor obvious. Her amusement
at his jokes seemed genuine. Danaer began to relax in
her company, enjoying the wine.

"Tell me, pretty one, do you give pleasure to a
man apart from his gift to Argan? Do you ever, for the
night, take that man as you would a . . . a qedra?"

"The question belies your young face, soldier. Or is
it because of the character of this night?"

"Mostly the night," Danaer admitted.

"As to the question—it depends on the man." She
pushed a stray curl off her forehead with a graceful
gesture.

"And am I such a man?"

"Shall we see?" She stood up, gathering her green
slit skirt with modesty unusual in her calling. Her
restraint contrasted with the general lewdness of the
surroundings, and ironically, it strengthened Danaer's
desire. He picked up the bottle and followed the
woman. She did not hurry, moving like a lady, not a

jade. Her concessions to his unspoken wishes made
Danaer vow to pay her well with his gift to Argan.

For a short while, in her little room above the inn,
they did no more than talk. Music and laughter continued to float up through the curtained door and window. She told him her name was Ildate, but she was
not offended when Danaer, more than half drunk,
called her Lira. He said stumblingly, "You are . . .
are Sarli, in part. Do you know the ways of the southern women? Do they hold themselves aloof even when
they want to take joy?"

"Some of the Sarli customs *are* strange. But I am
sure, in time, that a Sarli woman can learn to delight
in the body of a Destre man—more than she would a
man of her own people. *I* would." Ildate was skillful
with her hands as well as words, and Danaer gave
himself up to her talents, believing what she would
have him believe. She shrugged off his lame apology,
that he had spoken of another woman. "Sarli women
have hot blood, I promise you. It needs patience to
gain one's love, warrior. But her joy will come to you.
My father learned to gift Argan, did he not? And my
blood sings in joy to Argan . . ."

She proved that statement well. Her kiss was one to
fire Danaer with sweet and lustful imaginings. This
body was not denied him, and her welcome was full
and heated. Though it was her profession, Ildate
brought an eagerness to pleasuring, a delight quite
apart from the silver it would earn for her.

In such matings, it was said there was true worship
of Argan. Danaer gave his being unto that worship,
appeasing a hunger he had known since he left
Nyald. When, in his ecstasy, he whispered Lira's
name and lived in his dreams his strongest desires,
Ildate did nothing to shatter the illusion.

XVII

POOR LITTLE ENEMY WIZARD!

THE MARKUAND HAD TAKEN POSSESSION OF THE FER-
rymen's village and, with the labor of many Clarique
slave children, had made a part of it into a fitting
palace for their leader. It was to this place that the
warlords now came, on the eastern bank of the broad
river, a river thickened with Markuand blood.

They were angry and had overcome their fear of
him enough to cry accusingly, "You said your wizardry would conquer them!"

He did not seem to hear them, brooding over some
new magical device, a cunningly wrought ice-sphere
in which particles of light and shadow tossed and
danced. His refusal to look upon them infuriated the
warlords the more.

"They have turned back all the assaults!"

"And we have lost many soldiers!"

"How can enchantments defeat them if we have no
men left to fight? We have attacked those impossible
bluffs and deadly marshes, as you bade us. We have
used costly siege towers and thrown sixties of our
troops against the walls. What has become of the
sappers you said would dig tunnels to . . ."

"You have plenty more soldiers. The Emperor has
sent reinforcements." That voice, coming after his
long silence, chilled the generals. When they were ab-
sent from him, they forgot his awesome aura. Now
their fury began to fade into fear.

He did not put aside the ice-sphere but deigned to
regard them with a piercing stare. "Do not waste
yourselves defying me. You would find yourselves
exceedingly sorry if ever you attempted to usurp my
authority." A terrible smile split his face. "I hope you
have not forgotten that the enemy, too, has wizards."

254

One commander mumbled, "Wizards who have forestalled us, and you . . ."

The remark was overheard, and he smiled the wider, a grin that made the generals retreat a few steps. "It is true they have many arcane arts. And if you challenge me, I may leave you naked to the vengeance of their spells. Your doubt amuses me, for now. My attitude might change." In the shadows, his apprentices hid their eyes and moaned like terrified children.

He gazed into the ice-sphere, seeing things no other could. At last he said, "Yes, they have wizards. In particular, there is a pretty little wench who dwells in yonder city and opposes me fiercely. But she has weaknesses of the flesh, and she is young." Those who watched him were reminded of a pitiless hawk about to strike a fluttering dove. "She is far from her master and his other wizards. In any case, their wizardry is no match for mine."

He spun the ice-sphere between his fingers, and the shadows crawled across the light, turning its inner surface black as night. "But our foes are not the only ones who can seek allies. I too have found allies, some who did not heretofore realize what power we might wield when we act in unison. Some have been afflicted by concerns of the flesh. But now . . . my ally joins me, seeing her error. To be a wizard is to put aside all humanity." He spoke for his own ears, relishing what was to happen.

"So, you have lost men. But now the time is ripe. I have discovered the weakness of our youthful enemy, and my allies are within the city and ready to strike. They have done my bidding, stealing her focus, disarraying her charm-making." The master wizard clasped the arm of his chair and leaned forward, his expression intent. "I want your best assassins, those most adept in stealth and murder."

His attention locked on the foremost among them, and somehow the man found strength to reply. "They . . . they shall be at your command."

"And they will enter the city and slay the sentinels guarding the water gates. I will shroud you in magical fog until you are underneath the cover of the walls, and then the gates will be thrown open by our assassins. Those defending the walls will be trapped, and you may slaughter them at your leisure."

"But how . . ."

He grimaced at them, like a tutor with a group of dull-witted boys. "It shall be done, as I promise."

"We do not understand."

"Nor shall you. There will be little resistance," he said, and steepled his fingers. "Poor, pretty little enemy wizard! She is but an apprentice, and her master has been occupied by treachery within his own land. His thread connecting him to her is badly frayed, about to be severed. And then . . ."

The master wizard of Markuand formed a fist, snatching at empty air. When he opened his hand, the warlords gasped. A diamond lay upon the wizard's palm, and the priceless gem was shattered. He laughed cruelly and cried, "Deki!"

XVIII

MAGIC FROM THE SMOKING MOUNTAIN

THE WOWAN HAD TRIED TO WARN DANAER EARLIER. Her words had come to him through a fog of sleep, meaning little. Now he had awakened abruptly, trying to comprehend what had jolted him from dreaming. Ildate was gone, and she had taken with her all those feminine possessions which had made the room specially hers. Puzzled and disturbed, Danaer dressed.

Then that thing which had wakened him recurred: outside, in the streets, there were screams—and in the distance cries of agony and death. Danaer ran to the small window. Dawn barely streaked the sky above the towering stone houses. People were running in panic, knocking down the weak and elderly in their haste, all of them fleeing westward.

He quickly buckled on his sword and raced downstairs. The main room of the inn looked as if it had been the scene of a riot. The stout innkeeper shrieked in fear, "It was not me! I did not kill him, soldier, I swear!"

"Kill who?"

The man pointed to some overturned tables. The body of a troopman lay beneath the clutter. It was no one Danaer knew. "I swear I did not . . . you . . . you are an Azsed?" The innkeeper saw Danaer's eiphren, and relief swept his fat face. "Then you will understand. I could not stop them, you see. I myself am a man of peace, but the Dekan warriors found him here, only minutes ago. He was drunk from reveling all night and too proud to guard his tongue. Any Iit the warriors find now, they will—"

"You are making no sense. What warriors? Why are the Dekans killing unbelievers who helped them defend the city? And why are the people fleeing?"

"You do not know? The Markuand! They are here!"

"What? How?" Danaer exclaimed. "When has this happened?"

"In the hour just before morning, they say. Through wizardry—magic! A witch, some Iit woman . . ."

Surely the innkeeper did not refer to Lira? Furiously, Danaer shook him and demanded details. "What witch?"

"She . . . she walked atop the walls. Many saw her. Gaudy, she was, and clad in jewels and finery, a woman most beauteous and elegant and tall. And when any accosted her, she . . . vanished before their eyes, they say. I heard it from many lips! The same story, always! And while she worked her spell and held all attention, somehow the gate sentinels were slain and . . ."

Danaer set his helmet firmly about his ears, heading for the door. "I must to the walls."

"You fool! I tell you the Markuand are *within* the city! The goddess protect us!" the man babbled. "It is said they opened gates and magic tunnels through the walls themselves. Wizardry! Argan save me!" The man clasped his hands in pious dread. "Like flood waters through a burst dike they come, impossible to stop. Best to the west gate while you can. Deki is falling!" With that, the innkeeper rushed out into the street and joined the fleeing rabble, leaving behind all he owned.

Danaer's head spun with the shock of this news. If what the man said was true . . . he must get to Yistar's headquarters, and to Lira! If fortune was kind, she would already have fled the city. But she was stubborn and devoted to her sorkra responsibilities. It might be she remained, still fighting her evil opponent in the Markuand camp.

His anger and bitterness of the night before brought hurtful memories. He knew now that he had been bewitched—as the men on the walls had been! Danaer ran through the streets, ruing every word he had spoken when he and Lira last parted.

As he rounded a corner, he came upon a Markuand mounted on a Destre roan, pursuing a merchant's family. The civilians huddled in their cart and whipped their pony, but it was obvious they could not escape their well-armed foe. Danaer leaned back into the shadows until the Markuand drew abreast of his position. Then he shouted a command to the roan, and the horse came to a sharp stop, spilling its rider across its neck and half out of the saddle. Danaer struck before the Markuand could regain his balance, shoving the body off and claiming the mount for his own.

The civilians had been looking back fearfully, and now they waved their gratitude and called, "Argan favor you!"

"Argan favor us all!" Danaer kicked up the horse, riding hard toward the command center.

The building appeared deserted from without, but as Danaer galloped in through the open doors he was barely quick enough to dodge a bench thrown past his head. Yistar and several of his aides were sword to sword with their equal in number of Markuand. Danaer used his roan to advantage to help them. The Markuand were younger than those who had come against the walls. Were their generals now conscripting children to fill the ranks? Unblooded and inexperienced, they fell without much of a fight.

"Watch at the door, Aseyi. Make sure we are not surprised again," Yistar ordered one of his aides. The man went to keep lookout as Danaer jumped down from the roan. "Have you heard?"

"I . . . I was at an inn, Captain. Do you want me to report to the walls?"

Yistar was gulping for breath. "By the Black Mare's Mane, no! That is hopeless. We are forced to withdraw from Deki at once. Your units are already gone. Luckily Ti-Mori is safely away, and Qhorda as well. And they broke through at the bluffs now, Gordyan says. We cannot save Deki with twice the troops we have. The Siirn has been slain. Branra is getting the wounded away, gathering what is left us in the Square of the Ryerdon. Gordyan is there, too, trying to keep the Dekans from killing us as we retreat." The officer paused, then said with rage, "The Markuand knew everything! Every guard post! Every weakness in the walls!"

"My informant said magic . . ."

"Ai! And Lady Nalu says that apparition was indeed a witch from The Interior, the traitor her Web has been seeking."

"Betrayed by an Iit," Danaer muttered. "And now they conspire with Markuand, the Royal Commander's enemies in the capital."

"Rightly do the Azsed take vengeance on us. They will not forget who cost them Deki, and, by the gods, The Interior had best not! We fought well here, together, and then to be defeated by . . ." Yistar spat at the corpse of a Markuand. "We must hold here a trifle longer. Liyur, feed those papers in the fire at once. All of them. Nothing must give the enemy help. We will stall them until Branra gets our wounded to safety." He grinned at Danaer. "That devil-ecar. He wanted to stay here and kill more Markuand. But I sent him to cover the retreat. He has risked his blood enough already."

"Branraediir of the Bloody Sword, indeed. A warrior unequaled, save by Straedanfi."

"Bah! In two lifetimes I could not match that firebrand." But Yistar's eyes twinkled at the compliment. "We want him alive for the battles to come, though."

"Lira?" Danaer could contain his anxiety no longer.

"Upstairs, engaged in some sorkra business. Go fetch her. I tried to argue that she had run out of time, but I have no wit to deal with a wizard woman. Mayhap she will listen to you. Go!"

"They come again, Captain!" the lookout warned. Danaer hefted his sword, then was stunned as a woman's scream rang down the stairway.

Danaer took the steps at a run, in time to catch a Markuand climbing through a window at the top. He cut down the man, then hurried toward Lira's room.

As he flung aside the curtain at the door, Danaer's apprehension turned to fury. A Markuand struggled with Lira. Her face was contorted with distracted terror, a kind of half awareness of what was occurring. She was in a sorkra trance, and this brute had attacked her when she was thus helpless!

Danaer lunged forward, and the Markuand swung Lira around, using her as a shield. Lira thrashed in his arms, and Danaer called to her to be still, fearing she would goad the man to kill her. She could not hear him, transfixed in her wizardry. She was moaning, in a manner all too familiar. Danaer fought his dread, concentrating on what must be done.

The tip of his blade touched the slender sword of the Markuand. It was a testing, and this was no inexperienced youngster. This man knew how to handle a weapon, and his eyes were not so dull as many of his race Danaer had met in combat. The Markuand sensed Danaer's concern for Lira and kept her between them.

"Hear me, come to me," Lira keened, and the Markuand glanced at her uneasily. Danaer pressed the flat of his sword against the enemy's, trying to force the edge away from Lira.

The obsidian talisman began to thrill against his breast, strength flowing into sinew and bone, making him a living weapon of sorcery. The walls cracked with ice, and wind and an ominous darkness swept in upon them.

Danaer's sword was locked with the Markuand's. A brain-numbing singsong filled their ears. Danaer could neither move nor speak, but the Markuand could, and lifted his weapon. There was a wildness in his expression, and then he too was held motionless, his arm arrested as he prepared to bring down a death stroke.

The world was transformed. Danaer had felt too often the pervasive touch of magic which took him in as part of Lira's Web. But this was not the same. There was an awful emptiness, a reaching out with nothing to find.

A tremendous whining exploded among them. Danaer wanted to fling his hands over his ears. The obsidian burned against his skin, as hot as the smoking mountain which had given it birth.

A dot of light appeared in the cold darkness, resting lightly upon Lira's forehead. The blackness gathered, plunging the three of them into the totality of a starless, moonless night. Danaer's stomach heaved in rebellion as he knew a horde of entities—there and not there, human and inhuman, people and things Lira called to in her desperation.

Trapped amid strange voices and darkness, Danaer could somehow see Lira and the Markuand, their forms bright and dancing in the inky blackness. The Markuand's sword glittered as if lit from within by some supernatural force. Danaer marshaled his will against the man and the weapon and against all Markuand. He could not move, but he thrust with his mind, yearning to help Lira and free them from this menace.

Then, for the first time, Danaer heard a Markuand scream—a wordless shriek of utter despair.

Lira was rigid, only her lips moving, and before Danaer's startled gaze the Markuand began to . . . fall?

But no! He was upright, not falling. He was shrinking, receding from Danaer and Lira with great rapidity, dwindling in size, and screaming as he shrank. His voice, like his body, closed in upon itself, becoming ever smaller and smaller. Ice ran through Danaer's veins.

A small hand pressed his, the shock of human warmth reaching into his soul. Suddenly the cold and darkness were gone, like a burst bubble. Lira fell into Danaer's arms, and he discovered with immense relief that he could move those arms. She clung to him, shuddering violently. They were alone. The Markuand and the strange presences and the blackness and cold were gone.

"Oh, qedra, you . . . you were almost caught with him. If that had happened . . ." Lira broke off with a racking sob.

Finding his wits with difficulty, Danaer asked, "Where . . . is he?"

Lira's eyes were haunted. "He is trapped in the Web. Forever."

"Dead?" That, at least, was something Danaer could understand.

"No, not dead." Lira refused to speak more of this thing she had done with her sorkra talents. "The witch . . . the traitor . . . she who walked the walls and blinded men to her master's evil assassins . . ." Lira shuddered again, but now there was anger mixed with her fear. "She sent this Markuand to kill me. She wants me dead. And last night she countered my powers, almost destroyed me, with . . . with you."

Reluctantly he said, "She may have guided him, but he got into the building through a window. And we must get away before more of his kind come."

Danaer swept her into the protection of his arm, leading her out to the hall, looking warily to left and right. The corridor and the window were empty, and he steered Lira toward the stairs. Halfway down, they stopped. A clash and din of fighting rose from below, and then a Markuand ran up toward them, a dripping sword in hand. Danaer caught him by surprise, then pulled Lira out of the way of the body. They descended to the main room—into a scene of carnage. One man still stood amid the bodies, a Markuand, his sword bloody as he bent over Yistar.

Danaer was upon him before the enemy warrior

could react. It was only when Lira shouted him back
to sanity that Danaer realized he had been striking the
dead man over and over, butchering the remains.

He knelt and lifted Yistar's head. The officer's eyes
were already partially glazed, and a spreading wetness
covered Danaer's hand where he cradled Yistar's
shoulders. The Captain still held his sword. Plainly he
had been engaged with one of the enemy when another
had struck him down from behind. It seemed a cruel
twist of fate for Straedanfi, who had always come fear-
lessly at his foes. Danaer's throat thickened with grief.

Yistar blinked up at him. "Danaer? Ai, my Azsed."
He gripped the scout's wrist. His voice was slurred
and had an overstrong Nyald accent Danaer had not
heard Yistar use in years. "The snake," he moaned,
"that filthy, Bog'-cursed winged snake . . . !"

"It is gone," Danaer humored him gently, not arguing with his delirium.

"Great white wings mingled with scales and feathers,
with talons and dripping fangs like . . . like . . ."

"It fled from your sword, Captain. You have van-
quished it."

"Distracted me, and then . . ." Yistar was angered
by his defeat, but growing too weak to cling to the
thought. His gaze brightened. "Branra. Get to Branra.
He will need good men more than ever now."

"I will. And this is but one battle. The war will be
ours, Captain." Then Danaer sensed the man could
not hear him, would never hear him again. He pried
loose the fingers from his wrist and eased the body
down, closing the dead eyes.

He put away his sorrow, thinking what must be
done. The roan he had taken from the Markuand
waited beside the door, restlessly pawing the floor-
boards. Indeed, it had been wise to bring the beast into
the building, Destre fashion, to guard against theft.
Branra. Yistar had said to get to Branra, and where
had he said Branra would be? The Square of the
Ryerdon . . .

"Forgive me," Lira sobbed over Yistar's body. "I
was too frail, and they are so powerful. I have lost
Deki for you . . ."

"You were outnumbered, as we all were," Danaer consoled her. He caught Lira about the waist and lifted her onto the roan, then jumped up behind her.

"We cannot leave him like this!" Lira cried.

Danaer spurred the roan through the door. "I too wish to give Straedanfi a proper pyre, but the living need me more, you most of all." He put his riding skills to hard use, wending through the dangerous streets. Again and again he had to turn the roan into alleyways and filthy passages to hide from roving bands of mounted Markuand and some of Deki's own worst element, who used Deki's disaster as an excuse to slit throats and rob. Neither the Markuand nor the gutter sweepings seemed to have much of a plan, roaming and slaughtering at will. Danaer knew he might hope for a quick end if they were caught, but Lira would not fare so well. That grim knowledge made him the more determined to win free to the western gate.

Once he rode through a dank tunnel between structures and was forced to draw the roan to a sudden halt and mask its nostrils with his hand. Lira sucked in her breath, staring out into the sunlit square beyond their shadowed place as several Destre-Y rode by. Unlike many of the cutthroats in Destre garb, these were familiar, and Danaer bit his lip to keep from roaring out a name—and a challenge to fight to the death.

Hablit! The former chieftain of Vidik and his loyal followers prowled Deki's streets, roistering, grinning maliciously, celebrating the collapse of the city—and of the alliance between Gordt te Raa and the Royal Commander. Hablit had won his revenge and delighted in the bloodshed it brought.

Yet Danaer could not risk confronting him. With Lira in his keeping, it was foolhardy and pointless, a throwing away of their lives. He could not hope to reach Hablit before the others would cut him down. He could only watch until they had passed, and swear that he would take his own vengeance in the days to come, with the death of Yistar and many others repaid double.

Like animals or criminals, he and Lira moved in the half darkness cast by eaves and looming buildings, creeping through the streets, always turning west. Lira had mastered her grief now and was as a warrior's woman must be, silent and brave. Without asking, Danaer knew she was regaining her sorkra strength after the ordeal with the Markuand and the Captain's death.

Finally, ahead lay the Square of the Ryerdon, the first intersection Yistar's troops had crossed when they had come to Deki. Danaer patted the roan's neck and praised its sturdiness in bringing them safely here. It was a good mount, and he regretted that some Destre had been slain by a Markuand and his well-trained horse made plunder. But through that, Danaer and Lira had come to the place of meeting, near the gates.

Wagons were gathered in the square's center, and litters with wounded were being put into them. A last few ranks of soldiers were forming up and departing as rapidly as their Troop Leaders could make any order of the situation. Branra and Gordyan were directing this escape, their troops and warriors working together. Gordyan was sending his men off west to the gates with the wagons even as Danaer and Lira rode into the intersection.

As they dismounted, the big Destre swept them into a hearty hug of greeting and Branra grinned widely. But there was little time to enjoy this reunion. Danaer relayed the sobering news concerning Hablit's presence in the city and Yistar's death. Branra's swarthy face clouded with rage. "That will be avenged, I swear, and Hablit's treachery. But now we must away from here. Time draws very sharp."

Danaer helped to harness an ill-matched team to the last wagon while Gordyan rode toward a junctioning street, chasing Dekans away from killing several soldiers trying to reach the square. Danaer urged Lira to get into the wagon with the wounded, but she would not do so until the last injured man was aboard.

A great din filled the streets, and Danaer admired Branra's ability to make any sense out of the confusion. Then a troopman came riding from the inner city, shouting above the other noises, "They come, my lord!

They have flung wide the gates, and the eastern walls are entirely theirs!"

Branra added his weight to Danaer's arguments now, telling Lira, "It is proper that you should ride in the wagon, my lady sorkra. We have done our duty to Deki and must flee and continue the war elsewhere."

With much reluctance, she obeyed, barely in time, for the driver lashed up the team. Lira looked back at Danaer, calling to him, her words torn away in the uproar. He caught up the reins of his roan as horses and men bumped over panic-strewn cobblestones. Close beside Branra, Danaer rode around a pile of wrecked carts, following the wagon. Then something caught the corner of his vision, making him look upward.

An immense shadow was descending from Deki's lofty roofs, dropping down steeply into the square. Danaer gaped incredulously, jerking his horse to a stop, and Branra cried, "By the nine thousand devils of Bogotana, what is that?"

The underbelly was in darkness, but feathery body and wings were limned in white as the sun glanced off the diving creature—a snake! An unbelievable and hideous winged snake, gigantic and savage! Great flapping pinions reached out the length of three men's bodies on either side of a serpentine form, and its jaws were wide, terrible fangs dripping as it swooped, spiraling toward the center of the square, lizardy eyes seeking its prey.

Man and beast screamed and sought to flee, and grasping claws appeared from the snake-bird's underparts, talons finding flesh, tearing the head of a horse from the brute's body, then slashing death blows as a line of stragglers tried to follow the departing wagons. Blood and flesh were scattered in the demon thing's wake as it flapped and rose and swirled about again, coming for the attack.

Yistar's snake! The dying man had spoken true, not out of delirium! And this was the awful monster which had brought him to his death. Danaer's fear was overborne by hatred, and he forced his frantic roan to answer his command, riding breakneck, seeing where the snake-bird would try to strike next.

"My Lord Branra! Guard yourself! It comes for you as it came for Straedanfi!"

Superb horseman that he was, Branra pulled back his mount skillfully and the unholy serpent rushed by him, its murderous fangs and talons missing him by fingers'-breadths.

"Can it be slain?" Branra shouted.

Danaer remembered the attack in Ulodovol's chambers. "They *can* be killed. I have done so."

"Then at it!"

As the creature swooped by again, they fought their terrified horses and struggled to land a blow. Danaer exclaimed with triumph as he felt his sword bite clean and hard . . . into nothing! The terrible demon flew up unhurt, beating scaly white wings to gain height and turn and come again at them.

Danaer stared at his sword. There was no trace of blood on it, yet he was sure he had not misjudged. He *had* cut the thing!

At the edge of the square, Lira was climbing out of the wagon, dropping down to the stones, then holding up her arms. She was not safe, leaving the city, but staying to conjure at the Markuand snake-bird! The monster wanted Branra, but would he not want to destroy Lira even more? Danaer sucked in his breath, fearing for her.

But the demon was concentrating on Branra, closing, trying to rend him. Branra was the man who could best lead the survivors of the fallen city and hearten soldiers to turn and fight again. Well did the Markuand wizard select his prey!

And Branra would not be daunted, still trying to strike back, crying that he would have vengeance for Captain Yistar. The gaping snake's maw opened, glistening, deadly sharp fangs exposed. A leathery wing brushed Danaer's helmet and a stench gushed at him from the monster's mouth, a reek to steal a man's breath while he defended himself. The snake-bird hovered, beating the air, aiming for its kill.

Danaer wielded his sword in both hands, futilely, hacking at slime-bright scales and feathers, enraged by

his powerlessness. He deftly sheathed the sword and
drew his bronze belt knife, flinging it fair into the demon's ugly throat—to no effect!

Lira was swaying, gesticulating, and Danaer felt a
renewal of the cold and blackness gathering in response
to her spell-casting. But would it be in time, and could
she succeed without her Web? Danaer prayed to the
goddess and willed his being joined with her talisman,
then reached for his steel boot knife, though with little
hope.

Branra did not wait. He was hoarse from shouting
defiance at the evil snake and somehow yet found
voice to bellow, "Now!" The blade which had scourged
the Tradyan tribes slashed into the scaly neck just as
the demon tried to pluck Branra from his saddle.

Black steam poured from a terrible wound, and a
shriek from the Death God's realm split the air. Out-
spread wings spasmed in agony, showering scales and
feathers like rain. Falling, ichor spurting, the snake-
bird crashed into Branra's black, overtoppling the
horse and crushing it down to the cobblestones. Hurriedly Danaer rode out of its way as the monster
writhed in its death throes. Keeping reins tightly in
hand, not trusting the panicky roan overmuch, he
jumped down and ran forward to help Branra. The officer was stunned by his fall, about to be trapped beneath both animals.

"Quickly, my lord, take my arm!"

A ghastly serpentine head lay across the dead horse,
a black gore pouring forth, puddling under men and
beasts. Branra's own blood flowed from a bad scalp
cut. He clung to Danaer reflexively, kicking free. Staggering, he tried to put his sword back in its sheath,
needing Danaer's help, so dazed was he.

Danaer looked around apprehensively. This demon
was dead, but what if more should come while Branra
was still too weak to use his most potent sword?
"Mount my roan," Danaer said, shoving Branra's foot
into the stirrup.

"It is . . . your horse," Branra mumbled, arguing
even as he clambered into the saddle.

"We will ride double," Danaer said, wrapping

Branra's limp fingers tightly about the roan's mane and gathering himself to leap up behind the cantle.

Then a blow struck him, and a wave of excruciating pain boiled from his back. Danaer slumped heavily against the roan. Though restive, the animal stood his weight. Danaer shook his head and gasped, then gingerly slid his left hand across his chest and over his shoulder, groping to find what had hit him. His fingers touched the shaft of an arrow, and fresh agony nearly made him faint.

XIX

YOU GO INTO DANGER, DESTRE-Y

FIGHTING AWAY INCREASING DIZZINESS, DANAER craned his neck to locate the arrow and estimate its penetration. As he did, he saw a Markuand archer entering the square, riding for him and Branra. Perhaps, like the snake-bird, he was directed by his wizard master to slay Branra.

Danaer's legs threatened to give way under him. If he now attempted to mount behind Branra, it would mean death for them both. And he would not be able to fend off the approaching Markuand and then mount.

"Hold fast, Lieutenant," he said, then gave the roan a Destre command. Eager to leave the carcass of the monster serpent, the horse sped away, following the wagons toward the western gates. Branra, though only half conscious, stuck to its back as well as any tribesman.

With the roan's support gone, Danaer dropped helplessly to his knees. The Markuand was almost upon him, cursing an empty quiver, flinging down the bow and drawing sword, flailing his stolen roan and trying to catch up with Branra. Danaer was in his way, and would be but a moment's work to cut down. He saw

that the Markuand was already defeated, for Danaer
had sent Branra's horse off at a rocking gait, and the
enemy would never be able to overtake him. The
Markuand realized this also, turning toward him, angry
frustration in his manner.

"Kant, prodra Argan," Danaer whispered. He had
sent Branra to safety that his people, that Krantin,
might live. That was to die with honor, and he begged
the goddess to grant him a merciful death.

Suddenly the Markuand archer fell, landing supine,
a great bloody smear on the back of his neck. Dimly
Danaer identified the wound as one made by a Destre
sling. The enemy's stolen roan came to a halt when its
reins touched the cobblestones. It snuffled and pawed
as Danaer peered dizzily at it. A pair of large boots
were moving across his line of sight, closing in on the
Markuand as the archer attempted to rise. A heel came
down on the Markuand's neck with a hard snapping
sound and he moved no more.

A moment later, Gordyan was crouching beside
Danaer. Confusion and pain pounded at him as he
tried to speak. "An . . . an arrow . . ."

"I see it, maen," Gordyan said gently.

"Danaer!" Lira too was kneeling before him.

"The wagon. Get back in the wagon," he begged.

"Be still, my Sharp Eyes. There may be more wizardry afoot besides that bird. You need my sorkra arts.
Gordyan, we must help him."

"Ai! He cannot ride alone. Take that roan the
Markuand was using. Hold steady now, warrior. I must
break this shaft." There was a wrenching crack, and
from the pain Danaer was certain Gordyan had broken
a bone rather than the arrow. The big man pulled at
Danaer's armpits, heaving him to his feet, insistent.
"Get up. Stand up!"

A loud ringing filled Danaer's ears, and everything
seemed to have a peculiar yellow cast. "I cannot . . ."

"Gordyan?" Lira sounded very far away.

"It struck deeply. I have seen this before. Stay
awake a bit longer now, hyidu." Those powerful arms
lifted Danaer and carried him like a child. Gordyan

was trying to put him atop his own big blue roan.
Years of habit helped Danaer gain the saddle. The
sway of the horse under him churned his stomach and
jolted new hurt into his shoulder. By now nearly all
other noises were lost in the roaring within his head.
Gordyan was mounting and briefly brushing against
that torment at Danaer's back; then an arm closed protectively about his chest.

The roan galloped forward, the brisk gait driving a
soft moan past Danaer's clenched teeth. He tasted
vomit and choked it down. The nausea faded, and his
main concern became fighting back a shameful outcry
as the agony in his shoulder grew.

Sometimes his wits rallied and matters were clear.
At those times, he tried to assess their progress. Escape. That was the important thing. He could not remember why, but it was all that was real at this
moment, a desperate need.

Gray walls flowed by, and the ragged unsteadiness
of the roan's lope made Danaer's belly heave often.
He shut his eyes tight for long minutes. When he
opened them again, green countryside stretched out on
every side. Tiredly, he supposed they must have won
free of Deki and be entering the outlands. How far
had they ridden? He could not tell, and did not much
care. He roused and fell back into pain.

Finally the roan came to a stop. The animal was
lathered and blowing hard, for it had carried two men,
one of them Gordyan. Gordyan spoke close to
Danaer's ear, but he addressed Lira. "We must rest a
bit, or the horses will drop. And I must see if I can
staunch this blood."

Dismounting was torture. Danaer managed to get
down fairly well, but when his feet touched the earth
he collapsed. He sat on wet grass and let Gordyan and
Lira tend him, only half knowing what they did or said.

"Can we find some of your warriors, Gordyan? We
have lost the track of the wagons. The army must be
far ahead of us now."

"I fear my men are badly scattered. Destre-Y
always accept control lightly. We must ride on to the

Sink, or there will be no hope of getting away from the Markuand."

"Bogotana's Sink?" Lira wailed in dismay. "But Danaer must have water and food . . ."

"There is a fair oasis not far from here, just after we cross into the Sink. It is known to even very few Destre. Perhaps it will be safe for us to make camp there," Gordyan assured her. "But it will be slow going with Danaer. He can take little more jostling. The need now is to save his blood until I can build a fire and dig that barb free. What of the Markuand wizard? Does he hunt us with more of those snake-birds?"

"I think not," Lira said. She felt Danaer's brow and fussed over him. "Such creations as that take unfathomable wizardry to sustain. Further, he spent his powers breaching Deki's walls with magic. It may be that not even his terrible strength is inexhaustible. When Branra slew the demon, it hurt the Markuand sorely."

"Good!" Gordyan growled. "We will get away while he nurses his well-earned hurt."

Lira looked anxiously into Danaer's sweating face. "Qedra, do you hear me? Will you be able to ride again?"

He found his voice, though it was faint and unsteady. "I . . . I believe so. The ringing in my ears has stopped."

"Ah!" Gordyan cried, pleased by that.

Danaer rallied enough to say, "If you can reach the caravan, the surgeons can help me . . ."

"Not possible, hyidu. There is now very deep hatred between Destre and your army. We have passed numerous bodies of stragglers slain by plains people, not by Markuand. In time the anger may cool on both sides and let us approach your caravan without being killed on sight. But you need help *now*." Gordyan allowed no more arguments, nor had Danaer the strength to make them. "Hold still while I tie this."

After a bit the throbbing dropped to a bearable level. Gordyan had removed Danaer's mantle and used part of it as a crude bandage; the remainder he laid over Danaer's head; it was starting to rain, a cold and miserable shower. In the death struggle with the demon snake, Danaer had lost his helmet, but he still had his sword, which Gordyan cursed as a nuisance. He unbuckled it and gave it to Lira, then put Danaer atop his roan again.

The following time was a horror which must be borne. Sometimes Danaer sank into a state where no distraction could reach him, but the pain could. Now and then he roused enough to know the sky was darkening as the day wore on into evening. Once they stopped and Lira readjusted the makeshift bandage. She and Gordyan gave him some water and a bit of grain cake from the Destre's saddle pouch. The taste was satisfying but brief, for Danaer promptly vomited most of what he had swallowed. Then there was the ordeal of remounting and more riding toward the west. He no longer cared about anything, and when the ringing in his ears started once more, he had no strength to tell Lira or Gordyan of it.

The roan stopped. Danaer gazed about dully. It was night, and in the distance there was a campfire. It looked inviting. Why did not Gordyan take them there? The comforting warmth of his friend's big body disappeared from behind him, then Danaer felt a tug at his arm. "Slide off, maen. I will catch you." In a few moments Danaer was lying on his side, on sand, his head pillowed in Lira's lap.

Sand? Then they had reached the Sink. Gordyan had pressed them hard to come so far so quickly. Danaer's shoulder lessened its throbbing, and he was startled by a sudden clarity of thought and senses. Lira was caressing his forehead as he looked up at her. Her face was illuminated by a wavering golden glow far brighter than that campfire should have cast. "Lira?" She bent close to hear him well as he asked, "Where is Gordyan?"

"At the camp ahead. He said he would go and see what their clans were." The wisdom of this satisfied Danaer, but it sounded as if the fragile alliance of Malol and Gordt te Raa had been thoroughly undone. Gordyan, unsure of his fellow Destre-Y and checking their calling and tribes ere he entered their camp? And wary of all army men save Danaer?

"Lira, why can I see your face so clearly in the darkness?" Danaer asked in childlike wonder.

She turned eastward, her expression grim. "There is a great fire back there, qedra. It is Deki. But what would burn in that city of stone?"

"Bodies," Danaer said with tired frankness. "Thatch, fodder for beasts, any manner of thing which could tinder the conquerors' celebrations." He considered this and added, "But if the Markuand are looting, they will not be pursuing survivors. They may believe the desert, and our own rivalries, will destroy us for them."

Suddenly and silently, Gordyan was back with them. "They are none of mine, these warriors," he said with a low growl. "But we must have water and fire." The big man eyed Danaer worriedly, then took out his knife and slashed open the scout's tunic.

"What are you doing?" Danaer protested, struggling to rise.

Gordyan forced him back. "Making you into a proper Azsed." He cut the tunic into a Destre's loose vest, then tucked Danaer's breeches into his boots in the fashion of the plains people. Badges and insignia were sliced off and discarded. "You will pass for an ordinary Sarli with no trouble, Lira. Bury that sorkra cloak of yours, though. And that sword of Danaer's as well. I will tell them you are one of Qhorda's women who became separated from your little companions. Speak only Sarli, no Krantin, or they may turn suspicious. Lead the roans. I will say Danaer was unable to ride the last leg, and from his looks they will not doubt me. Bog'! This cursed thing is bleeding again. Up now, maen, just a bit further . . ."

Danaer could not stand alone, his knees sagging uselessly, and finally Gordyan carried him again. Danaer turned his head to the campfire and the Destre-Y gathered around it. He imagined he saw a ha-usfaen dancing and heard a delisich's silvery song. Then he realized it was only the ringing in his ears.

Gordyan was loudly complaining at someone, but the debate passed over Danaer, without meaning. He was stretched full length on the ground and then pulled up into a sitting position. The ringing noises quit abruptly, and Lira braced her hands against his chest to keep him from falling. Gordyan's voice eventually penetrated the pain. "You know me, stander. Do I ask much? Water and a cautery, in the name of the Siirn Rena." Gordyan hunkered by Danaer and said softly, "You have already borne much, hyidu. Prove yourself an Azsed now, or they will kill us all."

He was much pleased when Danaer met his gaze steadily and said with shakiness, "I will not disgrace Nyald Zsed."

If the arrow had struck more outward, Danaer knew he could expect to lose his arm. But this wound was more dangerous. His father's tribe friend had died of such a wound suffered in the clan wars. Pride ruled him, and he hoped the men watching them so narrowly would know any weakness came from loss of blood, not lack of courage. Lira put a small, battered copper pot of steaming water at his feet, and Gordyan was heating his knives in the fire.

"Take your arm with your good hand," Gordyan instructed. Danaer had barely time to comply when Gordyan started to cut away his shirt and bloody tunic. He worked at withstanding any wince or outcry. "Are these Markuand arrows barbed much, hyidu?"

"A slight barb, but sharp." Danaer managed a bitter smile.

"Then I shall have to dig a bit."

At what seemed the peak of his pain, Gordyan gasped in triumph, then splashed the hot water over the wound. He took his other knife out of the fire, its blade smoking.

The ringing in Danaer's ears came back powerfully, and Lira's face swam before him. Oddly, the pain subsided as the ringing noise built. A yellow blur spiraled in from the edge of his vision. He watched with mild curiosity while it came closer and closer, and the more it contracted the faster it curled in upon him, blotting out everything but Lira's eyes.

Finally those, too, vanished. The ringing sound sped

up out of his hearing and disappeared, and with it went all sensation.

XX

IN DREAMS THERE IS MAGIC

THE FEVER VISIONS BLURRED INTO ONE ANOTHER MAD-deningly, with no way to elude them. Danaer suffered again Yistar's death in poignant detail, knowing the ending of that gruff presence which had guided him so many years. His weapons availed nothing against the inexorable enemy, and once more he felt Yistar's life ebb through his hands.

That horror was gone, and Kandra was before him, exquisite, the paragon of Destre womanhood. She was smiling, bowing, turning . . . slowly, slowly. As people in a tapestry come to life, Danaer witnessed Kandra speaking to Gordyan. His blood friend took his mistress's hand and kissed her fingers. It was more than the action of an adoring servant. In his dream he saw that Gordyan was deeply stricken and help-lessly bound, held by a silken tress or the crook of a small finger. Sworn to serve lord and lady, and never to know the fulfillment of Kandra's promise.

That image was gone, too, and now Danaer lay en-circled by Markuand. They rained blows upon him with staves and swords and lances and knives, hurting and killing him, again and again. He died and lived once more, and suffered anew. Each blow had but one target—the fire in his shoulder.

Always, in those rare times when he came to him-self, Lira or Gordyan was there. His head would be lifted and water given him. He would sink back into fitful dreaming, despite Gordyan's pleas, and Lira's weeping. Their voices slipped away from him and he was allowed to drown.

Kandra again was in his dreaming . . . no, not Kandra. This was another woman assuming her form. The mirage, coming from the rainstorm—the rain sent by the Markuand wizard. This time Danaer knew the illusion for what it was, and in his nightmare he clutched at Lira's obsidian talisman and bade the false Kandra begone. Instead, she changed, became a cloaked figure, the traitor from The Interior. The hood was thrown back, and a lovely and evil face peered out at him, smiling. A man drew near her, leering at Danaer. He knew them both, thus revealed, as they stared their hatred at him. She was Kandra no more, but Chorii, the Prince's wanton mistress, and Diilbok himself abetted her in this treachery!

They hated him and hated Lira. The woman, especially, hated Lira. She stretched forth her hand tipped with sharp painted nails, as if she would claw his face, scar him, and thus bring pain to her dainty adversary from Sarlos.

Danaer moaned and writhed and fought to escape the nightmare, and the fever carried him elsewhere, away from that terrible pair. Now he gazed upon Malol te Eldri. The Royal Commander stood before a Destre council, swearing away his precious son's future, giving him to be consort to the successor of the Siirn Rena. It was a sacrifice far deeper than any at the council realized, Malol's only seed.

That dream faded, and Danaer held Ildate in his arms, slaking his lust, taking joy. The woman of ease smiled, and her image altered and became Lira's, welcoming him warmly, ardently. Danaer embraced her with delight, wanting this dream to be unending.

But such things could not be commanded. Lira was no longer joined with him, their bodies one. Yet she was nearby. She sat and watched as Danaer and Gordyan mingled blood and pledged their lives to each other. The fervent emotions were reborn for Danaer —his woman, his blood friend, the three of them by the fire . . .

And from the fire came a devil beast, a winged snake from the very depths of Bogotana's Realm. Danaer wanted to scream and run, but his feet were encased in stone, words choking his throat. The vicious claws struck his shoulder. Pain ripped at him, and Danaer thought of the talisman, focusing on the black stone.

Branra was there, and in the dream Danaer did not question how the nobleman came upon the scene. Branra was slashing with his sword, killing the creature from the wizard's world of the damned. The sword hilt glittered in the sun, a holy thing, studded with obsidian—the same material as the talisman. Chased with silver, bright metal and black stone blinding, being one with the charm at Danaer's breast, combining their powers to slay the snake-bird. One— all one—silver and obsidian, the creations of the smoking mountains of Krantin.

Osyta sat before him, mumbling prophecies, and behind her the volcano rumbled, birthing more glassy rock, cracking the mountains where the silver lay. She was chanting. "From Krantin must come a strength, a magic . . . it is the children of the smoking mountain. . . . You go into danger beyond your imaginings. You go into danger, Destre-Y!"

The warning echoed repeatedly, fading. Gradually Osyta's withered form dissolved, like all the other dream shapes, releasing him. He seemed to be rising to the surface of Deki's river. Danaer was a Destre and could not swim. But in this world he was leaving, he *could* swim, not wondering how, accepting it.

For a long while he had been vaguely aware of great heat, when the nightmares were particularly terrifying. There had been worse—periods when he had known nothing, his spirit held by the thinnest of threads and liable to snap at any moment and send him to join Osyta.

Now that was fading, as had the dreams. It was some minutes before he opened his eyes, but Danaer grew aware of sounds—the nickerings of horses, the slap of leather, men calling to one another, their accents Siank-thick. This last puzzled him, for Gordyan had said the warriors were strangers. Then Danaer realized his mind was unclouded. The sounds were real, not the companions of dreams. His shoulder still pained him, but not severely. He parted his eyelids narrowly, letting his vision adjust after long unconsciousness.

He was in a tent, sunlight streaming through an open flap to his right. At his feet, Lira was sewing a garment. She turned to catch the light for her needle and Danaer studied her face. Her cheeks had lost fullness and her eyes were rimmed with dark flesh. Guilt twisted at him as he recalled the many times he had wakened and found her always ready with comfort.

Danaer's throat was so dry that his first attempt to speak failed. He tried again, and when he called her name, Lira started with glad surprise. She knelt by him, pressing his bare chest, touching the amulet. "Qedra! When did you waken?"

"Just now. Is there water?"

She steadied the canteen for him, for he was very shaky. Danaer drank slowly, savoring, wanting to drain the skin yet fearful of using too much water if they were camped in the Sink. When he nodded that he had had enough for the present, Lira set down the canteen, then went to the tent flap and summoned Gordyan. The big man came in at once, very worried. But when he saw Danaer conscious and sitting up, he beamed. "Hai! The scout found his way back alone. How do you feel?"

"As if I were in Nyald, where the game is scarce."

"We all hunger, though you suffered most, with little food kept in your fevered belly."

"I can still taste some of that," Danaer said. "How long have I been out of my wits with this wound?"

"Half a ten-day." Danaer stared as Lira explained, "You fainted when Gordyan applied the cautery. And then the wound became infected despite it. I believe you were nearly dead when the herb-healer lanced it."

"I remember it not at all. An herb-healer? Are we in Siank, then?"

Gordyan chuckled sourly. "Not yet! This is a small camp of my men. We met with them a few periods' ride beyond that first fire. They managed to save some of our horses and equipment from the rout of Deki, but little food. The army emptied all the caches along the caravan trail, of course." Gordyan shrugged and grinned. He acted as if he very much wanted to drag Danaer into one of those rib-cracking hugs, but he forbore, careful of his friend's wound. "Maen, I am joyous to see you with us again!"

"It is a joy I share." Danaer brought his weight down tentatively on his right hand.

"Care," Gordyan warned him.

"The pain is well down. I would see if I can stand." Gordyan helped him up. Danaer swayed uncertainly, wincing at the sharp tingling in the soles of his feet. Cautiously, he took a few steps to the tent flap and peered out, seeing haggard warriors and roans with gaunt ribs. Lira was obviously hungry, and even Gordyan looked a bit thin. "Have you any food at all?" Danaer asked.

"We killed a roan a few days ago," Gordyan said, feigning unconcern.

"How goes the war, or have you news?"

Lira seemed troubled. "Gordyan's warriors learned that the Markuand keep their reputation, burning and looting, taking no men alive, and only the most beautiful women and sturdy children past their initial using." She added with unwonted fury, "I trust that shegolhi bitch who betrayed us delights that the women and men of her own land suffer because of her!"

Much disheartened, Danaer sat down again on the pallet. "How far are we from Vidik?"

"With these roans, it is hard to say. Perhaps a three-day."

Danaer doubted that the pitiful beasts could last that long. "What word of the army?"

"They are regrouping, what is left of them. The main camp is a period's ride distant, but . . ."

"There is your water and food, Gordyan. You said they collected the caches Lorzosh-Fila and Yistar had set along the way. They would not scorn to share with allies . . ."

"Much has happened while you suffered that fever, maen," Gordyan said morosely. "Much to destroy the Rena's alliance. Too many army stragglers were slain in the first rush of hatred for all Iit. Because of that, the caravan has grown most wary, even of refugee civilians, fearing a ruse that will mean more dead soldiers. The Destre are now beginning to realize it was but one treacherous harlot from The Interior who betrayed Deki, not all the people of the mountains. But I fear the army has been too sorely hurt to trust them. It turns in upon itself like a sand-crawler and keeps at bay anyone but army."

"What of Branra? What of Ulodovol and your sorkra web, Lira? Can you not speak to their minds and help us?"

She was silent a long while, then said, "I do not know what happened to Branra. And . . . and I cannot touch my Web. I cannot, and I dare not. The Markuand wizard may be hunting for us even yet. If I use my arts to communicate with the Traech Sorkra, he may find you through me, and lead the enemy to us."

Lira might have confessed she was crippled, stricken deaf and blind. Danaer took her hand in sympathy. He disliked her wizard dealings but knew how she must feel, thus cut off from all her own kind, here in the Markuand magician's conquered territory. Without her skills, they were *all* blind and lost, and the caravan as well.

"Gordyan, this war between Destre and army is senseless. It will mean death for both."

"I know, hyidu. The fugitive Dekans and the other Destre trying to cross the Sink are unlikely to reach Vidik unless we get food. The army has water and food but will not share it, out of fear. And because of that, they will be crushed when they *do* arrive at Vidik. If Wyaela te Fihar learns they refused to aid starving Destre-Y, she will treat them ruthlessly. The Rena and the Royal Commander have lost. Their alliance bound none but the two of us. I have failed my Rena. Deki is lost . . ."

"It was my fault," Lira corrected him. "I . . . she came at my heart, when I was least guarded . . ."

Danaer drew her into the crook of his unwounded arm, understanding what had robbed her of her skills at that critical moment, and his part in it as the witch's dupe. "You were overborne by awesome powers, as were we all. Not your fault, qedra, nor yours, Gordyan. There is no lack of honor among us, and Argan does not will that we accept defeat meekly. The army and Destre must reunite, or Markuand will wait till we slay each other, then take what is left."

"How? We dare not approach the caravan. Outriders would kill us before we could come close enough to vow our friendship," Gordyan said.

"There is a way," Danaer said in sudden resolve. "Gordyan, can you reconstruct enough of my uniform to garb me?"

The big man was doubtful. "Your shirt and tunic are bloody rags, and your helmet and sword are long gone."

"A scout need not always wear a helmet. And it would be best for me to go unarmed, anyway."

His friend eyed him warily. "I will try. But you are very weak yet."

"You will ride with me to the caravan's outposts. I can manage from there. If I cannot, well, I have faced starvation before in Nyald. Better for all of us to die quickly than from that slow dying."

Tents were pulled down and Gordyan went among his warriors, gathering a few garments necessary for Danaer's plan. Lira fashioned a tunic from scraps, and a Destre donated a shirt that would pass for army issue. With his breeches once more loose from his boots, Danaer's makeshift uniform was complete. He left off his tribal mantle, not wanting to risk flaunting that badge until he saw what his welcome would be. He must pass the scrutiny of the sentries. "If I can encounter Shaartre or a man from my units, all will be well," he said. "How do I look? Will I pass inspection?"

"You frighten me," Gordyan said. "Were this the old days, before the alliance, I would take you as the foe and strike."

"What, an unarmed man?"

Sheepish, Gordyan said, "I am sorry for the loss of your sword. But it had to be. Had those Dekans discovered you were a soldier, they would have given you a fresh wound in the throat, and then I would have had to kill them—and they are good Azsed-Y."

Danaer knew his friend would have tried to slay the entire camp, and perhaps come close to succeeding. There had been so many risks taken so far, and more to come. He worried over the authenticity of his dress. How many times in the past had sentries challenged him because he looked too much a Destre? And then he had worn a better uniform by far. But Danaer looked at Lira's pinched face and put aside his reservations.

The ride to the caravan's position told heavily on him. None of the others were wounded, but they too rode slowly. It was nearing evening when Gordyan called a halt and pointed down a slope, saying, "There is your army, maen, camping for the night."

The caravan was larger than Danaer had expected. Then he saw some flags of Ti-Mori's troops and part of Qhorda's Sarli rabble and knew those people had escaped the debacle and joined with the army. That would further tax the food supplies. Would they be willing to feed Destre as well, and accept the drain on dwindling resources?

Danaer kicked his hungry horse and rode down the slope, taking his time. Already the first challenges were coming as outriders loped to head him off. Danaer raised his hands waist-high, his palms upward.

"That is far enough, Destre!"

"I am army, and I would speak with your commander."

The sentries whispered to one another, occasionally glancing up at Gordyan's group on the hill above. One guard said, "You look not army to me: no helmet, no weapons . . ."

"I lost my equipment in Deki. I am Troop Leader Scout Danaer in the service of Captain Yistar, may his god favor him at Keth's portals."

"A Troop Leader, eh? When you devil worshippers imitate us, you do it by rank!"

"Is Lieutenant Branra with you? He will identify me," Danaer said.

"You would dare to let him confront you?"

Danaer took hope, for the soldier spoke in the present. So Branra was alive. Danaer's sacrifice had been rewarded. It seemed the officer had escaped Deki, slipping through the enemy wizard's magical net. He smiled wanly and said, "I like to think the Lieutenant owes me something, if only provisions. Will you take me to him, and permit my friends to stay there unmolested until I am vouched for?"

Finally the sentries nodded. "Dismount and come with me," one of them said.

Danaer's wound was aching and his knees shaky, but he did not protest. He followed the sentry through rows of wagons and tents, curious stares tracing his progress. A red and black banner flapping above a command tent was one of the most welcome sights Danaer had ever come upon. The sentry ordered him to wait, and Danaer leaned against a wagon. He refused to look at a pot of food bubbling over a nearby fire, but the scent made his empty belly tighten and complain.

When the guard returned, he eyed Danaer with wonder. "He is busy, but he will see you. For a famous slayer of your people, he is very tolerant of the Destre breed."

"Did you tell him my name?"

"I have forgotten it, but you may recite it to him, before he orders your execution."

Several officers were clustered in a circle within the tent. They pored over maps, arguing. Branra's back was to Danaer, but his posture made him immediately familiar. There was a bandage about the officer's head. After debating with an aide, Branra turned in response to the sentry's salute and saw Danaer. Shocked delight spread over the nobleman's square face and he hurried toward the scout. Danaer enjoyed the sentry's stupefaction at this friendly reaction. Then he saw that Branra meant to greet him with a comradely slap on the back. "I pray you, my lord, not that shoulder," Danaer said, and winced away.

"You are wounded? But how did you escape Deki? You said you would mount behind, but . . ."

"I took a Markuand arrow before I could, my lord. Gordyan and Lira helped me, or I would not be here. He and Lira and some of his men are waiting at the edge of your camp. I beg your favor and ask that I may take food and water to them."

"Hold! You embarrass me, Troop Leader. They shall be welcomed at once."

"Is that wise?" another officer asked. "The bandits will kill us in our sleep—"

Branra rounded on the man. "I have fought against the Destre-Y and fought with them—and I tell you this warrior is to be trusted with my life, he and all of his friends. He freely offered me his own life in Deki. Food and water are small repayment. Guard! Bring those people to me at once. Unharmed! Treat them with all gentleness."

Danaer sighed, and then an ominous shuddering overcame him and he sank to the ground. Branra cried, "It is his wound! Fetch surgeons!"

"No, my lord. This is because of an empty belly."

A bowl of hot gruel was thrust into his hands. Danaer had taken but a few bites when he began bolting the food. Branra caught his hand. "Slowly, or it will not stay down." With difficulty, Danaer obeyed. He had finished half the bowl when Gordyan and Lira were ushered into the tent. They too were fed, Lira sitting beside Danaer, color creeping back into her pale cheeks.

Gordyan ate a third bowl and shared some roast horsemeat Branra had given them. Then he winked approvingly at Danaer and Lira and turned to the young officer. "This is a bad pass for the alliance, Bloody Sword."

Branra grinned at the epithet, unoffended. He pointed at a map he held, and Gordyan noted what he had indicated and looked grim. "What do you suggest?" Branra asked amiably. "I cannot send out my troops to bring in Destre-Y. They would be killed." He glanced at Lira. "My lady, if you could employ your sorkra arts . . ."

She hid her face, shamed by her weakness. Danaer

said in her defense, "Her hunger prevents that at present, Lieutenant."

Branra accepted that without question, solicitous, sending a servant for still more of his own food.

Gordyan found a solution to the dilemma. "My warriors are your key, Branraediir. Let my men ride out with your soldiers and strike a truce, as Danaer did when he brought us to you. An Azsed can reach through the hatred of other Azsed-Y, for he can swear honor on his goddess. The refugees will believe that. They will hold their weapons if they are assured their safety is promised in the sacred tongue of Argan."

"Will they not suspect it as some trick and turn on your men?"

It was the same worry his aide had broached, but Branra merely presented it now as a thing to be weighed. Gordyan put it aside. "I think not. My Rena's colors, on our mantles, are known throughout the Vrastre. At even, is it not worth the attempt, to salvage the alliance?"

"We shall try it, Destre. Instruct your men, and I will summon my heralds." Gordyan showed few signs of his ordeal by hunger as he rushed from the tent. Branra gazed after him, bemused, then came over to Danaer and Lira. "I almost believe this plan can succeed. Before that giant arrived, I had given up hope for the Commander's union of Destre and The Interior. I had steeled myself to confess failure to him and General Nurdanth, that I had lost their army for naught—that is, if I lived to return to Siank at all. You have been a lucky mark for me, scout, or perhaps a curse. I have never known such close escapes as I have since I met you."

"How is your wound, my lord?" Danaer asked, thinking of one such escape.

"It was bad for a space." Branra fingered the bandage. "I credit that roan for my life. I was in no condition to ride the brute, but it got me safely out of Deki. I will return it to you with thanks. In truth, I had given you up for dead."

"Well you might!" Lira exclaimed. "He lay near Keth's portals so long he frightened me."

Branra smiled fondly. "That is no surprise to those of us who have eyes. I give you welcome back into our ranks also, lady sorkra, you and Danaer."

"I shall try to serve you better than I did the Captain." Lira's face was sad, but she squared her small shoulders. "Now that I know the tactics of the Markuand wizard and his treacherous conspirators, I shall no longer be such easy prey. The Markuand's evil lord does not know I live. When you slew the snake-bird, you wounded his powers. There has been no probing of my presence, no reaching toward the Vrastre. We have . . . fallen between the cracks of their fathoming," she said, trying to explain her arcane methods in terms they could understand. A sly smile curved Lira's mouth. "I shall endeavor to keep us well hidden, my lord."

"Put on a mask, eh? As they masked themselves from us at Deki with fogs and wizardry."

"Yes, my lord. I shall cast a glamour to conceal the caravan from them till we approach nearer to my Web. Once the Traech Sorkra knows of our plight, and of the witch's treachery, we will have much help."

"Ah! This time we shall be the tricksters and they the tricked!"

Lira added in a tiny voice, "But feed me well, I pray, so that I will have strength to work. I must . . . must do it all alone, for a while."

"You may have my own rations, if that will help," Branra promised. "Your skills are worth any price, lady wizard. Whatever you desire, but ask it. This will buy us time—and time is the thing we must have now, above all."

XXI

TAKE JOY OF ARGAN

DANAER HAD BEEN CHEERED TO LEARN THAT SHAARtre and a goodly number of his unit were among the survivors of Deki. But to his annoyance, he had not been allowed to join those comrades. At the insistence of Lira and the Lieutenant, he had been sent to the surgeons' wagons until they should feel he had sufficiently recuperated from injury and hunger. As soon as he could, by midday, he escaped their clutches and found a roan, then rode toward the head of the caravan.

Lira was mounted and riding in Branra's entourage, and Xashe and Rorluk had been reporting to the Lieutenant and were about to return to the point when Danaer arrived. They winked elaborately at Danaer as he saluted the officer and asked, "My lord, shall I resume my duties?"

Shaking her head, Lira silently expressed her disapproval, and Branra said, "Are you fit, Troop Leader?"

"Too fit to stay in those wagons, Lieutenant," Danaer replied, anxious to avoid more boredom and jouncing in the physicians' care. "I will regain my strength the sooner if I am active."

Branra waved to Danaer's apprentices, sending them forward. "I think they can serve us for now. You taught them very well. Without them, the caravan would never have found the landmarks through the Sink. Ride with my staff here, Troop Leader. You will act as liaison when Gordyan brings in more Destre."

It was not what Danaer had hoped, but it would keep him close to Lira, and he said, "Thank you, Lieutenant." At that, several of Branra's aides chuckled behind their hands, a thing that puzzled Danaer.

The nobleman noticed their amusement and told

them sternly, "How could he know his error? He was gravely wounded when the change occurred." They muttered lame apologies as Branra explained to Danaer, "I am now styled Captain, not my design but General Ti-Mori's. She bids me take the rank and command of Siank's contingent on this trek."

He seemed ill at ease, and Danaer fathomed the reason. "Captain Yistar would be most pleased. He never scorned advance for true merit, only for political purposes."

"I shall strive to honor his memory, though a heavy task, that."

When the caravan moved forward again, Danaer fell in, riding by Lira's side. It was no proper position for a Troop Leader, and he knew Shaartre and the others would call him an idler and similar gibes. No matter. The reward was worth the friendly torment it would bring later. Stirrup to stirrup, he rode with Lira. They spoke impersonally, for there were many of Branra's staff close by them. Now and then Lira would turn and look to the east. Danaer sensed her sorkra talents in play. "Pursuit?" he guessed, and dreaded the answer.

"None." A slow smile rounded her face, and Danaer was glad to see much of her proper color and flesh restored. "It is working. He still has not probed for us. He thinks us broken, slaying each other."

"It might have been so, and the journey still will not be easy." Danaer squinted at the sun. "I doubt we can reach Vidik before nightfall tomorrow."

"My Lord Branra feared we would have to deal with more mirages and evil storms and stampedes that were only illusions."

"Your glamour has hidden us safely."

Lira sighed. "But it has been bad, all the same." The caravan was no longer such an orderly column, for many civilians and refugee Destre-Y accompanied the train in ragged groups. Many horses had been sacrificed to feed the people, and water was rationed. Under the concealing magic Lira cast above them, they crept toward Vidik, out of the Sink.

Often Lira would stare into nothing for long minutes, and Danaer took care not to distract her at such times, aware of her need to shield them with enchantments, and to do this without aid from Ulodovol. She was dressed again as a boy, and Danaer suspected the clothes had been claimed from one of the dead. None could be squeamish about such things now. There was no dainty mare for her to ride or a sidesaddle to make her look the lady; only a rough-coated and dull-eyed black, a stolid and sturdy beast able to stand the privations of the trek better than many finer horses.

"I told the Captain what happened the night of the Markuand breaking through," Lira said after a lengthy silence. "About Chorii and the way Prince Diilbok has helped her—and she him, and Hablit as well, I think. We will have them all, in time, and I especially want her in my thrall. As soon as we reach Vidik and I can risk linking with my master, the Royal Commander will know the truth about them, too. He will arrest the Prince and that bitch. She should be torn limb from limb!"

Danaer said softly, "That is not like you."

"You are wrong, qedra. It is a part of me you have not seen. But I can be as a Destre woman, and my hatred for Chorii is strong. She is as evil as her Markuand conspirator, and she used you to try to hurt me. She will pay dearly for that."

"Her master was not invulnerable, so she must have her weaknesses as well," Danaer encouraged her, much impressed by Lira's fieriness.

"Ai! Weakness. We have discovered one, Danaer— a most important thing." Despite the fact that others were about, she sought his hand and smiled. "You learned it, too. Silver, and the sacred glass of the deeps of volcanoes. I felt the power of the white metal and obsidian there in Deki, when Branra slew the Markuand's demon snake. Not his sword alone, but combined with the power of the Rasven amulet, it created a great counterforce for good."

"Magic from the smoking mountains," Danaer murmured. When Lira asked what he meant, he told her of Osyta. She insisted on hearing every detail of the prophecy then. Danaer was reminded of the time he had mentioned the ha-usfaen, and Lira's fascination with that phenomenon. He had never thought of his people and their ways as a mystery. But Lira was genuinely interested.

"She was very wise, that old kinswoman of yours," Lira said when he had done. "I do not understand all of what you have said, though."

Danaer had veiled much of the story, and hidden some. "There . . . there were prophecies which concerned Argan's sacred law. Nothing to do with magic or the war," he apologized lamely.

She gazed at him questioningly, seeming to examine his soul. And she asked no more about the holy ways of the Destre, honoring Danaer's silence.

Once more she looked back to the east, probing another's presence now, and without the gentleness and concern she had used toward Danaer. Her expression was intent and wary, and only after a long while did she sigh and nod in satisfaction.

Though he had argued that he was fit, Danaer was grateful for the caravan's slow progress. His wound no longer pained him much, and he was recovering fairly quickly. Yet a full day's duty this soon after regaining his feet might have proved too severe a test.

Night fell, and still there was no Markuand attack, by weapon or by wizardry. No storms, no stampedes, no mirages. Lira's own strength was increasing steadily, and with it her confidence returned as well. Though separate from her web, she cast her spells expertly, hiding the column from unfriendly eyes. Her antagonist seemed nowhere about. Danaer remembered how Ulodovol had been prostrated by the attack of the demon beasts. He and Lira and Branra had done the same, with aid of silver and obsidian, for the enemy. For the moment, the caravan seemed comparatively safe and hidden.

The Wells of Ylami were far behind them, and the end of the Sink was near. Soldiers and civilians slept where they could in the cold desert darkness. Most were exhausted, but some woke often, tense and listening for evil winds or onrushing beasts where none should be. Nothing broke the natural quiet, though. Danaer had intended to stand guard outside Lira's tent, but she had none. She was housed in a private area of Branra's staff pavilion, one of the few intact tents left. Branra and Lira both assured him she would be well guarded, and Danaer reluctantly gave himself over to sleep, wrapped in a blanket a dead man had owned.

With dawn, the creaking wagons that had withstood the rigors of siege and rout rolled toward Vidik, horsemen and many people afoot following. Once more Lira hid them from pursuit, negligently, with only a part of her sorkra skills, another sign of her growing assurance. Often she chatted with Danaer or Branra, seemingly carefree.

Gordyan, too, spoke with them, riding in to confer with the nobleman on the progress of their motley groups. "Vidik lies not far ahead now," he told them past center-stand. "But it will not be the Vidik you remember. I have sent a message to Wyaela. By your leave, Lira. Do not be alarmed. It is word to give comfort to the Markuand wizard should he touch the messenger's thoughts—for I warned Wyaela to abandon Vidik. We will take on water and food and push toward Siank with all speed. But my messenger does not know the army will stop there. I have kept him in ignorance, deliberately."

"Abandon Vidik," Danaer said sorrowfully. "Deki, Vidik—all the bastions of Azsed are falling."

"We will win them back."

"That is so," Branra agreed. "And we will cleanse each city with Markuand blood and bring Destre-Y back into the fold of Krantin." He made no oath, for only once had Danaer heard Branra call on the gods. But his fierce tone made Danaer and Gordyan grin, deeming the officer a Destre in spirit, if not by birth.

"For now, I will keep my warriors well away from the caravan, and take in as many Dekans as I may. I will send the women with children to Suut, to the south. They will be out of the way of battle then," Gordyan said. "And we will keep the appearance of being bitter enemies, shall we not?" With that, he kicked up his roan and rode back toward his scattered bands of warriors and refugees.

A candle-mark later, Danaer began to see smoke

billowing up on the horizon to the west. Forewarned
by Gordyan, he knew what it meant, yet the sight cut
at him. It was painful to see Vidik die.

Grassland was on every side now and the wagons
rolled along briskly. The caravan had been brutally
culled of weaker horses and men. Any wagons that collapsed were broken up and the wood carried along.
Branra intended to deny any plunder he could to the
Markuand. Dead were buried quickly, alongside the
trail. Branra was callously practical, as he must be. He
ordered bodies stripped of clothing and weapons.
Prayers and grief must be short. Time was all-
important.

It was not quite nightfall when they camped by the
springs north of Vidik. On their left a pall of smoke
drifted on the soft Vrastre wind, the sunset tinging the
black cloud with spots of blood red.

There had been a flurry of excitement at sundown,
for General Ti-Mori arrived with a small unit of her
aides. She wanted to confer with Branra and deemed
it worth the risk. Danaer had lingered near the staff
area when the women galloped up to meet the caravan's young commander. In Deki he had been daunted
by the virago's manner; now he admired Ti-Mori's
seat, for she was a fine horsewoman, Branra's equal in
controlling her mount. Her elite guard, all female,
came with her, encircling Branra's nervous aides. The
General and Branra put their heads together, reaching
decisions quickly. "Three units?" Ti-Mori asked intently.

"It shall be as you order, General, as the Royal
Commander planned." Branra's tone was eager. "We
will send forward all our wounded and the unarmed
auxiliaries and civilians at dawn, with a skeleton
escort. As soon as we are provisioned, we follow."

Ti-Mori grinned. She was not handsome, and most
of her women were hard-featured, no soft females to
inspire a man to flirtation. But at this moment Danaer
was exceedingly relieved that Ti-Mori and her fanati-
cal little army were sworn to defend Krantin. "Ai! And
my units will turn back east. We will pick at the
Markuand, who now cross the Sink. We will see how

they enjoy my game—like a shamming golhi-pup dragging one leg and leading the shta-hawk into the jaws
of its greedy dam!"

"Leave some of them for our swords, or the Commander and the Destre will feel cheated," Branra said.
Ti-Mori turned to talk to her women, and Branra
glanced at Danaer and crooked a finger at him. "Seek
out Gordyan and ask him to come. I would give him
our news."

Danaer cast a sidelong glance at Lira, who was chat-
ting with some of Ti-Mori's junior aides. Then he rode
south, to where he knew Gordyan's Zsed would be, between the army's encampment and Vidik. The bright
glow of the burning city gave him more than sufficient
light to pick his way along the streams and hills.

As he neared the Destre, no one challenged him.
Danaer nodded in satisfaction. Deki was lost and Vidik
dying, but now an army scout could ride into a Zsed
and draw no sling stones or lances in hostility. Argan
had favored this joining of Destre and Iit, as Gordt te
Raa had prayed she would.

"It is the Azsed soldier!" Danaer recognized the man
who hailed him as one of Gordyan's guards and asked
after his friend. "He has ridden out to hurry in some
laggards. Is it a matter of importance?"

"A message from Branraediir. And I would see my
hyidu if I might. When think you he will return?"

The Destre held his fingers parallel to the horizon,
against the sinking sun. "About a candle-mark . . ."

"Too long to wait." Danaer knew this was one of
Gordyan's trusted men and relayed the message, then
rode back to the caravan. When he arrived, one of
Branra's staff took his report, saying the officer was
occupied elsewhere. Danaer began to feel with some
annoyance that he had lathered his mount to no purpose. However, the ride had tested his fitness well, with
pleasing results. He still was fresh, despite the long day.

He dismounted and walked the roan to cool it,
searching for Lira. By the time he found her, the horse
was breathing easy and he let it graze a bit. A flap had
been erected alongside a wagon, and Lira and two of

Ti-Mori's warrior women were talking there. Somewhat uncertainly, Danaer approached them.

"Is this your orderly, lady sorkra?" one uniformed woman asked, raking a calculating stare over Danaer. Her body was lean and muscular and her breasts were bound nearly flat beneath her tunic, her arms bare and scarred.

Lira laughed, but said a trifle sharply, "He has served me as an orderly, yes, and as a rescuer and confidant. But he is even more devoted to me in matters of the heart." At their displeased expressions, she added, "Do you begrudge me my appetites? I have not called your thirst for battle a dishonor to your sex."

They soon made their leave, marching as smartly as cadets new from The Interior. Guessing Danaer's thoughts, Lira said, "It is their way, and past changing. Most of their sort joined Ti-Mori when she defied her noble kindred and took arms, and at that time few of those women were much beyond their girlhood. They have never learned to be feminine in some things. But they are fearsome in battle."

"But when the war is at an end, these noblewomen and peasant girls will not be welcomed back into the castles and villages of The Interior, as warrior women would be among the Destre tribes."

Lira nodded and said morosely, "I *hope* the war will end, and that then there will still exist castles and villages in The Interior. When that time comes, Ti-Mori and her female soldiers must deal with their own lives." Her manner altered then. "But not all Destre women are warriors, I have heard. Many practice all the female arts, do they not?"

Before he could reply, Lira impulsively pulled his head down and greeted him with a passionate kiss. Pleasantly startled, he answered in kind. She drew him by the hand to a nearby knoll, where she had spread a piece of torn tent on the grass. They sat, and Lira put Danaer's arm familiarly about her waist and leaned against him. She was not wearing the uniform any more, but had wrapped a plain dark cloak about her small body, knotting it with frayed rope. It was not a pretty costume, yet to Danaer she seemed most alluring. Despite her kiss, there was a tenseness in her voice and manner. "Your wound is well closed? You are moving as strongly as before that awful moment in Deki."

"Gordyan's herb-healer and the army's surgeons fought to see who could heal me more quickly, and I profited from both."

He kissed her again, but Lira was pensive. "I cannot tell you of my fears when I saw you lying in your blood and racked with fever, so that every breath you took brought pain to those who cared for you. It is a reprieve from the gods to see you whole again, qedra."

"Argan favors me, and I wear your amulet. What can harm me?"

"I . . . I told you it was not sacred. But it is very powerful. It puts you under the protection of the sorkra Web, and in a way, whatever menaces the Web can menace you, through the obsidian."

Danaer's thoughts flew to times of terrible cold and blackness and things beyond an ordinary mortal's comprehension. "I have felt the touch of your magic. You speak as if *I* am a sorkra."

"Not precisely. But you have helped me when my Web could not, when I would have died without you. Can you not recall our combined wills when we sent the Markuand past saving?"

"Argan is the ruler of wills," Danaer said, disturbed. Then he brightened. "But if this thing is will, it is truly sacred to Argan, a gift of the goddess."

Lira caressed his face. "Yet it cannot put off death. When you were hurt, I was sure the gods punished me for my cruelty."

"Cruelty?"

"I dreaded that I should witness your death and carry with me forever afterward that I had denied you joy."

Danaer's wonderment was warring with stirrings of desire. "But it was Prince Diilbok's mistress, the witch, who controlled us both. I have no pride in the things I said that night . . ."

"That she put in your mouth. I should have been my own mistress and countered her evil charms. I *will* be mistress, henceforth. She cannot part us now, nor put words on our lips that are not our own."

"It seems we were caught in her snares, you by your sorkra calling, and I . . ." Danaer trailed off.

"Ildate?" He was astonished, and Lira glanced away from him, not angry but seemingly much shamed. "Forgive me. When you were near death, I probed your mind to assure myself and Gordyan that you were still alive. It was impossible to avoid stumbling through the dreams of your fever. Are you furious with me?"

Once the idea of Lira's mind entering his own had revulsed Danaer. Now he found he was not shocked. Rather, it seemed a form of joining, as man and woman joined bodies. "I must ask you to not scorn me instead. I believed the witch and did not understand when you spoke of your sorkra oath. If I had not pressed you that night, perhaps the enemy wizards would not have breached Deki's walls."

"No, it was too late even then, their net too finely woven." Lira studied him carefully. "Then you are not angry? To tell the truth, I am very jealous of Ildate, for she has known what I have not.'"

Danaer was delighted to find all Lira's reserve gone, and with it her Sarli primness. She said earnestly, "I would not deny you now, or deny myself. I have learned a bit of the Destre customs. Let me pledge myself to you and to your goddess, as the plains women do with the men they favor. I will sacrifice to Argan." Apparently Danaer's silence worried her, for she exclaimed, "Is there some Azsed ritual I have overstepped? Tell me if I offend some secret of your tribes, and—"

"There is no offense. It is only that I did not know the sorkra could pledge to Argan. Does it not violate the oath to your Web? And if we take joy, does *that* not break your oath as well and weaken your powers?"

Behind the love in her dark eyes shone something Danaer could not name. If it was doubt, she shrouded it at once. "No, I will be strengthened. For now, no other sorkra touches me, not even the Traech Sorkra. Tonight I am woman, not sorkra. Teach me what Ildate learned."

Danaer put her up on his roan and they galloped toward Vidik. With Lira sitting before him, the ground flew back beneath them and Vidik's spires and towers rose before them, smoke streaming from her walls, drifting east in the night breeze. Lasiirnte Wyaela would supervise Vidik's destruction until she had to leave, and the Markuand were drawing in sight of her ruined city. Danaer hoped she would not already have razed the temple. They found the gates open wide and the streets nearly deserted. Brick pavements were cluttered with debris, and inns and houses were empty. The people had fled.

Starkly magnificent, Argan's altar house dominated what had been the heart of Vidik. It was hulking stone and not yet scorched by the fires. Danaer helped Lira down and they entered the holy place. The interior gleamed with bright colors, and Danaer hated to think of the Markuand defiling the frescoes and tapestries. Better that Wyaela, in pious sacrifice, should destroy it and send it to the goddess. Danaer slid back his mantle, baring his head, as he and Lira walked toward the altar stones.

A lone priest stood before the fire, sadly bundling together tokens of worship, casting them into the flames. He turned toward them and began to say, "Yaen of the . . ." then hesitated as he saw Lira and knew her for no Destre woman.

"I would sacrifice to Argan," she said simply.

The priest shook his head, bewildered. "This is a passion few Iit may understand."

"I will try."

"For this warrior?" Danaer felt his inner being stripped clean under the priest's steady gaze.

"I seek not his soul," Lira assured the holy one. "Merely devotion of the flesh. Argan can never be rivaled by mortals."

The priest considered matters, then said, "If your woman wishes this, I will not refuse her, warrior. But it will be something to tell other priests once we reach Siank." He started a chant, not wasting time, for they were very aware of the conflagration consuming Vidik around them.

Lira fumbled within a fold of her cloak and took out an object which she held tightly. "Your sacrifice?" Lira gave the priest a gold coin, and then, at his nod, she went to the altar stone and flung her offering into the fire. Danaer saw a glint of metal and bright ribbon and knew it must be something of great value to Lira, for she was not a woman who would stint once her love was given.

"Yaen ve te Fihar," the priest cried. "Kant . . ." Danaer repeated the solemn prayer with him, and Lira waited till it was done. She did not know the language, but her attitude was all piety could demand.

As they left the temple, Danaer whispered to her, "Feel you now the goddess?"

"I would not lie to you. She is your goddess, qedra, and in that sense I know her well, but . . ."

"Through me you shall come to adore her, and to share her joy," Danaer promised.

"It were ever a good thing for an Iit to come to Argan," a deep voice welcomed them as they stepped out of the doors. Danaer and Lira stared in surprise at Gordyan. "I followed you here, but I did not want to interrupt holy matters."

Appreciative, Danaer asked, "Did your man give you Branra's message?"

"Ai. It has been dealt with. Then I saw you bound for Vidik and thought to overtake you, until I saw where you headed." Gordyan looked fondly at Lira. "Now you are sworn to my hyidu?"

"I am sworn." Her words rang sweetly in Danaer's ears. She touched his eiphren stone, and Argan's fire ran up his fingers to his soul and heated his blood.

"Come to my Zsed," Gordyan said.

"Branra . . ."

"I have spoken to Bloody Sword. He favors me in this, question it not."

Danaer let himself be persuaded, and he and Lira rode with Gordyan out of Vidik and to the nomad encampment. There were more tents and people about now than there had been a short while earlier when Danaer had delivered the Captain's message. Plainly refugees from Vidik had joined those of Deki and further swelled Gordyan's ranks of warriors and camp followers.

With a mysterious air, Gordyan led them to the largest of the Zsed's tents. It was no palace of cloth, as the Rena's was, for this was constructed of leavings from Vidik's disaster and Gordyan's retreat across the Vrastre. Nevertheless, it was obviously the property of this Zsed's chieftain—Gordyan. They dismounted and he ducked beneath the flap, beckoning Danaer and Lira inside. "Well appointed, eh?" he said with a laugh, indicating the meager possessions within, no more than a pallet and a few small pouches and blankets.

"It suits you as a warrior leader," Danaer said.

"Ai, it does." Gordyan rummaged through his personal blanket, the one he carried behind his cantle and that would contain his most precious belongings. When he stood up, Danaer was amazed that his friend was blushing deeply and sounding thick-tongued. "I . . . I know not the proper courtesies for such as this . . . but, Lira, to swear to Argan for my hyidu . . . then . . . well, it is that I would give you this."

Lira gasped as Gordyan clumsily dropped a golden chain set with rubies into her cupped palms. "Oh, how handsome it is!" she cried.

"Now, that is no caravan plunder," he assured her anxiously. "It was my dead sister's, and too fine a thing for me to lavish on any woman of ease. And I cannot see myself wearing it." Gordyan chuckled nervously at his poor joke, then held out his hand to Danaer. "Maen, I know you lost your belt knife in that devil snake. I would give you something to fill the empty sheath."

Danaer stared at an exquisite ceremonial dagger. It was no common blade but set with a silver hilt and guard, and the cutting edge was made of glassy black stone. Gordyan said with some embarrassment, "It is no proper weapon, of course. I had it to wear at vrentru, before I came into the Rena's service. Now I may wear only his badges and my lady's." He slapped his well-worn knife, the hilt wrapped in thongs of black and gold and green.

"I will treasure this, Gordyan, for never have I beheld such a fine knife, in truth."

Lira touched the obsidian blade and the silver, seeing, as Danaer had, the purity of the materials. They exchanged a speaking glance, their thoughts as one on the value of this gift. Indeed, it had value far beyond what Gordyan believed. In Danaer's keeping, allied as he was with Lira, this became a weapon against Markuand's magic.

Gordyan patted their shoulders. "You are kind to allow me to gift you with such trifles."

"We receive them most gladly." To Danaer's pride, Lira had learned the manners of Destre gift-giving, for she went on to say, "The honor is ours, warrior. These rubies will quite overwhelm my person."

"And the knife will make me look like a beggar wearing a Siirn's blade," Danaer added.

Gordyan beamed and said, "And now you will stay in my tent the night. This is another gift for my hyidu and his woman."

"I ought to report to my units," Danaer began.

"Do not anger me. I said I had dealt with Branraediir. You will stay. I would provide finer quarters if I could, but I am sure a pallet designed for me will be big enough for the two of you." With a loud laugh, Gordyan left, pulling tight the tent flap behind him, locking them away from the rest of the world.

Savoring the unexpected, Danaer and Lira looked at one another and at the things Gordyan had given them. Again Lira caressed the dagger. "My own talisman against wizardry," Danaer said. "Now you must take back your amulet, and the obsidian and silver will work together." Lira agreed. He slipped off the thong and gently threaded the head of Rasven down through her curly hair, returning it whence it had come, his hands lingering on her breasts.

Lira sighed and did not pull away from him. She held out the string of rubies. "It needs a companion," she said. "Do you think rubies and gold go well with obsidian?" He saw her intent and smiled. "Will you fasten it for me? There is a clasp, a cunning Destre device, no doubt." She spoke in that low, throaty voice which made his pulse race.

Awkwardly, he took the delicate jewelry. Lira tugged at her cloak, untying the rope. In a lithe, lovely motion, she cast both away and stood revealed in a bright dress. Somewhere she had found red cloth, perhaps purchased from one of the women of ease who followed the caravan. The gown was a mere wisp of fancy, caught by a thin little cord. Both would yield quickly to a touch. Danaer feasted his eyes and then his hands, and Lira came against him eagerly, a woman clad in silk and gems, responding to his every wish.

"To think that this spark lurked beneath your Sarli manners," he marveled as her passion matched his.

"My people are restrained until they have found their desire, and then we give ourselves completely," Lira said breathlessly. "A ruby necklace, and red is Argan's color, is it not? Do you wish to deck me in her jewels, to add a finishing stroke to the ceremony at her altar?"

He could not tell if she teased, but the necklace still dangled from his busy hands. Danaer slipped it against her throat, and as he did Lira pulled off her headband. Her dark hair tumbled about her shoulders and framed her face. It was as intimate a gesture as when an Azsed woman took her eiphren pendant from her forehead. Both actions could only be a prelude to Argan's most joyous worship.

In the next instant, Lira's lips and body were one with Danaer's, her intensity feeding the fire that ruled them both. Briefly, Danaer was aware that the rubies and the handsome dagger had dropped to the earth beneath them. Then he forgot all about such trifles.

XXII

ANDARU

DANAER SEEMED TO SEE AN IMMENSE CLOUD OF DUST
stirred by hundreds of men and beasts. Weapons
flashed and rang and screams filled the air. Everywhere
there was blood. He did not want to be part of this
thing, yet he must. Old Osyta was woven through its
fabric, and her prophecy. It was a terrible battle, and
Iit and Destre-Y fought side by side, Krantin reunited,
as his kinswoman had said it would be. Andaru—the
time of glory to come, to crown the destiny of the
plains people. Andaru would come swiftly on wings
of blood and fire, against evil forces powerful beyond
dreaming.

The cloud-obscured battle raged, and Osyta's leathery face wavered before Danaer. Accompanying the
din he heard a heavy, ominous rumbling. It was the
smoking mountains of Krantin, waking, joining the battle.

A woman lay dead. It was not Osyta, whose haggish
image danced transparently across the scene. Through
her wizened face Danaer saw the beautiful corpse. Detail was strangely blurred, however; he could not
clearly discern her face and hair nor even what sort of
garments and jewels she wore. The woman was young,
he knew, broken and lifeless and covered with blood.
Wails of grief rose from around the body, and Danaer
would have joined that mourning.

Osyta's quavering voice tore into his soul, a cry
echoing from the regions beyond the world: *Andaru,
and you will witness it, kinsman!*

This was the sacrifice, the unknown woman. Her
blood was to begin the long-promised day of rebirth for
Azsed and all Krantin. Danaer struggled, trying to
learn her identity, growing frantic. But a blood-red veil
remained between him and the body.

303

He *must* know who she was—who was to be slain to bring Osyta's prophecy into being? Was it Lira?

Osyta spoke again, words she had not given him ere she died: *She will be an Azsed woman, and evil magic is part of her death and sacrifice. It must be, kinsman, for it shall give us Andaru.*

A scream of fierce denial caught in Danaer's throat as he came awake. He was lying on Gordyan's pallet. Lira was curled up at his side, still asleep. He was bathed in his own sweat, his heart pounding as from the exertions of battle, his hand clenched on a sword that was not there. After a shudder of horror, he calmed himself. Gradually he tried to put aside the awful vision. It was merely a dream, though one most terrible. Lira moved and yawned, then smiled and clung to him. Dawn was near, and they chased the remnant of his nightmare into nothingness with joy in Argan.

Danaer had hoped that would make an end of the thing. But it had not. It returned to haunt him through the hours that followed. He had said nothing of it to Lira, not wanting to alarm her. But again and again the vision came back. And always he feared that this time the veil would fall away and he would see what he dreaded—that the woman was Lira, slain in the battle, her death the price of Andaru.

Too dear a price! He would not pay it!

When day had come, he had parted from her, with much regret, then resumed his duties at the point. Once when he had returned to consult with Branra over the caravan's progress, he did not see Lira. And to his unsubtle inquiries Branra replied that she had withdrawn to one of the wagons. Danaer knew, with misgivings, what that must mean: Lira was casting spells, and seeking her Web, now that they were safely beyond Vidik. When he had returned to her the graven obsidian, he had assumed he would again be an ordinary man, untouched by her wizardry. Now he knew it was not so; the familiar tingling warmth was at his belt, where Gordyan's dagger rested. Though he was not a sorkra, he realized now that he was still linked to her wizardry, could not escape it.

At nightfall, Lira greeted him warmly, but he detected an earnestness of purpose in her manner that he had not sensed since they had left Deki. While the business of the camp eddied around them, they spoke softly. "You have touched minds again with Ulodovol," he guessed, before she could tell him so.

Lira nodded, very somber. "I have informed him of all that happened. He says that the attacks upon The Interior ceased quite abruptly at the moment the snake-bird died."

"It may be a ruse, some trick of the Markuand and Chorii."

"Perhaps," she admitted reluctantly. "We will find them. Now we have bait to catch Chorii of the Valley of the Hawks. We have her lover."

"Diilbok? How will that serve? Surely she but used him while he suited her evil schemings. If Malol has discovered his treachery and removed him from his rank, Chorii will not care. She will find another tool."

Lira smiled up at him. "Women do not always command their hearts in these matters. I think it very possible she may come to his aid. Certainly he loved her, for the Traech Sorkra says Diilbok never showed such deviousness before he became Chorii's man. He abandoned his safe castles and easy life and sought out his cousin's plans, leaving the mountains, all for Chorii's sake. If she returns even a part of such devotion to him, our bait will trap her."

"You have learned all this, across many a king's-league, with never a word on parchment nor horseman to carry it?" Danaer marveled again at her arts.

"I am recovered, as you are, and able to serve the Captain once more."

"Mine was a wound of the body, not of wizard's charms." Danaer drew her close and whispered, "And what of your body, my woman? Shall we find a place apart from the caravan and take joy?"

For the briefest moment, he felt an odd hesitation. Whatever disturbed her, she put it aside. "Come to the command tent near dawn. I will be waiting outside. That will be a time when I can . . . when I will freely welcome your love, qedra." Again she paused, worry in her eyes. Then she said, "I wish it could be now." Like a woman newly initiated to this lusty delight, she clung to him for a minute, then ran back to Branra's staff area.

Danaer stayed where he was for a while, muttering curses and mastering his frustration. Till morning! He would survive his eagerness, he supposed. Lira had taken oath, as he had. And as he must go where his officer commanded, so must she now leave him.

But only till dawn. He remembered the promise and smiled in anticipation, then hurried to find his units. When the night began to ebb, he woke and stole through the camp, avoiding sentinels. Lira had not forgotten, and none of her doubts or hesitation came with her. The reward of that early waking was all Danaer had hoped for, a sating of their senses.

The day and the night that followed were the same. By day Lira must practice her sorkra skills. She reached out to her Web, and then she turned and cast the glamour over caravan and the outspreading warriors of Gordyan's train. Somehow, she both maintained the glamour and spoke to her Web, and no mirages or storms pursued them. At night, she again came out of her shelter near dawn to share joy with Danaer. He feared to distract her, knowing well the burden she carried. But Lira seemed to relish his kiss and their mating, a blissful escape that made her woman, not oath-bound sorkra. They must rob the lords they served of this time with each other, at least until the battle was won.

Until the battle was won . . . and the price paid in blood.

Three days after Vidik, drawing very near to Siank, that same grim thought recurred another time to Danaer. He could not fend it off. The vision's horror had not faded but had grown in intensity.

"Bedding your woman does not please you?" Gordyan remarked slyly. "Surely Lira is no shrew or hag to give you rough sleeping?" Danaer realized he had been riding beside his friend for many a minute without speaking, and Gordyan taunted him to bring him out of woolgathering. Gordyan grinned and said, "It is good that your apprentices know the landmarks. You have not been heeding them for a quarter-period."

"It . . . it is a dream which troubles me," he confessed, the secret broken at last. His fear must be mirrored in his face, for Gordyan sobered at once, taking his words most seriously. It was a thing he could tell his blood friend, if no one else, and Gordyan listened to it all.

"Ah!" Gordyan shook a fist at the sky. "The priests speak of such omens, Danaer, that some people, not all of them sorkra or far-seers, have the foretelling gift at times. Smile, Argan! Let us slay the Markuand and you can feed on their carcasses! Maen, this prophecy of your kinswoman is most wondrous! It is at one with your dream."

"Andaru," Danaer said slowly. He and Gordyan spoke in the Azsed idiom, though neither Xashe nor Rorluk showed any impolite tendency to eavesdrop. The young men rode ahead of them, honoring Danaer's conversation with his friend. "Andaru," Danaer repeated. "But to know it must be a woman's death that brings its beginning . . ."

"Warriors know that some of them will fall in battle, hyidu. Then their names sing to Argan. It is much glory."

"It was terrible to see." Danaer shivered. "I woke with a cry frozen on my lips. I have not been able to speak of it till now, not even to Lira. Most especially not to Lira!"

"A woman." Gordyan was gentle with Danaer's fear. "Could you see the woman's face?"

"No! And it is that which tortures me! I saw Iit and Destre-Y fight Markuand, and wizardry was mixed with the weapons. And I knew that the woman lying dead was an Azsed." Danaer nearly choked on those words. "Gordyan, Lira sacrificed to Argan. She is pledged to me. *She* is Azsed. If it is her death that must fulfill this prophecy—"

"Still, hyidu!" Gordyan gripped his shoulder hard. "You have interpreted it wrongly. Lira is no warrior woman. How can she die in battle?"

"She is part of it, the Royal Commander's sorkra,

who has fought most fiercely with the Markuand's master wizard." Danaer yearned to accept Gordyan's argument. He had begun to fear sleep, dreading that the dream would return. But it had not. Argan acted most powerfully when man and woman took joy in her name, and it was said the prophetic visions that came then were the truest.

He felt somewhat eased, though, now that he had told the dream to his friend. Gordyan did not dismiss the omen. Rather, he sought an explanation that would comfort them both.

"Ti-Mori," the big man said suddenly, pouncing on her name. Danaer eyed him, puzzled. "There is she who will die, that Iit devil. Warrior woman, indeed. Even now she fights the Markuand, engaging them and their wizard. If she does not gauge her fight-and-turn scheme perfectly, she *will* die."

"But the sacrifice must be an Azsed woman, and Ti-Mori is an unbeliever."

Gordyan's hand still lay on his shoulder, and now he shook Danaer lightly. "It will not be Lira. If an Azsed woman must die to gain us Andaru, it will be . . . will be . . . Wyaela!" They looked at one another. The Lasiirnte of Vidik was much respected, but she was neither friend nor lover. Gordyan hammered at his idea. "Ai! Wyaela to Fihar. She is with my warriors and her own, and she vows to stand on the line of blood when we meet the Markuand in battle. She is a most fierce war mistress, maen. And she is Azsed."

"She does not scorn lance and sword," Danaer said, agreeing. "I would mourn her death . . ."

"As would we all, and sing her fame to the portals of Keth. Wyaela would die content in such glory. And if it comes to pass, we shall be the first to proclaim her part in Andaru. But . . . for now, say nothing. It might alarm her followers from Vidik and endanger the coming battle. We must pray all goes well and that your woman and her wizardly companions continue to hide the truth of our alliance from the Markuand."

"And from others," Danaer added.

"Ai! And it is time I assembled my men, Danaer.

I must go forth to rejoin the Rena. When next we meet, it may be side by side in battle." They clasped hands tightly as they had across the fire when they mingled blood. "To the death of Markuand!"

"And to the destruction of their evil wizardry!" Danaer added.

During the past days, Destre bands moving beside the caravan had begun to drift away, taking their own diverse paths westward over the grassland. Groves and streams broke the Vrastre now, and the land was green and rich. There were many places to camp, many places to lie and wait and hope to be first to spot the Markuand as they came and carry the warning to the Rena.

Branra knew of their going but locked the knowledge out of his conscious mind, away from wizard spying. The Destre-Y were supposed to be his enemy, and on Lira's instructions he brooded much on his campaigns amid the Tradyans, making his thoughts those of a merciless lord of The Interior whose only relation with the plains people was to kill as many of them as he could.

Couriers pursued them now, brave men who ran between Ti-Mori's retreating army and Branra's columns, risking capture and torture should they encounter Markuand skirmishers ahead of the battle line. The word was brought—Markuand had crossed the Sink and fallen upon Vidik, and had raged to find it in ashes and its wells befouled. At great labor, they had been forced to bring more water with them from the river they had conquered. Their slaves suffered, but so did many of their own kind. Yet the Markuand warlords had no pity and seemed heedless of the waste of lives and sweat. Undeterred, grim, they came after Ti-Mori and struck at her warrior women again and again, each blow costing both armies dearly.

Branra's caravan rolled upland, toward its rendezvous with the main forces of Krantin. Each sunset found them farther west, closer to Siank, where the army of The Interior and the tribes of the Destre-Y gathered to meet the last attack of the Markuand, the attack that must decide all.

They climbed, a more gradual ascent than the one out of Deki. They had traveled this way long days ago, not knowing the full extent of the peril which lay ahead. Now, lean and hardened and blooded, the caravan made its return journey. The wagons were few, and many soldiers rode roans rather than blacks. Uniforms were not standard, and weapons were whatever a man had been able to save from the rout. But they were a better army than when they had left, in many ways.

The column wound up through a pass at the end of two parallel ridges. A broad, grassy plain lay beyond, and Siank, set against a backdrop of snow-capped mountains. A vast array of tents and rude dwellings and provision wagons was drawn up on Siank Plains, far too many to have been accommodated within the city walls. Siank would already be bursting from the refugees of her sister Destre cities to the east. The surviving wagons of the caravan were sent on, and troops were assigned campsites along the myriad streams of the Plains. Danaer and his apprentices were told they might return to their units. The great trek was done.

The Vrastre and Bogotana's Sink had been crossed twice, and many good comrades had died. The friends they had left behind at Siank garrison greeted them with cheers. Their ranks had been swelled by tens of tens of conscripts from The Interior, peasant boys and city rabble forced to be soldiers and properly fearful in their ignorance. There would be a second city of tents north of Siank, where the Destre community would also enlarge to become the mightiest Zsed the plains people had ever known. Gordt te Raa would lead his own army, a great band of warriors gathered from Deki to Barjokt and from Ve-Nya to Kakyein. There might even be a few warriors from Nyald Zsed, Danaer knew, but he would keep the honor of his clans himself, in uniform.

He saw many faces he had almost forgotten in the ordeals of the trek. Confusion was all around, and he could only nod to most of these comrades he had known since Nyald Fort. Danaer sought out an enclave of staff, hoping to see Lira before he must go to his units. An immense canopy had been set up at the rear of the Plains, hard by Siank. A forest of pennants surrounded the open tent, the badges of many lords of The Interior who had come to serve the Royal Commander. Above them all floated Krantin's bold, dark banner and the black and gold flag of the Brotherhood of the Zseds. The alliance still held fast.

The canopy's sides were drawn up to admit the breeze, and Danaer peered curiously into the tent. Malol te Eldri was there, looking more pale than Danaer remembered. There was tiredness in his posture, which spoke of many sleepless nights. General Nurdanth was with him, studying maps. He too looked very worn; the bulk of those who had died at Deki had been from Siank garrison, and Nurdanth was well known to weigh heavily the loss of even a single man. Gordt te Raa and Lasiirnte Kandra were there also. It gave Danaer a momentary start to see the princess; then he reminded himself this was no illusion. This woman would not seek to betray him or make him abandon his oath. Indeed, she took no notice of him, concerned, as was her lord, with whatever General Nurdanth was indicating on his map. The Destre monarchs were dressed in their finest raiment, their bright mantles and jeweled weapons contrasting with the drab uniforms all around them.

There was one more person among these leaders, perhaps the most powerful one of them all—Ulodovol. The master wizard, unlike Malol, seemed stronger and more prideful than when Danaer had looked upon him last, as if he had taken strength from his adversary's besting at Deki. He gazed at the map expressionlessly, his mind walking paths common men could not.

Branra and his aides had ridden up outside the tent, and the officer caught sight of Danaer, pausing to salute him. "Well done, Destre. Now just a bit more work and we will finish this campaign, eh, and avenge Yistar." Danaer was giving only a fraction of his attention to the nobleman, for Lira was among Branra's staff, and he hurried to help her down from her horse. Branra was saying, "I trust your wound is fully healed, Troop Leader. It would be too bad to be confined and miss a vrentru such as this promises to be . . . however, I do not think there is doubt that you are fit. If you do not mind, though, now other men must call upon the Lady Nalu's services for a while; only in her capacity as sorkra, I hasten to say, lest you challenge me for my impudence." He winked familiarly, ignoring the ranks between them.

Branra was laughing, and Danaer suspected his skin was showing a blush. Still chuckling, Branra went on into the tent while Danaer seized a moment to be close to Lira.

"There is no time, qedra," she said. "I must go to the Traech Sorkra." Ulodovol's distant gaze had shifted and locked upon her. He might have been speaking, save that his lips did not move. Lira trembled, then whispered, "Keep ever close the dagger Gordyan gave you. It is mated to my amulet, as I am to you, my love." She glanced at Ulodovol and then stood on her toes, embraced Danaer, and kissed him. There was defiance in her action. Almost at once, she left him, running into the tent.

Danaer was tempted to edge closer and try to hear what might be said within, particularly what the two sorkra would say to one another after their separation and all that had happened.

"La! That is the end of fine company for you, for the present, youngling!" Shaartre poked Danaer in the ribs teasingly. "I came to fetch the mooning bride-groom, lest you lose your way."

Sighing, Danaer grinned and went along with him. They led their horses through the crowded unit camps. Shaartre chatted amiably about the latest gossip, for he was ever sharp-eared in such matters. Once he teased Danaer and asked if he intended to sneak off to his lady's tent ere dawn, as had been his wont of late. He saw Danaer's reaction and apologized.

"There will be no chance for that until the battle is done," Danaer said, accepting what must be. "She is much occupied with sorkra dealings and her wizard master."

"Well, with the gods' blessing, you will both be free

to enjoy yourselves soon," Shaartre said. He and Danaer were not green, and they spoke of what was to come without boasts, hoping for the best but knowing there would be much blood and death.

Now that Lira had returned to her mentor, Danaer was grateful that Shaartre had come to show him the path, for this was a greater assemblage than any he had ever known. Soldiers and quartermasters and weapons makers and troopmen's wives and camp women were everywhere. There were dismantled wagons formed into barricades, and trenches and pitfalls dug as last-ditch defenses to protect Siank. Countless cook fires stewed homely fare and even an occasional haunch of woolback or motge.

"There is a special business," Shaartre said, lowering his voice. He pointed discreetly, concealing the motion behind his side. Danaer saw one tent set well away from all others and ringed about with furze and brambles and lines of ropes, patrolled constantly by stern-faced guards, some of Nurdanth's most trusted veterans. "Have you ever seen a prince in chains?"

A man sat before the tent. His chair was gilded, and he dined upon delicacies and Daran wine poured into crystal goblets, tended by his servant. Danaer lacked Shaartre's forbearance and gaped in amazement. "Diilbok!" he exclaimed.

"They say Malol and Nurdanth keep him here so that he will be under their eyes every minute of the battle, and witness what his treachery almost cost."

"And if we lose, will Malol claim his head?" Danaer wondered. "I owe him no pity, for he accused me falsely and almost killed Lira and me, in conspiracy with his mistress and Hablit. Yet I did not think Malol would dare such a thing. Diilbok is his cousin, and the King's."

"I spoke with the Royal Commander's orderly a while ago," Shaartre said. "The strange part is that when Malol came for him, the Prince seemed to expect it and even went willingly into his captivity. He treats it as a jest. Mayhap he thinks they will not risk harming him and offending the King . . ."

"Or it may be he believes his witch of a mistress

will work magic to free him," Danaer said darkly. "What does he hope to win from this betrayal? To reign among the Markuand?" Did the Prince, by surrendering so easily, spin a new form of treason, buying time for his woman to escape Ulodovol's sorkra web?

Prince Diilbok played the fop, dabbling his fingers on a napkin and quaffing his wine with a great show of dainty manners. He was unconcerned by his shameful imprisonment, exuding arrogance and confidence.

Shaartre remarked, "The Royal Commander has ordered that the Prince be encouraged to drink, enough to put him into a stupor."

Malol's orders, or Ulodovol's? Was this a tactic to befog the Prince's mind so that his witch could not come to him with her evil arts?

"Whatever favor he enjoyed in Kirvii, for certain this does not impress Malol." Shaartre shrugged. "At least they have not done us any further harm since Deki."

Danaer knew that Malol te Eldri was hampered by rank and birth. Diilbok was too close to the crown to be dispatched lightly, though Branra and Yistar had both muttered of political assassination. Apparently that was a thing Malol would not countenance. Danaer did not envy the Royal Commander, for the situation was thick with deadly thorns, even should he be victorious in the battle.

"Was not Deki enough?" he said with great bitterness. "Come. Let us to the units and have a good meal, ere we go to fight the Markuand."

XXIII

An Unnatural Brand

THE GIGANTIC SLEDGE HAD BEEN DRAGGED UP OVER the desert and across the grassy plains. Whenever the terrain was rough, the white-clad drivers looked back fearfully, dreading that some slight bump or jar might anger their passenger. They sought the smoothest parts of the trail to give him ease. But when they did, his minions would ride close and flog the horses, demanding speed, saying their master must not be delayed. Always the sledge's curtains remained shut, and none dared ask whether the occupant lay ill or dreamed upon some new and awful conjuration.

Driven till their hearts burst, horses were taken from the traces and replaced with others. Yet no rest was allowed and the sledge went on. When this day's fighting had ended, the warlords were dismayed to see that the sledge—again—sat overlooking their key positions. Its occupant had followed them since the fall of Deki.

Now his minions summoned them, and the generals came at once. They had not seen him since the conquest of the river city, though his hidden presence had pursued them through the vastness of this alien land. In their souls, they had hoped to be rid of him and his dark rule.

The curtains were at last drawn, and they saw that he lay reclining upon many cushions. He seemed very pale, and there were whispers that he had been badly stricken by some countering magic. Perhaps he had summoned them only to hear his dying words, after which they could make their plans for tomorrow's victory.

"Yes, you shall have victory," he said suddenly. He stepped out of the sledge and glared at them, and in the shadows the soldiers watched, awed. "You *did* think upon victory, did you not? Yet I sense doubt."

"It . . . it is so, Master. The journey and the battles have been most arduous. We have been obliged to call reinforcements from the campaigns in north and south . . ."

"No matter. The defeat of Krantin is vital." Again he reached into their minds and revealed their secret fears. "You are wondering if the enemy alliance is truly shattered. It is not." They gasped in shock and he went on. "But it is severely taxed. They have carried before them tales of what occurred in the river city, and that will breed faintheartedness among them."

"This . . . she-devil who now blocks our way . . . ?"

"A mere delaying tactic. You will crush her, along with the rest, when her guidance is gone, the enemy's chief wizard. When a beast's head is cut off, it will die." He drew himself up proudly. "I shall wield a weapon they can never parry. We shall defeat them utterly."

Nearly all of them were cowed now, dumb and submitting to the yoke of his power. But one, the bravest, who had always nursed defiance, could not hold his tongue. "Is it the same magic weapon you used in the river city? We lost many sixties there through such magic . . ."

"A minor miscalculation."

"And the enemy nearly slew you. It may be their wizards know the same tricks that you do, and employ them against you."

The eyes of their master flashed horribly. The night was moonless, but now a greater darkness gathered, the outspilling of a demon's cauldron, pouring over the warlords. With a hideous shriek, the challenger fell, writhing, his hands clutching his head to shut off a howling none but he could hear. He begged his companions to kill him and end his misery. Appalled and helpless, they watched him while the wizard wreaked his vengeance.

His victim wailed and guarded his throat against an unseen attacker. Even as he did, gouts of blood covered lips and hands and flowed from his ears and nose. His eyes started from his head and his tongue thrust out, life choking from him.

Then he vanished. Only bloodstained dust was left. There was no clothing or trace of the warlord, save his gore.

"Is there any other who questions my ability to match *any* wizard's magic and more?" The stillness had been profound, but now it seemed to deepen. The shadows receded, leaving them in firelight once more. None spoke. They scarcely dared breathe. His smile widened. "Attend my pleasure. You will wait here until I call you to hear the battle plan."

He strolled to his tent, and they remained where he had left them. The wizard's apprentices scampered before him and on every side, eager to serve his wishes. Within the luxurious tent creature comforts had been prepared, transported to this place at great risk and difficulty. It was a palace under cloth, on the edge of a battlefield. A throne sat before his brazier, and the ice-sphere of light and shadows rested on a bronze tripod. A girl-child, a Dekan of Clarique ancestry, knelt beside the chair. She was listless, enduring her fate.

Others also awaited him—a craggy-faced and scowling Destre warrior and a beautiful black-haired woman. The Destre was barely courteous, but the woman spread wide her purple skirts and curtseyed deeply, showing her full breasts. Then she pressed her palms together in adoration and spoke. The tone was deferential, though the words were alien, unknown to him. The Markuand wizard did not trouble to probe her thoughts, as he had probed many another mind to learn what he wished. He had found a readier tool. He sat in the throne and clasped a strong and hurtful hand on the girl's fair brow. The little Clarique whimpered, and from her tender mind he learned the meaning of his allies' speech, using the slave as he would an arcane machine.

"Master Wizard of all Markuand, I am Chorii of Krantin, she who would be your handmaiden in sorcery and in the empire to come." The woman glanced at her sullen companion.

With a grunt, he said, "Hablit of Vidik, outcast of the Brotherhood of the Zseds."

The wizard eyed Chorii with appreciation and Hablit with disdain. He sought what he needed in the child's brain. "I greet you, my allies in conquest. All is ready for the morrow?"

Through the medium of the helpless slave, Chorii said, "Exactly as you have commanded, Master."

"Good. I have removed the last thorn among my warlord generals, a splinter taken from my least finger. Now we shall have our triumph."

Hablit remained sour, disinterested in such plotting, a man of action. Chorii had been the pampered mistress of a royal lord. Yet now she stood meekly before this magician who had guided her into danger and supreme treachery. Her dark eyes glowed. "I wish to be your apprentice . . ."

"And so you shall, my dear. And for what you have done, how shall I reward you? Do you want nothing more than that?" He took up the ice-sphere and its contents coruscated. Then Prince Diilbok's image appeared within it. Chorii leaned close to admire the vision, her normally sharp expression much softened. The Prince slept, his pale cheek on a downy pillow, his full lips twitching as if he spoke within a dream. "As you see, my dear, he is well treated. His noble cousin will not harm him, I promise you."

Chorii tore her attention from the illusion. "Such tenderness toward him will not make me merciful to them."

"Ai!" Hablit drew his dagger. As the wizard's minions recoiled in shock, the Destre stabbed through the billowing tent wall in his frustrated anger, ripping the cloth asunder. "So would I do with him who cast me out!"

His vehemence reached the Markuand through the Clarique child, and she screamed in pain, assaulted both by his fury and by her master's cruel hand. The slave and the Destre amused the sorcerer, but Chorii regarded Hablit warily. She did not judge his wrath so lightly.

"You want the head of this Gordt te Raa, eh?" the wizard asked.

"His blood!"

"You shall have both, and he will suffer long ere he dies. Before tomorrow is done, we will conquer all those who oppose us." He held out his free hand, demanding their oath. Chorii laid slim, bejeweled fingers on his, and after a moment's hesitation Hablit added his scarred brown paw to the pact of blackest wizardry.

"Those fools actually believe they may have countered my magic," the master said. "And perhaps they did achieve some small success at the river city. But I was not fully prepared then. I will never be so careless again."

Hablit shuffled about uneasily, disliking all traffic with these things. Hate had overruled his fear and made him strike a bargain as well with a witch from The Interior.

"I have arranged the force point you require, Master," Chorii said. With all other men she had ever wished to please, she had played the coquette. Now she did not, wanting his interest in her dark arts, not in her body.

"A focus at which to strike." He spoke softly, but the significance of that phrase pained the slave child. "When it is done the first time, there must always be a focus. Afterward, it is more easily repeated, as it was at the river city. But now there will not need be a *second* time."

Chorii begged, "Master, teach me this wondrous thing! It is marvelous beyond any spell I have ever known. When you used me to serve you at Deki and carried Hablit and me within the walls . . ." Hablit shivered, not wanting to remember. The Markuand and the witch laughed at his cowardice. He was a tool who would suit their evil purposes and then be discarded.

"It is beyond your powers, my dear, beyond the powers of any other mortal," the wizard said with great pride. Her crestfallen expression made him offer his lovely conspirator a crumb of comfort. "But you will both accompany me once more, when I strike—tomorrow."

She looked forward to the experience, but Hablit

clenched his jaw, ruing the price he must pay for his vengeance. Chorii touched her breast and said, "I have put my secret mark upon my Prince—here. I set it myself with most potent and binding spells."

"Your lover did not protest?" The wizard licked his lips. "Truly, he is enthralled with love for you, yielding up his very soul and the conquest of his land and kinsmen."

"He has been most devoted to our cause, as well as he was able; and Markuand *will* make him a monarch in his own right, when you have won Krantin?"

"His own little kingdom, as we agreed." He waved his hand and the ice-sphere misted. When it cleared, Prince Diilbok again slept in the image formed there. Now his garment appeared to melt, revealing his naked skin. In that place Chorii had touched, an unnatural brand glowed, throbbing and purple. The sleeping man twisted about on his pallet, his carnal dreams plain in his face. Hablit looked away in disgust and Chorii laughed.

Beside the wizard, the Clarique child stared into nothing, her jaw sagging and drooling spittle, her mind emptied save for the stream of languages moving through her bone and flesh. The wizard turned to his minions and commanded, "Bring my warlords. I shall show them what they must do and how they will provide the diversion which will make the battle fall into our hands."

As they left, he gazed into the sphere. "Dream on, Prince Diilbok. Soon we will give you handsome new titles, my faithful cat's-paw. Sate yourself with lustful dreams. Tomorrow you will help us conquer Krantin and crush forever this alliance of the plains people and those of the smoking mountains."

XXIV

The Price Is the Blood of Azsed

DANAER HAD AWAKENED TO THE GLOW OF FALSE dawn and knew he had been summoned, just as he had been many ten-days past, when the goddess sent him to Osyta. Stealthily, he moved through the great camp, led by the strange urging, approaching the smaller tents near the Royal Commander's pavilion. He did not go close, for this area was the most heavily guarded of any place on the Siank Plains. He waited in a grove, and soon, as he had sensed must happen, Lira left a tent and came directly to him, into his arms. For a few moments neither of them had words or breath to spare.

Then, with a deep sigh, Lira warned, "I . . . I cannot stay, qedra. I do not know what made me come here, or you await me."

"The goddess," Danaer said simply. He took her face in his hands and felt her trembling. "The battle is upon us, is it not?"

"Yes. Ti-Mori's army is now less than a quarterday's ride east, closely pursued by the Markuand. And there are so many of them!" She shivered despite the warmth of his embrace. "Danaer, I glimpsed what the Traech Sorkra saw in his probings. Only a glimpse. It . . . it is forbidden to do so for one of my lowly rank. But . . . I have done it before." She frowned, puzzled. "This time it was unusually difficult, for some reason. Ah, no matter. But these Markuand, qedra —a vast, ghost-white arrow of an army, aimed at Krantin's heart!"

"Krantin's heart will withstand that arrow and fling it back," Danaer murmured. "The warriors of the Zseds are eager to engage them, for last night all the priests and ha-usfaen and delisich of all the clans gathered and sought Argan. Branra gave me leave to go, and it was splendid. A most fearsome ritual. None who witnessed it can fear Markuand. Nor do many of my comrades in uniform feel differently, though they worship other gods." He patted her shoulder and said, "Ti-Mori will pretend to flee and will come to us, and we will close the trap. It is an old trick, one Straedanfi knew well and used often."

Lira was not comforted, and Danaer was shut outside, unable to help. If the thing that afflicted his woman were a human enemy, he would sever its life in an instant. But no one could fight wizardry but another wizard. "Danaer, come with me," she said suddenly, hope in her voice. "I will have the Royal Commander assign you as liaison."

"We have no more need of liaison," Danaer started to say. Then he understood. "You want me there because you will be there—in Malol's command tent?"

"Yes, and also Master Ulodovol and General Nurdanth. But I have been told Gordt te Raa and Kandra must ride with their tribespeople." Danaer nodded. He would have been astonished if any Destre Siirn had done otherwise. Lira went on. "The Traech Sorkra and I must cast the Web protectively around the Royal Commander, to shield him and his plans. We will be his eyes and ears throughout the battle, swifter than any couriers can be. Ulodovol thinks the Markuand may guess, in part, that we have laid a trap. Yet so far we have concealed its exact design. Come with me, beloved. You will be safe there—"

Danaer hugged her with such force that she gasped for mercy. "*You* will be safe! Hai! *I* will not hide in a tent at the rear of the battle! I will stand on the line of blood and keep any danger from coming near you!"

"Please . . ."

Danaer silenced her pleadings with kisses. "I am a warrior. I cannot shun honest challenge," he said.

Lira wept with disappointment and he gentled her more. At last she gave up begging. "I wish—oh, qedra! But it will be as you say. I see that. You have your calling, as I do mine." She dried her tears, and with one more brief embrace, she slipped away from him

and went back to the tents, to Ulodovol, to her sorkra
Web. Danaer stared at the closed flap long after she
had disappeared behind it. If she were not a sorkra,
he would have sent her to safety, perhaps to Nyald
Zsed or, even farther west, to the Barjokt tribes of the
Tradyans. But she was sworn to Ulodovol's service.
Yet he had learned she would stay in the Royal Commander's tent, the most secure position in all the battlefield. Surely she would be well protected there.

He pressed the silvery hilt of his new dagger, knowing that he had the weapon against the enemy's magic
now. There would be Andaru and victory, and life for
Lira Nalu, woman of Danaer of Nyald Zsed.

The candles burned away swiftly after that, time
rushing upon them all. News ran through the camp,
and officers roused their men, delivering the same message Lira had whispered to Danaer concerning Ti-
Mori. There was a scramble for weapons as dawn
broke. Unessential wagons and personnel were sent to
the rear, but that would be no farther than Siank. The
alliance had its back to the mountain wall. At the
ritual the night before, the Destre-Y had sworn that
whatever else happened, they would not let one
Markuand touch Siank, Argan's holy city, the last
stronghold of Azsed.

Cavalry and infantry sorted into their units, following the bellowings of Troop Leaders and the chain of
command Malol had established. No one in the ranks
knew the whole of the battle plan, but Malol's reputation put away their worries. Had he not mastered
all the rebel lords who opposed his cousin's dynasty?
And had he not struck this alliance no one believed
could be wrought? They would follow, trusting Malol
and Gordt te Raa.

They climbed. Horses snorted and heaved their sides
and bleated for rest. "Let them rest at the top!"
Branra shouted, and Danaer and Shaartre and the
other Troop Leaders relayed his stern order. Men
whipped their blacks with the reins and dug in heels,
and they continued upward, wading through the tall
grass and brush of the hilly Vrastre.

At last they stood upon a ridge. Until now Danaer

had been too busy to look around the landscape. Now he remembered maps and that they had passed through the same valley below only yesterday. They stood atop Yeniir, the southernmost of two prominent ridges. Opposite was a height equal to this one, called Thaante. The hills cradled an arrow-shaped valley, the easiest and best route to Siank Plains. If the Markuand reached the western end of this pass, there would be no stopping them.

Danaer checked the looseness of his new sword in its sheath. He had been provided a leather shield and slung it at ready position from his saddle, then tested the handiness of the two lances slung in the scabbard under his stirrup.

"Position your units here," Branra said, coming along the ridge and personally directing the placement of his cavalry. "Watch for the pennants down slope when you begin your charge. Those mark the blinds where our archers lie. *Our* archers. Tradyans. Do not run them down, or Stethoj of the West will have my head. I promised him an honorable battle for his warriors, not a trampling by the army. Scout." Danaer rode out of line and saluted smartly. "The next forces east are Destre-Y. Go give them the word that we are in place and ready."

As Danaer loped along the crest, he saw that the slope was much overgrown and afforded good cover. There was plenty of brush to conceal archers and Destre slingmen. If the Markuand tested Yeniir, they would be hunting for their targets, while the hidden defenders could aim downward, to great effect.

To his pleasure, Gordyan looked to be the chieftain of the Destre on Branra's flank. It was only when he drew near and dismounted that Danaer discovered his friend was not in command of the assembled warriors. Gordyan's bulk had hidden the true chieftain here.

"I *will* take sword and lance in this battle!" It was a woman's voice.

"The Rena wishes you would not," Gordyan said gently, most deferentially.

Kandra stood before him. She tossed her head, her hair like a shimmering flag, her green eiphren sparkling. "I am Lasiirnte of Ve-Nya, and I will command."

Gordyan was almost abject. It was a tone Danaer had never heard him use. "Forgive me, Lasiirnte, please. You are a most skilled rider, but you are unblooded, as befits the consort of the Rena. I . . . I know I speak out of place, but serve the Rena otherwise, I beg you. Offer Malol and Nurdanth advice on the fighting methods of our people and how to employ them best . . ."

"That is their realm, not mine. Do you think I would let Wyaela best me?" Kandra's black eyes flashed with indignation. She pointed across the valley at Thaante's height. "She makes her stand there. And I will hold here! It is done. We are warriors both."

"Lasiirnte," Danaer broke in, "your favor, but Gordyan speaks with much wisdom in this thing."

"Ve-Nya will follow only me, and that is an end of it," Kandra snapped. Her face was bright with the same battle fervor that inspired all the Destre-Y today. "How would Argan deem any chieftain who would not lead her tribe to war? The Iit commander must hide behind his flags, safe from the line of blood. But we are Destre-Y. *I* am Destre-Y! The Rena defends Thaante's center, and I will meet the Markuand, lance to lance, here. My brother died at Deki. Now Ve-Nya Zsed has none to lead them but me, his chosen successor. And they will have that right," she finished with ferocious pride. Her attention swung to Danaer again. "Soldier, do you bring me a message?"

Impressed by her regal manner, he conveyed Branra's report. Kandra accepted it with a curt nod and turned away to speak with some of her warriors. Gordyan's gaze met Danaer's and he said, "I will be close to her left hand, with my personal guard. Yet the Rena is most worried, and so am I. But he will not deny her this." Danaer smiled wanly as Gordyan shook his head and went on. "Truly, she is a chieftain, just as Wyaela is. You . . . you say Branraediir is on our flank? Good! Bloody Sword will not desert us when we need him."

When Danaer got back to his units, an air of expectancy hovered over them. Danaer had seen its cause during his short ride along the ridge. Mountainous clouds of dust rolled up in the Vrastre east of the valley. The reason for those clouds must be close, and it could only be that tens of hundreds of feet and hooves broke the earth and stirred it to powder.

Everyone watched the clouds eagerly, standing by his horse and awaiting the commands. Shaartre and Rorluk and Xashe and many of Danaer's comrades murmured their restlessness. Courage was building, and they tired of doing nothing. Veteran and merchant's son and peasant herdsman were at one with each other. Like Danaer, most of these units had trekked to Deki and lost many a brave friend. They had learned that the tales of the Destre were not all true, and that in this battle the enemy was Markuand. Though the men of The Interior lacked the customs that bound Destre warriors, Danaer had seen their valor through the years and did not scorn it. On every side now they took oath, swearing to acquit themselves well and perhaps to avenge a dead man the Markuand had slain.

Danaer made his own vow silently: For Argan, and to gift Straedanfi. May he bear with him to his god every second Markuand I slay. Drink their blood and curse their souls, Keth, Dread Guardian of the Portals.

A white pennant was raised on the slope below. Across the valley a finger of fire stabbed into the late-morning skies, spewing orange sparks. It was a device Danaer had never heard of or seen, and the loud explosion that accompanied it made the horses nervous. There had been rumors of some new signaling invention, a secret among the lords. Now it seemed Malol was using it to manage the movements of his noblemen.

Men examined their weapons and fidgeted. Now the valley was being buried in dust. Danaer put his distance-trained vision to work. Under the cloud there were horses, many of them army blacks with a scattering of roans and a few of the reddish-colored steeds the Clarique favored. With them were men and women warriors, pretending to be in headlong flight. Green banners fluttered, the tattered standards of Clarique which had survived the debacle at Jlandla Hill.

Ti-Mori! Rejoining her countrymen at last! Like a shamming golhi-pup which dragged its leg . . .

A great noise washed up from the valley's entrance, and still greater quantities of dust. A furious rear-guard action was taking place, to make the pretense seem more real. As it reached the farthest end west in the pass, Ti-Mori's ragged banner was planted defiantly and moved no more. The she-wolf turned to face the Markuand.

Behind her, through the tongue of the pass, more riders now rushed to her support. The Royal Commander's infantry, bearing their own standard.

All along the two ridges, the fighting groups now raised their flags. Branra's blood-red pennant floated over Danaer's units, and to his right rose the black flag of Gordt te Raa's realm, marking the position of Lasiirnte Kandra and Gordyan.

Sound roared, an assault on the ears, and dust heaved like the smoke thrown out in the tumultuous eruptions of Krantin's mountains. Amid the cacophony, Danaer heard an ominous singing he remembered vividly from Deki—archers, loosing their deadly shafts. If the Tradyans were shooting from their blinds along the slopes, they must have targets. They could see Markuand scaling the heights, heading up toward Danaer's position and all the others.

Danaer swung his arm to make sure the last of his wound's stiffness was gone, then waited tensely. He gathered reins and a tag of his roan's mane. White-clad invaders were coming into view out of the dust, climbing Yeniir, riding fast. Branra too galloped back and forth, exhorting his men to stand a moment longer. Then he gave a mighty shout and they all lunged to the attack, lances set, thundering downhill.

Hurriedly the Tradyans ducked into their blinds and bushes, close to their markers, fearful of being run down.

Danaer had scaled the outer slopes of Yeniir and knew that by now the Markuand's horses would be staggering. The two lines of cavalry met in a grinding collision of screaming animals and splintering weapons and cries of wounding and death. Danaer's first lance rammed into a Markuand chest, and his roan, obeying knees and reins, crashed into the light-boned gray the enemy rode. Man and animal went down, dragging Danaer's spear with them. Immediately he drew his second lance and closed with another foe.

White seethed in the valley and up onto the slopes, an endless wave of Markuand. It was not a matter of finding a target but of selecting a worthy one, trying to guess which alien would be an officer whose death would cost his army dearly. Danaer soon lost his second spear much the same way as the first and drew sword, setting to work.

There were shrieks and yells to the rear as the infantry moved down behind the cavalry, occupying the space they had overridden. They aided the Krantin wounded and finished off dying Markuand. Many of these men were also veterans of Deki, and though the Royal Commander had said his army should be merciful when it could, Danaer knew the soldiers were not likely to honor his order. The archers crept out of hiding, following the horsemen down, seeking fresh vantage points from which to aim their arrows.

They took a fearsome toll, these Tradyans. A few of the Markuand also drew bow, but they lacked the Tradyans' power and most certainly had little of their skill.

Again and again, the white-clad invaders came against them. The cavalry maintained its line with great difficulty, struggling to keep the Markuand from reaching the crest of Yeniir. At each new onslaught, the ranks were thinned. Danaer tried not to think about reserves or relief, knowing there could be none. All of Krantin was now engaged.

More skyworks burst above the valley. Now the horses had other things to distract them and did not notice the explosions. One such signal was for Branra's units, and he called for more effort. Somehow, they pressed forward a length or so. Danaer was one man among thousands, yet he felt a tension binding them all. And he sensed another, countering tension in the

Markuand, commanding that they too hold and conquer.

Obeying the commands of their officers? Or of their wizard?

Danaer had kept no count of the Markuand he had slain, but he readied himself to send many more to Keth. Then Branra was traversing the slope at a reckless pace, flogging his roan with his reins. "Get to the Destre-Y! Bid them thrust along our flank! We are sorely pressed!"

Danaer wended his way through the carnage, angling east. He galloped past archers and throat slitters and toward the banner of the Rena's consort. Reaching it, he dismounted at a run and was startled to see a group of Destre standing behind the line of blood. Their lances dangled limply in their hands. Warriors? Not slaying Markuand? What had happened? Were they bewitched, as the Sergeant of the Post had been in Deki? Danaer shoved his way through the strangely quiet throng, to come upon a scene that stunned him.

Kandra lay on the grassy slope, her servant Esbeti beside her and weeping as she tried to comfort her mistress. Gordyan also knelt, his big hands stroking Kandra's brow and hair with infinite tenderness. A Destre herb-healer labored over the Lasiirnte, his expression showing the hopelessness of his task. There was a gaping slash above Kandra's belt and a great quantity of blood. Danaer wondered that the woman still lived, but she did. Gordyan's face was a bleak mask which did not quite hide his terrible anguish. The herb-healer spread his hands. "There is nothing I can do . . ."

Gordyan seized his garment and shook him. "Lasiirnte will not die! You will save her!"

The Azsed physician said sadly, "She will be with the goddess soon. I have potioned her, and she does not suffer."

With a strangled gasp, Gordyan flung him away. He gazed at the circle of warriors. "How did this happen? I will kill the man who let her be hurt!"

They wept openly, and one managed to say, "All who were guarding her were slain. Lasiirnte fought most bravely, a true warrior woman." The man pointed to something that might once have been human. The body was so butchered Danaer's belly heaved at the sight, though he had seen much slaughter. Several other Markuand lay near the strewing of shattered skulls and brains and entrails as well as the bodies of many Destre-Y who had died trying to protect their Lasiirnte.

Choking with grief, the man went on. "They . . . they all came at once. They seemed to appear out of nowhere. We did not see them until . . . until it was too late!"

Wizardry! Markuand—unseen by keen-eyed Destre-Y in time to save Kandra. Danaer knew this must be the work of Prince Diilbok's mistress. Chorii had taken the guise of Kandra and failed in that deceit. Now she had taken her vengeance, and Kandra lay dying.

Gently Gordyan resumed stroking Kandra's hair. His eyes, and his soul, met Danaer's. They had drawn the same terrible conclusion. Andaru. The price of victory was the blood of a woman of Azsed. Danaer had thought he would not care what sacrifice was made, so long as Lira lived. But now his heart ached and rage tore at his spirit. Not Wyaela but Kandra was to be the sacrifice. The woman with the eyes of a diamond-black, the Rena's beloved consort . . .

A groan rumbled in Gordyan's constricted throat. Suddenly Kandra spoke with surprising clarity. "I ask something of you." He bent very close, never ceasing that steady caressing. "We must not lose this position. The Rena desires it, and I desire it."

"We shall not, Lasiirnte, I swear to Argan!"

"And you will tell the Rena that I regret my failure . . ."

Danaer dropped down beside her and took the dying woman's hand. "You have not failed, Lasiirnte. You are giving us Andaru. It was prophesied to me so. You will go to greet the goddess with more glory than any Azsed-Y has ever known."

There was deep grief in Gordyan's face, but now loving gratitude joined it. Kandra smiled weakly, a spark of delight illuminating her last moments. "Truly? You give me great joy, Nyald-Y, great joy." Then she turned her head and said with increasing faintness, "Bear my mantle, Gordyan. Upon my lance, as it was done in the old days. Give my warriors that standard. And have no sorrow. It is Argan's will . . ."

She twisted in his arms, her eyes shifting, no longer seeing the world. "Esbeti? Esbeti? Draw the curtains, little one, it grows cold . . ." With a small sigh, she was still, the life melting from her. Kandra's woman began to chant with the singsong of hysteria, taking the pendant from her mistress's hair. She held the faith-jewel toward the heavens to guide Kandra to the portals, her voice tinged with madness as she keened the prayers.

Gordyan eased Kandra's head onto the grass, staring at her as a man disbelieving what he knew was true. Like Danaer, he had seen much death, but this one was past bearing. Then he rose and caught up Kandra's bloodstained cloak and speared it onto a Destre lance. He lifted it above his head, and because of his great height all could see it well. "Warriors!" he roared. "Warriors of Ve-Nya and Azsed! For Lasiirnte Kandra! In her name! It is Andaru! Andaru! Conquer! *Conquer!*"

Danaer had the wits to scream, "Bring the attack to your left, Gordyan!" Then he too was burned by Argan's holy flame of passion. Men cried with rage and leaped onto their roans, sweeping down Yeniir, led by Gordyan. Headlong they rushed toward Branra's beleaguered units.

"Har-shaa! For Kandra! For Andaru!"

The shout was stronger than any weapon, flung into the faces of the attacking Markuand. A few of the army's fighters brushed shoulders with the now-goddess-governed Destre-Y, and they took up the challenge without knowing its meaning. They were shaken by this berserk charge of the tribesmen. A human avalanche of roans and Destre warriors careened into the line of battle. Markuand reeled from the shock, beginning to go down as before an invincible storm.

For the second time Danaer could recall, he saw fear on a Markuand face. On many Markuand faces. They did not fear wizardry now, as had the man he and Lira had sent into nothingness. Now they feared sword and lance. Their master's magic potion that controlled their pain was not sufficient to shield them from this awesome Destre fury.

Gordyan and the warriors knew no tempering of sanity, lusting for a revenge that would not be turned aside. Danaer screamed the same defiance and slashed limbs and bodies and wanted still more Markuand blood to spill, his battle thirst unslaked. He would thrust through every hated white tunic, slay every one of the enemy.

Death to the Markuand—and most especially to their wizard and his treacherous allies in sorcery.

They had descended halfway down the slope, more and more forming a solid line with the army, two branches of a river joining, drowning the Markuand between them. The Destre fell on the Markuand's flanks while Branra assaulted them frontally.

They had held! They had swept Yeniir clean of the invaders! Shaartre struggled through the melee to Danaer, calling, "Danaer, youngling! What is this? Never have I seen Destre so possessed. Danaer? Do you not know me, old friend?"

The full import of the last few minutes struck Danaer and he slumped in the saddle, too stunned to reply at once. Gordyan too was by his side. The big man's face was still grief-tortured and he wiped at his eyes. Then he stared over Danaer's shoulder. Branra too was spurring to join this little gathering, but it was not Branraediir's approach which disturbed Gordyan.

An elite Destre guard lanced down Markuand blocking their path, clearing the way for the Siirn Rena. Gordt te Raa's magnificent roan was lathered and staggering from the punishment he had given it, an unheard-of thing for a Destre. "Word was brought . . ." he began, then saw what he had feared he would in Gordyan's expression. The Destre leader's powerful hands knotted reins and his mount's mane as he struggled to contain his anguish.

"Lasiirnte . . ." Gordyan could say no more.

Though the battle din surrounded them, they seemed to be held in a profound silence for a long moment. Gordt te Raa jerked his head several times to one side and then the other, his jaw clenched. He was Rena, and he must ever be the strongest of all his people.

"Kant, prodra Argan," he murmured at last, his voice shaking only a trifle, his sorrow nearly mastered now.

Branra obviously felt he should offer some condolence. He grasped what had happened and thought to speak on behalf of the Royal Commander and all those of The Interior who were Gordt te Raa's allies. "Can we help in any way, Sovereign?" he asked.

"Give the Siirn a moment, my lord," Danaer advised the nobleman.

"Call him *Rena!*" Since he and Gordyan had become hyidu, his friend had not spoken with such anger to him. Yet Danaer knew what drove Gordyan, taking no hurt.

He shook his head sadly. "You know I cannot. The prophecy is not yet fulfilled, when Andaru shall come to be and the Azsed Rena shall be the Rena Azsed." Gordt te Raa stared at him, his intelligent eyes glistening. Even in his grief, he understood.

Ashamed of his outburst, Gordyan gripped Danaer's arm in apology and said, "Ai! Forgive me. Rena, it is so. Her . . . her sacrifice will buy us Andaru. A holy vision proclaims it."

It was the only consolation that would have meant anything to the leader of the Destre-Y. Gordt te Raa nodded curtly, drawing his mantle across his breast, preparing to leave. There was no blood fever in his face, but a cold dedication, tinged with deep mourning. "So Argan wills. And many more will die, to accompany her to Keth's gates—an army of Markuand I myself will slay."

With that, he turned and rode back into the melee, his guards clearing the way around him, all of them lancing down the enemy ruthlessly and methodically as they went.

"I do not know if I can accept Andaru at this awful price," Gordyan said. "I have failed him, and Lasiirnte . . ."

Danaer feared his friend was about to make some reckless vow in his grief, some suicidal oath to atone for a thing that had been foredoomed. He started to speak and say again that the goddess would not be denied.

Then he reeled in the saddle, grunting with shock, clutching his belly. Branra had drawn rein and begun to head back to his command, but now he paused, concerned. Shaartre leaned toward his comrade in arms, and Gordyan said, "What is it, hyidu?"

They thought alike, that Danaer had been struck by the enemy. They feared to see blood flowing, ready to catch him if he fell.

But there was no wound, though Danaer felt indeed as if arrow or spear had pierced him—a weapon of raging fire. The dagger! Silver and obsidian burned where his hand lay and all along his middle, under the sheath. Flame moved from his fingers into his veins and bone.

And out of the dust a figure took shape, shimmering in midair before him. Lira! She held out her hands pleadingly, her lips moving, and he heard, "Danaer, help me! He is here! *They* are here!"

"The sorkra! It is wizardry, Bloody Sword. . . ."

"Ai! But what sort—!"

Shaartre and Danaer's unit mates were pointing in fear, and Branra and Gordyan gawked in amazement at Lira's image. They saw it, too, and seemed to hear her as well! The power of her magic—and the desperate need that fed it!

"More Markuand tricks," Gordyan guessed. "Trying to bewitch him."

"I think not." Branra narrowed his eyes, looking first at the illusion and then at Danaer.

"Treachery!" Lira shrieked at Danaer. "They are attacking the Traech Sorkra and the Royal Commander! Help us!"

Danaer yanked his roan's head around, brutalizing the animal in his frenzy. Branra was shouting, "Wait,

Troop Leader, we will—Sha-artre! Fetch a squad and follow him quickly. Now! Spare nothing!"

"Hyidu," Gordyan called, striving to catch up with his friend. But Danaer was far ahead of him already, beating a cruel tattoo on his horse's ribs.

If only the roan could fly, as the Markuand's demon snake had flown!

The dagger's flaming summons never ceased, though he had left Lira's magical illusion behind. He cursed his blindness as he galloped through pockets of the battle, along the base of Yeniir, heading for the pass. Why had he been so quick to assume Kandra's death had fulfilled Osyta's prophecy? Kandra was dead and Wyaela te Fihar might yet die, as would many another woman and man in this war. But— there had been no face on the body in his dream! An Azsed woman's death must be the sacrifice—an Azsed woman who was also a sorkra, the bitter rival in wizardry of evil Chorii and the Markuand?

He began to beat on his horse's shoulders with the flat of his sword and with his reins and swept his heels from ribs to rump, calling more speed from the foaming beast.

Up out of Yeniir's slopes and through the pass, where the forces of Malol and Ti-Mori had broken him a clear path—the goddess be praised! Danaer fought the roan's failing strength and the hordes of camp followers who clustered on the Plains, hoping to see the show yet fearful of coming too close to the conflict. They dived out of his way, seeing his panic, and he rode on wildly.

The command tent was looming before him. Where were the guards? This was Krantin's heart, and it had been locked within a protective ring of many good soldiers.

They lay on the ground. All the sentries were still, their eyes open and staring at the sky, though there was no wound on them. They were held in the living death of witchcraft!

Danaer's roan collapsed, utterly foundered, and he jumped free, staggering and catching his balance, then running for the tent. All the flaps were tightly closed . . . to shut out what?

In the distance behind him there was a thunder of approaching hoofbeats. Gordyan and Shaartre would be bringing help. But he must not wait. The dagger scorched his side, and with one stroke Danaer swung his sword and slashed an opening through the tent wall, plunging inside.

Cold! And blackness! And amid it were whirling points of eerie light, twinkling spheres seemingly formed of ice, hovering, shining upon the combatants; Lira and those she sought to help, and those who would destroy Krantin's power forever.

Like the sentries, Malol's staff aides were entranced, lying at his feet. He and Nurdanth held out their swords, fighting with steel as Lira and Ulodovol fought with wizardry.

Against them stood four people Danaer had learned to hate. Prince Diilbok and his beautiful mistress, the outcast Hablit, and a man Danaer had never seen yet knew at once.

The Markuand sorcerer, the evil genius who led the invaders and conspired to betray the alliance and this land!

He was very different from Ulodovol, but in some fashion much the same. The Markuand was not elderly, and he was strongly built, his eyes dark, not Irico pale. His robes were mingled white and iridescent, not drab brown as the sorkra's were. He and Ulodovol were the champions here, standing no more than two arm-lengths apart, their features contorted in a savage duel of magic.

Like Malol and Nurdanth, Hablit and the Prince held weapons. But they could not reach each other. Futilely, frustrated, they prodded at a barrier of air between the two factions.

And all the while Lira and Diilbok's woman gesticulated and cried countercharms, aiding their masters and seeking to shatter the other's will.

The cold and blackness tried to close in upon Malol's little party, filling all the rest of the tent. Only where Ulodovol stood did light remain, even though

the torn tent wall flapped and let in the sunlight.
There were . . . things in that cold blackness. Presences and gibberings and dreadful forces Danaer remembered too well from previous encounters. He
sought to move, to go to Lira's side and help her in
this crucial struggle. Ulodovol's gaunt arms were
raised, and sweat poured from his white hair and
down his beard. His limbs trembled from the stress of
his magic-making.

The wizards warred with eyes and lips and each
called on his unseen minions. The Markuand was
younger, physically strong, his sorcery of unimagina-
ble potency if he could rule entire armies and bind
their tongues against any pain. Ulodovol was frail,
weakening, and soon the Markuand and Chorii must
break through his counterspells!

Lira's gaze flicked momentarily toward Danaer, ap-
pealing. His sword had become a great rock, too
heavy to hold, torn from him by Chorii's vengeful
spell-casting. He was Lira's man, and as much a target
as her hated foe, the little sorkra from Sarlos.

The sword slipped from his nerveless fingers and
fell in the dirt. No matter. He was still armed, with
fire and the magic of the smoking mountains. Danaer's
grip tightened on the dagger hilt.

There was a rush of air as the tent flap was torn
back, and then Gordyan was exclaiming, aghast,
"Argan guard us!" Abruptly, his voice and those of the
men with him choked into nothing. They had hoped to
support Danaer, but now they were entranced, prisoners within their own bodies, as he was.

Danaer forced his thoughts toward Lira and
Ulodovol, feeding them strength through his will and
the dagger. At that, though sorely beset by the whirling darkness, Ulodovol seemed to grow still taller,
hope entering his wrinkled features. More presences
gathered, friendly ones, from Lira's Web, and now
they touched Danaer—and he could move!

He wanted to reach the source of evil, the
Markuand, but others were opposing him, the tools of
that mighty wizard and Chorii. Hablit turned slug-
gishly to counter Danaer's attack, for he had no sor-

ceress who guided him with her love and magics. But
Diilbok did, and the Prince became a most dangerous
foe, his nobleman's blade out, pointed for Danaer's
breast.

Danaer, too, had his woman to aid him, and now
several of the hovering ice-spheres burst, shattering
brilliant fragments over the scene, momentarily blinding the three men. Blinking against that radiance,
Danaer tried to strike at Diilbok, the nearest enemy,
aware at the last instant of his stroke that the Prince's
mistress was flinging herself before her lord to shield
him.

The obsidian-edged knife bit deeply, reddening to
the hilt, and Chorii shrieked. Her cry was a tangible
thing which nearly knocked Danaer from his feet.

Hablit was bellowing, "Help me kill him, you whoreson Iit!"

But Prince Diilbok had abandoned the war. He
had dropped his sword and was cradling his dying
mistress. Chorii gazed up at him in stunned disbelief,
her eyes misting, blood spreading over her breasts as
her lover embraced her and called her name. Diilbok
was crooning piteously, oblivious to the conflict.

As Chorii's life ebbed, Danaer again felt Lira's
touch and the wizardly caress of her Web, making
him their weapon. Unbearable tension filled the tent.
Two immense waves of sorcery mounted, rising to
their heights.

It must be now!

Hablit's lips were flecked with froth in his rage, and
Lira smiled faintly. Her master's tremors lessened,
new vigor in his limbs. Somehow Danaer knew the
moment was at hand, and he knew Ulodovol's firm
resolve—that the Markuand wizard would not escape
his just punishment.

Malol, Nurdanth, Gordyan . . . all of them were
stirring, not yet themselves again, but recovering. The
enemy magician was losing his power over them. And
as he did, Hablit twisted this way and that, his helpless
fury growing.

The wizard *was* going to escape. But how? How
had he fled at Deki, when Branra and Danaer had

trapped him in the tunnel? And how had he destroyed that city, magically carrying Chorii and Markuand soldiers inside the walls where they could betray the Dekans? How, indeed, had he reached the Royal Commander's tent, bringing Chorii and Hablit with him? They had released Prince Diilbok and—

"I know your secret, and I will have you!" Ulodovol exulted, and as he did, Danaer freed himself from the alien's spell and rushed to Lira, holding her close and thrusting his dagger toward the Markuand's heart.

And the Markuand and Ulodovol vanished!

With a violent wrench, Danaer was being torn out of his body, and Lira from hers. They were being swept upward, towed, like a star lancing through the sky and dragging with it fiery wakes. They were leaving the tent and being carried up into the air!

Yet below were his friends and enemies—and himself! He and Lira stood immobile, frozen, their bodies emptied of life.

This was worse than any dream, for Danaer knew he was awake and that all he felt was truly happening. He was floating ever more rapidly, and the tent was falling behind. Lira's presence was very near, as close as his body held hers, and the strange scene below him was receding, just as the Markuand soldier had shrunk into nothing. Was he separated forever from the world of the living, as the enemy soldier had been?

In the tent, Hablit was lunging for Danaer's body, his spear aimed for the scout's back, striking to kill.

Then Danaer could see no more! He was too high in the air!

Had Hablit slain him? Was this how it felt to be lifted up to Keth's portals? No! He was certain he was not yet dead. His flesh and bones had been left far below, but his being was here, with Lira and Ulodovol and the invisible magic net of their Web. He was joining them in pursuit of the Markuand leader.

He would have gasped had he lungs to fill. How could he see and hear if he had neither eyes nor ears? Danaer could not understand these things, but the battlefield lay far down, spread out under him like the maps in Malol's tent. He saw a living chart, thick with people and beasts and war. The white-clad Markuand army was rallying, and troops of The Interior and Destre warriors stood side by side as the enemy launched murderous counterattacks. The war was far from won, could yet go ill for Krantin, if . . .

Danaer thought he could see Branra's red pennant, the flag of Gordt te Raa, Ti-Mori's warrior women, and even the bloodstained green mantle that marked Kandra's followers. They must not lose! The sacrifice had been so great. It could not be wasted.

He thrust away his terror, trusting in the goddess and Lira's benign magic, adding his hunger for enemy blood to that of the Web.

Out of the clouds before him, framed against a bright sky, Ulodovol and the Markuand wizard winked into being, their bodies real. For a few incredible heartbeats, the two wizards floated in air, men of magic, great powerful birds taking human form above the battle of their peoples.

Ulodovol belied his age, flinging a malicious and lusty cry of triumph at his adversary. He knew! Some precious and terrible secret was his!

The Markuand's dark eyes widened and rolled, looking downward, and horror contorted his strong face. Ulodovol gently fanned the air, swimming in nothingness, secure.

"You have overreached, and you have lost." He spoke almost with pity. "You wanted to lead Markuand's final charge to victory! Now you will be the cause of its defeat. Go! Join them! Fly to the head of your army!"

Ulodovol was suspended, serene, borne up by his Web like a lanky and brown old spider.

But the Markuand began to flail his arms and legs, his magic and power completely broken. Still a man, not a formless, floating spirit or image, he fell, tumbling over and over.

With the Web, Danaer watched the descent to its inevitable end. The wizard smashed to earth directly before his foremost soldiers and warlords. His body was shattered, but his robes were unmistakable, and as he had fallen he had screamed, and men had stopped fighting to gaze up in wondering and dread, tracking his terrible headlong rush. The warriors of Krantin gawked in bewilderment, not understanding. But Markuand warlords set up a doleful cry, seeing him who had led them so far from their homeland now dead.

Who would guide them now? Who would tell them what to do? His evil potions, too, lost their power. And now the common soldiers looked about in fear, and those who had endured wounds began to cry out in pain, a wail of agony rising from an army that had been notorious in its silence.

And they began to run, many throwing down their arms the better to flee. Startled, the defenders of Krantin took some moments to react to this thing. Then they took up the chase, their yells of triumph drowning out the Markuand despair.

The sounds of those two great masses mingled, rattling in Danaer's senses as sounds had when he had been wounded and was about to faint. He was being drawn backward, ever faster and faster, more swiftly than any hawk could dive.

Ulodovol had vanished from the clouds, and now he retraced the invisible path in the sky, his Web towed with him, and Danaer along with it.

They were in the tent again.

Danaer blinked and licked his lips, savoring a slow return of the dissociated sensations he had lost. Lira was in his arms, and he was giddily aware of his heart's pounding and the pulse of blood through his body. He looked down at his hand, flexing his fingers tentatively around the hilt of the bloody dagger, enjoying the thrill of contact once more with solid objects.

He was alive! He and Lira and Ulodovol were alive, and back in their own bodies!

Friends crowded around them, whooping with joy. When Ulodovol appeared a trifle weakened by his experience, Malol and Nurdanth themselves rushed to fetch him a chair, not allowing any of the now-awakened sentries and guards to perform that task, honoring the wizard by serving him themselves. Ulodovol sat down gratefully, mopping his brow. "It is done," he panted. "He is dead, and the battle is ours, Royal Commander."

"Hyidu?" Gordyan was pressing Danaer's arm.

Danaer felt like a man waking out of a nightmare. All around him were friends and allies. The enemies were no longer a threat. Chorii's eyes were glazed, and Diilbok took no heed of what went on, continuing to hold his woman and murmur to her as if she could hear him. Hablit lay dead close behind Danaer and Lira. Gordyan's knife was bloody, and Danaer could guess what had happened while he had been held prisoner in wizardry.

Gordyan grinned and said, "Am I not sworn to guard your back? And it was plain you could not protect yourself or our little sorkra at that moment. Thank Argan that when the great wizards disappeared, I could move in time to save you both!"

Danaer started to speak his gratitude, then felt Lira sigh and slump limply against him. Much concerned, he carried her to a nearby couch and put her down carefully, anxiously feeling her forehead. Gordyan leaned over his shoulder, as worried for Lira as the officers had been for her mentor.

To Danaer's relief, in a few moments Lira's eyelashes fluttered and she began to stir. At first she was confused, then focused on him and took his hand. "We . . . we succeeded, qedra. The Traech Sorkra won."

"Ai," Gordyan said heartily. There was still much pain in his expression, the anguished memory of Kandra's death. That would not leave him soon, but he tried to cheer his young friends. "You are back safely with us, free of that enchantment that held you like stone figures."

Danaer shuddered. "I . . . I was flying, up in the clouds, and I saw Ulodovol vanquish the Markuand wizard while we all floated high above the battlefield. I was . . . *flying!*"

"Not precisely," Ulodovol said. The gaunt old man was regaining his strength rapidly, sitting up straighter and tidying his robes. "We did not become like birds, as you believe. Rather, for a few heartbeats, the Markuand and I were transported away from this tent and through the sky, where I brought him to bay as you and my Web supported me and witnessed what came about."

"Master, you fathomed his most arcane power," Lira whispered reverently.

Ulodovol's pale eyes gleamed and he slapped the arms of the chair exuberantly, a man who had gambled and won. "I did! It is so! I have been pondering this riddle deeply since he first employed that hidden art against me and the Web. He believed himself invulnerable, and indeed so it seemed, for a while. It was with this special magic he has so long thwarted our efforts, turned back our own considerable powers so often. And in his lust to conquer, he scorned me, thinking no other wizard could discover his secret." Forming a spidery hand into a fist, Ulodovol said, "But I did, and now this lore is ours. I have mastered it." He shook his head sadly. "Such a magnificent thing, and to have wasted it to such evil purpose. Be assured, Royal Commander, my Web will use this skill only for good."

"I . . . I do not understand," Malol stammered. "What is this thing you learned from the Markuand? Some magical device? I see none here."

"It is a peculiar skill, my lord, a tremendous skill— enabling me to transport people and objects instantly across the space it might take a rider many minutes or candle-marks to travel. Or a hawk many minutes to fly." Danaer wished he had not been reminded of that last, but listened intently as the wizard went on. "He could, with this new art, conjure demons and transport them. As I said, employing his greatness to evil ends. Against this skill, barriers are as nothing. Walls, armies, even rivers are no hindrance. It is not easily accomplished and takes great effort and must be carefully used, but with it a sorkra may move invisibly from one place to another. Ah, the possibilities . . ."

Malol cried out, "That is how they conquered Deki!"

"True, my lord. Your brave soldiers did not fail you. They were betrayed from within. The Markuand wizard transported himself or his minions across the river and inside the walls. He could not move very many at a given time, for the cost in effort is most severe even to the greatest wizard. But now we understand how he beguiled us. Lord Branra said the Markuand vanished from the tunnel. And we were told Chorii and the assassins suddenly appeared inside Deki's walls, striking at the defenders' backs." Ulodovol looked at the dead sorceress and her Prince. "She was his apprentice, and Hablit was drawn into their ranks through his hatred. Diilbok joined them willingly, served as their ally. They transported themselves across our battle lines, even freeing him from close confinement, flying here to thrust at you, Royal Commander."

Nurdanth clasped Malol's shoulder and exclaimed, "But the secret was discovered, and they are defeated. Sorkra, no reward can be enough to repay you."

The wizard did not hide his pride. "I gave you my vow, my lords, and I am bound to serve your banners against the powers of evil and Markuand. My Web assisted me so that I could pursue and trap that evil genius ere he made good his escape this last time." He eyed Lira and Danaer and added, "Though the Web was larger, by one member, than I had expected. It was support that was much needed."

"You were part of the Web, qedra," Lira said. "Without your strength we might have—oh, Danaer!" She began weeping, near hysteria, and Danaer embraced her tightly, for this needed no magic to counter.

Gordyan watched them fondly, then winked at Shaartre as he and other soldiers gathered around them. "Did you hear? He is a sorkra, just like these other white wizards."

Shaartre laughed, his earlier terror at the enchantments fading. "In truth, I have long suspected that. What other man could have straddled so well the division between the plains people and the army and lived to tell about it? This latest bit of magic must have been but small work for a wizard of his abilities, eh?"

Danaer looked up and said sourly, "I am no sorkra. Never that!" Lira's tears were lessening and she clung to him, smiling weakly. "I need no wizard's spells at all now. Lira will be sorkra for us both. I swear by my eiphren, I want no more of flying without my body or seeing and hearing what common men cannot! I have had enough wizardry to last any warrior ten lifetimes!"

XXV

Te Rena Azsed

RECOVERING FROM THE SURPRISE OF ULODOVOL'S pronouncements, Malol te Eldri went over to Prince Diilbok and looked down at his treacherous cousin. Even those who had been congratulating the wizard broke off their talking and watched Diilbok with pity. His eyes were unnaturally bright and he did not weep. Instead he fondled his mistress as if she were still alive, and spoke in the same wise, laughing and planning what they would do in the days to come.

". . . and we will hang bright streamers from the castle walls, ai? Just as at the festival when the minstrels sang so gaily. Do you remember? And when Summer's Height is come, we will journey to your beloved Valley of the Hawks, just as I promised you we would do when the Markuand had won. I will be one of their kings, and you . . . you shall be queen, my love . . ."

Very softly, Malol said, "She is dead. She will never be queen. Her evil master is destroyed, and so is all your scheming."

"I shall order my artisans to make you a pretty

little crown, set with jewels and beaten gold and precious pearls from far Clarique," Diilbok babbled. He rocked back and forth, holding his broken dreams in a warm embrace. "A beautiful crown for your lovely hair, and a gown of cloth of gold. For you . . . just for you, my pretty . . ."

His kinsman shook him and cried, "Diilbok, she is dead! Your witch is dead!"

Diilbok replied, but not to Malol. He answered Chorii, responding to questions only he could hear, his voice sweet with madness. "Oh, of course! You shall have as many slaves as you desire, ever obedient and perfect servants, my love. And grand furnishings for our palace . . ."

Malol drew away from him, his expression bleak. He gestured furtively to Shaartre and the guards. "Fetch a litter for her body. Humor his delusion. Say you are conveying them to the palace, and return him and the corpse to his tent. Give him whatever he asks for. I will send for the surgeons to prepare a posset to give him sleep, so that we may take her from him and give her burial. Go." Somberly they obeyed, and because they acted with seeming deference and did not deny that Chorii still lived, Diilbok went with them, still chattering insanely, laughing and merry.

As they left, Nurdanth told Malol te Eldri, "It is for the best. We would have been bound by his rank, despite his betrayal. Now . . . his sentence has been rendered by the gods. We will confine him the rest of his days, no threat to Krantin, an object for nothing but pity."

"Ai! It will be hard to tell Tobentis, but . . . it is the way of things."

Ulodovol had been silent the while. Now he rose from his chair and approached the couch where Lira lay, tended by Danaer. His momentary frailty was gone, and he seemed much angered. "And it is the way of the Web to contribute one's skills when it is required. Lira Nalu, you could have hurt the Web fatally by withholding your arts!"

Lira clung to Danaer fearfully, and he wondered if he should draw his dagger again, wary of the white-bearded elder's wrath. She said timidly, "I . . . I brought Danaer to aid us, Traech Sorkra. If it were not for his courage . . ."

"It was because you kept back your gifts that we had need of help from an . . . an outsider!" Then Ulodovol's pique abated and he said with sincere puzzlement, "Why? Your mind was one with mine when the Markuand transported himself and Chorii and Hablit among us and began his dark attack. Why did you then shrink from the circle? I felt your presence weakening, becoming distracted. Most unlike you, my child. What is wrong? Does hunger still afflict your powers?"

Gordyan and the soldiers were listening, not saying anything, respectful of Ulodovol, not wanting to interfere in these internal matters of wizards. But Danaer glared at Lira's mentor and held her close, resenting his sharp tone and accusations.

At last Lira said in a tiny voice, "I . . . I do not hunger, Traech Sorkra. But it is true my gifts were weakened. I am sorry. It may be because there is . . . another life within me, just beginning."

"Female!" Ulodovol roared.

Danaer was torn between astonishment and growing pride. He stared at Lira, a new and strong, protective instinct filling his being. More than ever, she was his woman, to be shielded from all harm.

Ulodovol's expression softened. "How could you have thrown away your gifts, my dear? Such promising talents, too. You were warned to keep yourself aloof from the yearnings of the flesh." He seemed disappointed to find that his apprentice was young and human.

Lira lifted her little chin defiantly. "I am sorkra, but I am also a woman, and I will not deny my nature. I have taken an oath that transcends the calling of wizardry. I am sworn to Danaer now."

"Ah! You will learn why a sorkra must not succumb to such joy, child. Carnality is not for us. Your gifts will weaken further as the child fills your belly."

"Will I lose my sorkra abilities?" Lira asked, sounding rueful. In contrast, Danaer was delighted.

He patted Lira's shoulder in sympathy over her coming loss of wizard's skills. Yet he anticipated eagerly a time when the cold and darkness and unseen presences could no longer claim her from him.

"Not entirely." Ulodovol's rheumy eyes actually twinkled kindly. "You will still be part of the Web, but not an intimate of our circle. And you will find, as have other sorkra who surrendered to the joys of the flesh, that more and more your life will be taken up with other matters than the Web. You have found a new calling, and a new loyalty, for a while." He sighed and glanced at Danaer.

There were horses galloping up outside the tent, and the guards poked their heads through the rent left by Danaer's sword. Then they snapped back and came to sharp attention as Branra rushed through that opening. At his heels came Gordt te Raa. Branra was panting with eagerness, full of good news. Grief still ruled the Siirn Rena, but he looked as if he too might have welcome words to deliver to the Royal Commander. Gordyan left Danaer's side, going to his lord, nodding, ready to serve, still sharing the wound they had both suffered at Kandra's death.

"My Royal Lord!" Branra exclaimed, carelessly wiping a bloodied sleeve across his dusty forehead. "The field is ours! They are in rout! I stayed to be certain it was not a trick, but it is not. They are witless, headless snakes, countless numbers of headless snakes, and they are slithering out into the Vrastre, hunted to earth."

Gordyan said, "I shall go to kill my share of them."

"Do not bother." Gordt te Raa caught his man's arm, restraining Gordyan's vengeance. Wondering, Gordyan stared at him as the Destre leader went on. "It is no longer fit work for a warrior. There is no honor in this slaughter, no more than cutting the throats of bleating woolbacks." He spat into the dust, his contempt bitter.

Branra was aware of the anguish ruling his companion and nodded fervent agreement. "That is true, Commander. Ti-Mori still lusts after them, and she leads the army to strike them down while the

Markuand flee. I do not know if even the coming night will stop her. But as for me, I wanted to tell you they are broken. Completely ours."

Malol te Eldri smiled wanly and patted his protégé's shoulder. "I give you thanks. We owe many debts to the sorkra in this."

"Wizardry and arms were both needful," Ulodovol said generously. "It was a victory we all desired. The Markuand wizard employed his arts shamefully, a black stain on the whole of magic, for he bent his mighty skills to evil." The brown-robed old man drew himself up and said haughtily, "That is not true sorkra. Sorkra must ever be the sword of righteousness and peace. And now we shall have that peace, my lord, after this victory is complete and the last Markuand driven beyond Clarique's islands."

Gordt te Raa's dark face was haunted. "Your victory comes at an unbearable price, sorkra." Gordyan winced as from a hard blow and looked pleadingly at Danaer. The scout rose, and Lira got up, too, her strength returning.

Branra was whispering in the Royal Commander's ear, and Malol and General Nurdanth stiffened with shock, learning of Kandra's death. With deep dismay, they turned again to Gordt te Raa, struggling to find words to speak their hearts. "In truth," Malol said, "the price is dear beyond calculation."

Danaer dared to interrupt. "It was the prophecy of Argan." The Royal Commander and the Destre chieftain eyed him intently. "It is Andaru's beginning, the ancient promise finally brought to us. And we were always told that its cost would be terrible, to buy what was to come for us all."

Nurdanth nodded, but the legend was foreign to Malol. He did not know the Destre ways, and Danaer explained, "Lasiirnte's death is the great sacrifice that will reunite the peoples of Krantin. In times to come, we will be as we once were in the days of Ryerdon, no longer torn by hatred and war between ourselves. Andaru means that . . . the Azsed Rena will become the Rena Azsed."

Lira drew very close to him and added, "It means, my lord, that someday in the future one of the plains people will rule all of Krantin."

Danaer gazed down at her with love and awe. How did she know? He had not spoken fully of this sacred promise of Argan. But then . . . Lira was an Azsed, too, now.

The Royal Commander met Gordt te Raa's steady stare, their thoughts combining despite their differences of birth and custom. The Destre said slowly, "I am not the one who will take that throne. I have no desire for such rule, not now." Gordyan eyed his lord morosely, then brightened as Gordt te Raa visibly steeled himself to bear his grief and move into the world that was to be. "The child who will succeed me, and your son, Malol te Eldri . . . they are bound and will be one when the years are right. She is Azsed, and he will learn to love her and bind his heart to hers. Then, indeed, will Andaru be fulfilled." He turned to Danaer and Lira and finished, "Then, at last, a warrior like this Nyald soldier will finally be able to call the leader of the Destre-Y Rena, and with no breaking of his oath to Krantin."

Malol extended his pale hands and Gordt te Raa clasped them tightly. They had done so once to seal an alliance. Now they vowed themselves to the future of their land, the land their inheritors would rule.

Gordyan nodded to Danaer, learning to accept the pain, looking to days to come. Lira leaned her head tiredly against Danaer's chest, content to remain there. Danaer too looked forward to days to come. Now Lira's talisman would become little more than a pretty ornament, and so would his dagger. Osyta's prophecies of danger and evil were done. And her promises had also been of joy, and that too he had known, and the future would hold much more. Andaru was beginning, and he had been a part of it, he and Lira and Gordyan. Malol and Gordt te Raa spoke of Krantin's heirs, and Danaer smiled, thinking of his own heir, a tiny little thief who had already begun to rob his mother of her sorkra powers and leave her merely a woman—Danaer's woman.

The prophecy was fulfilled, the dark times had been put behind them, and he looked to what must come with confidence. The land would survive, and so would they.

Glossary

Andaru the prophesied time of glory for the plains people, when their leader will become the ruler of all the land.

Argan one of the three major deities of Krantin. She is goddess of the plains people; her special provinces are fertility and fire, and she is known as the ruler of wills.

Azsed the religion of the plains people, and sometimes also used as an alternate name for them. It means "law"—the law of Argan.

Bhid the river which runs through Nyald; it arises in the mountains and flows south to Sarlos and beyond to the unknown sea. For the greater part of its length, it is not navigable.

blacks common name for the preferred breed of horses of The Interior of Krantin; they are a very sturdy animal, useful in mines and on farms.

Bogotana the evil god, monarch of the realm below the earth.

Clarique name of the land and the people east of Krantin. It is an island country and the people are tall and blond, mostly dependent on fishing and the harvest of the sea.

Deki the oldest established settlement in Krantin, situated at the most westerly bend of the river separating Clarique and Krantin.

delisich priestess of Argan who is gifted with a spectacular singing voice and uses her talent to summon her goddess during rituals.

Desin one of Krantin's deities. Desin is a composite of numerous older supernatural beings, pictured as a changeling god, able to be human (of either sex) or animal. A common form is that of a black mare, one of the moon's shadow makers.

Destre (or Destre-Y) The plains people of Krantin, a loose confederation of family groups and their tribes. They live on the Vrastre and in the cities of that area. All Destre-Y are believers in Argan's worship of Azsed; but city dwellers sharing that same belief, while called Azsed, are called Destre-Y only as a courtesy.

ecar a large wild feline common throughout the provinces.

eiphren the sacred jewel of Azsed bestowed on the children of her people when they reach puberty. The gems symbolize their devotion to Argan and are treasured throughout life, never parted from them, even to ease extreme poverty. Women generally wear them as hair ornaments and men as rings.

fael a term meaning "faithful," referring to one who keeps an oath or is to be trusted, even though an enemy.

golhi a ferocious carnivore, now becoming rare, but still much feared and respected for its courage and deadliness.

harshaa the shouted challenge of the plains people, a call to defend oneself; or, in proper circumstances, a call to the goddess to witness some particular achievement by one of her people.

ha-usfaen   the priestess of Argan who dances and then transforms herself to assume the physical form of her goddess during ritual.

herb-healer   the physicians of the Destre-Y. They rely much on primitive charms and simples but usually serve their tribesfolk well enough through sickness and injury.

Iit   one who does not worship Argan. In the Destre idiom, it is a very derogatory term, far more insulting than "unbeliever."

Irico   the northern land and its people, a tall, white-haired, forest-dwelling culture. It is also the name of the river issuing from the land and flowing south between Clarique and Krantin.

Keth   the guardian of the gods' portals, he who will admit the dead to the land beyond or condemn them to wander eternity as unappeased spirits.

Kida   demigod of madness; his lash strikes one accursed, and the victim will be driven insane either for a short while or permanently.

Lasiirnte   in effect, "Princess," the title of a woman leader among Destre-Y.

maen   a term of close, friendly address, meaning "mine" or "my."

mantle   a narrow striped cloak worn by Destre peoples to mark their clans and tribes.

Markuand   the aliens from the land far across the great eastern sea beyond the outermost islands of Clarique.

motge   a bovine common to all the provinces. It provides meat and leather and is both wild and domesticated, depending on the area where it is found and the people who harvest the animal.

Mountains of the Mare a designation for the mountainous interior of Krantin. The term describes one of the god Desin's changeling forms, that of a "moon mare," whose black "shadow" covers the lunar disc during the dark phase.

Nidil the death god, he who comes out of the far north, past even Irico's winter cold, and slays mortals.

Nyald a much-reduced Destre community on the southern edge of The Interior. The city is now prospering as the Destre decline because of plague and hunger.

Peluva most ancient of Krantin's major deities. A sun god.

qedra a Destre endearment: "treasure."

Rasven reputedly the first man to recognize within himself the gifts of white wizardry; he brought together others of his own kind to establish the first sorkra Web.

Rena sovereign of all Destre tribes, a leader embodying the spirit of the people of Argan.

roans the horses of the plains people, a hardy breed well adapted to survival in grassland or desert.

Ryerdon the original home area of the people of Krantin, it was located on the coast of Clarique, not far from the Irico River.

Sarlos the southernmost province of the land. The terrain varies from inhospitable marshes to high deserts to fertile river deltas. Her people are short and of dark complexion.

Siirn   the title of a male leader among the Destre-Y—
not merely a leader of his clan but of the entire
tribal grouping.

sorkra   a wizard, practitioner of conjuring and mind
touching and other arcane arts, ideally for good.

Straedanfi   an epithet the Destre give to a particularly
tenacious foe. Literally: "long-fanged beast."

Tradyan   the Destre tribe inhabiting the far western
Vrastre (q.v.). Their customs of dress are different
from other plains people, but they are devoted to
Argan and loyal to the Brotherhood of the Zseds.

Traecheus   once the Empire of the Eastern Islands, a
fierce rival of Ryerdon, it fell because of civil wars
and natural disasters, and its people became the
Clarique in later generations.

Vrastre   the name given to all the lands below the
mountains and fertile valleys of Krantin's Interior.
It includes grassland and high desert such as
Bogotana's Sink and ends, in the east, when the
land begins to drop down to Deki's river.

vrentru   a Destre festival, sometimes to celebrate a
particular time of their religious calendar, sometimes merely to honor a gathering of the clans and
tribes.

Zsed   a nomadic community of the plains people.
Some have become semipermanent, where hunting
is close at hand. Others move constantly to follow
game and the caravans which the people plunder.

ABOUT THE AUTHOR

JUANITA COULSON began writing at age eleven and has been pursuing the habit off and on ever since. Her first professional sale, to a science-fiction magazine, came in 1963. Since then she has sold thirteen novels, several short stories, and odds and ends such as an article on *Wonder Woman,* science-fictional recipes, and a pamphlet on how to appreciate art.

When she isn't writing, she may be singing and/or composing songs, painting (several of her works have been sold for excessively modest prices), reading books on abnormal psychology, biography, earthquakes and volcanoes, history, astronomy, or almost anything that has printing on it, gardening in the summer and shivering in the winter.

Juanita is married to Buck Coulson, who is also a writer. She and her husband spend much of their spare time actively participating in science-fiction fandom: attending conventions and publishing their Hugo-winning fanzine, *Yandro.* They live in a rented farmhouse in northeastern Indiana, miles from any town you ever heard of; the house is slowly sinking into the swampy ground under the weight of the accumulated books, magazines, records, typewriters, and other paraphernalia crammed into it.

Most of Juanita's books to date have been science fiction, but she has also written the historical romance, *Dark Priestess,* available from Ballantine, and is currently working on a new fantasy novel set in the same world as *The Web of Wizardry.*